A Bilingual Edition of
Three *Sewa-mono* Plays by Chikamatsu Monzaemon

Woman-Killer in Oil Hell
Drumbeats over the Horikawa
Lovers' Suicides at Imamiya

Adapted and Translated by Masako Yuasa

対訳
湯浅版 近松世話物戯曲集
「女殺油地獄」「堀川波鼓」「今宮の心中」

翻案・英訳 湯浅雅子

社会評論社

Dedicated to my mother and my sister, and to the memory of my father

本書を母、姉、そして今は亡き父に捧ぐ。

CONTENTS

FOREWORD by Bunzō Torigoe 4
PREFACE 6

Chapter I

INTRODUCTION 16
MEASURING SYSTEM IN THE EDO PERIOD 32
STAGING OF THE CHIKAMATSU PROJECT 38

Chapter II

Woman-Killer in Oil Hell
    Performance Poster 44
    Stage Photos 45
    Design 46-47
    Play Text 50
    Notes 172

Drumbeats over the Horikawa
    Performance Poster 186
    Stage Photos 187
    Design 188-189
    Play Text 190
    Notes 278

Lovers' Suicides at Imamiya
    Performance Poster 292
    Stage Photos 293
    Design 294-295
    Play Text 296
    Notes 394

BIBLIOGRAPHY 408
POSTFACE 412

目次

　　序　島越文蔵　5
　　はじめに　7

第Ⅰ部

　イントロダクション　17
　江戸時代のもののはかり方　33
　近松プロジェクトの舞台　39

第Ⅱ部

「女殺油地獄」
　　　　公演ポスター　44
　　　　舞台写真　45
　　　　舞台図　46-47
　　　　戯曲　51
　　　　註　173

「堀川波鼓」
　　　　公演ポスター　186
　　　　舞台写真　187
　　　　舞台図　188-189
　　　　戯曲　191
　　　　註　279

「今宮の心中」
　　　　公演ポスター　292
　　　　舞台写真　293
　　　　舞台図　294-295
　　　　戯曲　297
　　　　註　395

参考文献　409
おわりに　413

FOREWORD

Bunzō Torigoe

I am not sure exactly when I first encountered Dr Masako Yuasa, although I remember well that she came through the introduction of Professor Yasunari Takahashi, a Shakespearian scholar at Tokyo University. Dr Yuasa was at that time a lecturer at the University of Leeds in the UK, so it must have been in the nineteen-nineties, when I was the curator of the Theatre Museum.* I suppose that research in the library of Museum must have been one of the purposes of her visit. Having said this, as she used to be able to travel home once a year for only a short period of time, our communication was chiefly by telephone and letter. The main subject of our discussion was her intention to stage *jōruri* by Chikamatsu in her own English adaptation. She has fully realised the plan. She brought her theatre ensemble of British student-actors to perform at one of the auditoriums at Waseda. Now the scripts of these productions are to be published, much to my delight.

Jōruri by Chikamatsu are broadly classified into two categories, *jidai-mono* (period pieces/stories) and *sewa-mono* (domestic or contemporary pieces/stories). I further subdivide his twenty-four *sewa-mono* into three categories, which are eleven *shinjū-mono* (lovers'-suicide pieces), eight *shobatsu-mono* (punishment pieces) and five *kakō-mono* (fictional pieces). The plays collected in this book consist of one *shinjū-mono* and two *shobatsu-mono*. *Sonezaki Shinjū* (Lovers' Suicides at Sonezaki) and *Shinjū Ten no Amijima* (Lovers' Suicides at Amijima) are regarded as master pieces of the *shinjū-mono* category. These are stories of a courtesan and her client committing a double suicide. But Dr Yuasa did not select one of these, instead she staged *Imamiya no Shinjū* (Lovers' Suicides at Imamiya), a story taken from the account of a double suicide committed by shop employees. I think that this choice demonstrated her notable discernment. The subject matters of the other two plays selected could be placed into further categories, *Horikawa Nami no Tsuzumi* (Drumbeats over the Horikawa) - *kantsū-mono* (an adultery piece), and *Onna Koroshi Abura no Jigoku* (Woman-Killer in Oil Hell) - *hanzai-mono* (a criminal piece). Both are master works and highly accessible to a modern audience.

I am happy to write this introduction in the belief that this book will increase knowledge and understanding of Chikamatsu's work.

(Emeritus professor of Waseda University)

*The TSUBOUCHI Memorial Theatre Museum of Waseda University

序

鳥越文蔵

　湯浅雅子君が私の前に現れたのは何年前か定かでないが、東大教授でシェークスピア研究家の高橋康也氏の紹介だったことは記憶している。イギリスのリーズ大学講師の肩書があったので、一九九〇年代で、私の演劇博物館＊館長時代と重なる。演劇の本の利用も目的の一つだったのであろう。とはいえ、日本に帰国するのは一年の中、短期間でしかないので、手紙や電話での交信が主であった。交信の内容は近松門左衛門の浄瑠璃の英訳を、彼女の台本による英語での上演に関することであった。イギリスの学生を引連れて来て、早稲田大学の講堂での上演はすでに実現している。その台本がこの度上梓されるという。喜ばしいことである。

　近松の浄瑠璃は時代物と世話物に大別される。世話物二十四篇を更に種別すれば、私は心中物（十一）、処罰物（八）、仮構物（五）の三種としている。本書に選ばれた作品は心中物から一篇、処罰物から二篇となる。心中物は遊女とその客との心中を扱った「曽根崎心中」「心中天の網島」などが名作としてもてはやされているが、湯浅君はそれらを選ばず、商家の雇用人の心中を題材にした「今宮の心中」を採り上げた。これも一つの見識であろう。他の二篇は姦通物（「堀川波鼓」）とも犯罪物（「女殺油地獄」）ともいえる内容で、現代にも通じる名作である。

　この書で近松を理解する人が一人でも多くなることを願い、私の序文とする。

（早稲田大学名誉教授）

＊早稲田大学坪内博士記念演劇博物館

PREFACE

About the Chikamatsu Project

    The purpose of the Project was to introduce one of the most acclaimed Japanese playwrights, Chikamatsu Monzaemon's works to the international audience by staging them in the English language in British theatre environments. In order to realise this, we chose **Woman-Killer in Oil Hell, Drumbeats over the Horikawa**, **Lovers' Suicides at Imamiya**, and gave the focus on the texts of *jōruri*, which is a mixture of narration and speeches for a *jōruri*-chanter to recite, being accompanied by *samisen* in *ningyō-jōruri or Bunraku* (the traditional Japanese puppet theatre). My English adaptations are written in the style of a straight play, reworked as period drama using actors, but kept faithful to the original.

    Traditional Japanese theatre such as *Nō*, *Bunraku* and *Kabuki* are performed in the stylised forms which have been passed on from generation to generation. Needless to say, the people's devotion to life-long training and learning in these theatres has made it possible to hand down the unique precious forms of theatre until today. But, at the same time, because of this distinctive nature, traditional Japanese theatre could have been regarded as something to be studied and appreciated, but not to be practised. This might account for it not being staged much in International Theatre circles. The ultimate aim of the project is to change this tendency and to place the works of Chikamatsu in the repertoire of the international stage in the same way as those of Shakespeare and of Chekhov are accessible to all.

    Writing a stage script faithful to Chikamatsu's original was a good opportunity to learn the art of Chikamatsu's theatre. The basic structure of *sewa-jōruri* (a domestic or contemporary piece) is three-act.[1] Because of this framework, the development of the drama was easy to follow, and the characters and the subject matter were clear to see. In the *jōruri* text, the descriptions such as the characters' positioning on stage or stage settings are not written in detail. But they are not difficult to find by examining the context of the play and with the help of the stage rules of *Bunraku*. In addition a *jōruri*-chanter tells the audience many things apart from characters' speeches, and entrances and exits. In my adaptation I created the Chorus to compensate for this, and let the Chorus take on this role of the chanter. As for the three *jōruri* in the project, there have not been specific problems in transforming them to a play without music. I think that this was due to Chikamatsu's talent as a playwright and his stance as a theatre practitioner, who wrote a script in day-to-day contact with his performers and audience as a residential *jōruri* writer.

はじめに

近松プロジェクトについて

　近松プロジェクトは日本の演劇史上最も優れた戯作者（劇作家）と称賛されている近松門左衛門の作品を英語上演することにより、近松の芝居の素晴らしさを世界の人々に紹介することを目的として行った国際演劇プロジェクトです。この目的の達成のため、プロジェクトでは「女殺油地獄」「堀川波鼓」「今宮の心中」の三作品を選んで近松の浄瑠璃に焦点を当てました。浄瑠璃は語り・ナレーションと台詞の融合体です。人形浄瑠璃、又は文楽（日本の伝統的な人形芝居）では、浄瑠璃の太夫が文楽の三味線弾きの伴奏で語ります。私の翻案は時代劇の台詞劇で、人形ではなく人間の俳優によって演じられるものですが、近松の原作に忠実であるように心がけました。

　能、歌舞伎、文楽などの日本の伝統演劇は決まった型の通りに演じられます。それは歳月をかけ世代を超えて伝承され続けてきたものです。伝統演劇の舞台に携わる人々の生涯をかけた弛まぬ努力が、今日も尚、他に類を見ない貴重な演劇形態の伝承を可能にしていることは言うまでもありません。しかし、また、この特質が日本の伝統演劇をややもすれば、自らが演じるものではなくて、学び鑑賞する対象であるもののようにしているのではないか。さらには、このことが日本の伝統演劇が世界の演劇サークルに深く浸透しえないでいる理由ではないかと思われます。近松プロジェクトは世界のこのような見方を変え、近松門左衛門の芝居をシェークスピアやチェーホフの芝居のように、色々な国の演劇人の手の届くところに置き、様々な形で上演されることを究極の目的としています。

　近松の浄瑠璃を原作に忠実に戯曲に翻案する仕事は彼の演劇を学ぶ素晴らしい機会でした。世話浄瑠璃は基本的に上之巻、中之巻、下之巻の三幕構成[1]で書かれています。このように劇の骨組みが確立していることにより、ドラマの発展が分かりやすく、登場人物や作品のテーマなどがはっきりと見えます。浄瑠璃では人物の舞台上の立ち位置やト書きの細かなところは書き込まれていません。しかし、こうした部分は作品の流れや文楽の決まり事を通してあまり苦労なく読み取ることが出来たように思われます。また、浄瑠璃には台詞や人物の出入り以外にも様々なことが太夫によって語られます。私の翻案では台詞やト書きとして書き表しにくい部分はコーラスを登場させて、コーラスに太夫の役を一部担わせました。プロジェクトで舞台化した三曲では浄瑠璃を戯曲に変えるにあたり、特に難しい点はありませんでした。これは、文楽や歌舞伎という庶民の芝居小屋で、日々客席と舞台に接して創作をしてきた、近松の戯作者としての才能とその立ち位置がもたらしたものだと思います。

PREFACE

Three *jōruri* chosen for the project were written based on actual events, in the same way most of his *sewa-jōruri* were. Chikamatsu's characters enter and exit, being led by his beautifully rhyming powerful language. They are lively and full of life's truths. Their complex human relationships torn between obligations and feelings, the strict social and moral codes of the feudal regime, their Buddhist beliefs and the Confucian influences penetrate through Chikamatsu's *jōruri* as an honest depiction of people's everyday lives in the Edo period. It is hard to believe that they were written three hundred years ago, and yet the stories being told still hold a strong sense of the truth and appeal deeply to our minds across time and culture.

The adaptations collected in the book are the revised versions of the staging texts of the project, but the alterations given are minimal. The notes on social and historical backgrounds are newly added to this publication. Also the book is presented bilingually. The book aims to be read by people, both at home and abroad, who are interested in theatre, culture and society and language of Japan. I hope that the book will be read as a book of a play as well as that of cultural exchange.

Staging the adaptations was carried out in collaboration with the drama departments of two British universities, Leeds and Hull. **Woman-Killer in Oil Hell** was staged at Leeds in 2004 as the first play of the project. Then the project changed base to Hull and continued there. The second play, **Drumbeats over the Horikawa** in 2006, and the third play, **Lovers' Suicides at Imamiya** in 2008 were both staged at the Donald Roy Theatre, a licensed theatre of the university. The staff and cast of each production consisted of the students and the members of staff of each university, and all the rehearsals were held in the theatres, the studios and the rehearsal spaces of each university department. It should be noted that the staging was the product of the efforts and the energy, the arts and the skills of all who were involved in the project.

The project was also financially supported by the grant foundations such as the Great Britain Sasakawa Foundation, the Anglo-Daiwa Japan Foundation and the SPRET.[2] The second and the third plays had opportunities of touring Japan as part of the COE[3] of Japan of the Osaka City University and the TSUBOUCHI Memorial Theatre Museum of Waseda University. The performances in Osaka were supported by the OCU[4] and the City of Osaka,[5] and those in Tokyo by the TM Theatre Museum of Waseda University.[6] The tour was made possible by the support of the leading authorities of the field of the Chikamatsu research[7] and the academics in theatre studies in Japan.

The following is the list of the performance dates and the venues of each play:

はじめに

　プロジェクトに選んだ三曲は近松作品の多くの世話浄瑠璃と同様に、当時実際に起こった事件を題材として書かれています。近松の登場人物たちは美しく韻をふみ、リズム感に満ちた力強い言葉に導かれて登退場します。彼らは人間の真実に溢れ、生き生きとしています。幾重にも絡む複雑な人間関係、義理と人情の狭間で迷い苦しむ人々の姿、厳しく立ちはだかる封建社会、心の支えとなっている儒教思想や仏教信仰など、当時の人々の生活が手に取るように映し出されています。近松の浄瑠璃は江戸時代の人々の日常の正直な描写です。けれど、三百年あまり前に書かれたものとは思えないほど、今もなお人間の生の真実を伝え、時を越え、国境を越えて私たちの心に訴える力を持っています。

　この本に掲載している翻案戯曲は、プロジェクトの台本を出版に際して必要な箇所に限り手を加えたものです。新たに作品の時代や社会背景に関する註も加えました。また、日本語版も載せて日英対訳の形にしました。本書は、国の内外を問わず、広く日本の演劇、文化、社会、言語などに関心のある人々に読まれることを目的にしています。純粋に芝居の本として読まれるだけでなく、文化交流などにも役立つようになって欲しいと願っています。

　翻案の舞台化はイギリスのリーズ大学とハル大学の二つの大学の協力を得て行いました。第一作目の「女殺油地獄」は英国リーズ大学で2004年に上演し、二作目からは拠点を英国ハル大学に移して「堀川波鼓」を2006年に、「今宮の心中」を2008年に同大学内のライセンス・シアターであるドナルド・ロイ劇場で上演しました。各プロダクションの演技者やスタッフは各々の大学の学生と教職員が務めました。リハーサルはすべて舞台化を行った大学のリハーサル室、スタジオ、劇場で行いました。舞台作りはプロジェクトに参加した人々全員の努力と熱意、舞台芸術に対する理解と技術の結集であったことをここに明記しておかなければなりません。

　プロジェクトはこのイギリスの二大学の協力だけでなく英国笹川基金、日英大和基金、SPRET[2]からの資金援助も受けています。二本目と三本目は大阪市立大学と早稲田大学坪内博士記念演劇博物館の協賛を得てCOE[3]の研究の一端として日本ツアーを行いました。大阪公演は大阪市立大学[4]と大阪市[5]、東京公演は早稲田大学演劇博物館[6]の支援を受けて行いました。日本ツアーは日本の近松研究の第一人者と言われる方々[7]、またその他の演劇研究に携わる日本の研究者たちの尽力のおかげで実現しました。
　以下は近松プロジェクトの公演日程の詳細です。

PREFACE

Play 1: **Woman-Killer in Oil Hell**
Performances at Studio 1, the Workshop Theatre at Leeds, UK, 15-17 March, 2004

Play 2: **Drumbeats over the Horikawa***
(*The title of the play was **Tsuzumi-Drumbeats over the Horikawa** for the first production.)
Performances at the Donald Roy Theatre at Hull, UK, 15-18 March, 2006
Japan Tour: at the Seika Small Theatre, Osaka, 30-31 March and at the Ono Memorial Auditorium of the University of Waseda, Tokyo, 4-5 April, 2006

Play 3: **Lovers' Suicides at Imamiya**
Performances at the Donald Roy Theatre at Hull, UK, 5-8 March, 2008
Japan Tour: at the Seika Small Theatre, Osaka, 30-31 May and at the Ono Memorial Auditorium of the University of Waseda, Tokyo, 5-6 June, 2008
At the Greenside, Edinburgh, 18-23 August, participating in Edinburgh International Theatre Festival Fringe

It has been an exciting journey to rewrite the works of Chikamatsu who is considered to have reached a high degree of perfection in his art, and to stage adaptations of his works in the English language. I sincerely hope that I have done enough to fulfil the aims of the Chikamatsu Project.

Notes

1   *Jidai-jōruri* (a period piece) is normally written in five acts.
2   Sir Philip Reckitt Education Trust
3   The 21st Century Global Centres of Excellence Programme of Japan Society for Promotion of Science.
4   The first Japan tour was supported by the theatre research group in the Urban-culture Research Centre of the Graduate-school of Literature and Human Sciences of Osaka City University. Professor Hiroyuki Sakaguchi and other academics of the group were busily involved in realising the performances in Osaka. By the second tour Prof Sakaguchi had left the OCU for another university, but kindly continued to act as a mediator between Osaka city and the project. Prof Mikaki and Prof Fukushima of the OCU kindly helped the project once again. Some of the post

はじめに

第一回作品　　湯浅版「女殺油地獄」（英題 *Woman-Killer in Oil Hell*）公演
　2004年3月15日〜17日　英国リーズ大学英文学部
　　　　　　　ワークショップ・シアター　スタジオ1

第二回作品　　湯浅版「堀川波鼓」（英題 *Drumbeats over the Horikawa*）公演
　（初演時の作品名は *Tsuzumi-Drumbeats over the Horikawa*）
　2006年3月15日〜18日　英国ハル大学ドナルド・ロイ劇場
　第1回日本ツアー　　3月30日、31日　精華小劇場（大阪）
　　　　　　　　　　　4月4日、5日　早稲田大学小野記念講堂（東京）

第三回作品　　湯浅版「今宮の心中」（英題 *Lovers' Suicides at Imamiya*）公演
　2008年3月5日〜8日　英国ハル大学ドナルド・ロイ劇場
　第2回日本ツアー　　5月30日、31日　精華小劇場（大阪）
　　　　　　　　　　　6月5日、6日　早稲田大学小野記念講堂（東京）
　エジンバラ演劇祭参加公演　8月18日〜23日　グリーンサイド（エジンバラ）

　近松門左衛門の浄瑠璃は完璧に近いといわれています。その浄瑠璃を英語の翻案戯曲に書き直し、上演するのは一演劇人として胸の躍る経験でした。私のこの仕事が近松プロジェクトの目的達成に適ったものであることを心から願っています。

註
1　時代浄瑠璃は基本的に五段（五幕）で書かれている。
2　Sir Philip Reckitt Education Trust の略。
3　日本学術振興会による21世紀グローバルCOEプログラム。

4　第一回目は大阪市立大学大学院文学研究科都市文化研究センターの演劇研究グループの支援を受けた。阪口弘之先生を中心にグループの諸先生方の奔走で大阪公演が実現した。第二回目は、阪口先生は他大学に移籍されていたが、大阪市との橋渡しをして下さり、三上雅子、福島祥行両先生にも再び市大側の仕事を引き受けていただいた。上演では市大の院生達や劇団浪花グランドロマンの人々の協力も受けた。友人の幸村三千代さんや喜多直美さんたちが着付けを担当、また山村若禄秀先生には動きのアドバイスをいただいた。

PREFACE

graduates of the OCU and some members of the Naniwa Grand Roman Theatre Company worked for the production voluntarily. Also my friends, Michiyo Komura and Naomi Kita, worked as a dresser, and my dance teacher, Yamamura Wakarokusyū, gave some advice to my actors.

5   Yutori & Midori Section for Advancement of the Culture of the Osaka City Hall supported the project and let us use the Seika Small Theatre for the venue of our performances. In Osaka the student actors did a home-stay, which was one of the volunteer activities of the Osaka International House Foundation. The Hull students enjoyed experiences of Japanese lives as well as performing in Japan.

6   The tour was carried out under 'the UK-Japan Project for Staging Chikamatsu Plays' jointly sponsored by University of Hull, the OCU and Waseda University. Professor Mikio Takeuchi, then the curator of the Theatre Museum of Waseda University, supported the project.

7   Emeritus professor Bunzō Torigoe of Waseda University (the fifth curator of the Theatre Museum of Waseda University) and Emeritus professor Hiroyuki Sakaguchi of Osaka City University (Head of Research Centre of Classic Performing Arts of Kobe Women's University).

5　大阪市ゆとりとみとり振興局文化部の支援を受けて精華小劇場で上演出来た。学生俳優達は大阪国際交流センターのアイハウスボランティアによるホームステイで大阪公演の滞在期間を過ごした。日本家庭に滞在し、日本人の普通の生活も体験出来たことは日本ツアーをより意義深いものにした。

6　ハル大学、大阪市立大学、早稲田大学の三大学の共同主催で「日英近松劇上演プロジェクト」の名のもとに行われた。東京公演は二回とも当時早稲田大学演劇博物館館長であった竹本幹夫教授（第七代館長）の支援で成就した。

7　鳥越文蔵早稲田大学名誉教授（第五代早稲田大学演劇博物館館長）。阪口弘之大阪市立大学名誉教授（現・神戸女子大学古典芸能研究センター所長）。

Chapter I

第 I 部

INTRODUCTION

Jōruri and Story-telling

In the history of Japanese music, one of the unique characteristics is that the vocal music accompanied by a musical instrument developed more than the instrumental music. The vocal music is divided into two categories, *utai-mono* (a singing piece) and *katari-mono* (a story-telling piece). For example *rōei*, *saibara*, *jiuta*, *nagauta* and *kouta* are *utai-mono*, while *heikyoku*, *jōruri*, *sekkyō*, *saimon* and *rōkyoku* are *katari-mono*. The former is generally understood as Singing and the latter as Telling.

Katari-mono is a style of a story-telling with a tune which could be traced back to *katari-be* (a story-teller) of the Yamato/Nara period in the 7th century Japan. But the real origin of *katari-mono* as an art form is thought to be *heikyoku* of the 13th century. *Biwa-hōsh* (a blind Buddhist monk) started chanting a sutra accompanied with a stringed instrument, *biwa*[1] in the 10th century. By the 13th century *heikyoku* became the most popular piece in *katari-mono*. *Heikyoku* was composed based on **Heike Monogatari** (The Tale of the Heike),[2] epic war poetry in the Kamakura period about the rise and fall of the Taira clan. At first *heikyoku* was the entertainment for the upper-class people, but as the number of *biwa-hōsh* increased, only the *biwa-hōshi* with good skills and a respectable social standing were required. Consequently *biwa-hōsh*s who were left unemployed looked for their audience among the common people and *heikyoku* became the entertainment for the masses. Then in the 15th century *jōruri* was born as one of the new stories in *heikyoku*.

Jōruri was an abbreviation of **Jōruri-hime Jūnidan Zōshi** (The Story of Princess Jōruri in Twelve Chapters). It was a love-story of Princess Jōruri and Minamoto no Yoshitsune[3] who fought the battles against the Taira clan along with his elder brother Yoritomo[4] when he raised his army against the Taira. The Minamoto clan won the battles and destroyed the Tairas. But after that, Yoshitsune fell out with Yoritomo, and fled to the north part of Japan to avoid assassination. On this journey Yoshitsune met Princess Jōruri when he stayed in Yahagi of Mikawa. The important element of the story was not the romantic part but the miraculous story of Yakushinyorai, the healing Buddha, who saved Yoshitsune's life from all the dangers. Princess Jōruri was a pious believer in Yakushinyorai and it was her faith that saved Yoshitsune. Buddhism was the most important background of the society in the middle ages and the world of entertainment was framed by its strong influence. The masses longed for a virtuous deed. In the course of development in The Story of Princess Jōruri in Twelve Chapters, the

イントロダクション

浄瑠璃と語りもの
　日本の音楽の歴史におけるユニークな特質の一つは、楽器などの伴奏のついた歌謡が楽器のみの音楽よりも発達してきたことである。この伴奏つきの歌謡には〈歌い物〉と〈語り物〉の二種類がある。朗詠、催馬楽、地唄、長唄、小唄などは〈歌い物〉、平曲、浄瑠璃、説経、祭文、浪曲などは〈語り物〉に入る。前者は歌を歌うのであり、後者は物語を語るのである。

　〈語り物〉はメロディーに合わせてある話を語る形式で、七世紀の大和奈良時代の頃の語り部に始まっている。しかし、〈語り物〉を現在の形にしたのは十三世紀に流行した「平曲」であるといわれている。十世紀ごろから盲目の琵琶法師が琵琶[1]を弾きながら経典などを語り聞かせることを始めるが、十三世紀になると「平曲」が最も人気のある語り物の演目となった。この「平曲」は平家の興亡を描いた鎌倉時代の軍記物語「平家物語」[2]を題材にした物語である。「平曲」は最初、上流階級の人々の娯楽として楽しまれていたが、琵琶法師の数が増えるにつれて、語りも上手く、社会的地位も高い琵琶法師が求められるようになった。その結果、仕事に就けない琵琶法師たちは平民の中に自分たちの観客を求めるようになり、「平曲」が一般大衆の娯楽となって広がった。「浄瑠璃」は十五世紀頃この「平曲」の中の、新たに加えられた話の一つとして出てきたものである。

　「浄瑠璃」は「浄瑠璃姫十二段草子」を短くした呼び名で、浄瑠璃姫と源 義経[3]の恋物語を語ったものである。源義経は兄頼朝[4]の挙兵に応じて平家打倒の戦いに加わる。幾つかの合戦で源氏が勝利し、平家が滅びて、源氏の世となる。しかし、その後、義経は兄頼朝と不仲になり、兄の追手から逃れるために北に向かう。旅の途中、三河の国矢矧に滞在しているときに義経は浄瑠璃姫と出会う。この物語で重要なのは二人の恋の成り行きよりも、義経をさまざまな危険から救った薬師如来の奇跡の話にある。浄瑠璃姫は薬師如来の敬虔な信者で、彼女の厚い信仰心が義経の命を救ったことが大切なところなのである。仏教は中世の日本社会の重要な精神的背景であり、娯楽もまたその影響を強く受けていた。「浄瑠璃姫十二段草子」が広く語られるようになるにつれて、

way of chanting was newly devised and elaborated, and its tunes and chanting style were used for many other stories. Eventually *jōruri* took over the position of *heikyoku* as a new chanting style of story-telling.

Meanwhile around the middle of the 16th century *sangen* (a three-stringed musical instrument) was brought to Japan through Ryūkyū (present-day Okinawa) and evolved into *samisen*. The players of *samisen* used *bachi* (a plectrum) or artificial fingernails made of horn and produced a more refined and stronger sound of music. Soon *samisen* took over the position of *biwa* and *jōruri* musically matured. *Jōruri* made a rapid progress with the development of *samisen*.

Ningyō-jōruri (or Ayatsuri-jōruri) or Bunraku

It is not clear exactly when *jōruri* came across with *ningyō-shibai* (puppetry). However, it has been said that it was around the end of 16th century when Menukiya Saburō, a *jōruri* chanter from Kyoto, and Hikita Awajinojō, a puppeteer from the Awaji Island, performed **Kyō-meguri** (Sightseeing of Kyoto) together or otherwise when some chanter did it with a puppeteer from Nishinomiya.[5] Those people created a new form of theatre called *ningyō-jōruri* (a performance of puppets and *jōruri* together). Gradually *ningyō-jōruri* evolved into the present form in which three puppeteers manipulate a puppet, a *jōruri* chanter tells a story and a *samisen* player plays an accompaniment.

Originally *jōruri* was born in *Kami-gata*, the Kyoto and Osaka region. In the Edo period it was introduced to Edo (present-day Tokyo), a newly built capital of the Tokugawa Shogunate, where the culture was still young and rough, powerful and dynamic. *Jōruri* absorbed this Edo culture and returned to the Kyoto and Osaka region. Since this period various schools of *jōruri* recitation had been established by the middle of the 17th century.

There was a son of a farmer who sang in a good voice while working in a rice field in Tennōji village of Osaka. His name was Gorobei.[6] Since he was small, Gorobei learned *jōruri* by ear from a *jōruri* teacher in his neighbourhood who always chanted it. The boy was the young Takemoto Gidayū. He was spotted by a *jōruri* chanter Kiyomizu Rihei, became Rihei's disciple and then was given a professional name, Kiyomizu Ridayū.

The master Kiyomizu Rihei was the best disciple of Inoue Harimanojō, one of the eminent *jōruri* chanters in Osaka who had taken the vibrant and powerful features of *Kinpira-bushi* of Edo and added them into his original style of recitation. Before long Ridayū (Gorobei) became an accompanist for his master and grew famous. At that time Uji Kadayū[7] of Uji-*za* (the Uji Theatre) in Shijō Kawaramachi was very popular in Kyoto. Uji Kadayū heard of Ridayū's good reputation and invited him to join his troupe. Having gained his

その語り方も工夫されて、より精巧なものになり、浄瑠璃の節や語り方が他の物語にも多く使われ始める。やがて「浄瑠璃」が「平曲」に代わって語り物の地位を奪うことになる。

　一方、十六世紀の中ごろに、後に三味線となる三弦という楽器が琉球（現在の沖縄）からもたらされる。三味線は爪の代わりに撥や動物の角を人間の爪のように作ったものを用いて弾かれ、琵琶よりも洗練されて強い音を奏でた。間もなく三味線が琵琶に代わって用いられるようになり、浄瑠璃は三味線の発達とともに目覚ましい進歩を遂げることになる。

人形浄瑠璃（操り浄瑠璃）と文楽

　浄瑠璃がいつごろ人形芝居と結びついたのか厳密な時期は分っていない。が、恐らく十六世紀末であるだろうと考えられている。京都の浄瑠璃語りである目貫屋長三郎というものが淡路の傀儡子である引田淡路掾という人物と提携して「京めぐり」という演目を上演したのが最初であるとか、他の浄瑠璃語りが西ノ宮の傀儡子とともに人形芝居を始めたのが最初であるとも言われている[5]。いずれにせよ、こうした人々によって新しい芝居の形である操り浄瑠璃、又は人形浄瑠璃（人形と浄瑠璃語りが一緒に公演する舞台）が産み出された。操り浄瑠璃は徐々に、三人の人形遣いが一体の人形を操り、太夫が浄瑠璃を語り、三味線弾きが太夫に合わせて伴奏する現在みられる形になってゆく。

　浄瑠璃はもともと上方（京・大阪）に生まれ、江戸時代中期に幕府の所在地である江戸（現在の東京）に紹介された。新しく都となった江戸の文化は上方と異なりまだまだ若く洗練されていなかった。が、そのぶん力強くダイナミックであった。浄瑠璃はこうした江戸の文化を吸い取って上方に戻り、十七世紀中ごろには多くの流派が出来た。

　大阪の天王寺村に畑仕事の合間にいい声で歌っている百姓の息子がいた。名前を五郎兵衛[6]といい、小さいころから近所に住む浄瑠璃の師匠が歌っているのを聞いて浄瑠璃を覚えた。後の義太夫である。五郎兵衛は清水理兵衛という浄瑠璃語りに認められ弟子入りし、清水理太夫という名を貰う。

　清水理兵衛は、力強い江戸の金毘羅節を自身の語り口にいれ大阪で人気も技芸も秀でた井上播磨掾の高弟であった。やがて、理太夫（五郎兵衛）は理兵衛のワキ語りとして舞台に上がり評判を取るようになる。当時、京都では四条河原町に宇治座を開いた宇治嘉太夫[7]が人気を得ていた。大阪の理太夫の評判を耳にした嘉太夫は理太夫を宇治座に招く。理太夫はその招きに応え、師の許可を得て、京都の宇治座に移ることになる。

master's permission, Ridayū moved to Kyoto to join Kadayū's troupe.

Uji Kadayū was born into the family of a paper merchant in present-day Uji in Wakayama city. At first he studied *yōkyoku* (*Nō* song), and then moved to *jōruri*. Kadayū did provincial tours, developed his style of recitation during this time, and then arrived at Kyoto, the city which had been the capital of Japan since the 8th century and whose culture was mature and sophisticated.[8] Kadayū's chanting style appealed to the aesthetic sense of the Kyotoites. Because of the training in *yōkyoku* and his experience of *Heikyoku*, Kadayū's chanting style, *Kadayū-bushi*, is said to be refined and elegant. He established his popularity in Kyoto and became one of the best chanters of the old *jōruri* in the Kyoto and Osaka region.

> "Kadayū and Gidayū (Ridayū) formed the relationship of master and disciple, otherwise Kadayū was regarded as Gidayū's senior. Kadayū recited *jōruri* with a soft touch while Ridayū adopted stirring manner, and their opposing characteristics, the elegance versus the magnificence, compensated for each other's weakness, produced an exciting stage and gained a good response. But Kadayū and Ridayū quarrelled in staging **Saigyō Monogatari** (The Story of Saigyō) and left each other for good."[9]

There was a disagreement about the theatre management between Kadayū and a proprietor of the Uji Theatre, Takeya Shōbei. In 1677 when Shōbei also opened his new theatre at Shijō Kawaramachi in Kyoto, where the Uji Theatre stood, he invited Ridayū as the main chanter of the new theatre. But, as Kaganojō's reputation much exceeded that of Ridayū, only small audiences came to hear Ridayū. Half a year later Shōbei closed his new theatre and left Kyoto with Ridayū and the troupe for a tour of the western region. It took Ridayū a further ten years before he learned his craft and returned to Osaka, the bustling and hustling townspeople's town and the centre of commerce of that time. Ridayū changed his name to Takemoto Gidayū after his benefactor Takeya Shōbei and opened the Takemoto Theatre in Dōtonbori in Osaka in 1684, where his master's old master Inoue Harimanojō used to perform.

Ningyō-jōruri went into a decline, after having lost two main residence theatres, Takemoto-*za* (the Takemoto Theatre) and Toyotake-*za* (the Toyotake Theatre) in Dōtonbori by fire in 1724. However, in the early 19th century Uemura Bunrakuken,[10] a theatre proprietor originally from the Awaji Island, built a new theatre for *ningyō-jōruri* close to Kōzubashi (near the present-day National Bunraku Theatre), and restored *ningyō-jōruri* in Osaka. The Uemura family maintained this theatre, Bunraku-*za* (the Bunraku Theatre), and held the right of performance of *ningyō-jōruri* for generations. Bunrakuken's name *Bunraku* has been used for *ningyō-jōruri* because of this. Nowadays *ningyō-jōruri* may be better known as *Bunraku*.

宇治嘉太夫は和歌山県宇治の紙商の家の息子として生まれた。最初、謡曲を勉強していたが途中で浄瑠璃に転向した。嘉太夫は地方巡業をしている間に自身の語りを習得し、やがて京都に座を構えるに至る。京都は八世紀以降の日本の首都[8]でその文化は成熟し洗練されたものであった。謡曲の基礎を身に付け、浄瑠璃のもとである「平曲」も学んできた嘉太夫の語りはそうした京都人の好みにうまく適合し、嘉太夫の語りは上品で優雅だという評判をとった。嘉太夫は京都で揺るぎない人気を確立して、上方における古浄瑠璃語りの第一人者となった。

　　「嘉太夫と義太夫（理太夫）は師弟というか先輩後輩の関係にあったようです。嘉太夫はやわらかい語りで、義太夫は豪快な語り口でした。柔と剛がうまく調和して公演は評判をとったようですが「西行物語」の上演でけんか別れをしてしまいます。」[9]

　このころ宇治座の興行主であった竹屋庄兵衛は宇治嘉太夫と座の運営で意見が合わずにいた。庄兵衛は1677年に宇治座のある四条河原町に新たに操り浄瑠璃の小屋を開き、若手の理太夫を引き抜いて興行を始めた。しかし、嘉太夫の人気は高く、理太夫の浄瑠璃を聞きに来る客は少なかった。興行は失敗に終り、半年後には座を閉じて一座は西国の地方巡業に出ることになる。地方を回る間に研究を重ね、十年の後に、理太夫は自らの語りに開眼する。理太夫は活気に満ちた商都大阪に戻り、竹屋庄兵衛に因んで名を竹本義太夫と改め、1684年に恩師の師であった井上播磨掾の道頓堀の芝居小屋跡に竹本座の櫓をあげたのである。

　人形浄瑠璃は、道頓堀にあった竹本座と豊竹座の両座を1724年に共に火事でなくして一時衰退する。しかし、十九世紀初めに淡路島出身の興行師文楽軒[10]が高津橋近く（現在の国立文楽劇場の近く）に小さな浄瑠璃の小屋を開いて再興させる。植村家は代々この小屋、文楽座を守り人形浄瑠璃の興行権を握っていた。今日、人形浄瑠璃は文楽と呼ばれて親しまれているが、これは、文楽軒の名前が浄瑠璃の代わりに使われていたことによっている。

INTRODUCTION

In 1909 the Uemura family handed over the right of performance to the Shochiku.[11] In 1963 when the Shochiku pulled out of Bunraku, Bunraku-*za* changed its name to Asahi-*za* (the Asahi Theatre), and then Bunraku restarted its activity under the newly formed *Bunraku Kyōkai* (the Association for Bunraku). In 1984, exactly 300 years after the opening of the Takemoto Theatre, *Kokuritsu Bunraku Gekijō* (the National Bunraku Theatre) was opened near Dōtonbori in Osaka. Here the Asahi-*za* ended its life as a regular Bunraku theatre.

Chikamatsu, Monzaemon (1653 - 1724)

Chikamatsu Monzaemon was a prolific playwright. There are more than 150 *jōruri* and *kabuki* plays which have the signature of 'Chikamatsu Monzaemon' as a script writer; if we include the ones without signature, the number rises to over 200. His scripts were all written for staging; it is understood that Chikamatsu wrote the original text on his own, and that a chanter and a *samisen* player could make minor alterations to work the text and the tune better. Perhaps more serious alterations would have been asked by the actors in *kabuki* so that their performances would satisfy the demand of their audience.

Chikamatsu was born in Yoshie of the fief of Echizen (present-day Sabae city of Fukui prefecture). Chikamatsu's father was a samurai of the Echizen fief and his mother was a daughter of a fief doctor. The real name of Chikamatsu Monzaemon in his childhood was Sugimori Jirokichi and, his adulthood, Sugimori Nobunari. When he was in his early teens, his father left his job, became *rōnin*, a master-less samurai, and so his family moved to Kyoto.

In Kyoto Chikamatsu worked for the Dōgami family, one of the families of the court nobles. In those days court nobles did not have political power, but they kept a tradition of enjoying high culture such as poetry, music and dance, and often were the patrons of *kabuki* and *ningyō-jōruri*. Chikamatsu's broad knowledge was thought to be achieved during this time. One of the members of the Dōgami family was writing *jōruri* for Uji Kadayū. Chikamatsu was a messenger between the court noble and Kadayū, and it was how he was introduced to the world of *jōruri*. He began writing *jōruri*, receiving instructions from Kadayū in his formative years.

Chikamatsu's first known *jōruri* was **Yotsugi Soga** (The Heir Soga) in 1683, which he wrote for Kadayū, then called Kaganojō, at the age of thirty-one. The success of the production of The Heir Soga at the Uji Theatre made Kaganojō more popular in Kyoto, and Chikamatsu made his debut as a *jōruri* writer with the piece. As a matter of fact Chikamatsu had been writing several plays for Kaganojō since he was twenty-five, but it was the time when a position of a *jōruri* writer was not recognized, which explains that Chikamatsu's name was not found in Kaganojō's *jōruri* script at all before The Heir Soga.

植村家は1909年に興行会社松竹[11]に文楽の興行権を譲る。その後、1963年に松竹が文楽から撤退し、文楽座は朝日座と名前を変え、文楽は新たに財団法人文楽協会として出発する。竹本座が開かれてからまさに三百年後の1984年に、道頓堀に近い現在の位置に国立文楽劇場が建設され、関西の文楽の定席であった朝日座はその長い幕を閉じることになる。

近松門左衛門（1653－1724）

近松門左衛門は多作家で浄瑠璃と歌舞伎台本を合わせて、署名のあるものだけで百五十曲以上書いている。署名のないものをも含めると二百曲以上になるといわれている。彼の作品はすべて舞台化のために書かれたものであり、近松単独の作であるといわれている。浄瑠璃本は太夫や三味線弾きが言葉と曲の兼ね合いのため少し変えることがあり、歌舞伎本は客の要望を満足させるため、役者が多くの書き換えを求めたと推測されている。

近松は越前国吉江（福井県鯖江市）の生まれである。父は越前藩主に仕えた武士、母は藩医の娘であった。本姓は杉森信盛、幼名は次郎吉であった。近松が十代の初めに父が致仕し、浪人となり、一家は京都に移り住む。

京都で近松は公家の堂上家に仕えたといわれている。この時代、公家は政治的には無力であったが、詩歌や歌舞音曲を楽しむ伝統を保っており、しばしば浄瑠璃や歌舞伎の後援者になっていた。近松の幅広い教養はこの時代に培われたものであると考えられている。当時、堂上家の公家の一人が嘉太夫に浄瑠璃を書いており、その使いをしたことが近松の浄瑠璃の世界を知るきっかけになり、近松は嘉太夫のもとで浄瑠璃を書き始める。

現在知られている近松の最も早い時期の作品は、1683年に彼が三十一歳の時に宇治加賀掾（前名宇治嘉太夫）に書いた「世継曽我」であり、近松はこの作で浄瑠璃作家として世に出る。一方、宇治座での「世継曽我」の成功で加賀掾は京都での人気をより高めることになる。実際には、近松は二十五歳のころから加賀掾に浄瑠璃を書いている。しかし、当時まだ浄瑠璃作家の地位が確立されていなかったことで、「世継曽我」以前に近松が書いた浄瑠璃の加賀掾の正本には近松の名前が載っていない。

INTRODUCTION

Kiyomizu Ridayū, now Takemoto Gidayū, who had been back in Osaka, asked Chikamatsu for permission to stage a revised version of The Heir Soga as the opening production of the Takemoto Theatre. The Heir Soga saw another big success in Osaka. In 1685 when Chikamatsu was thirty-three, he wrote **Shusse Kagekiyo** (Kagekiyo's Success) for Takemoto Gidayū. This was going to mark the start of a successful and prosperous collaboration between Chikamatsu and Gidayū.

From this time on *jōruri* written before Kagekiyo's Success are known as *ko-jōruri* (the old-*jōruri*) and after it, as *shin-jōruri* (the new-*jōruri*). Gidayū is regarded as the founder of the new *jōruri* recitation. His chanting style is called *Gidayu-bushi*[12] and the name *gidayu* is now synonymous with *jōruri*. Meanwhile we first find the signature 'Chikamatsu Monzaemon' at this time when he was about thirty-four and making claims for his position as a playwright. This was not the custom of the time and he was criticised for that.

There were three people with whom Chikamatsu worked closely as a playwright. Their names are Uji Kaganojō, Takemoto Gidayū, and a *kabuki* actor, Sakata Tōjūrō.[13] The collaboration between Chikamatsu and the three significantly changed the world of *jōruri* and *kabuki*.

Sakata Tōjūrō was born as a son of a theatre proprietor of Miyako Mandayū-*za*, the Miyako Mandayū Theatre, in Kyoto. He began acting when he was six. In his twenties he learned naturalistic acting from one of the experienced female role actors. When he was thirty-two, he played the part of Fujiya Izaemon, Yūgiri's lover, in **Yūgiri Nagori no Shōgatsu** (The Sorrow of Parting of Yūgiri on New Year's Day) in Osaka; his performance had a sensational reception. Yūgiri was a real courtesan in Shin-*machi*, Osaka who lived between 1654 and 1678. She was much admired and after her death, several *kabuki* plays about Yūgiri called *Yūgiri-kyōgen* (Yūgiri play) were written, employing her as main character. Tōjūrō always played Yūgiri's lover, Izaemon, in the first productions of Yūgiri plays and a role of Izaemon became his signature part.

Kabuki was becoming very popular and theatres competed for audiences then. It was coming to the peak of the *Genroku Kabuki*[14] era, one of the most prosperous times in *kabuki* history. *Kabuki* actors looked for a good play which would grab the audience's attention. Chikamatsu began writing a kabuki play around this time. In 1693 when Chikamatsu was forty-one, he was commissioned by Tōjūrō to write a play, **Butsumo Mayasan Kaichō** (Revealing the Image of Mother Buddha of the Mount Maya). It was a story about an internal squabble over the headship rights of a feudal lord. His step mother and brother try to take over from the rightful heir. Tōjūrō played the role of a dissipated heir to the lord, and there was a scene in a licensed quarter written specially for Tōjūrō to do his *yatsushi* (to dress incon-

24

大阪にもどり、今は竹本義太夫となった清水理太夫は近松に「世継曽我」の改訂版を竹本座の旗揚げで上演する許可を貰う。大阪の竹本座での「世継曽我」は再び大きな評判をとる。1685年にそれまで加賀掾に書いてきた近松が初めて義太夫に「出世景清」を書きおろす。この仕事がこの後、近松と竹本義太夫の二人に繁栄と成功とをもたらす共同作業の始まりになる。近松三十三歳の時である。

　この時から浄瑠璃では「出世景清」以前の曲を古浄瑠璃、以後の曲を新浄瑠璃といい、新浄瑠璃を語る義太夫の語りは義太夫節[12]と呼ばれるようになる。義太夫は新浄瑠璃の語りの開祖と言われ、今日、浄瑠璃のことを義太夫と呼ぶのはここに由来している。一方、近松は三十四歳になったころから自作の浄瑠璃に署名を入れて自身の作家としての地位を主張し始めるが、当時の慣習に従っていないとして批判を受けている。

　近松が戯作者として近しく仕事をした三人の演者がいる。前述した浄瑠璃の太夫、宇治加賀掾と竹本義太夫、そして、もう一人は歌舞伎役者坂田藤十郎[13]である。近松がこの三人とした仕事は浄瑠璃や歌舞伎の世界を大きく変えた。

　坂田藤十郎は都万太夫座の座元の息子として京都に生まれ、六歳のころから舞台に上がる。二十代のころ、経験を積んだ女形から、これまで学んできた歌舞伎の型ではない写実的な演技の教えを乞う。三十二歳のとき、大阪で上演した「夕霧名残の正月」で夕霧の恋人藤屋伊左衛門の役を演じて大評判をとる。夕霧は1654年から1678年に大阪新町の遊郭に実在した太夫職の名妓である。人々から称賛されていて、死後、彼女を主役に立てた芝居である「夕霧狂言」が多く書かれた。藤十郎はこの「夕霧狂言」で、最初の作品からずっと伊左衛門の役を演じており、伊左衛門が彼の当たり役となった。

　このころ、歌舞伎はその歴史の中で最も栄えた時期の一つである元禄歌舞伎の時代[14]を迎えており、歌舞伎の人気が高まると同時に競争もますます激しくなってゆく。その結果、歌舞伎役者は観客の心を掴む役の書かれたいい芝居を探すことに心を注いだ。近松が歌舞伎を書き始めたのはこのころである。1693年、四十一歳の時に近松は藤十郎に「仏母摩耶山開帳」を書いている。芝居の筋書きは武家のお家騒動で、主人公の継母と義弟が世継ぎを争って画策する話である。藤十郎は正統のお世継ぎ、放蕩ものの第一子を演じている。この芝居には特別に藤十郎の〈やつし〉と呼ばれる演技のために遊郭のシーンが書き込まれている。

spicuously or to be in the disguise) acting.

"A young lord or a young master of a large shop in a shabby paper kimono appears on stage. He is a wreck of his former self. But he is still easy-going, generous and acts in an elegant manner, somehow amicable and humorous. This device in *kabuki* is called '*yatsushi*' and Tōjūrō was good at playing it; he was excellent in both movements and delivering speeches which were often Chikamatsu's writing"[15]

The play is thought to be the first *kabuki* play with the signature of 'Chikamatsu Monzaemon.' When Tōjūrō became the proprietor of the Miyako Mandayū Theatre in 1695, he invited Chikamatsu as playwright in residence; there he wrote for Tōjūrō for the next ten years. There are about thirty existing *kabuki* plays by Chikamatsu from this period in which Tōjūrō played a leading role. In comparison Tōjūrō's acting was less stylized for *kabuki* and had an element of realism through which he tried to express the character's true feelings. The direction was paralleled by the one taken by Chikamatsu in *jōruri*. Their collaborative work helped to bring some natural and realistic acting called *wagoto* (soft and gentle style of acting)[16] to *kabuki*.

Chikamatsu made a trip to Osaka when he was fifty-one. There he was asked by Gidayū to write a new *jōruri* based on a recent incident in Osaka; a shop assistant, a nephew of the owner of a large soy sauce shop, committed lovers' suicide with a young courtesan in Dōjima, at the Sonezaki Shrine in Osaka. A double suicide was a forbidden act and so the happening was a major scandal among the Osakan. Kabuki was quick to present the incident on stage, but not yet in *ningyō-jōruri*. Chikamatsu wrote a *jōruri*, **Sonezaki Shinjū** (Lovers' Suicides at Sonezaki) in 1703; the production of the *jōruri* at the Takeda Theatre was an instant big success. It has been said that the theatre earned so much money as to be able to pay off all its debts.

Jōruri had been written based on classics or historical occurrences until this time. Lovers' Suicides at Sonezaki was the first ever *jōruri* written based on a contemporary event. After this new piece, *jōruri* were divided into two categories, *jidai-jōruri or jidai-mono* (a period piece) and *sewa-jōruri or sewa-mono* (a domestic or contemporary piece). Chikamatsu and Gidayū were the founders of *sewa-jōruri*.

Chikamatsu became a residential *jōruri* writer of the Takemoto Theatre at the age of fifty-three, and wrote altogether twenty-four *sewa-jōruri* for the theatre in addition to many *jidai-jōruri*. Takemoto Gidayū died at the age of sixty-four in 1714 when Chikamatsu was sixty-two. After the death of Gidayū, Chikamatsu fostered the next generation of *jōruri*

「若殿や商家の若旦那が零落してみすぼらしい紙衣姿(かみこ)で現れるのを「やつし」と称する。どこかかつての鷹揚さが抜けきらず、おかしみのある演技を見せる。この「やつし」の芸を藤十郎は得意とした。それに加えて「しゃべり」の芸も得意であった。この「しゃべり」の芸は近松の書いたセリフが元になっている」[15]

「仏母摩耶山開帳」は近松門左衛門の署名の書き込まれた最初の歌舞伎本と考えられている。1695年に藤十郎が都万太夫座の座元になったとき、近松は藤十郎に都万太夫座の座付き作者になるよう頼まれる。こののち十年間、近松は都万太夫座で藤十郎のために歌舞伎を書き、現在その歌舞伎本が三十本近く残っている。藤十郎の演技は歌舞伎としては型の芝居ではなく、比較的写実の芝居であった。こうした演技方法で藤十郎は登場人物の内面的な部分も表現しようとした。これは近松が浄瑠璃で求めてきたものと同じ方向性であったようである。戯作者近松と役者藤十郎の二人の共同作業は和事[16]と呼ばれる自然で写実的な歌舞伎のカテゴリーを元禄歌舞伎に編み出すことになる。

五十一歳のとき近松は大阪に旅をする。その折、竹本義太夫から最近大阪で起こった心中事件を浄瑠璃に書くことを依頼される。大きな醬油屋の主人の甥の若い手代と堂島の若い遊女が曽根崎の神社の森で心中した。心中は天下のご法度で、事件は大阪の人々にとってひどく扇情的な出来事であった。歌舞伎はいち早く事件を舞台に乗せていたが、人形浄瑠璃ではまだ誰も取り上げていなかった。1703年、近松は義太夫に浄瑠璃「曽根崎心中」を書いた。そして、「曽根崎心中」の竹本座での上演は大成功をおさめるのである。「曽根崎心中」の成功は、竹本座がこれまで抱えていた借金をすべて返済することができたと言われるほどのものであった。

「曽根崎心中」以前に書かれた浄瑠璃はすべて歴史上の出来事や故事が題材であり、「曽根崎心中」は当時の世の中で起こっている出来事に取材した初めての浄瑠璃であった。以降、前者は時代浄瑠璃、後者は世話浄瑠璃と呼ばれ、浄瑠璃は大きく二つの種類に分けられることになる。近松と義太夫がこの世話浄瑠璃の創始者であった。

近松は五十三歳で竹本座の座付き作者となり、時代浄瑠璃以外に二十四作の世話浄瑠璃を書き下ろす。1714年、近松六十二歳のときに竹本義太夫が他界する。享年六十四歳であった。義太夫の死後、近松は竹本座で次代を担う戯作者の育成に力を注ぎ、自身の没後に迎える人形浄瑠璃全盛時代の基礎を築き、七十二歳で没する。

INTRODUCTION

writers in the Takemoto Theatre. He built a solid foundation for the coming golden age of *ningyō-jōruri* until he died at age seventy-two.

Between 1703 and 1722 Chikamatsu wrote twenty-four *sewa-jōruri or sewa-mono*. They are subdivided into four categories based on their theme: they are *shinjū-mono* (a lovers'-suicide piece), *hanzai-mono* (a criminal piece), *kantsū-mono* (an adultery piece) and *kakō-mono* (a fictional piece). There are eleven lovers'-suicide pieces, five criminal pieces, three adultery pieces and five fictional pieces in his *sewa-jōruri*.

Three plays of the Chikamatsu Project are all *sewa-jōruri* from the different categories. **Onna Koroshi Abura no Jigoku** (Woman-Killer in Oil Hell) first staged in 1721, is a punishment piece, **Horikawa Nami no Tsuzumi** (Drumbeats over the Horikawa) in 1707, is an adultery piece and **Imamiya no Shinjū** (Lovers' Suicides at Imamiya) in 1711, a lovers'-suicide piece. The project chose these *jōruri* to give a broader representation of Chikamatsu's contemporary output.

Notes
1. An oriental stringed musical instrument. A Japanese lute has a bent neck and four of five strings.
2. Of unknown authorship
3. Minamoto no Yoshitsune (1159-1189) was a general, the ninth son of Minanoto no Yoshitomo who was also a general. Yoshitsune's childhood name was Ushiwaka-maru.
4. Minamoto no Yoritomo (1147-1199) was the third son of Yoshitomo, the founder of samurai or militarist government, became a shogun in 1192. The first shogun of the Kamakura Shogunate/Bakufu.
5. Urayama Masao, *Nihon Engeki shi*, Tokyo: Ōfū-sha, 1978, Page75
6. Gorobei (1651-1714), became Kiyomizu Ridaū, then Takemoto Gidayū. After receiving the title of honour in 1698, he was called Takemoto Chikugonojō.
7. Uji Kadayū (1635-1711), called Uji Kaganojō after receiving the title of honour in 1677.
8. Although the Tokugawa Shogunate opened his government in Edo (present-day Tokyo) in 1603, Kyoto was kept as the capital of Japan until the return of political power to the Emperor by the Tokugawa Shogunate in 1867, followed by transferring the seat of the Imperial Court to Tokyo in 1869. Japanese emperors resided in Kyoto Gosho (Kyoto Imperial Palace) till that time.
9. Torigoe Bunzō, *Chikamatsu e no Shōtai*, Tokyo: Iwanami Shoten, 1989, Page 6.

近松が1703年から1722年の間に書いた二十四篇の世話浄瑠璃は主題によって、〈心中物〉〈犯罪物〉〈姦通物〉〈仮構物〉の四種に分けられる。作品数の内わけは〈心中物〉が十一篇、〈犯罪物〉五篇、〈姦通物〉三篇、〈仮構物〉五編である。

　近松プロジェクトでは〈心中物〉〈犯罪物〉〈姦通物〉の異なったカテゴリーからそれぞれ一篇ずつ選んで上演した。「女殺油地獄」(1721年)は〈犯罪物〉、「堀川波鼓」(1707年)は〈姦通物〉、「今宮の心中」(1711年)は〈心中物〉である。異なったカテゴリーからの選択は世話浄瑠璃を出来るだけいろいろな角度から考察するためであった。

註
1　東洋の弦楽器。木製の扁平な茄子(なす)の形の胴に4、5本の弦を張ったもの。日本のものはふつう4〜5個の柱(じゅう)をつけて撥(ばち)で奏する。
2　作者未詳。
3　源義経(みなもとのよしつね)(1159〜1189)。武将。幼名牛若丸(うしわかまる)。源氏の大将源義朝の九男。母は常盤(ときわ)。
4　源頼朝(みなもとのよりとも)(1149〜1199)。源義朝の三男。鎌倉幕府初代将軍。武家政治の基礎を築く。1192年に征夷大将軍に任ぜられる。
5　浦山政雄他『日本演劇史』桜楓社、1978年、75頁。
6　本名五郎兵衛(1651〜1714)。初名清水理太夫、後に竹本義太夫と名乗る。1698年ごろに受領した後、竹本筑後掾と称する。
7　宇治嘉太夫(1635〜1711)。1677年に受領した後、宇治加賀掾と称する。
8　1603年に徳川家康は江戸(現在の東京)に幕府を定めたが、1867年の大政奉還、1869年の東京遷都まで京都が日本の首都であり、その時までずっと天皇は京都御所にいた。
9　鳥越文蔵、『近松への招待』、岩波書店、1989年、6頁。

INTRODUCTION

10   Uemura Bunrakuken (1751-1810)
11   Shochiku Co., Ltd. The company was founded in 1895 as a kabuki production company. It is a Japanese movie studio, which also produces and distributes anime films.
12   Gidayū's chanting style was formed on the ground of Harima-*bushi* by Inoue Harimanojo. As it had the influences of the chanting style of Uji Kaganojō, *Heikyoju*, *yōkyoku* and so on, it acquired the ability to express more than the old style.

13   Sakata Tōjūrō I (1647?-1709): Other well-known Chikamatsu plays for Tōjūrō are **Keisei Awa no Naruto** in 1695, **Keisei Hotoke no Hara** in 1699 and so on.
14   It is the time about fifty years around the Genroku era (1688-1704). Kabuki became spoken drama and *sewa-kyōgen* (a domestic or contemporary play) appeared in this era. "Kabuki developed greatly as an art. The first official playwright was listed in 1680, and star actors began to emerge. In the Kyoto-Osaka region, Sakata Tōjūrō I developed *wagoto*, an acting style for the realistic portrayal of young men in love. Meanwhile in Edo (present-day Tokyo) Icihkawa Danjūrō I invented the bombastic acting style called *aragoto*, which became enormously popular with the plebeian audience." (Ronald, Cavaye. *Kabuki, a Pocket Guide*. Rutland, Vermont & Tokyo: Charles E Tuttle Co., 1993, Page 20.)
15   Torigoe Bunzō, *Kyojitsu no Nagusami Chikamatsu Monzaemon*, Tokyo: Shinten-sha, 1989, Page 222.
16   See Notes No. 14.

10　植村文楽軒（1751 〜 1810）

11　松竹株式会社。日本の映画、演劇の制作、興行、配給を手掛ける。歌舞伎の興行はほぼ独占的に手掛けている。創業1895年。

12　義太夫節。義太夫の始めた新しい浄瑠璃は播磨掾の語り口を基本にしていたが、それは加賀掾はもとより他派のいろいろな長所、平曲、幸若、謡曲、説教、祭文から流行歌まで幅広くふくめたもので、従来の浄瑠璃よりも表現が多彩で新鮮に聞こえた。

13　坂田藤十郎（1647 ? 〜 1709）。その他、近松が藤十郎に書いた芝居は「傾城阿波の鳴門」（1695年）、「傾城仏が原」（1699年）など。

14　元禄歌舞伎。元禄時代（1688年〜 1709年）のおよそ五十年の間の歌舞伎のこと。歌舞伎が台詞劇になり世話狂言（世話浄瑠璃）が始まる。「歌舞伎は舞台芸術としておおいに発達する。1680年に初めて戯作者のリストが発表され、人気役者が出始める。上方では坂田藤十郎が恋する若者を写実的に表現する演技で和事を発達させる。一方、江戸（現在の東京）では市川団十郎が大げさな演技の荒事を発案して、それが庶民の間で人気を博する。」[Ronald, Cavaye, Kabuki, A Pocket Guide. Rutland, Charles E Tuttle Co., Vermont & Tokyo, 1993, p. 20.]

15　鳥越文蔵『虚実の慰み　近松門左衛門』新典社、1989年、222頁。

16　註14参照。

MEASURING SYSTEM IN THE EDO PERIOD (1603-1867)

1 Time of the day

In Edo time the clock was adjusted in accordance with the sunrise and the sunset. Start of the daytime was called *Ake-mutsu*, the 6th hour of dawn, which was about half an hour before sunrise when the eastern sky was becoming light. Start of the night time was called *Kure-mutsu*, the 6th hour of dusk, which was about thirty minutes after the sunset when the lights began coming on. *Ake-mutsu* and *Kure-mutsu* were adjusted in every fifteen days.

An Edo hour was about two hours by the present clock. There were twelve Edo hours in a day: six Edo hours each in the daytime and the night time. The length of an Edo hour was not the same in the daytime and the night time, as well as in a different season.

There were two ways of counting the time, one way was by numerals and the other was by twelve animal signs. The details are seen in the following diagram.

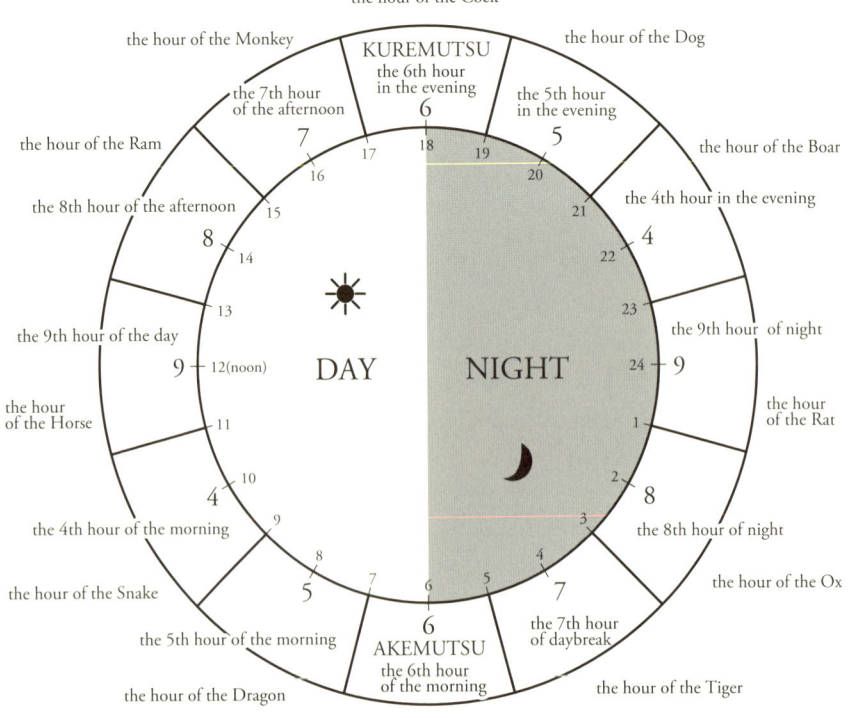

江戸時代のものの数え方

1　時刻

　時刻制度は日の出と日の入りを基準とする不定時法で、日の出の半時間ほど前、東の空が明るくなり始める頃を「明け六つ」、暗くなって照明が必要となる頃を「暮れ六つ」とした。「明け六つ」と「暮れ六つ」の時間は十五日ごとに決められた。

　「一とき」はおよそ現在の二時間で、昼と夜をそれぞれ「六とき」に分け、一日は「十二とき」からなっていた。不定時法であるので季節によって昼と夜や「一とき」の長さは異なった。

　「とき」は数で数える場合と十二支で数える場合の二通りあった。詳しくは下の図に示した。

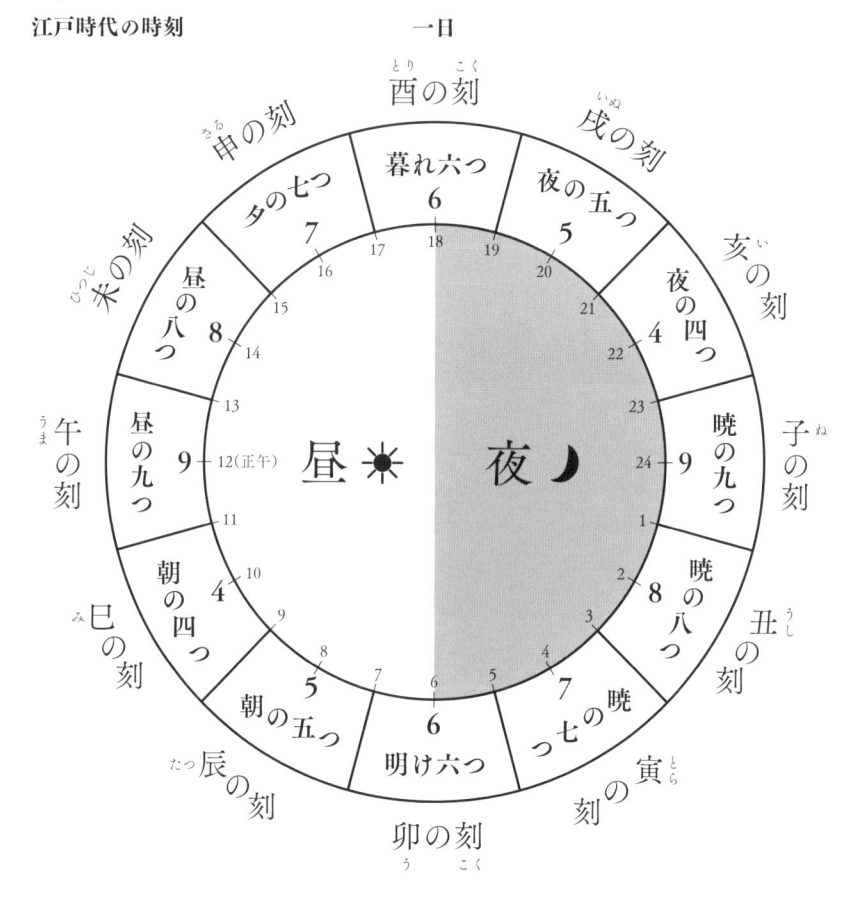

江戸時代の時刻　　　　　　　一日

酉の刻　戌の刻　亥の刻　子の刻　丑の刻　寅の刻　卯の刻　辰の刻　巳の刻　午の刻　未の刻　申の刻

暮れ六つ 6／夕の七つ 7／昼の八つ 8／昼の九つ 9（正午）／朝の四つ 4／朝の五つ 5／明け六つ 6／暁七つ 7／暁の八つ 8／暁の九つ 9／夜の四つ 4／夜の五つ 5

昼　夜

MEASURING SYSTEM IN THE EDO PERIOD

2 Calendar

The calendar in the plays is the old Japanese calendar which the Tokugawa Government employed from 1684. It was a mixture of the lunar and solar calendars, produced by Shibukawa Shunkai (1639-1715). In this calendar a month lasted from a full moon to the next full moon. A long month consisted of 30 days and a short month of 29 days. The long months and the short months were adjusted every year for the months and the seasons to cohere. A 'Long-Short Month Calendar' was put on sale every year.

The present calendar has been shifted about forty days forward from the old calendar. In **Woman-Killer in Oil Hell** the incident happens on the fourth of May. But the fourth of May then is the middle of June in the present calendar, and it is the climate when changing kimonos for the summer is necessary.

3 People's age

People's ages were counted by *kazoe-doshi*, 'the person's calendar age.' According to this calculation, when a person is born, he/she is one year old, to which a year is added every New Year's Day. This means that the characters in the plays could be a couple of years younger than their numerical age.

4 Monetary system

Three different metals, gold, silver and copper were used for the money in the Edo period.

Gold Coin was counted by a quaternary-coded decimal arithmetic. An oval gold coin was one *ryō*-gold; one *ryō*-gold was four *bu*-gold, and one *bu*-gold was four *shu*-gold. (1 *ryō*-gold =4 *bu*-gold =16 *shu*-gold) One *ryō*-gold minted in *Keichō* period was about 17.7g.

Silver was the currency by weight and the denomination was *monme*. One *kan monme*-silver was one thousand *monme*-silver; one *monme*-silver was ten *bu*-silver. (1 *kan monme*-silver = 1000 *monme*-silver = 10,000 *bu*-silver)

Copper Coin was called *sen*, which derives from *Kaigentsūhō-sen* brought over from China. One copper coin was one *mon sen*-copper; one thousand (*mon*) *sen*-coppers were equal to one *kan* (*mon*) *sen*-coppers. (1 *kan sen*-coppers = 1000 *sen*-coppers)

The official quotation was 1 *ryō*-gold = 50 (later 60) *monme*-silver = 4000 *sen* coppers around 1700. This however was altered by the market price.

江戸時代のものの数え方

2　暦

　劇中の暦は一六八四年に渋川春海(しぶかわしゅんかい)(1639〜1715)によって考え出された暦、旧暦である。これは太陰歴と太陽歴を混ぜたもので、ひと月を満月から次の満月までとして、大の月を三十日、小の月を二十九日としている。この暦では毎年大の月と小の月を変えて、月日と季節がずれるのを防いでいる。江戸時代には毎年、大の月と小の月の記された大小暦という暦が売り出された。

　旧暦と新暦（太陽暦）には四十日ほどのずれがある。「女殺油地獄」の事件が起こる旧暦の五月四日は新暦では六月中ごろであり、衣替えが必要な気候になっている。

3　年齢の数え方

　年齢は「数え年」で数えた。「数え年」とは、生まれたその年を一歳とし、以後正月ごとに一歳ずつ増やして数える年齢である。登場人物たちの年齢は「数え年」で書かれているので、今日の数え方だと実年齢は一、二歳ほど若くなる。

4　貨幣

　貨幣は金・銀・銭(せん)（銅）三種の異なった貨幣からなる三貨制度(さんかせいど)を用いた。
「金貨(きんか)」は小判(こばん)一枚を一両(りょう)とし、その四分の一を「分(ぶ)」、分の四分の一を「朱(しゅ)」とした四進法を用いた。（一両＝四分＝十六朱）金一両は慶長小判1枚で4.73匁、約17.7グラム。
「銀貨」は重さが貨幣の価値となる秤量貨幣(ひょうりょうかへい)で基準単位は匁(もんめ)（目(め)・文目(もんめ))であった。一貫(かん)は千匁(もんめ)、一匁(もんめ)は千分(ぶ)。（一貫＝千匁＝一万分）

「銭(せん)（銅貨）」は一個が一文(もん)で千文を一貫文(かんもん)とした。（一貫文＝千文）銭(せん)は唐の開元(かいげん)通宝(つうほう)銭が渡来して標準とされ、一文の目方(めかた)を一文目(いちもんめ)と呼んだことによる。

　三貨の価値は時代により変動した。1700年頃は、公定相場は金一両＝銀50匁（のち60匁）＝銭四貫であった。

35

5 Measurement for length, weight and volume

Shakkanhō is a traditional Japanese measurement, measuring length by *shaku* and weight by *kan*. Japan joined the Treaty of the Meter in 1885, but *Syakkanhō* was used in combination with the metric system of measurement until 1958.

(1) Units of Length

There are *ri, chō, ken, shaku* etc. for the units of length. One *ri* is thirty-six *chō*. One *chō* is sixty *ken* and equal to about 109 meters. One *ken* is normally 6 *shaku* and is equal to 1.82 meter. (1 *ri* = 36 *chō*=2160 *ken* =about 3927meter)

(2) Units of Weight

There are *kan, monme* (or *me*) for the units of weight. One *kan* is one thousand *monme*. One *monme* is equal to about 3.75 gram. (1 *kan* =1000 *monme* = about 3.75kilogram)

(3) Units of Volume

There are *koku, to, shō, gō* for the units of volume. They were used measuring rice, sake and oil etc. One *koku* is ten *to*. One *to* is ten *shō*. One *shō is* ten *gō,* equal to about 1.8 litres. (1 *koku* = 10 *to* = 100 *shō* = 1000 *gō* = 180.39 litres)

A samurai's annual stipend was paid by rice or gold. It was thought a grown-up person would need five *gō* of brown rice for food and other necessary things per day. Rice was used as a system of measurement.

5　長さ、重さ、かさの単位

　日本古来の度量衡法で、長さの単位を尺、重さの単位を貫、かさ（容積）の単位を升、とする尺貫法を用いた。日本は1885年（明治18）にメートル条約に加入したが、1958年まではメートル法と併用されていた。

（1）長さの単位

　　「里」「丁・町」「間」など。一里は三十六町で3.927キロメートル。一町は六十間で約109メートル。一間はふつう六尺で1.82メートル。
　　（一里＝三十六町＝二千百六十間＝約3.927キロメートル）

（2）重さの単位

　　「貫」「目（匁・文目）」。一貫は千匁。一匁は約3.75グラム。
　　（一貫＝千匁＝約3.75キログラム）

（3）容積の単位

　　「石」「斗」「升」「合」など。米、酒、油などを量るのに用いた。一石は十斗。一斗は十升。一升は十合。1891年に一升を1.8039リットルと定めた。
　　（一石＝十斗＝百升＝千合＝約180.39リットル）
　　「石」は大名・武家の所領地の石高を表す。人が一日に必要な食糧やその他の物を玄米に換算して計算した。成人で一人一日五合必要と考えた。

STAGING OF THE CHIKAMATSU PROJECT

The stage we used for the project had three areas; they were the main stage, *the hanamichi* and the side-stages. The side-stages were Stage Right and Left of the main stage, both visible to the audience.

Needless to say, the main stage and *the hanamichi* (an elevated walkway through the auditorium) were the main performing area. The platform of several tatami-mat sized rostra raised to the height of about 40cm* was placed Upstage of the main stage. The platform was used for the places higher than ground level, such as the inner part of a house or a river bank. The *hanamichi* was used as part of a street.

All the actors entered the side-stages in Blackout before the start of a performance. The actors who should be on stage from the start of the play moved to the main stage from there. The rest of the actors waited for their turn, sitting on the actors' waiting benches put on the side-stages. While in the side areas, they also played the roles of the chorus and produced sound effects. Some sound effects were also created by the stage-managers at the wings of the stage.

As we performed a Chikamatsu *sewa-mono* play with about ten actors, it was common for an actor to play more than one character; as a result the costume change had to be quick and seamless. The actors went behind the curtains when they had a major costume change, but minor costume changes were done on the side-stages. Also the props for the actors to carry were placed on the prop tables set on the side-stages.

* It is the height called *tsune-ashi* in *Kabuki*. The standard height in *Kabuki* is called *jōshiki* which is seven *suns* (about 21cm). *Tsune-ashi* is the height of two *jōshiki*, and is often used for houses of a merchant, a low-ranking samurai and a farmer.

近松プロジェクトの舞台

　近松プロジェクトの舞台では本舞台、花道、脇舞台（サイド・ステージ）の三つのエリアを設けた。脇舞台は本舞台の上手と下手の両端から舞台袖までの観客席から見える部分である。

　言うまでもないが、本舞台と花道を主な演技空間とした。本舞台奥に畳四~五畳ほどの広さで、高さが約四十センチメートル＊の台を組んだ。この部分は座敷や土手などの地面よりも少し高い場所に用いた。花道は文字通り道として使った。

　出演俳優全員は開幕前の暗転で上手と下手の両脇舞台から登場した。板付きの俳優も先ず脇舞台から登場し、そこから本舞台に移動した。板付きでない俳優は脇舞台に置かれた「俳優待機ベンチ」で各自の出番を待った。脇舞台では、俳優達はコーラスの役をしたり、効果音を出したりした。全員が本舞台に出ている場面の効果音は、舞台転換のために袖で待機しているステージ・マネジャーが受け持った。

　近松世話物劇を十人前後の俳優で演じたので、一人の俳優が一つ以上の役を受け持つのは普通であった。そのため、異なった役への衣装替えは、手早く行われなければならなかった。大掛かりな衣装替えには舞台袖の暗幕の後ろを用いた。が、少しのことはすべて脇舞台で行った。持ち道具も脇舞台に小道具台を設置して、そこに並べた。

　　＊　歌舞伎で常足（つねあし）と呼ばれる高さ。歌舞伎の決まりごとである定式（じょうしき）の台の高さは
　　　　七寸（すん）（約21cm）で、この七寸が二つ重ねて常足の高さとする。常足は商家
　　　　や下級武士や百姓の家などに使われる。

Chapter II
第Ⅱ部

WOMAN-KILLER IN OIL HELL
A Play in Three Acts

Original Jōruri
Onna Koroshi Abura no Jigoku
By
Chikamatsu Monzaemon

Adaptation and translation
By
Masako Yuasa

「女殺油地獄」
三幕六場

原作

近松門左衛門

翻案・英訳

湯浅雅子

Performance Poster（公演ポスター）
Woman-Killer in Oil Hell（「女殺油地獄」）
Leeds in March 2004（2004年3月リーズ大学）

Stage Photos（舞台写真）
Woman-Killer in Oil Hell（「女殺油地獄」）
Leeds in March 2004（2004年3月リーズ大学）
Photographs by Workshop Theatre at Leeds（撮影リーズ大学ワークショップシアター）

ACT ONE Zenbei, Yohei and Kichi　上之巻　善兵衛、与兵衛、吉

Part One of ACT THREE Kiyo and Kichi
下之巻　その一　清と吉

Part One of ACT THREE Kichi and Yohei
下之巻　その一　吉と与兵衛

Original Design for *Woman-Killer in Oil Hell*   ACT ONE
「女殺油地獄」舞台図原案　上之巻
Tokuan Embankment　徳庵堤

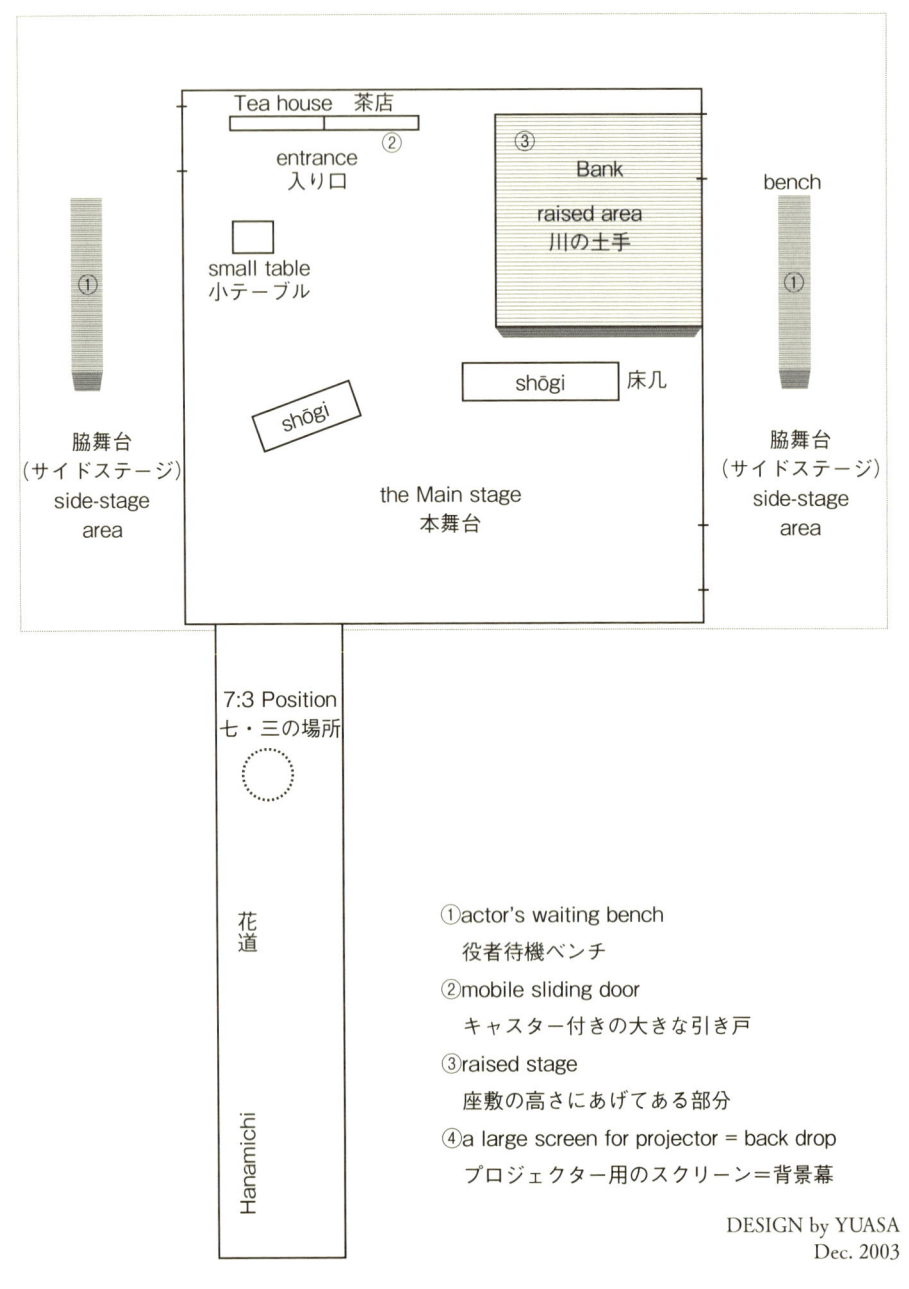

④　　　　　　　screen　スクリーン

Tea house　茶店

②　entrance
入り口

③ Bank
raised area
川の土手

bench

small table
小テーブル

shōgi

shōgi　床几

①

①

脇舞台
(サイドステージ)
side-stage
area

脇舞台
(サイドステージ)
side-stage
area

the Main stage
本舞台

7:3 Position
七・三の場所

花道 Hanamichi

① actor's waiting bench
　役者待機ベンチ
② mobile sliding door
　キャスター付きの大きな引き戸
③ raised stage
　座敷の高さにあげてある部分
④ a large screen for projector = back drop
　プロジェクター用のスクリーン＝背景幕

DESIGN by YUASA
Dec. 2003

Original Design for *Woman-Killer in Oil Hell*　ACT THREE
「女殺油地獄」舞台図原案　下之巻
Teshimaya　豊島屋
④　screen　スクリーン

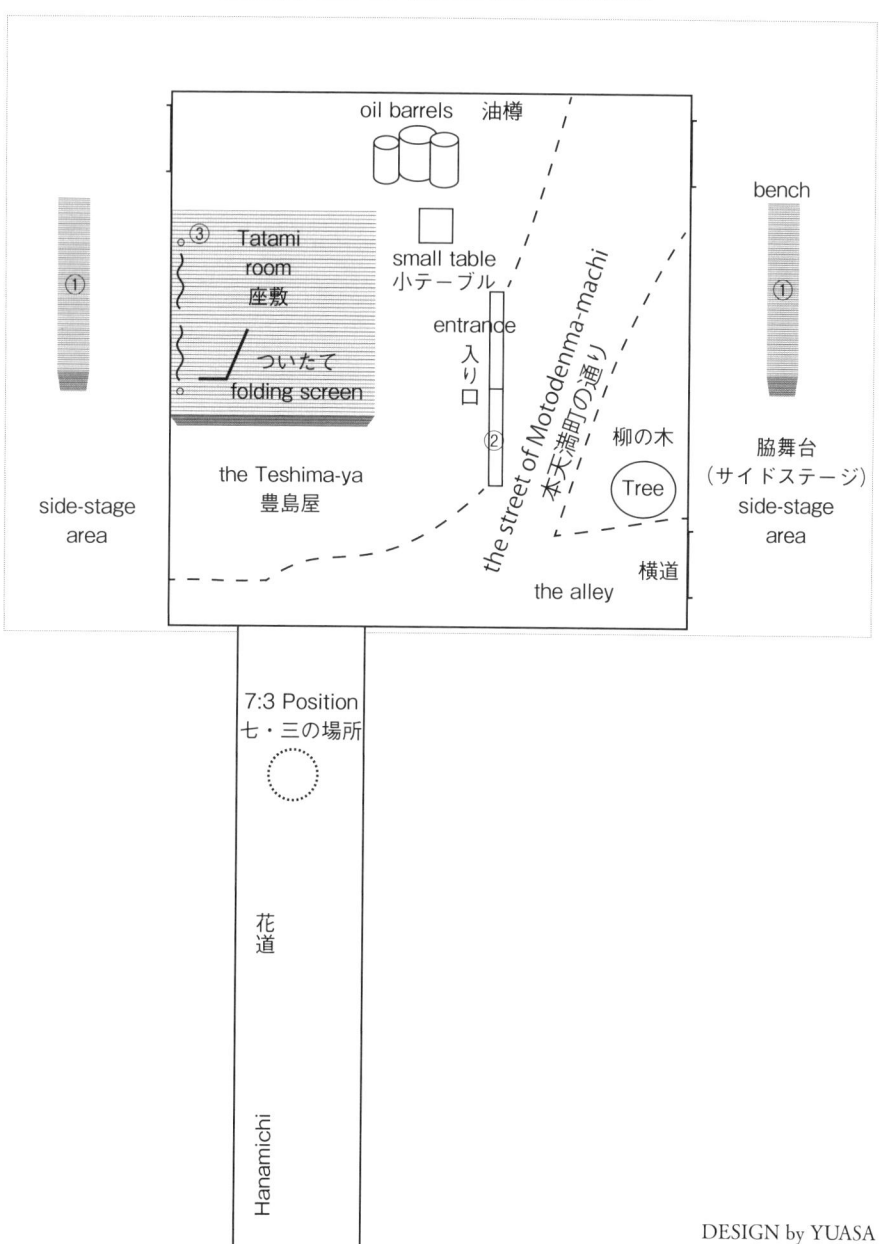

oil barrels　油樽

③ Tatami room 座敷

small table 小テーブル

ついたて folding screen

entrance 入り口

②

the street of Motodenma-machi 本天満町の通り

柳の木 Tree

the Teshima-ya 豊島屋

the alley 横道

① bench

① 脇舞台（サイドステージ）side-stage area

side-stage area

7:3 Position 七・三の場所

花道 Hanamichi

DESIGN by YUASA
Dec. 2003

47

WOMAN-KILLER IN OIL HELL

The original *jōruri* was first performed at the Takemoto-za on the 15th of July in 1721. The proprietor of the theatre was Takeda Izumo. The *jōruri* reciter was Takemono Chikugonojō. The *jōruri* was written by Chikamatsu Monzaemon when he was sixty-nine.

Reference
'Onna Koroshi Abura no Jigoku,' *Nihon Koten Bungaku Zenshū Chikamatsu Monzaemon Shū 1,* edited by Torigoe Bunzō, translated into current Japanese with notes by Yamane Taneo, published by Shōgakukan in 1997. (Page 205-265)

The adaptation was first staged at Studio 1 of the Workshop Theatre, School of English of the University of Leeds from 15th to 17th March 2004, with the following cast and crew:

KAWACHI-YA TOKUBEI	Michele Chung
SAWA	Katheryn Owens
YOHEI	Jonathan Bonnici
KACHI	Helen Love
TESHIMA-YA SHICHIZAEMON	Michael Taylor
KICHI	Tiphaine Tailleux
KIYO	Michele Chung
ZENBEI	Michael Taylor
WHITE FOX	Michael Taylor

CHORUS and narrations were performed by the members of the cast.

Direction and original design	Masako Yuasa
Construction manager	Tim Skelly
Lighting	Jo Wright
Sound	Dominic Howard
Projector	Camilla Cook
Costume	James Huntington
Props	Katharina Brendel and Masako Yuasa
Stage Managers	Nick Wiltshire and Miriam Camidge

The adaptation for the performances in 2004 has been revised with companion notes for the publication. This is the only play which was not staged as a whole play in the project.

「女殺油地獄」

初演　1721年7月15日　竹本座。座本竹田出雲。太夫竹本筑後掾、
　　　作者　近松門左衛門（六十九歳）の作品。

参考資料　日本古典文学全集『近松門左衛門集①』「女殺油地獄」（205～265頁）
　　　　　鳥越文蔵　編、山根為雄　校注・訳　小学館　1997年3月20日出版。

　湯浅版初演は2004年3月15日～17日に英国国立リーズ大学英文学部ワークショップ
シアター・スタジオ1で以下のスタッフ、キャストで上演した。

河内屋徳兵衛	ミシェル・チェン
沢	キャサリン・オーエン
与兵衛	ジョナサン・ボニチ
かち	ヘレン・ラブ
豊島屋七左衛門	マイケル・テイラー
吉	ティファニー・タイユー
清	ミシェル・チェン
善兵衛	マイケル・テイラー
白稲荷法印	マイケル・テイラー
コーラスとナレーション	出演者全員
演出・舞台原案	湯浅雅子
舞台装置	ティム・スケリ
照明	ジョー・ライト
音響	ドミニク・ハワード
プロジェクター	カミラ・クック
衣装	ジェームズ・ハンティントン
小道具	湯浅雅子、キャサリナ・ブレンデル
ステージ・マネジャー	ニック・ウィルシャー、ミリアム・カミッジ

　この本に掲載したテキストは出版のために2004年の初演台本を改訂したもので、新たに註も付けた。「女殺油地獄」に限り全編を通しての舞台化はしていない。

ACTS AND SCENES

(The Play is in Three Acts with Six Scenes)

ACT ONE
    The Tokuan Embankment in Nozaki
    The eleventh of April in 1721

ACT TWO
    At the Kawachi-ya
    The second of May

ACT THREE
  PART ONE
    At the Teshima-ya
    The fourth of May
  PART TWO
    SCENE ONE At Shinmachi
    The sixth of June
    SCENE TWO At Sonezaki
    The same day
    SCENE THREE At the Teshima-ya
    The eve of the thirty-fifth day of the death of Kichi

CHARACTERS

KAWACHI-YA TOKUBEI, an oil-merchant and owner of the Kawachi-ya oil shop at Motodenma-machi[1] in Osaka. TAHEI and YOHEI's stepfather and KACHI's real father; he used to be a clerk of the Kawachi-ya. When the former Kawachi-ya Tokubei died, he was asked to marry SAWA in order to succeed to the former master's name and the business.

SAWA, the wife of the previous and the present KAWACHI-YA TOKUBEI, and the mother to three children

TAHEI, the previous TOKUBEI's first son, aged 26

YOHEI, the previous TOKUBEI's second son, aged 23

KACHI, the present TOKUBEI's daughter, aged 15

YAMAMOTO MORIEMON, SAWA's elder brother, a samurai and OGURI HACHIYA's chief footman

「女殺油地獄」

劇の構成

(三幕六場)

上之巻
　　　野崎・徳庵堤の場
　　　　一七二一年　四月十一日。
中之巻
　　　河内屋の場
　　　　五月二日。
下之巻
　　　その一
　　　　豊島屋の場
　　　　　五月四日。
　　　その二
　　　　(一)　新町の場
　　　　　　六月六日。
　　　　(二)　曽根崎の場
　　　　　　同日。
　　　　(三)　豊島屋の場
　　　　　　吉の三十五日のお逮夜。

登場人物

河内屋徳兵衛（かわちやとくべえ）　　大阪本天満町[1]の油屋河内屋の主。先代の河内屋に奉公していた。先代亡き後こわれて婿に入る。太兵衛と与兵衛の継父。かちの実父。

(河内屋) 沢（さわ）　　先代及び現在の徳兵衛の妻。三人の子供の実母。

(河内屋) 太兵衛（たへえ）　　先代の第一子。二十六歳。
(河内屋) 与兵衛（よへえ）　　先代の第二子。二十三歳。
(河内屋) かち　　末娘。十五歳。
山本森右衛門（やまもともりえもん）　　沢の兄。太兵衛や与兵衛の伯父。小栗八弥（おぐりはちや）の家臣で徒歩頭（かちがしら）。

WOMAN-KILLER IN OIL HELL

TESHIMA-YA SHICHIZAEMON, an oil-merchant and owner of the Teshima-ya oil shop across the Kawachi-ya.
KICHI, SHICHIZAEMON's wife, aged 27
KINU, KICHI and SHICHIZAEMON's first daughter, aged 9
KIYO, KICHI and SHICHIZAEMON's second daughter, aged 6
DEN, KICHI and SHICHIZAEMON's third daughter, aged 2
KAME, a widow and the procuress of the Tennōji-ya, a restaurant and brothel[2] at Sonezaki,[3] the new licensed pleasure quarter of north Osaka
KOGIKU, a courtesan of the Tennōji-ya, YOHEI's favourite
THE MAID, a maid of the Tennōji-ya
RŌKU, THE WAX, Kogiku's client, a rich countryman from Aizu,[4] the northern part of Japan where wax is produced
YAGORŌ the Brush, Yohei's work and playmate whose topknot is brush-shaped
ZENBEI the Vermillion,[5] Yohei's work and playmate whose face is the colour of red lacquered goods

OGURI HACHIYA, a samurai, the retainer of the lord Nagai of Takatsuki, Moriemon's superior
OGURI HACHIYA's FOREMAN
OGURI HACHIYA's FOOTMEN
THE VISITORS 1, 2 and 3, the worshippers to Nozaki Kannon
THE TEAHOUSE PROPRIETOR at the Tokuan Embankment
THE VILLAGERS of Nozaki

THE LEADER, a leader of the Twelve Lights, a group of young oil merchants who believe in mountain asceticism; the group goes to the Ōmine Mountain in Nara, one of the sacred mountains, for the annual assembly and training.
TWELVE LIGHTS 1, 2, 3 & 4, the members of the Twelve Lights
WHITE FOX,[6] a Buddhist exorcist and mountain ascetic
WATA-YA KOHEI, an employment agent and usurer[7]

KAMURO[8] OF SHIN-MACHI,[9] a little girl attendant of a courtesan at Shin-machi
MATSUKAZE, a courtesan of the Bizen-ya, a brothel in Shin-machi, the licensed pleasure quarter in central Osaka
A MAN IN AN AMIGASA HAT[10] Matsukaze's client
KAMURO OF SONEZAKI, KOGIKU's little girl attendant at Sonezaki
GORŌKURŌ, a paper merchant and a prominent member of the True Pure Land Sect of

「女殺油地獄」

豊島屋七左衛門	河内屋の筋向いの油屋豊島屋の主。
（豊島屋）吉	七左衛門の妻。二十七歳。
（豊島屋）絹	長女。九歳。
（豊島屋）清	次女。六歳。
（豊島屋）でん	三女。二歳。
かめ	北の新地曾根崎[3]の料理茶屋[2]天王寺屋の後家の女将。
小菊	天王寺屋の女郎。与兵衛の馴染み。
下女	天王寺屋の女中。
蝋九	小菊の客の会津の金持ち。会津[4]は蝋燭の産地だったことから廓でこのあだ名で呼ばれている。
刷毛の弥五郎	与兵衛の油屋仲間で遊び仲間。髷が刷毛のような形をしている。
皆朱[5]の善兵衛	与兵衛の油屋仲間で遊び仲間。皆朱は朱塗の漆塗り。赤ら顔なのでこのあだ名で呼ばれている。
小栗八弥	高槻の領主永井氏の家臣。森衛門の上司。
先払い	
徒士の者達	
野崎観音への参詣客１、２、３	
徳庵堤の茶屋の亭主	
野崎村の在郷の人々	
先達	若い油商でつくっている山上講「十二灯組」のリーダー。
「十二灯組」講中の人１、２、３、４	
白稲荷法印[6]	祈祷師の山伏。
綿屋小兵衛	口入れ屋[7]。
新町[9]の禿[8]	
松風	新町の遊郭備前屋の女郎。
編笠[10]の客	松風の客。
曽根崎の禿	天王寺屋の小菊に仕える禿。
帳紙屋五郎九郎	豊島屋の信仰する浄土真宗[11]の信者仲間の長老。

Buddhism[11]
THE FELLOW BELIEVERS 1, 2, 3, 4 & 5, the members of the True Pure Land Sect
THE TOWN MAGISTRATE
THE TOWN MAGISTRATE'S SUB-PREFECT
THE TOWN MAGISTRATE'S MEN
TOWNSPEOPLE OF MOTODENMA-MACHI

CHORUS

「女殺油地獄」

同信者仲間1、2、3、4、5
町奉行
町奉行配下の与力
町奉行配下の役人達
本天満町の人々

コーラス

ACT ONE

The Tokuan Embankment in Nozaki

The eleventh of April in 1721
The approach to the Nozaki Kannon,[1] the Temple of the Deity of Mercy in Nozaki, runs across the stage. The mountains and the fields in the background are in the beautiful tender green of early summer. The temple is located off-stage to the left. The quay of the Tokuan Embankment of the Catfish River where house boats sail up is off-stage to the right. The hanamichi,[2] an elevated walkway running through the auditorium, is another approach to the temple joining the other on stage.

There is a small teahouse upstage centre. A yoshizu[3] sunshade stands against the building to avoid direct sunlight. A couple of shōgi[4] benches are placed outside the teahouse. At the front of the teahouse tea trays are put out for the visitors to the temple. The Catfish River runs behind the teahouse.

The place is crowded with people visiting the ceremonial exhibition of an image of Buddha, the Deity of Mercy, at the Temple that began in March. People are enjoying a good outing as well as paying homage to the temple.

CHORUS [*singing merrily*]: (a song)
   The water is smooth; it's like rowing like a new boat.
   Yoi-na Yoi-na!
   Good! Hoi! Good! Hoi!
   Sa-yoi-yo-yei, sa-yoi-yo-yei!
   Good! Hoi! Good! Hoi! Good! Hoi! Hoi!
   You and I, and I and you,
   [*Intoxicated*] Let's get in the right tune and enjoy the swing.
   Shi-ton-ton, shi-ton-ton, shi-ton-ton-ton
   Let us enjoy a secret rendezvous in our house boat![5]
   Sa-yoi-yo-yei, sa-yoi-yo-yei!
   Good! Hoi! Good! Hoi! Good! Hoi! Hoi!
   I want to pour you sweet drops of sake in the golden moonlight.
   Then we'll row in our boat all night long.
   Shi-ton-ton, shi-ton-ton, shi-ton-ton-ton

「女殺油地獄」

上之巻

野崎・徳庵堤の場
（のざき・とくあんづつみ）

　一七二一年四月十一日。
　新緑の山里を背景にした野崎観音[1]への参道の徳庵堤付近。舞台の上手袖が野崎観音のある方角、下手奥袖の方角に徳庵堤の船着場がある。花道[2]からの参道が本舞台で合流している。

　舞台中央に出茶屋店がある。初夏の強い日差しをよけるため、茶屋には葦簾[3]が立てかけられている。茶屋の店先には参拝客のためのお茶が用意され、床几[4]が二、三置いてある。茶屋の裏手を鯰川が流れている。

　参道は三月に始まった野崎観音の御開帳に参詣する老若男女で賑わっている。人々は観音様への御参りを兼ねての春の遊山気分を楽しんでいる様子である。

コーラス（にぎやかに）
　（唄）船は新造船の乗り心地
　ヨイナ　ヨイナデ
　サヨイヨエー　サヨイヨエー
　君と我　我と君とは　（酔った調子で）調子に乗った　乗ってきたー
　しっとんとん　しっとんとん
　しっぽりと　逢瀬楽しむ　屋形の船[5]の　旅のしとねよ
　ヨイナ　ヨイナデ
　サヨイヨエー　サヨイヨエー
　君の杯　大杯を　さしてさされて　暮れぬ月　月の夜通し　戯れ遊べ
　しっとんとん　しっとんとん

VISITORS TO NOZAKI 1, 2 and 3 come onto the hanamichi.

VISITOR TO NOZAKI 1: It's a lovely day! So delightful.

VISITOR TO NOZAKI 2: Indeed. It's a comfortable, warm spring. We're still in April, but it feels as if it's summer.

VISITOR TO NOZAKI 3: Truly so. I feel quite hot, although it's comfortable. Perhaps Nozaki Kannon, our Deity of Mercy, is taking care of visitors like us who come to the ceremonial exhibition of her Eleven-faced image. [*Laughing*]

VISITOR TO NOZAKI 1 [*also laughing*]: If so, we should be very thankful that the Kannon cares about people like us.

VISITOT TO NOZAKI 2: There have been ceremonial exhibitions of the images of Buddha for three consecutive years; the year before last it was the image of the Thousand-armed Kannon at the Nachi Mountain Temple,[6] last year the image of the Mercy Kannon of the Hōryū-ji Temple,[7] and this year it's the Eleven-faced Kannon here at Nozaki. In ancient times Buddha appeared as Hokke in the sacred mountain, at present Buddha resides in the Western Pure Land as Amida, transformed as Kannon in this world. Buddhist blessings for past, present and future have been with us for three years. We are truly blessed.

VISITOR TO NOZAKI 3: It is wonderful to be blessed, but as the weather is wonderful too, there are many visitors, aren't there?

VISITORS TO NOZAKI 1, 2 and 3 stroll to the centre stage leisurely.

CHORUS: The Catfish River flows lesurely and a house boat to Nozaki floats happily.
The refreshing winds in a mountain village blow across the river.
The winds have a cool chill, but April sun sparkles with the face of early summer.
A beautiful flower of the Tennōji-ya, sweet and darling Kogiku, is in full bloom.
Her client, a countryman from Aizu, is over the moon with his flower princess, the courtesan at Sonezaki.
The more man's face slackens, the more the mouth of his purse is loosened.
Let him spend more money on his precious sweetheart!

KOGIKU, a courtesan of the Tennōji-ya, enters from the direction of the quay with THE MAID. KOGIKU wears a hat with a veil that hides half of her face, but she still attracts people's attention as she is spectacularly pretty and wears her obi[8] high which is unusual for an ordinary townswoman.

「女殺油地獄」

　　　　　　野崎への参詣の人々１、２、３が花道から来る。

参詣人１　ええ天気で、気持ちよろしいですな。
参詣人２　ほんに、ぽかぽか陽気で。まだ、四月というのに、夏みたいに温うて。

参詣人３　ほんまにもう暑いくらいですなあ。でも、気持ちよろしいなあ。きっとここ野崎の観音さんが御開帳の御参りに来る私らに気い遣てくれたはりますんやろ。（笑う）
参詣人１　（笑って）そうですやろか。観音様に気い遣てもらえるなんて、有難いことでおますなあ。
参詣人２　一昨年は那智山６の千手観音の御開帳、去年は大和法隆寺７の救世大悲観音の御開帳、そして今年はここ野崎の御本尊十一面観音さんの御開帳と御開帳が三年続いていますさかいなあ。仏様はその昔は霊山で法華、今は西方浄土で阿弥陀、この世で観世音の姿となっておわします。その仏の過去、現在、未来にわたる御利益が三年間も続いてますのや。ほんに、有難いことです。

参詣人３　有難いのはよろしいけれど、お天気もええので、えらい賑わいですなあ。

　　　　　　参詣人の三人、ゆっくりと散策しながら本舞台の方に歩く。

コーラス　ゆらりゆらりの鯰川　ゆらりゆらりと野崎参り
　　　山里の川面渡るさや風は　まだ肌寒ではありますが
　　　四月半ばのお日さまは　初夏の顔してきらきらきら
　　　愛し可愛いや天王寺屋の小菊　遊里のあだ花咲き匂う
　　　きららうきうき会津客　大事のお金を湯水と使う
　　　蝋九の顔はゆーるゆる　財布の紐もゆーるゆる

　　　　　　船着場の方角より遊女小菊が下女らと来る。小菊の顔は被りものと布で半分しか見えないが、胸高に粋に締めた帯８やその派手な美しさが素人の町女にはないものなので人目を惹いている。

59

KOGIKU [*capricious*]: Dear, dear! It was awful. It's much nicer to go on foot like this than to go on a boat and to be looked at by the people on the bank.

    KAME, the owner of the Tennōji-ya, follows KOGIKU from the direction of the quay.

KAME: Dear, dear Kogiku-san,[9] you mustn't leave your client. Wait, wait for us! [*She catches up with KOGIKU and THE MAID.*]

    THREE VISITORS come across KOGUKU, THE MAID and KAME in the main stage. They stop and gaze upon them in rapture.

CHORUS: Kame, the owner of the Tennoji-ya restaurant and brothel in Shinchi, the pleasure quarter of Osaka, does not waste her time.
She has no time for indulging herself weeping at being a widow.
Busy with her business as a procuress, she goes between her courtesan and the rich Aizu countryman.
The Catfish River flows lesurely and the house boat to Nozaki floats happily.
Drink and drunk, and drunk and drink.
Heart pounds, body sways.
Please forgive us Kannon-san!
Namu Amidaaabutsu Amidabutsu.
Namu Amidaaabutsu Amidabutsu.

    RŌKU, THE WAX, who looks like a typical rich countryman, comes after KOGIKU and KAME.

WAX [*short of breath*]: Kogiku-dono! Please wait for me. You said to me, "I won't visit Nozaki unless we take a house boat." That's why I specially hired a nice boat for you to sail up the river to Nozaki. Then suddenly you got off the boat. Can't you hear me? Wait for me! Hey, Kogiku, Kogiku-dono!

    KOGIKU ignores WAX and walks on merrily with KAME and THE MAID towards the temple in the light of the dazzling new green leaves. Soon WAX catches up with them and all walk off in the direction of the temple merrily.

「女殺油地獄」

小菊　（わがままそうに）ああ、いやだ、いやだ。あんなにじろじろ見られて屋形船でゆくよりも、こうして土手を歩いて行く方がなんぼかよい。

　　　　天王寺屋の女将かめが小菊ら追って船着場の方角から来る。

かめ　まあまあ、小菊さん、大切なお客様の蝋九さんを置いて行ったらあきませんがな。ちょっと待っておくれ。（小菊たちに追い付く。）

　　　　御参りの三人は、花が咲いたように艶やかな小菊ら一向に見とれて立ち止まる。

コーラス　女将のかめはしゃかりきで　今日は野崎で一儲け
　　北の新地の料理茶屋　後家だとゆうて　泣いてはおれぬ
　　花車の仕事に精出して　遊女とお客の　お取り持ち
　　ゆらりゆらりの鯰川　ゆらりゆらりの野崎参り
　　酔って酔われて酔わされて　心うきうき　身はゆらゆら
　　観音さんもごめんやす
　　南無阿弥だーぶつ　阿弥陀仏
　　南無阿弥だーぶつ　阿弥陀仏

　　　　少し遅れて蝋九が船着場の方から追いかけて来る。蝋九は見るからに田舎者の金持ちの風体。

蝋九　（息を切らせて）小菊殿！待ってくだされ！『屋形船でしか野崎参りはしませぬ』と、言われるから、せっかく船を用意して川を上ってきましたものを。途中で降りてしまわれるとは……。待てというのに。待って下されんか！これ、小菊、小菊殿！

　　　　小菊は蝋九の呼ぶのも知らんぷりでかめや下女達と共に眩い新緑の光の中を観音寺に向かって歩いて行く。皆はこの陽気にうきうきとした様子である。蝋九も追い付き、一行は参詣の人々に混じり野崎観音のある上手に

61

Three VISITORS TO NOZAKI also walk off after them.

CHORUS [*singing lively and merrily*]: (*A song*) Some are leaving.
[*Imitating playing the samisen*] Chin-tsuru!
Some are going home.
[*Imitating playing the samisen*] Chin-tsuru!
Others are coming here to pray.
[*Imitating playing the samisen*] Chin-tsuru!
[*Imitating playing the samisen*] Chin-tsu chiri-tsute chiri-tette!

KICHI, the wife of TESHIMAYA SHICHIZAEMON, an oil merchant of Motodenma-machi, comes from the hanamichi holding Den, her two-year-old third daughter, in her arms and leading KIYO, her six-year-old second daughter, by the hand. KICHI is a willowy beautiful woman and has glossy black hair which is well groomed with hair oil from their own shop. KICHI does not look like the wife of a merchant who is a mother of three. She is twenty-seven and in the prime of womanhood.

KIYO: Mother, I'm thirsty.
KICHI: Are you, sweetheart? Then, shall we have some tea in the teahouse over there? [*Walking up to the teahouse and to the interior*] Hello! We'll borrow your shōgi and have some of your tea!

KICHI tells KIYO to sit on one of the shōgi, leaves DEN in the care of KIYO and goes to fetch a tray of tea. She places the tray on the shōgi, gives tea to KIYO and DEN, and then drinks tea.
YOHEI, the second son of KAWACHHI-YA TOKUBEI, an oil merchant of Motodenma-mach, across the TESHIMA-YA, comes from the hanamichi with YAGORŌ, the Brush and ZEMBEI, the Vermillion. They are workmates as well as playmates at the licensed pleasure quarters. They are carrying a nest of lunch boxes and a five-shō[10] sake-barrel for the picnic lunch. They carry them by 'a-monk-seeking game'[11] in that they trade off the load when they come across a monk. They are swaggering about and occupying the whole road. They appear to be drunk and are a nuisance to the other visitors.

YOHEI: I'm certain that Kogiku is taking this road. She should be toddling down here with that rich countryman from Aizu. I won't let her get away from me.

「女殺油地獄」

　　　去る。
　　　　御参りの三人も参道を舞台上手の野崎観音の方角に歩み始める

コーラス（にぎやかに浮かれ気分で）（唄）　行く人も
　　（三味線を弾く真似で）チンツル
　　帰る人も
　　（三味線を弾く真似で）チンツル
　　来る人も
　　（三味線を弾く真似で）チンツル
　　（三味線を弾く真似で）チンツチルツテ　チリテッテ

　　　　参拝の人々に混じって、花道から本天満町の油商豊島屋七左衛門の妻お
　　　吉が二才の末娘おでんを抱き、六才の中娘清の手を引いてやって来る。お
　　　吉はほっそりと柳腰で、油屋だけに手入れの行き届いた艶やかな黒髪をし
　　　た美しい女、三人子持ちの商家の女房とは思えない二十七歳の女ざかりで
　　　ある。

お清　　母様、ぶぶが欲しい。
お吉　　おお、おお、喉がかわきましたか。ほなあそこの茶店で一休みしてぶぶもらいま
　　　ひょなあ。（茶店のところまで来てから、店の奥に声をかけて）ちょっとここ、お
　　　借りしてお茶いただきます。

　　　　吉は店の前の床几の一つに清を座らせてでんを見させておいて、茶を汲
　　　んで来る。清とでんにお茶を飲ませながら、自分もお茶を飲む。
　　　　花道を河内屋の二男、河内屋与兵衛が商売仲間で遊里通い仲間の刷毛
　　　の弥五郎、皆朱の善兵衛らと連れ立ってやって来る。三人は提げ重箱や
　　　酒の五升樽[10]を坊主持ち[11]している。道いっぱいにのさばりかえり、他の
　　　参拝客の迷惑など頓着ない様子から既にかなり酒が入っているのが窺える。

与兵衛　　小菊めが女のヨチヨチ歩きであの奥州会津の田舎の金持ちと参詣から戻るの
　　　もこの道のはずや。逃しはせんぞ。

KICHI [*noticing YOHEI and in a friendly manner*]: Yohei-san, Yohei-san! Hello, we're here! Why don't you come and join us?

YOHEI [*noticing KICHI*]: Goodness, it's O-Kichi-sama![12] Are you making a visit to the Nozaki Kannon with your daughters, too? [*By way of compliment*] I would have come with you if I had known. [*Noticing she is not with her husband*] So is Shichizaemon-sama staying at home today?

KICHI: No, he isn't. We came together, but he has a few places to drop by, so he's coming a little later. He should be here before long. Now, now, why don't you join us, all of you?

YOHEI: [*prompting YAGORŌ and ZEMBEI*] Then, shall we have a break here?

> *KICHI offers the shōgi next to her. The three men sit on it and start smoking. The way they sit and smoke shows that they are typical men of pleasure.*

KICHI [*watching the visitors light-heartedly and to YOHEI, at ease as a friendly neighbour*]: Yohei-sama, really, the visitors to the Kannon! Aren't they a lively bunch of people? What wonderful kimonos the wives and daughters of rich families are wearing! Oh, look over there! The woman in the violet-blue kimono with a different colour around the lower back[13] and with a striped satin obi . . . she must be from a pleasure quarter. And a woman in a striped crepe kimono with a dappled cloth obi over there, she could be a courtesan at Shin-machi. Don't you think that she has class and considerable charm? I can see why young men want to escort these beautiful courtesans on an occasion like this. Yohei-sama, you must have someone like them to come with, too [*mischievously*] . . . for example, Kogiku-san of the Tennōji-ya at Sonezaki or Matsukaze-san of the Bizen-ya at Shinmachi. [*Laughing*] Are you surprised that I know a lot about you? Why aren't you with any of them today?

YOHEI [*flattered*]: That's the thing, O-Kichi-sama. I wanted to dress them in a beautiful kimono and take everyone's breath away in Nozaki, so I did my level best to get it together in a short time. But Matsukaze said, "I've been engaged," and Kogiku said that she wouldn't come whoever pleaded with her, as at the moment the direction of Nozaki was unlucky because her alignment of stars means she is not safe. Then, early this morning a rich countryman of Aizu called Rōku the Wax escorted Kogiku to Nozaki down the Catfish River by river boat. If this Aizu countryman defeats me in securing Kogiku, I will lose face. So, I came here with two of my good friends [*looking at YAGORŌ and ZEMBEI*] to fight him for her.

> *YOHEI's words, 'fight him,' prompt YAGORŌ and ZEMBEI to roll up their*

「女殺油地獄」

お吉　（与兵衛に気付いて、親しげに）与兵衛さん！与兵衛さん！こちら、こちら！こちらへお出でなさいまし。

与兵衛　（お吉に気付いて）や、お吉様[12]。お吉様もお嬢様連れでお参りでございましたか。（上辺(うわべ)だけのお愛想(あいそ)で）そうと知っておりましたらご一緒いたしましたものを。（吉が独りなのに気づき）今日は、七左衛門(しちざえもん)様はお留守番ですか。

お吉　いえいえ、家(うち)の人も一緒です。二、三寄る所があって少し遅れて後から来ているのです。でも、もうすぐここに来るはず。まあ、さあさあ、お連れの方々もこちらへどうぞ。

与兵衛　（弥五郎(やごろう)と善兵衛(ぜんべえ)を促して）そしたら、ここらで一服しょうか。

　　　　　与兵衛と連れの二人はお吉に勧められるままに床几(しょうぎ)に腰を掛けて煙草を吸い始める。三人共、見るからに道楽者(どうらくもの)の様子が物腰(ものごし)に表れている。

お吉（参拝の人々を目で追いながらうきうきと、近所付き合いの気安さで）与兵衛(よへえ)様、まあ、なんと賑(にぎ)やかな参詣(さんけい)の方々ではございませんか。ええしゅの娘さん方や奥様達のお召し物の見事なこと。あれ、あそこに来る桔梗染めの腰替わり[13]の着物に縞繻子(しまじゅす)の帯をした方、あの方は玄人(くろうと)さんですよ。それから、そこの縞縮(しまちぢみ)の着物に鹿(か)の子帯の人は新町(しんまち)の郭(くるわ)のお女郎(じょろう)さんやないですやろか。やっぱり格があって一段と艶(あで)やかではございませんか。若い方々がこんな折にはああした美しいお人を連れて歩きたいのも物の道理ですわなあ。与兵衛様も、こんな折には連れてお参りしたいお人がおられるはず。（いたずらっぽく）……曾根崎新地(そねざきしんち)の天王寺屋(てんのうじや)の小菊(こぎく)さんとか……新町の備前屋の松風(まつかぜ)さんとか……。（笑って）よう知ってますでしょ。今日はまた、どうしてご一緒ではございませんのです？

与兵衛（おだてられ、気を良くして）まことに、お吉さまの仰有る通りです。今日は見事な拵(こしら)えでお参りの衆をびっくりさせようと、この間からあせって手を尽くしましたが、備前屋の松風は『先約(せんやく)がある』と言いやがるし、天王寺屋の小菊めは『野崎は方角が悪いからとなたの仰せでも行きません』とぬかしよりましたんや。ところがどうです。小菊の奴は蝋九たらいう会津(あいづ)からの客に揚げられて、今朝早うから川御座船(かわござぶね)でこの野崎にお参りに出たと言うやないですか。会津の田舎者に負けたとあってはこの与兵衛の顔が丸つぶれです。それで、（刷毛と皆朱をみて）友だち二人連れて一喧嘩(ひとけんか)かましたろうと思うてこうしてやって来ましたんや。

　　　　　与兵衛の喧嘩という言葉で、刷毛も皆朱も腕まくりをしたり袖をさすっ

65

sleeves to intimidate an unseen enemy, as if they were fighting an ogre. KIYO has finished drinking tea and is picking some flowers near by.

KICHI: Now, now, Yohei-sama. You've just given yourself away. You are making a pilgrimage to Kannon-sama not for your faith but as a complacent man of pleasure. Your parents are so worried about you that they've even found out your favourite courtesans' names. When they come to our shop, they often say to us, "Our son is always at your shop whenever he has time. We'll be truly grateful if you have a word with him, as good neighbours. We beseech you." I think my husband Shichizaemon may talk to you some time. Now I guess, you must be wondering why on earth the young wife of an oil shop merchant wants to make impertinent remarks in a teahouse like this on the way to Nozaki. She should keep her mouth shut and just look after her children. But please listen to what I say. Just now I saw you thrusting through the happy crowd, making them frown and attracting people's attention. I can't keep quiet when I see people point at you and say, "That's the second son of Kawachi-ya Tokubei, who runs an oil shop in Motoden-ma-machi. Look, the prodigal son is swaggering about, leaving bills for restaurants and brothels unpaid." Yohei-sama, how about taking your big brother Tahei-sama as your role model and becoming a good tradesman who wouldn't waste even two *sen*-coppers?[14] People say, 'The more sparrows live in a nest, the more savings there are.' Why don't you help your parents' shop and set them at ease. It's for your own sake. [*Perceiving unwelcoming mood of YOHEI and his friends*] Dear dear, you are not speaking to me any more. I must have said something wrong. [*Calling KIYO*] Kiyo, come, my child! Shall we walk to the temple again? [*Bowing to the three*] We are going. Goodbye for now. If you see my husband on your way, please tell him that we are waiting for him in the main building of the temple. [*Taking some change out of her purse, leaving it on the shōgi and addressing the interior of the teahouse*] Thank you for the tea. I've left some money for it here.

KICHI holds DEN in her arms, leads KIYO by the hand and walk off stage left. The way they exit indicates that KICHI is a good and loving mother to her children, with whom she has a close relationship.

ZENBEI [*watching KICHI depart and giving a broad grin in the manner of a dissipated man*]: Yohei, wasn't that the wife of the Teshima-ya across from your father's shop? She's got a pretty face, and very attractive, but pity, she's awfully uptight!

YOHEI: She's only twenty-seven. Indeed she is pretty and very attractive, but she's already borne quite a few children like herring roe. She looks worn out by family cares. . . It's a

「女殺油地獄」

たりして、まるで鬼を相手に喧嘩するかのように凄んでいる。
　お茶を飲み終えた清は辺りの草花を摘み始める。

お吉　まあまあ、与兵衛様。語るに落ちるとはこのことだす。何やもっともらしそうに話しておいでになりますけど、それやったら信心からの観音様参りやのうて、喧嘩好きの道楽参りやありませんか。親御様はあなたが通われるお女郎様の名前まで知っておられるほど心配なされているというのに。『うちの息子は暇さえあればお宅に入り浸っております。近所同士のよしみ、どうか一度意見してやって下さい。夫婦してお願い申します。』と言うて、常々から家に来られます。夫の七左衛門もいずれあなたにお話することと思います。油屋の若女房が子供の世話をしておればよいものを、こんな野崎参りの道中の茶店でなにを自分に差出がましく意見する、もってのほか、と内心思っておられることでしょう。けどなあ、まあ聞いて下さい。大勢の御参りの群衆を突き退け押し退け来るあなたの目に立つ姿。『あれは本天満町の油屋、河内屋徳兵衛の二男坊。道楽者が茶屋の払いもろくにせず、ああして肩で風を切って歩いておるわ。』と、人が後ろ指さすのを黙って見ておられません。どうだす？与兵衛様。お兄様の太兵衛様をお手本になされて、二文の銭[14]でも無駄にせんような商人魂持たれては？雀の巣も巣食うほどにたまるといいます。心配なさる親御様を救うと思うて、どうぞ商いの手助けしてあげて下さいな。他人の為やのうて御自分の為にだす。（与兵衛と連れの二人の白けた様子を見て）あれあれ、お気に召さぬか返事がない。（清を呼んで）お清、おいで、早うお参りに行きまひょ。（与兵衛達に会釈して）ほんならこれで。道で家の人に逢うたら、本堂で待っていると言うて下さい。（小銭を出して床几に置き、茶店の中に向かって）どうもごちそうさまでした。ここにおぶのお代金置いときます。

　お吉はおでんを抱き、清の手を引き上手に向かう。母と娘が仲良く楽しそうに歩いて行く。

皆朱の善兵衛　（いかにも放蕩者らしい感じで、お吉の後ろ姿をにやにや見送りながら）与兵衛、あれはおのれの筋向かいのわしらと同業の油屋、豊島屋の女房やないか。どことのう艶のある物越の美しい顔して、えらい堅い女子やないか。
与兵衛　歳もまだ二十七や。色気はあるけど数の子みたいにようさん子産んで所帯臭うなって……あの、真面目くさっとるのが珠に疵。見かけだけでうま味のない飴

pity that she's so uptight. She is like wheat gluten in the shape of a bird,[15] gorgeous but tasteless . . .

The three burst into laughter.

CHORUS [*singing lively and merrily*]: (a song)
Let's sing a chin-tsuru in Aizu dialect.
[*Imitating playing the samisen*] Chin-tsuru!
As a handsome kabuki actor, Jinzaemon,
[*Imitating playing the samisen*] Chin-tsuru!
As a leading actor, Kōzaemon
[*Imitating playing the samisen*] Chin-tsuru!
As a romantic actor, Shirōza
[*Imitating playing the samisen*] Chin-tsu chiri-tsute chiri-tette!

At the same time as the CHORUS begins, KOGIKU and the others enter from stage left returning from the temple. They are in a merry mood and looking slightly intoxicated. WAX is encouraged to sing the Chin-tsuru song in Aizu dialect and trying to oblige. The others sing the refrain along with the CHORUS and back WAX by humming a samisen tune.

YAGOYŌ [*noticing KOGIKU and the others*]: Look over there! They are coming!
KOGIKU [*noticing YOHEI and his friends, quickly to KAME*]: O-Kame-san, I'm getting tired of walking; I think I'm going back to the boat. [*KOGIKU hurriedly tucks up the hem of her kimono and tries to run away to the quay.*]

YOHEI quickly moves in front of KOGIKU and blocks her way. ZENBEI and YAGOYŌ move behind KOGIKU and her company in order to block the rear. They have taken off their zōri,[16] pushed them in their obi, rolled up their kimono sleeves, and are threatening them.

ZENBEI: Yohei, no need to hurry! First you talk to Kogiku and save your face! If this Aizu country candle tries to interfere with you, we'll chop off its wick and snuff it out.

WAX is panicked by ZENBEI's ferocious attitude. KAME and THE MAID are frightened and shivering, protecting KOGIKU.

「女殺油地獄」

　　　細工[15]の鳥や。

　　　　　三人はお吉を肴にして笑いこける。

コーラス（にぎやかに浮かれ気分で）（唄）
　　　会津訛りの　替歌で　チンツル
　　　当世人気の　二枚目甚左衛門で　チンツル
　　　立て役の　幸左衛門で　チンツル
　　　思い入れなら　四郎三で　チンツル
　　　チンツチルツテ　チリテッテ

　　　　コーラスと同時に、参詣を終えた小菊たちが、ほろ酔いの上気分で上手から戻ってくる。田舎者の蝋九は皆に持ち上げられて流行歌のチンツル節を唄わされる。一行はコーラスが歌うのに合わせて、てんでに口三味線で蝋九をもり立てる。

刷毛の弥五郎　（小菊達に気付いて）そらそら！来たぞ、来たぞ！
小菊　（三人に気付き、慌ててかめに）花車さん、こうして参道を歩くのにも飽きてきた。また来た時の船に戻りとうなりました。（小菊は言い終えるや否や、急いで裾を絡げて船着場の方に逃げて行こうとする。）

　　　　与兵衛がぬっと小菊の前に立ちはだかる。
　　　　皆朱の善兵衛と刷毛の弥五郎は仁王立ちで小菊ら一行の後ろを塞ぐ。善兵衛と弥五郎は既に草履[16]を脱いで腰に差し、腕捲りして凄んでいる。

善兵衛　与兵衛、急がんでもええ！まず、小菊と談判してお前の男立てえ！もし、この会津の蝋燭が光出しよったら、わいら二人で芯切って踏み消したる！

　　　　善兵衛の剣幕に蝋九はあわてふためき、かめや下女はうろたえて小菊を囲んで震え上がる。

YOHEI: Listen, Widow, I'll borrow your Kogiku for a while. I, Kogiku's regular, Kawayo, am asking. I don't think that you can have any objection! [*YOHEI grabs KOGIKU by her arm and takes her to one of the shōgi; he is pulling an angry face like an ogre.*] You whore! Cheap prostitute! You said to me, "Nozaki is in the wrong direction. The alignment of stars for me is not safe at present, so I won't go there whoever pleads with me." You refused to come here with me! But it seems you don't mind about the wrong direction if you're with your favourite client. Now, I want to know why.

KOGIKU [*in a calm and intimate tone*]: Kawayo-san, my love, please don't be a boor. Everybody knows about you and me. "When they hear Kogiku's name once, they always hear yours three times." That's how they make fun of us. I didn't want to come here with you because I didn't want anything wrong to happen to you by bringing you down in this direction because the stars are against it. You didn't think about any of my considerations. Instead, enticed and spurred on by your friends, you act like this. [*KOGIKU draws YOHEI to her and holds him tight affectionately.*] I swear to all gods, goddesses and Buddha my true love for you, my love.

YOHEI [*over the moon*]: You mean it? Kogiku, I'm so happy.

WAX [*unable to absorb the turn of events and sitting down next to KOGIKU noisily*]: Kogiku-dono! I don't understand you. Last night you said, "I don't know what kind of destiny you and I have, but Aizu-sama, I haven't met anyone I love as deeply as you in all Osaka." I thought it was the greatest honour to my home country that I had been made advances to by a courtesan at Sonezaki in Osaka. I was only too glad. So spending my precious money like water, I hired a boat ride for you and me. I didn't come this far to be insulted by you. You must say what you told me last night here in front of that man once again. Until I hear it, I won't cross any streets or pass through any borders to Aizu. I won't go back to my country, Kogiku-dono!

YAGORŌ [*approaching WAX*]: Hey, you eastern country bumpkin! We'll have the courtesan! Leave her and just return to your native land!

ZENBEI [*from the other side of YAGORŌ, also approaching WAX*]: Or, shall we entertain you to a dinner with some muddy Osaka water as a souvenir of your trip?

YAGORŌ and ZENBEI are about to grab WAX.

WAX [*not intimidated and seeming to be itching to fight*]: How dare you! You scoundrels! Back east we've heard about you villains in Osaka; there are men with tattoos on their arms, who threaten good people, seek a fight and steal things from their pockets. Having been

「女殺油地獄」

与兵衛　おかみ、ちょっと小菊殿、借りるで！馴染みの河与が借りるんや、文句は言わせん。(小菊の腕を掴み、茶屋の床几のところに連れて行き座らせる。怒りで鬼のような顔で) おい、売女！安女郎様！『野崎は方角が悪いからとなた様の仰せでも行きません』とこの河与を断っておいて、好いた客とならこっちの方角でもええというそのわけ聞かせてもらおうやないか！

小菊　(和やかな口調でしんみりと) 河与さん、野暮なこと言わしゃんな。小菊と言う名が一つ出たら与兵衛と言う名が三つ出るほど深い深い仲と言いはやされているあなたとわたし。一緒に連れ立って野崎参りに来ないのは、悪い方角に連れ出して愛しいあなたにもしものことがあってはと思うから。その気も知らず、人におだてられ、けしかけられてそのようなさまで。(与兵衛をぴったりと抱き寄せ) わたしの心は神様仏様に誓って偽りのないこと。

与兵衛　(でれっと有頂天で) ほんまか？小菊。嬉しいやないか。

蝋九　(二人の様子に我慢が出来ず、小菊の横にどんと座り) 小菊殿、あなたもわけが分かりませぬ。『いかなる縁か知りもせんが、会津様、あなたほど愛しいお人はこの大阪中に無ぁい。』と、昨夜、私に言い申したではないですか。新地の遊女にくどかれたとあって、郷里への面目も立つ、私にとってもこの上ない喜びと、大事のお金を湯水のように使っての舟遊び。このようなところまで嬲られに来たのではありもせん。その男の前ではっきりともう一度、昨夜のように言ってくださらんと、とやとやの通りもむやむやの関も越しもうさん。それを聞くまでは郷里には帰りもうさん。小菊殿！

弥五郎　(蝋九に詰め寄って) やい、東国のもさ！この女郎はこっちに貰う。置いて帰れ！

善兵衛　(弥五郎の反対側から蝋九に詰め寄り) それとも、東国への土産に上方の泥水ご馳走しょうか。

　　　　弥五郎と善兵衛が蝋九に掴みかかろうとする。

蝋九　(怯まず立ち上がり、腕に自信のある様子で) 何だと！このならず者めらが！腕に入れ墨して人を脅し喧嘩をふっかけては懐中物を狙う輩がいるというのは東国でも聞いておりもうす。己れの身の始末も出来ぬ貧乏人のくせに女狂いしおって。

stricken by poverty and not knowing how to make ends meet, you are chasing after women. What did you say? You want to give me 'muddy Osaka water' as a souvenir of my trip? Take the muddy leg of the eastern countryman instead!

WAX kicks YAGORŌ's chin with all his might. YAGORŌ rolls over towards the bank behind the teahouse and falls into the Catfish River. ZENBEI throws himself at WAX, saying 'Take This!' Then WAX kicks ZENBEI in the crotch really hard. ZENBEI cannot stand the pain and crawls off to stage right stretching his neck like a kite.

YOHEI: I'm not the kind of man who runs away when his friends are knocked down. I shall hang you upside down and bury you! [*YOHEI gets hold of WAX by his shoulder.*]
WAX [*freeing himself from YOHEI*]: Shut it! You impudent greenhorn! I shall teach you never to brag like that!

The two start grappling with each other.

KOGIKU: Good gracious! How boorish! Oh, I don't know what to do. [*She tries to get between the two men.*]
KAME [*stopping KOGIKU*]: Oh, please don't hurt yourself, Kogiku-sama! It would be most unfortunate if something happened to your precious body. [*KAME stands close to KOGIKU with THE MAID to protect her from the fight.*]

The visitors on the approach to the temple say, "There's a fight!" "There's a fight!" and gather. THE TEAHOUSE PROPRIETOR quickly closes the teahouse. No one stops the fight.
YOHEI and WAX go off to the embankment while fighting and fall into the Catfish River together. Then off-stage it seems that they start throwing river mud at each other.

OGURI HACHIYA enters on a horse with his men from stage right. He is making a visit to the Nozaki Kannon for his master, Lord Nagai of Takatsuki, north of Osaka. OGURI is in formal ceremonial attire, a kamishimo.[17] *His FOOTMEN are all in a dark orange haori*[18] *with a family crest on it. His FOREMAN makes way for OGURI by swinging his hand from side to side and saying "Hey. Hey. Hey."*
YOHEI and WAX down on the river edge do not notice the procession and contin-

「女殺油地獄」

なにを上方の泥水！奥州者の泥足食らえ！

　　　　蝋九は足でおもいっきり弥五郎の顎を蹴りあげる。顎を蹴られて弥五郎はコロコロと茶屋の裏を流れる鯰川の土手の方に転がり、そのまま川に落ちる。蝋九は次に、「こいつめ！」とかかってきた善兵衛の股座を嫌というほど蹴る。善兵衛は痛みに耐えかねて鳶のように首を伸ばし腹這いで下手に逃げ去る。

与兵衛　友だち投げられて黙っているような男やないぞ。おのれ、逆さにして頭から地面にぶち込んだる！（蝋九に掴み掛かる。）
蝋九　（与兵衛の腕を振りほどいて）なにお、ちょこざいな、青二才が！二度とその口きけんようしてやるべえ。

　　　　与兵衛と蝋九、取っ組み合いの喧嘩を始める。

小菊　無粋なことを。まあ、どうしましょう。（二人の喧嘩を止めに入ろうとする。）

かめ　（小菊を止めて）ああ、怪我しやさんすな、小菊様。大事な体にもしものことがあってはなりまへん。（下女と共に小菊の体を庇う。）

　　　　参道を行く人々が口々に「喧嘩や！」「喧嘩や！」と集まってくる。
　　　　茶店は慌てて店を閉める。喧嘩の仲裁をする者もない。
　　　　与兵衛と蝋九は取っ組み合いを繰り返し、組み合ったままで土手の堤の崖を踏み外し川に落ちる。二人はそのまま川原で泥や藻屑などを手当たり次第に投げ合っている様子である。

　　　　下手から小栗八弥が馬に乗り供の一行を従えて登場する。小栗は主君高槻領主永井氏の代参で野崎観音に参詣に来ている。小栗は裃姿[17]、御供の徒士の者達は揃いの家紋の入った濃い柿色の羽織[18]を着ている。一行の先払いの者が「はいはい、はいはい」と手を振って人を払いながら進んでくる。

　　　　河原の与兵衛と蝋九は小栗一行に気付かず喧嘩を続けている。運悪く与

ue fighting. When YOHEI throws mud at WAX, the mud unfortunately hits OGURI by mistake. OGURI and his horse are covered with mud, from the kamishimo to the harness. The horse is frightened and grows restive. THE FOOTMEN chase YOHEI, saying, "Catch him!" OGURI wipes the mud on horseback.

KOGIKU, KAME and THE MAID quickly hide themselves in the crowd to avoid trouble.

YOHEI tries to run away across the river. But YAMAMOTO MORIEMON, OGURI's chief footman, hits YOHEI's leg from behind. YOHEI cries out in pain, falls over and is apprehended from behind by MORIEMON.

YOHEI [*almost in tears*]: Please, o-samurai-sama. Please forgive me. It was a mistake. Sir, please forgive me. Have mercy on me! Please!

MORIEMON [*holding down YOHEI*]: You rogue! You've smeared my master's kimono and the harness of his horse. You will not escape your wrong deed by claiming it was a mistake. Fool! Raise your face! [*MORIEMON forcefully raises YOHEI's face and is astounded when he sees YOHEI.*] Goodness!

YOHEI [*also astounded*]: Goodness! You're my uncle Moriemon-dono!

MORIEMON: Good gracious! You're my nephew, Yohei. [*Managing to recover from the shock*] Listen, Yohei! You are a townsman; therefore any shameful matters won't disgrace you. But I am a samurai who receives an allowance from my lord. Therefore it is impossible for me to forgive a rogue, ever more so when the rouge turns out to be my nephew. I have to cut you down at this point! Stand up! [*He makes YOHEI stand up.*]

OGURI [*on horseback*]: Listen, Moriemon! It looks like the sheaths of your swords have come loose . . . If your swords leave their sheaths, hurt someone and the blood runs before our visit to the Temple, we will have to go back without paying homage at the temple for our lord. You must keep your swords sheathed until we accomplish our mission as it is most important to fulfil our duty. You heard me, Moriemon? [*Hurrying MORIEMON*] Follow me, Moriemon!

MORIEMON [*moved by OGURI's kind words and looking up at OGURI*]: Yes, sir! [*To YOHEI*] You fool! I will cut you down on my way back! [*While saying this, MORIEMON motions YOHEI to leave the place as soon as possible.*]

The FOREMAN starts making way for OGURI by swinging his hand from side to side and saying "Hey. Hey. Hey." OGURI and his men go off to stage left as if nothing happened. Onlookers disperse on their various ways.

「女殺油地獄」

　　　　兵衛の投げた泥が偶然小栗八弥にあたる。小栗の裃、着物から馬具、馬にいたるまで泥がかかり、馬が暴れる。徒士の者達が口々に「逃がすな」と与兵衛を追う。小栗は馬上で泥をぬぐう。

　　　　災いを逃れる為、小菊達は素早く見物衆の中に身を隠す。

　　　　与兵衛は川の向こう岸に逃げようとするが、後ろから徒士頭の山本森右衛門に脛を払われ「ぎゃっ！」と転び、背中から取り押さえられる。

与兵衛　（泣きべそをかいて）お侍様、どうぞお許し下さい。過ちでございます。どうぞ、お許しを。お慈悲を。お慈悲を。
山本森右衛門　（取り押さえたままで）この無礼者！小栗様のお小袖や馬具にまで泥をかけおって、過ちですまされると思うのか！愚か者が、顔を上げい！（与兵衛の首を捩じ上げて顔を見て仰天し）やっ！

与兵衛　（同じく、仰天して）やっ！これは！伯父上の森右衛門殿！
森右衛門　何と！与兵衛めか！（何とか気を取り直して）やい、与兵衛、お前は町人ゆえどのような恥辱を受けても疵にはならぬ。しかし、御主君より俸禄をいただいてお仕えする武士の身のこの森右衛門、無礼者を取り押さえてそれが甥と分かっては尚更助けるわけにはゆかぬ。この場で斬って捨てる！早う立て！（与兵衛の腕を掴んで引き立てる。）

小栗八弥　（馬上から）これ、森右衛門。見たところそなたの大小の鞘口の詰め、ちと弛そうであるが……もしも刀身が抜け、けがでもして血を見るような事があっては、観音様への御殿の大事の御代参叶わず、ここから戻らねばならぬことになる。下向まで十分に鞘口に注意してしっかと閉めてお供のお役目果たすよう心せよ。よいな……森右衛門。（促して）供をせよ！供をせよ！

森右衛門　（小栗の情け深い言葉に有難く、一度顔をみつめて、頭を下げる。）はっ、はあーっ！（与兵衛に）おのれ、下向時には首を討つぞ。（言いながら、他人には分からないように、手で早くこの場から去るよう合図する。）

　　　　先払いの者は再び「はいはい、はいはい」と言いながら手を振って、群衆を払って行く。その後を小栗一行は何事もなかったかのように進み上手に退く。見物衆もそれぞれの方向に散って行く。

YOHEI [*relieved and absent-minded*]: Save us! Merciful Buddha! Buddhist Priest! Oh, what shall I do? I'll be slashed by my uncle on his way back from the temple. I'll be dead! Oh, what have I done! I must run away. It's the only way. [*YOHEI abruptly dashes off, but as he is extremely upset and confused, he has completely lost any sense of direction.*] That's the way to Nozaki . . . oh, no, I can't tell which way is for Osaka. This one must lead to Kyoto . . . so is that mountain the Kuragari Peak standing between Osaka and Nara . . . ? Or is that the Hiei Mountain in Kyoto? No, no! I can't tell which way to go! I'm completely lost.

> *YOHEI gets more and more distraught and looks around in confusion.*
> *KICHI returns from stage left with her daughters. YOHEI sees KICHI and rushes towards her.*

O-Kichi-sama! Have you paid homage at the temple?
KICHI: No, we are not on the way back from the temple. We managed to go several chō[19] from here, but it was getting so crowded, we've come back to the place where we originally arranged to meet my husband. [*Noticing YOHEI's odd manner and astounded*] Good gracious! What's the matter with you?
YOHEI: I, I'll be cut down if I stay here when they come back. . .Please take me back to Osaka. I beseech you. Please help me! [*Kneeling down and pleading to KICHI in tears*]
KICHI [*staring at YOHEI*]: You're covered with mud. Yohei-dono, are you all right? Have you gone mad?
YOHEI: I don't blame you if you think I've gone mad. The thing is, while Kogiku's client and I were fighting, we started throwing mud at each other, and by mistake the mud I threw hit the samurai on the horse. If they see me on their way back, I will be cut down and killed. [*Following KICHI and not letting her go*] Please, I beg you! Please help me.
KICHI: What have you been doing? I'm appalled and dumbfounded! My heart goes out to your parents who are so anxious about you. As your neighbour, I cannot leave you like this . . . oh, what shall we do? [*Looking around*] All right! Let's go into the teahouse and borrow a back room from them. Then, before anything, let's wash the mud off your kimono and clean your face. After that you should go back to Osaka as soon as possible. Promise me Yohei-san. You must never do this again. Do you hear me? [*Addressing the interior of the teahouse*] Excuse me, please! We're borrowing your back room for a minute. [*Turning around to KIYO*] Kiyo, will you please wait here and look after Den for a moment. [*KICHI sits KIYO on the shōgi and puts Den next to KIYO.*] Now, my dear, listen. When your father arrives, you must let your mother know. Is that all right? Be a good

「女殺油地獄」

与兵衛　（緊張が緩み、ぼーっとして）南無三、仏様、お坊さま！ああ、とないしょう！伯父殿の下向時には切られる。切られたら死んでしまう。ああー、えらいことになってしもた。逃げよ。逃げるしかない。（思わず駆け出すが、気が転倒していて方向がよく分からない。）こう行くと野崎……ああ、どっちが大阪の町かよう分かれへん。こっちが京都のはず……あの山が大阪と奈良の境の闇峠か……それとも京都の比叡山か……ああ、どっちに逃げたらええんやろ。とないしょう。とないしたらええか分かれへんようになってしもた。

　　　　与兵衛、益々狼狽して、キョロキョロと回りを見渡す。
　　　　この時、上手からお吉たちが戻って来る。与兵衛、お吉を見つけて走り寄る。

　　お吉様！参拝を終えられましたか。
お吉　いいえ、参拝を終えての下向ではないんです。七、八丁[19]行ったら大変な人出なのでうちの人との待ち合わせのこの場所まで戻って来ました。（与兵衛の様子に気付き、驚いて）まあ、与兵衛殿、どうなされました？
与兵衛　わたしは、わたしは、今ここに居ては切れる。どうか大阪まで連れて帰って下さい。お願いします、助けて下され。（泣きながらお吉を拝む。）
お吉　（初めて与兵衛が泥まみれなのに気づき）まあまあ、顔も体も泥だらけやありませんか。気でも違われましたか。
与兵衛　そう思われるのもごもっとも。小菊の連れと喧嘩しているうちに泥の投げ合い掴み合いになり、運悪くわたしの投げた泥が馬上のお侍にかかってしもたんです。一行の下向時に出くわしたら切られてしまう。（吉にまとわりついて離れようとせず）頼みます！お吉殿！お願いします！助けて下され！
お吉　何ということを！呆れてものも言えまへん！親御様のご苦労を思うと胸が痛うなります。向かい同士で知らん顔もできず、ほんに困りましたなあ……（あたりを見回して）そや、この茶屋の奥を借りてまずその着物の泥を落として、それから顔もきれいにして……そうして、少しでも早う大阪へ帰ったがええ。よろしいな、与兵衛さん、二度とこんな真似しはりませんようにな。（茶店の奥に）すいません、ちょっとここお借りします。（清に）お清、ちょっとの間、ここに居ておでんのお守りしててくれるか。（吉はお清を床几に座らせ、おでんをその横に寝かせて）ええか、父様がみえたらこの母に知らせておくれ。ええな。頼みましたよ。（お吉は与兵衛を促して茶店の奥に入って行く。）

girl, sweetheart. [*KICHI disappears into the teahouse with YOHEI.*]

> *The bright sunshine of the early summer shows that it is almost noon. A silence spreads over the empty approach to the teahouse. KIYO nurses DEN for a while. Soon DEN goes to sleep. KIYO gets curious about KICHI and YOHEI who disappeared into the teahouse. She gets up and starts peeping into the teahouse through yoshizu.*
>
> *SHICHIZAEMON, carrying a lunch box in his hand, comes in hurriedly through the hanamichi followed by KINU, the nine-year-old eldest daughter of SHICHIZAEMON and KICHI.*

SHICHIZAEMON: The talk with the clients took longer than I thought. Your mother and Kiyo must have been waiting for us with an empty stomach. We'll soon be there. You must be hungry, too, O-Kinu.

KINU: Yes, I am, Father. As we walked so fast, I'm thirsty, too.

SHICIZAEMON: Of course, you are, my dear. I'm so sorry.

KIYO [*noticing SHICHIZAEMON*]: Father! Sister! I'm here! [*KIYO runs towards SHICHIZAEMON and KINU.*]

SHICHIZAEMON: Oh, O-Kiyo. I'm sorry! Have you been waiting for us long? You must be hungry, sweetheart . . . but, where's your mother?

KIYO: Mother's gone into the teahouse with Yohei-sama. They untied the obi . . . and undressed in the back room.

SHICHIZAEMON: What? Your mother and Yohei untied the obi and were naked in the back room of this tea house. . . ?

KIYO: And after that, cleaned up with paper and washed . . .

SHICHIZAEMON: What? Then cleaned up with paper and washed. . . ? [*Driven to a frenzy of anger and jealousy*] I've been deceived! Hell! I'm so angry! [*To the interior of the teahouse*] Oi! O-Kichi! Yohei! Come out! Come here quickly! If you don't, I'll come in!

KICHI [*off-stage, from the inside of the teahouse*]: Is that my husband? Where have you been, forgetting your children's lunch time?

> *KICHI comes out of the teahouse first. YOHEI comes out after her. YOHEI's kimono is wet and some mud is still stuck in his hair. He looks like a drowned rat.*

YOHEI [*trying to save face*]: Oh, it's Shichizaemon-sama. I'm really ashamed of myself. I had a silly fight and fell into river mud. Your wife was helping me to clean the mud off. I'm

「女殺油地獄」

　　　初夏の日差が昼に近づいてゆく。
　　　人通りの途切れた出茶屋店付近をひととき静寂が襲う。
　　　お清は暫くおでんをあやしているが、おでんはすぐに寝てしまう。葦簾の奥の母と与兵衛のことが気になり、お清は葦簾の隙間から茶店の中を覗き始める。
　　　昼のお弁当を手に提げた豊島屋七左衛門が九才になる姉娘のお絹と一緒に急ぎ足で花道から来る。

七左衛門　話が長引いてえらい遅うなってしもた。お前の母様や妹がさぞお腹を空かせて待っていることやろ。もうすぐや。お絹もえろうお腹空いたやろ？

お絹　はい、父様。急いで歩いたので絹は喉も渇きました。
七左衛門　そうか、そうか。喉も渇いたか。
お清　（七左衛門を見つけ）あれ、父様！姉様！（走り寄る。）

七左衛門　おお、お清、待たせてすまなんだなあ。お腹空いたやろ。で、母様は？何処におられる？
お清　母様はここの茶店の奥で河内屋の与兵衛様と二人、帯解いて……べべも脱いでおられます。
七左衛門　何！母様がここの茶店の奥で河内屋の与兵衛めと二人で帯解いて！裸になって！
お清　その後は紙で拭いたり洗うたり……。
七左衛門　その後、紙で拭いたり洗うたり！（嫉妬と怒りで逆上して）だまされた！ああ、口惜しい！（茶店の奥に向かって）おい、お吉！与兵衛！出て来い！早ここへ出て来い！出て来んかったらそこへ踏み込むぞ！
お吉　（茶店の奥から）家の人か？子供のお昼の時間も忘れて何処で何をしておいでやったんです。

　　　お吉が茶店から出てくる。与兵衛もお吉の後から出て来る。与兵衛の髪にはまだ泥が残り着物も濡れて濡鼠のようになっている。

与兵衛　（体裁をつくろって）これは七左衛門様。どうも面目ございまへん。しょうもない喧嘩をして泥にはまり、おかみさんのお世話になっておりました。これもご

immensely obliged to you, Shichizaemon-dono; you have always been a good and kind neighbour to me. I'm truly grateful to both of you.

SHICHIZAEMON [*forgetting to greet YOHEI because of his anger and the ridiculous sight of YOHEI*]: O-Kichi, you ought to know where to stop when you want to take care of people. A young woman unties a young man's obi, and then wipes him down . . . It's very misleading! It really lacks manners. Better leave people to their own business…Now, we must go and worship at the temple. Otherwise the sun will have set.

KICHI: That's right. We'd better hurry. We have been waiting for you for so long. We can talk about it on the way . . . now, everyone, let's go! Let's go!

> *KICHI holds DEN in her arms. SHICHIZAEMON is carrying a lunch box. KINU and KIYO start walking hand in hand, a little ahead of their parents, to stage left. KICHI and SHICIZAEMON also walk to stage left, laughing and talking, while keeping an eye on their children. The family look very happy.*
>
> *YOHEI is left alone and watches the family until they are out of sight; then he sits on the shōgi absent-mindedly.*
>
> *THE TEAHOUSE KEEPER and several VILLAGERS of Nozaki come from stage right.*

TEAHOUSE KEEPER [*noticing YOHEI*]: You have been hanging around here for some time. Are you on your way to the temple or on your way back from the temple? Which is it?

VILLAGERS: Really we don't understand you. What the hell do you want?

TEAHOUSE KEEPER: If you don't want anything from us, will you please go? Go! Go away! [*He chases off YOHEI.*]

> *The sound of a horse's hooves and "Hey, hey, hey" from OGURI's FOREMAN are heard from off stage left. Then OGURI and his FOOTMEN enter. OGURI is on foot.*
>
> *YOHEI sees them and comes to himself. He tries to run away in a fright, but MORIEMON is quick enough to catch YOHEI.*

MORIEMON [*holding down YOHEI*]: Yohei, last time you were released because we were on the way to the temple, but now we have paid homage for our lord and we're on our return journey. There's no need to sheathe our swords any more. [*Putting his hand on his sword*] I will cut you down!

「女殺油地獄」

　　　近所で日頃から何かとご親切にしていただいている七左衛門殿のおかげです。どうも、かたじけございまへん。
七左衛門　（泥だらけの与兵衛の姿に可笑（おか）しいのと腹が立つのとで与兵衛に挨拶するのも忘れて）お吉、他人の世話やくのもええかげんにしておけ！若い女が若い男の帯解いて、その後紙で拭くとは。何とも紛らわしい。不作法この上ない。人様のことはもうええから……さあさあ、みんなでお詣りしょう。早（はや）行かんと日（ひ）いが暮れてしまうがな。
お吉　ほんまにそうだす。早行かんと。もう、待ってましたんや。話の続きは道々にして……さあ、みんな行きまひょ、行きまひょなあ。

　　　　　吉はでんを抱く。七左衛門はお弁当を提げている。お絹とお清は手を繋いで先に上手に向かって歩き出す。お吉と七左衛門は子供たちを目で追い、笑いながら上手に去る。一家の幸せそうな様子が見える。

　　　　　一人取り残された与兵衛は幸せそうな豊島屋親子の姿をじっと見送る。そして、所在なげにぼーっと床几（しょうぎ）に座り込む。

　　　　　茶屋の主人や在郷（ざいごう）の人々が数人出てくる。

茶屋の主人　（与兵衛に気づいて）さっきから同じところにウロウロしておりなさるが、お前さんは参詣か下向かどっちじゃ？

在郷の人々　ほんに合点がいかんわ。何の用かいな？
茶屋の主人　用がなかったら、さあ、行った、行った。（与兵衛を追い立てる。）

　　　　　この時、上手から小栗八弥の先払いの「はいはい。はいはい。」の声と馬の轡（くつわ）の音が聞え、下向の小栗八弥の一行が現れる。小栗八弥は徒歩である。
　　　　　与兵衛は一行に気付き我に返り、狼狽（うろた）えて逃げようとする。森右衛門が与兵衛を目ざとく見つけて捕らえる。

森右衛門　（与兵衛を捩じ伏せて）与兵衛、さっきは参詣の途中ゆえそのままにしたが、今は無事それも済ませての下向。もう、刀を慎（つつし）む必要もない！（刀の柄（え）に手をかけて）討って捨てる！

OGURI: Wait! Wait, Moriemon! Why do you say that you'll cut down that youth?

MORIEMON [*bowing to OGURI*]: Please allow me to say, sir, that this is the rogue who did you wrong a moment ago. If this man weren't my relative, I might ask you for a pardon. However this man's mother is my younger sister by blood and the man is my real nephew. Therefore however noble-heartedly Oguri-sama may speak of him, I cannot spare his life. Truly, sir, I do not know how I could compensate for what he has done to you.

OGURI: Well then, tell me Moriemon, what wrong has the youth done me?

MORIEMON: He threw mud over you and smeared you and your horse on our way to the temple; that 'disrespect' is the crime the man committed.

OGURI: What did you say? Did you say the man smeared me with mud? Look at me, Moriemon. I'm clean, not covered with any mud.

MORIEMON: No, sir. Sir, I meant the kimono before you changed. . .

OGURI: That's right. Once I change my kimono for a clean one, there's no stain on it any more. Therefore it is as if no mud had ever dirtied my kimono.

MORIEMON: I don't mean to dispute you, sir, but you're making a return journey on foot because this youth dirtied the saddle and the saddle flaps of your horse. Sir, this man is a serious criminal who has behaved insultingly to my master.

OGURI: Now Moriemon, you must listen to what I'm about to say. A saddle flap is a thing to protect a horse from mud. If there were never any mud to avoid, we wouldn't saddle a horse in it. Therefore there is no disgrace, disrespect and crime to be found when the saddle flap of my horse is covered with mud. However, of course, even one drop of cloudy water, if it smeared my family name and honour, would not be washed away or rinsed out. That is a disgrace for samurai to act on. Someone like this youth is mere muddy water to me. My name, Hachiya, stands for *hasu*, a lotus which blooms on the surface of water, while its root is in the mud. I bloom out of mud, but I am not stained by mud. Save him. Let go of him, Moriemon.

MORIEMON: Yes, sir. [*Thankful, he sits upright with his hand on the ground and bows.*]

    OGURI and his FOOTMEN go off to the right. MORIEMON releases YOHEI and follows them.
    THE VIILLAGERS see off OGURI and his FOOTMEN.
    YOHEI bends low and keeps sitting with his hand on the ground.

    Blackout.

「女殺油地獄」

小栗　待て待て！森右衛門！その者を討って捨てるなどと、何故そのようなことを申す。

森右衛門　（小栗に向かい頭をさげて）恐れながら、こ奴は最前の無礼者にございます。他人ならばどうぞお許しなされて下さいますようと執り成しも致しましょうが、こ奴の母は私の妹。こ奴は私の実の甥(おい)。小栗様が如何に仰せになろうとも助けるわけにはまいりませぬ。このままでは申し訳が立ちませぬ。

小栗　それで、その者が如何なる無礼を致したと申すのか。

森右衛門　先ほど小栗様の御身やお馬に泥をかけて汚した無礼の大罪でございます。

小栗　何と申す？私の身を汚したとな？これ、私を見よ、どこも汚れておらぬではないか。

森右衛門　いえいえ、お召し替えにならぬ前のお着物が……。

小栗　そうであろう。着替えてしまったら泥がかからなかったも同然ではないか。

森右衛門　お言葉ではございますが、お馬の鞍(くら)や鐙(あぶみ)にも泥がかかり小栗様がこのように徒歩でお帰りなされることになりました。こ奴は我が主人に恥辱を与える無礼者でございます。

小栗　黙って私の申すことを聞け。馬の胴にかける馬具は泥を避けるもの。泥をよける必要がないなら、そのようなものを用いることはあるまい。それゆえ、泥障(どろよ)けの「障泥(あおり)」に泥がかかっても、恥辱も無礼も罪もない。たった一滴の濁った水であっても、名字家名(みょうじかめい)にかかるものならば、洗っても落ちず濯(すす)いでも取り去れない。武士の恥辱とはそういうことをいうのだ。そやつのような下賤(げせん)な輩(やから)は私の目から見れば泥水だ。私の名前は泥から出て泥に染まぬ「蓮(はす)」を名に持つ「はちや」。私の名は汚されてはおらぬ。助けてやれ。

森右衛門　ははーっ！（森右衛門は有難さに両手をついて畏まる。）

　　　　　小栗八弥の一行、下手に去る。森右衛門は与兵衛を放して一行に続く。
　　　　　在郷の人々は一行を見送る。
　　　　　与兵衛は小さくなり地面に両手を付いている。

　　　　　暗転。

ACT TWO

At the Kawachi-ya

The second of May, about a month later.

The roofs of town houses are seen in the background, where colourful banners for the Boys' Festival Day[1] are flying in celebration here and there in the beautiful May sky.

The oil shop and residence of KAWACHI-YA TOKUBEI centre stage to left. The street of Motodenma-machi runs from the hanamichi to upstage right. The shop of Kawachi-ya opens out to the street. There is a willow tree by the street downstage right. A narrow alley runs downstage across the street.

A large noren,[2] on which the shop name 'Kawachi-ya' is dyed, is hung at the front of the shop. The entrance hall is earth-floored, but the shop is a room with a wooden floor whose level is lower than the other rooms. Many oil barrels are lined up on both the floor and the shelves in the shop. A few ladles and measures are seen on a small table in the corner of the shop. There is a doorway to the storeroom behind the shop.

There are two tatami-matted[3] rooms next to the shop towards stage left. The rooms are raised about 40cm above ground level. The first room is a living room but the area close to the shop is used as a counting room. There is a doorway to the inner part of the house at the back of the first room. A long noren is hung over the doorway.

A futon has been rolled out in the second room and KACHI, the daughter of the Kawachi-ya, is lying. The fusuma[4] sliding doors between the two tatami-matted rooms are open to let in the fresh air and a byōbu[5] screen is placed to screen off the futon.

THE TWELVE LIGHTS,[6] a group of young Buddhist oil merchants, enter from the hanamichi. They are in the attire of a mountain ascetic. They wear a Buddhist rosary and a covering for the waist, and carry a conch, a pilgrim's staff and a water flask around the waist. They chant the Heart Sutra[7] in unison while blowing the conch horn now and then. They are on their way back from the assembly on Mount. Ōmine.[8] There are some inexperienced members but the group has paid homage to the mountain many times; one of the members, who has undertaken the ascetic practices at the peak of Mt. Ōmine more than four times, has been named as THE LEADER.

THE TWELVE LIGHTS: Gyatei gyatei gyatei hara-gyatei, harasō-gyatei, Gyatei gyatei hara-gyatei, harasō gyatei. Onkoro onkoro sendarimatōgi, onabiraunken.

「女殺油地獄」

中之卷

河内屋の場

　五月二日。前景のほぼ一月後。
　舞台後方に本天満町の町並みが見え、五月の青空の下、町屋の家々の屋根には色とりどりに端午の節句の絵幟[1]がはためいている。
　舞台中ほどから上手に向かって油屋河内屋徳兵衛の店と住まい。花道から舞台下手側奥へ本天満町の通りが走っている。河内屋はこの本天満町の通りに面している。舞台下手、通りの傍に一本の柳の木。通りを横切って舞台手前を路地が走る。

　店の入り口には「河内屋」の屋号を染め抜いた暖簾[2]がかかっている。店内は床が座敷よりも低くなっている板敷きの落間で、床や棚に油樽がところ狭しと並んでいる。店の一角に台があり、その上に油を量るための枡や柄杓が幾つか置いてある。その奥には物置きへの入り口がある。

　店から上手に向かって、座敷[3]、次の間と続いている。座敷の店に近いところは帳場である。座敷の中ほどには奥向きへの出入り口がある。

　今、次の間に一組の蒲団が敷かれていて、河内屋の末娘おかちが寝ている。風通しがいいように座敷との境の襖[4]は開けてあり、かわりに目隠しのための屏風[5]が立てられている。

　花道から、法螺貝を吹き鳴らし、手に金剛杖、首に数珠、腰に腰当をして水飲みをぶら下げたものものしい山伏姿の油屋仲間の若い衆でなる「十二灯組」[6]の講中が、口々に『般若心経』[7]を唱えながらやって来る。一行は大峰山の山上講[8]からの下向の途中である。講中には新人も混じっているが、組はこれまでに幾度も参詣しており、先導者は大峰山入りを四度以上も果たし先達の院号を受けているほどである。

講中一同　掲諦　掲諦　掲諦　波羅掲諦、波羅僧掲諦、掲諦　掲諦　波羅掲諦、波羅僧掲諦。唵呼嚧　唵呼嚧　施茶利摩登枳、唵阿毘羅吽欠。

THE TWELVE LIGHTS stop when they come to the Kawachi-ya.

LEADER [*addressing the interior of the Kawachi-ya*]: Yohei! Are you in? We've completed our annual training on Mt. Ōmine successfully and thankfully have returned home safely. [*Looking into the shop and then entering.*]

TWELVE LIGHTS 1 [*entering the shop after the LEADER*]: Yohei! Aren't you in? You must've known that we were returning from the mountain today. All our close friends came to meet us at Kuwazu[9] in Higashi-Sumiyoshi. As you were the only person who wasn't there, we've dropped by to see whether or not you are all right.

TWELVE LIGHT 2 and 3 enter the shop, too.

TWELVE LIGHTS 2: Yohei! Are you feeling unwell? We have a good souvenir for you. It's a wonderful story we heard on the mountain.

TWELVE LIGHTS 3: Here goes. A blind boy aged 12 or 13 from the western country paid homage to Mt. Ōmine so that his deepest wish would be granted. While he was praying to the statue of the Great Ascetic En,[10] his wish was heard and his eyes were opened. The boy could run down the slope of bamboo grass without a stick when he descended the mountain. The people seeing this said, "What a wonderful sight! It's a sign of a rich rice harvest for this year."

TWELVE LIGHTS 1: Yohei, do you understand what this means? 'A blind boy's eyes were opened' means a long-closed rice granary will be opened.

TWELVE LIGHTS 2: And 'descending the slope easily' is a prophecy that rice prices will go down smoothly.

TWELVE LIGHTS 3: Did you get that? Isn't it a good thing to hear?

All the members pray to the Great Ascetic En together.

LEADER: If you are free this evening, come to my house. I would like to talk about what we did on the mountain and to forget my travel fatigue.

As there is no reply from the house, THE TWELVE LIGHTS decide to leave the Kawachi-ya and start chanting the incantation of the Heart Sutra loudly once again.
KAWACHI-YA TOKUBEI rushes out of the inner part of the house through the doorway of the living room.

「女殺油地獄」

　　　　　　「十二灯組」の講中、河内屋の店先まで来る。

先達　（店の中に向かって）与兵衛、在宅か？講中みな無事で大峰山での修行をありがたく終えてきたぞ。（中をうかがってから店に入る。）

講中１　（続いて中に入り）与兵衛、おらんのか？今日の下向はお前も知っているはず。仲の良い友たちは皆東住吉の桑津９まで迎えに来たぞ。お前一人の姿がなかったので、心配で寄ってみた。

　　　　　　講中２、講中３も続いて店に入る。

講中２　与兵衛、具合でも悪いのか？有難いご利益のみやげ話があるぞ。

講中３　なんでも西国者の両眼のつぶれた十二、三歳の子供のめくらが大願をかけて山上参りをして役の行者様[10]の尊像を拝むうちに両眼が開いてあの小篠の坂を杖もつかずにすっすっと下ったとか。それを見ていた山上講の連中が、『ああ、有難い。この秋は豊作のお告げだ。』と言ったとかだ。

講中１　与兵衛、分かるか？子供のめくらはこめくら、即ち、米蔵開くということ。

講中２　やすやすと下り坂を降りるのは、米の値段が下がり始めるということのお告げやそうや。

講中３　ええ、どうや？有難いやないか。

　　　　　　講中一同、有難く拝む。

先達　暇なら夕方にでもわしのところに来るとよい。色々とお山での話をして旅の疲れ晴らしたいわ。

　　　　　　与兵衛も家人も出て来る様子がないので、講中一同は河内屋を後にすべく再び大声で『般若心経』の呪文を唱え始める。
　　　　　　店の主河内屋徳兵衛が座敷の奥から走り出て来る。

87

KAWACHI-YA TOKUBEI: Oh, oh, the party of young oil sellers! Are you on the way back from Mt. Ōmine? You have completed the ascetic practices on the mountain and got back home safe. Well done! How commendable of you! Compared to you, good youth, it's regrettable to say, but we don't know where the hell my useless son has gone to pay his homage. This year too, he got four thousand and six hundred *sen*-coppers from us and four thousand from his big brother Tahei in Junkei-machi,[11] nearly ten thousand in total. You said that he didn't even go to meet you. He is a rogue forgetting the power of all the gods, goddesses and Buddha. A damned rogue! Please tell him off severely for his wrong doing as his good friends. I beg you.

SAWA comes in through the doorway of the living room with a tea tray.

SAWA: Well, well, welcome home. How good to see all of you return safely! Everyone, please have a cup of tea. [*Deeply dejected*] Perhaps this must be punishment for our Yohei having lied to the Great Ascetic En of Mt. Ōmine. His little sister O-Kachi has got a cold and been in bed for about ten days. She has seen three doctors but her temperature hasn't gone down…On the one hand the Boys' Festival Day is getting closer, and on the other we've found a good husband for our daughter and the marriage has been decided by mutual agreement…now the man's family wants to do it sooner. We don't know what to do. I am sure that this is a divine punishment for Yohei's lie to the Great Ascetic En. Young people of the Twelve Lights, please say your prayers for forgiveness.

LEADER: If it was a divine punishment from Mt. Ōmine, it would have been directed at Yohei himself. The sacred Great Ascetic En would not punish Yohei's sister who is quite irrelevant to what Yohei has done. I think her illness is caused by something else. Such illness needs neither a doctor nor medicine. Have you ever heard of an exorcist called White Fox? People gave the mountain ascetic this nickname because his cures are like the magic of the white fox, the messenger of the god of the Harvest. He is much talked about. Perhaps Yohei has heard about him, too. I'm sure once White Fox performs the incantations and prayers, your daughter's temperature will soon go down. I shall drop by his place on the way home and ask him to visit your daughter. He would come immediately if I asked.

SAWA [*delighted*]: Oh, I am grateful! [*Praying with her hands pressed together*] This must be the will of the Great Ascetic En. I have to go to my daughter's doctor for her medicine now. You must excuse me, but all of you, you should stay and rest.

LEADER: Thank you very much for your kindness. But we'd like to celebrate our safe return

「女殺油地獄」

河内屋徳兵衛　おお、おお、若い衆か。下向ですか。皆、無事に大峰山での修行を終えられてのお帰りか。ほんに御奇特なことです。それに引き替え、うちの野良めは山上参りだ、行者講だと嘘をついて、今年も私から四貫六百文、順慶町11の兄の太兵衛のところから四貫と全部で十貫近いお金を取っておいて、何処にお参りに行ったのやら。お前様方のお迎えにも出やがらんと。神仏も考えん罰当たりの道楽者。友だちやと思うて、きつう意見してやって下さい。お頼みします。

　　　　　　座敷の奥からお沢がお茶の盆を持って出てくる。

お沢　まあ、まあ、お帰りなさいませ。皆無事の下向、ほんにめでたいことでございます。皆様、ひとつお茶でも召し上がって下さい。（沈んで、しみじみと）うちの与兵衛が大峰山の役の行者様に嘘をついた罰か、あれの妹のおかちが十日もの間風邪をひいて寝込んでいます。医者も三人変えましたが未だに熱も下がらず……端午の節句は近づくわ、婿取りの相談が決まり先方様は急がれるわで、どうしたものかと夫婦して困っております。これもみな与兵衛の野良めが行者様に嘘ついた祟りです。お若い衆、どうかお詫びの御祈祷をお頼み申します。

先達　いや、お山の祟りならば与兵衛に罰が当たるはず。役の行者とも言われる尊い仏が、関係のない妹様に祟ったりなされません。娘御の熱病はまた別のことと思われます。そのような病には医者も薬も要りません。聞かれたことはございませんか。不思議なほど良く治るので異名を白稲荷法印と呼ばれている、今、世間で評判の山伏を？多分、与兵衛も聞き知っているはず。この山伏に祈祷してもらえば一度に熱も下がります。これからすぐに法印のところに立ち寄ります。私から頼めば嫌とは言わんはず、すぐに来てくれることでしょう。

お沢　（喜んで）まあ、有難いこと。（手を合わせて）これも行者様の思し召し。私はこれからお医者様のところに行かねばなりません。けど、お前様方はここでゆっくり休んでいってくだされ。
先達　有難うございます。が、私らも早う親や妻子の顔を見て無事の下向を一緒に祝お

with our wives and children as soon as possible.

> *The members of the TWELVE LIGHTS thank SAWA and TOKUBEI, start chanting the incantation of the Heart Sutra and blowing a conch horn now and then, and depart for their own homes.*
> *SAWA goes off downstage right.*
> *TOKUBEI sees all off outside the shop.*
> *Soon YOHEI's elder brother TAHEI comes in hurriedly from the direction in which SAWA has gone.*

TOKUBEI [*noticing TAHEI*]: Oh, Tahei. Did you come to pay a visit to O-Kachi? How good of you, but really you didn't have to do this. It's nearly one of the seasonal settlement days[12] and you must be extremely busy with writing bills for all the accounts of credit sales or other things. Anyway, do come in. [*TOKUBEI leads TAHEI to the living room and sits down.*]

TAHEI [*following TOKUBEI and sitting*]: I met Mother on the way here, so I've already talked to her about this. . . . Just a moment ago a courier delivered a letter from Uncle Moriemon in Takatsuki. The thing is, what's written in his letter is something unthinkable. Please have a look. [*Taking the letter out of the bosom of his kimono and showing it*] It says, "Last month when I accompanied my master to the Nozaki Kannon, I happened to come across our Yohei the scoundrel who was also making a visit to Nozaki. He was fighting his friend and the mud he threw at this friend of his hit my master and my master's horse. Thus he disgraced my master. I made up my mind to cut him down on the spot and to commit hara-kiri.[13] However my wise master let Yohei go without punishment and ended the matter peacefully. But after the incident in Nozaki, wherever I went, everyone in Takatsuki, from the retainers to the townspeople, was talking about the incident. I cannot put on an appearance of composure and continue to serve my master unashamedly any more. I have decided to ask for leave, to go down to Osaka in a few days and to think about how to save my honour as a samurai. Otherwise I won't be able to live as a swordsman any more . . ."

TOKUBEI [*grasping his knees with mortification before TAHEI finishes reading*]: Alas! As was expected, at last the fool has gone too far! I knew something like this would happen sooner or later. Now, we know that Moriemon-dono is in trouble . . . in addition, our O-Kachi is very ill. What's worse, nobody knows what our fool could do next. [*He holds his head in his arms.*]

TAHEI: As things have come this far, you don't need to think twice! Please kick him out of

「女殺油地獄」

うと思います。

　　「十二灯組」の講中は徳兵衛と沢に礼を言い、再び法螺貝を吹きならし、「掲諦 掲諦 掲諦 波羅掲諦 波羅僧掲諦……」と『般若心経』の呪文を唱えながら、それぞれ自分の家のある方向に帰って行く。
　　お沢は舞台下手前へ去る。
　　徳兵衛は店の外まで出て人々を見送る。
　　与兵衛の兄、河内屋太兵衛が舞台下手、お沢の去った方角から急ぎ足で来る。

徳兵衛　（太兵衛を見て）おお、太兵衛。おかちの病気見舞いに来てくれたんか。節季前[12]で売掛金の請求書書きやなんやらで忙しい時に、わざわざ来てくれんでもよかったのに。まあお上がり。（先に座敷に上がって座る。）

太兵衛　（徳兵衛の後について、座敷に上がって座り）母様には今、道で会いましたので立ちながら詳しいお話を致しました……。たった今、高槻の伯父上森右衛門様から飛脚に託した手紙を受け取りました。それが、思いもよらない事を書いてこられたのです。父様、どうぞご覧ください。（懐から手紙を取り出して徳兵衛に見せて）ここに、『先月、我が主人のお供をして野崎にお詣りせし折、極道者の与兵衛のお参りと行き会った。与兵衛めは友達と取っ組み合いの喧嘩をしており、けんか相手と遣り合う拍子に我が主人に重ね重ねの無礼を働いた。即刻その場で与兵衛を切り殺し自分も切腹[13]の覚悟を決めたが、我が主人の聡明で穏便なご配慮のおかげで、その場は事無く済んだ。しかしながら、その後、御家中及び御城下の町人にいたるまでがその件でもっぱらの噂。おめおめと平静を装い御奉公を続けることも出来ず、暇を願い出て四、五日中に大阪へ下り、武士の面目立つべき思案をせずば、再び刀を差して武士に戻る事も出来ず……』と書いてあります。

徳兵衛　（太兵衛が手紙を読み終わらないうちに、膝を掴んで、口惜しげに）ああーっ、案の定、大変なことをやらかしおった！きっとどこかで大きな間違いを起こすに違いないと思っていた！森右衛門殿の難儀。かてて加えておかちの病気。まだこの上にあの野良が何をしでかすやら知れたものではない。（頭を抱え込む。）

太兵衛　もう、こうなったからには考えることなどありません！あいつをこの家から叩

this house! If I may say so, Father, you are too soft on him. It's not right that you should feel constrained before Yohei and me just because you are our step-father. Although you aren't our natural father, you married our natural mother and raised us benevolently. You are our true father. You do not hesitate to hit O-Kachi who's grown up to be someone's bride, but you've never hit Yohei and so have made the fool all puffed up. Your restraint towards him hasn't done him any good. The fool knows how to take advantage of you. Please kick him out of this house and send him to me. I shall find him a suitable shop to work in so as to flog the laziness out of him!

TOKUBEI [*mortified*]: Oh, it's so regrettable! You're right. I'm your step-father, but, still a father. Certainly a father would have no hesitation in scolding his children. But you two are the sons of my old master, the late Kawachi-ya Tokubei. When the master died, you were seven and the fool was only four. But the fool remembers how I addressed you and him and how he talked to me when I was a senior shop assistant at the shop. Back then I also called your mother 'mistress.' Your uncle, Moriemon-dono thought over the oil retailers' monopoly share[14] and said to me, "There is no one to be able to succeed to the share in the Kawachi-ya at this point. If you leave the shop now, the widow and her two sons will lose the means of their livelihood. Will you please stay and keep the trade going? I beseech you." He pleaded with me earnestly. So I married the widow of the master, assumed the professional name of Kawachi-ya Tokubei, became your step-father and kept the shop open. It was worth doing. You've grown up to be a respectable merchant, already independent and running your own shop. I was hoping to let Yohei expand our business, employ a shop assistant, then build a storehouse . . . but whatever I planned for him and his future, he was like a purse with a hole in the bottom. It was like scooping water with a basket . . . for every one *monme*-silver he earns, he will spend one hundred . . . for every word I have with him, I will receive a thousand . . . Originally our relationship was that between the master's son and his employee. It's natural that my talking to him has no effect on him. [*Gritting his teeth with mortification*] Oh, hell, what a position to be in…

TAHEI: Listen, Father, he sees through your heart. He takes advantage of your being honest and tramples on your feelings, and does as he likes. Because you kindly stayed with us and succeeded to the Kawachi-ya, we didn't have to close this oil shop. We neither had to sleep under a bridge nor to stand outside someone's gate to beg. I have never forgotten your merciful love to us for a moment. It's as deep as our real father's. Mother regrets that you are too conscientious and honest about having been our employee. She is anxious that you might feel diffident about her too because she is the mother of the boy whom you never wants to upset . . . it's sad that she needs to feel awkward with you

「女殺油地獄」

き出して下さい！大体、親仁様(おやじさま)が甘すぎる。私と与兵衛がお前様の実の子でないからと遠慮されるのがいけない。実の子でのうても産みの親の母上と連れ添い育ててくれたお前様は私共の真の父上。もうすぐ婿を取る程大きゅうなったおかちのことはぶったり叩いたりされながら、あの阿呆(あほ)めには手一つ上げずにつけあがらせる。万事に遠慮されるのがみな本人の害になりました。叩き出して私のところへおよこし下さい。どこぞ厳しいお店に奉公させて、あいつの性根(しょうね)叩き直してやります！

徳兵衛（無念顔で）ああ、口惜(くちお)しい。義理の仲とはいえ確かに親は親、子を叱るのに遠慮はないはず。けど、お前達兄弟は私の親方の子。親旦那様が亡くなられた時には、お前は七つで野良(のら)めが四つ。『ぼん様、兄様』と、この徳兵衛に呼ばれ、『徳兵衛、どうしろ、こうしろ』と手代(てだい)の時の私に命じていたのをあいつはちゃんと覚えている。嬶も元は、『おか様の、内儀様(ないぎさま)の』と呼んだ人。伯父の森右衛門殿が小売商の株仲間(かぶなかま)[14]のことを思案なされて、番頭(ばんとう)やったこの私に『今、そなたが見捨てては残された後家も子供も路頭(ろとう)に迷う。どうか、私の言うことを聞いて欲しい。』と、折り入って頼まれたので、親方の奥方と夫婦になり名跡(みょうせき)を継ぎ、親方の子の父となって育て店を守ってきた。その甲斐(かい)あって兄のお前は独立して商売なされる程になった。与兵衛には商いの手を広げさせ、手代の一人も置き、蔵も建てる程にしてやりたいと……いくらこっちで思うても、あいつは尻のほどけた銭差(ぜにさ)し、籠(かご)で水汲(く)むのと同じの後ろが抜けっ放し。一匁(いちもんめ)儲(もう)けたら百匁(ひゃくもんめ)使い、小言一言(こごとひとこと)言うたら千言(せんこと)言い返す性根(しょうね)……。元が主人筋と奉公人筋の間柄では小言の効き目の無いのも当たり前。（くやしさに歯をくいしばり）ああ、我が身の立場が口惜(くちお)しい……。

太兵衛　それそのようなあなたの正直なところを見透かして、あの道楽者がやりたい放題であなたのことを踏み付けにする。親仁様が残って河内屋の名跡を継いで下さったおかげで、橋の下にも寝ず、人の門(かど)にも立たず、店も閉じずにやってこられた。実の親にも変わらぬあなたのお慈悲、忘れたことはありません。母様は親仁様が奉公人筋であったことに律儀で正直すぎるのを逆に悔やんでおられます。子供に遠慮されるからには、その子を宿した自分にも遠慮されているのではないかと……要らぬ気兼ねを重ねられて……。何の因果(いんが)ですやろ。あの恥じ晒(さら)しの与兵

about that . . . What have we done to deserve these sufferings? I've had enough of Yohei who only brings dishonour on my family. I, Tahei, beg you. Please chase him off; send him far away, even to Edo[15] or Nagasaki.[16] Mother says that she never wants to see him again and if he died, that would be the end of it. She vows in front of Buddha that she won't keep any lingering attachment to Yohei. When his natural mother feels this way, why do you hesitate? Please, Father, please renounce him.

KACHI is woken up by TOKUBEI and TAHEI's conversation.

KACHI: Oh, it hurts. Mother! Where's Mother! Isn't she back yet?

At this point the exorcist WHITE FOX in the attire of a mountain ascetic enters from upstage right and stops in front of the Kawachi-ya.

WHITE FOX: Hello! Excuse me! Is this Kawachi-ya Tokubei-dono's house? I am White Fox, a mountain ascetic. The Leader of the Twelve Lights asked me to pay a visit to your sick daughter.

TAHEI [*to TOKUBEI*]: Oh, you asked for a prayer for O-Kachi. That's a good idea. Well, I must be going. I should write a reply to Uncle Moriemon as soon as possible. Good-bye for now.

TAHEI greets WHITE FOX at the shop entrance and goes off to stage right.

TOKUBEI [*to the outside of the shop*]: Kawachi-ya Tokubei is here. Please, do come in. Thank you for coming so soon. Please come this way.

TOKUBEI leads WHITE FOX to the room where KACHI lies. He puts the screen away and sits by KACHI. WHITE FOX sits by her, too.

YOHEI comes home from the hanamichi. He has spent all his money in the pleasure quarter. He walks in a leisurely manner, carrying two empty oil barrels dangling on a pole.

CHORUS: Look! Yohei is coming home.
  The fellow can't walk steadily.
  But he knows how to glide over the world smoothly.

　　　　　　　　「女殺油地獄」

衛にはほとほと愛想がつきました。この太兵衛がお頼みします。どうか、江戸[15]、長崎[16]へも追い下して下さい。母様も仏様に誓うて、死によったらそれまでのこと、二度とあいつの顔は見とうない、少しも未練はないと言っておられます。母様がこう言われる以上何の遠慮がございます。どうか、あいつを勘当して下さい。

　　　　　徳兵衛と太兵衛の会話を聞いて、末娘のおかちが目を覚ます。

おかち　ああ、苦しい！母様！母様！母様はまだ戻られませんか。

　　　　この時、舞台下手奥より山伏姿の白稲荷法印が来て河内屋の門口に立つ。

白稲荷法印　御免。河内屋徳兵衛殿はこちらか。山上講中に頼まれて白稲荷法印がお見舞いにあがりました。

太兵衛　（徳兵衛に）おかちの祈祷を頼まれましたか。それはいい。高槻の伯父への返事を急いで出したいので、私はこれでお暇いたします。

　　　　太兵衛は店の門口で白稲荷法印に会釈して、来た方向に急ぎ足で去る。

徳兵衛（店の外に）徳兵衛はこちらに居ります。早々とお出向きくださり有難うございます。どうぞ、こちらへ。

　　　　徳兵衛は白稲荷法印をおかちの寝ている部屋に案内し、立てていた屏風をたたんで、おかちの側に座る。法印もおかちの側に行って座る。

　　　　色町で遊んでお金を遣い果たした与兵衛が、空の油樽をぶらりぶらりと担いで花道から帰って来る。

コーラス　しっかり地に　足つけて　踏みしめて歩くことは　知りまへん
　世の中を　滑り渡りの　河内屋与兵衛

A frequenter of the pleasure quarter
Drained of all the sales money,
Nothing, not even a drop of oil, is left, after the excitement last night.
Don't ever be deceived by the sweat on his forehead.
It's the hot summer sun that's making him sweat!
The oil barrels on his pole are as light as a feather,
For they're empty, just like his purse.
Walking leisurely, slipping and sliding,
He's got something wicked up his kimono sleeve.
Frogs! Worms! Men! Women! Everyone!
Excuse me! Please!
Oh, what a bliss! It's another fine day.
A happy-go-lucky fellow's coming home in broad daylight!

YOHEI [*entering the Kawachi-ya*]: Oh, that's odd, a mountain ascetic at home. [*Walking onto the first room and looking into the second room*] Why, it's White Fox whom I know by sight. Are you here to perform incantations for curing O-Kachi? If your prayers could dispel whatever evil spirit she's been possessed by, I would cut my head off. [*Noticing SAWA is not around*] I see . . . Mother must've gone to the doctor for O-Kachi's medicine. O-Kachi's illness is a fatal one that even the legendary Indian doctor Giba wouldn't be able to cure. Mother shouldn't worry too much. [*Putting on a serious look*] By the way, Father, I've got something more important to tell you. I told Mother about this when it happened, but then completely forgot about it. As I just remembered it this morning, I came home leaving my sales half-finished. The thing is, when I paid a visit to the Nozaki Kannon last month, I happened to meet my uncle Moriemon-sama. He said to me then, "How good to meet you here. I was about to send a courier to your parents. I'd like to ask a favour of you. Will you please tell them? The truth of the matter is that I've embezzled my master's money for three thousand *monme* in silver. If I fail to pay it back by the coming settlement day, I must commit hara-kiri. Otherwise, I will be hanged. Please tell your parents to send me three thousand *monme* in silver by your hand confidentially, and please make sure to keep it secret from your elder brother Tahei, as he is a man who does not understand justice and obligation." Father, if you let our uncle commit hara-kiri by refusing a mere few thousands *monme*-silver, your reputation will be damaged. You'll lose face. It's already the second of May today. The next settlement day is just the day after tomorrow. Will you please prepare the money for him setting everything else aside? If I leave for Takatsuki tomorrow at dawn, I should be able to be back here by noon.

TOKUBEI [*disgusted with YOHEI's lie*] Even if he is your uncle, if he is a samurai who has

「女殺油地獄」

売り上げ金も　絞られて　滓も残らん色町通い
でぼちん濡らす　玉の汗は　夏の日差しのせえでっせえ
肩に担いだ油桶　中は涼しい空っぽで
空の財布と　どっちこち
腹に一物　悪巧み　抱えて　ブラブラ　ツールツル
どっちもこっちも　カエルもミミズも
ごめんやっしゃあああー
今日も極楽　ええ天気
極楽トンボの　昼帰り　でっせええぇー

与兵衛　（河内屋に入って）おや、珍しい、お山伏。（座敷に上がり、奥の座敷を覗いて）なーんや、顔見知りの白稲荷殿やないか。おかちの病気治癒のための御祈祷ですか。妹の体に憑いた憑き物が山伏衆の祈りで退いたら、この与兵衛の首やる。（お沢の居ないのに気付いて）ふーん、そうか、母上は薬を取りに行かれたのか。まあまあ、お釈迦様の生きておられた時代にいたという、天竺の名医ギバでも治せん死病やというのに、無用の心配なさって。（尤もらしく）それはそうと、なあ、親仁殿、おかちの病気よりももっと大変なことが起きましたんや。その時は、母様に言いましたけど、その後、ずーっと忘れていました。今日、ふとそのこと思い出しましたよって、商い止めて帰ってきましたんや。先月、野崎にお参りした時、伯父森右衛門様に行き逢いました。伯父様は『これは良いところで出会った。わざわざ飛脚を遣るところであった。お前の親に伝えて欲しいことがある。主人のお金を銀三貫目余り使い込み、この節季までに返済せねば切腹か縛り首になる。お前の兄の太兵衛は義理も法もしらん奴だから、くれぐれもあいつには内緒で三貫目調達して与兵衛に持たせてくれるように。』そう言われました。二貫目や三貫目ほとのお金で伯父様に腹を切らせては、お前様の外聞悪く世間体が立つまい。今日はもう五月二日。節季と言っても、明後日のこと。何事もさしおいて今日中に三貫目の金を用意してください。明日の夜明けに出かけたら昼までには高槻まで行って来られます。

徳兵衛　（与兵衛の嘘に呆れて）いくら伯父でも主君の金を遣い込むような侍は腹切ら

stolen his master's money, it will be best for him to commit hara-kiri. What? Did you say a mere few thousand *monme*-silver? I haven't seen any of your sales money since last year, but it should make three or four thousand altogether. If you want to help your uncle, why don't you give him your money? When we're busy arranging a husband for our daughter and she is not well, I have no time for your silly story. [*Taking no notice of YOHEI*] I'm so sorry to have kept you waiting, priest. Please take a good look at O-Kachi.

TOKUBEI gently helps KACHI to sit up. KACHI looks worn out.

YOHEI [*annoyed by the failure of his plan, picking up the abacus from the sales counter, throwing himself down in the middle of the living room and resting his head on it*] Humph! You think you can arrange a husband for O-Kachi successfully. Try it then! I shall sit back and watch.

WHITE FOX [*looking at KACHI's face fixedly*]: How old are you?

KACHI: I'm fifteen.

WHITE FOX: When did this begin?

KACHI: It started on the twelfth last month.

WHITE FOX [*with a knowing look*]: I see, the twelfth is the memorial day of Yakushi Buddha[17] and the fifteenth is that of Amida Buddha,[18] and it follows . . . [*taking out a book from the bosom of his kimono, spreading it open and counting the days on his fingers*] originally, as it written in one of the sermon jōruri ballad,[19] Yakushi Buddha and Amida Buddha were once a husband and wife . . . therefore, this means . . . your daughter wants to take a husband as soon as possible . . . her illness means she is possessed by some evil spirit.

TOKUBEI nods his head in agreement with WHITE FOX.

WHITE FOX [*encouraged and getting into the swing of things*]: The white fox is a messenger of the Great God of the Harvest, and what it says never differs a hair's width from the truth. Like medicine, every incantation and prayer has a different function in the same way as every god, goddess and Buddha does. It is the Twenty-one Shrines on Mt. Hiei that cure a fever; the Atsuta Shrine is for poor blood circulation, the Atago Shrine for a headache; Ashuku Buddha is for diseases of the feet and legs, while Acala, the God of Fire, can freeze the robbers and elopers by his spell, the Shrine to the Wind is for a cold, the Shrine to Grey-hair is for senility. Then the Jizō, the guardian deity of children, who's famous for his great mercy and compassion, cures homosexuals. If you want a good hand

「女殺油地獄」

せた方がまし。何を？軽々しく三貫目ほどの金だと？お前の商いの儲け、去年から一文も見てないが、全部合わせたら三貫目や四貫目はあるはず。伯父にお金を遣りたければその金を遣るといい。間もなく婿を迎える大切な娘が病気だというのに、お前の馬鹿げた相談聞く暇はない。（与兵衛の言うことなど取り合わないで）法印様、お待ちどうさまでございます。どうか、おかちの容態ご覧なされてください。

　　　　　　徳兵衛は優しくおかちを抱きおこす。おかちは窶れた顔をしている。

与兵衛　（胸算用が外れて腹を立て、帳場にあった算盤を取り、枕にして座敷の真ん中にごろりと横になり）おお、おお、見事に婿が呼べるもんなら呼んでみさらせ！見物さしてもらうわ。

白稲荷法印　（じっとおかちの顔を見て）歳は幾つかな？
おかち　十五。
白稲荷法印　病気の始まりは？
おかち　先月の十二日。
白稲荷法印　（尤もらしく）ふーん、十二日は薬師如来[17]の縁日。十五日が阿弥陀様[18]の縁日、とすると……（懐から書籍を取り出して広げて、指を折って日数を数え）そもそも、説教浄瑠璃[19]の中の法蔵比丘の浄瑠璃にもあるように、阿弥陀と薬師はご夫婦でおられるから……ふんふん、即ち、この病気は一時も早く婿殿を呼び入れ夫婦になりたいと願う気持に、少々他の憑き物が憑いて……。

　　　　　　徳兵衛は法印の言葉を尤もという顔で頷いている。

白稲荷法印　（調子に乗り）稲荷大明神の使者白狐の教えは髪の毛一本ほども違わぬ。加持祈祷も薬と同様で神仏にもそれぞれの役がある。熱を冷まし冷やすのは比叡山二十一社。暖めるのには熱田明神。頭の病気は愛宕権現。足の病は阿閦仏。駆け落ち者や盗人を動かぬよう金縛りにするのは不動明王。風邪のお祈りは風の宮。老人のお衰には白髭神社や白髪薬師。若衆の病気の祈りには大慈大悲の地蔵菩薩。カルタの絵の高い点の札の祈祷には麻布の明神や釈迦牟尼仏。博打の胴元

at cards, the gracious god of Azabu will answer your prayer. Bookies' gambling prayers will be heard if you ask the deity of the Six Shrine named after the numbers of a dice and so forth. But above all, my speciality is the market price of *sen*-coppers and *ryō*-gold coins, rice and wheat. Their rise and fall of their rates are in my power. When the owner wishes for a bullish market, I will ask all the gods on the Takamagahara Plain High Heaven. Then for the people who have just sold their stock and wish for its rate to continue to fall, I shall ask the Temple of Saga or the Yasui Shrine which stand at the foot of the mountains. For both buyers and sellers the rate needs to be neither high nor low; that is for the Takayasu god in Kawachi in a place which neither high nor low. Thus, the power of faith is unshakable . . . Normally I receive thirty *ryō*-gold coins in reward for my service and I wouldn't mind receiving it anytime. Now let me start an incantation . . . . [*WHITE FOX waves the priest's staff and rubs the Buddhist rosary. While saying a prayer, he is about to make a sign with his fingers.*]

KACHI [*raising herself in anguish and stopping WHITE FOX*]: No, no! I don't want any prayers and incantations! If you want to cure my disease, you must stop arranging a husband for me! [*KACHI is as if possessed by the late KAWACHI-YA TOKUBEI.*] "My son Yohei is suffering from debts which he fell into through the error of his youthful ways. His suffering has become my torment in the land of the dead. Now it tortures me in hell. I want you to allow Yohei to marry the woman he promised to, even if she is a courtesan. You must pay a bride-price for the woman, take her in as Yohei's wife and let Yohei inherit the shop. [*The spirit becomes stronger.*] If you dare to take a husband for Kachi, she will surely die. You must listen to what I say! Do you understand?" [*Suddenly looking around restlessly and writhing in agony*] Oh! Oh! It hurts! Oh, it's so painful! Help me . . . !

TOKUBEI is taken aback by this.

WHITE FOX [*not wincing at all*]: Where have you come from? Leave her at once! The magical power of the mountain ascetic is boundless! [*Shaking the priest's staff energetically and tinkling loud*] Leave her! Go away! My incantation will exorcise evil spirits! Kyūkyū Nyoritsuryō, Kyūkyū Nyoritsuryō, Kyūkyū Nyoritsuryō . . .

YOHEI [*abruptly getting up*]: What on earth do you think you're doing? You quack mountain ascetic! Stop that silly prayer! [*He takes hold of WHITE FOX in the second room and pushes him off the shop floor.*]

WHITE FOX: You don't know the mystic power of the mountain ascetic! Take this! [*WHITE FOX quickly gets up from the floor, runs up to the living room, shakes the priest's staff and*

「女殺油地獄」

の祈りには四三五六のさいころの目にちなんだ六社大明神などがある。とりわけこの法印の得意とするのは銭、小判、表物の相場の商い、上げようと下げようと思いのまま。持ち主が値上がりを祈るときには、買いに出て高値を祈る高天が原の八百万の神。売り終わった方々のため値下がりを祈るには高いお山を一時麓に下がった嵯峨の釈迦堂や安居天神。売り手と買い手の両方の祈りには高からず安からず、中を取って河内の国の高安明神。法力のあらたかなることは棚から物を取るがごとく確かなり。謝礼金は大体三十両。何時でも受け取る。さあ、一祈り……。（錫杖を振り立て、苛高数珠をもみ、呪文を唱えながら指で印を結ぼうとする。）

おかち　（辛そうに身を乗り出して白稲荷法印を止めて）嫌や、嫌や。お祈りも祈祷も要らん。このおかちの病気治すために、婿取りの相談止めて欲しい！（先代徳兵衛の霊が乗り移った様になり）「あの与兵衛が若気の過ちから借金して苦しんでいる。その苦しみが冥途にいる私の苦しみとなり、地獄で鬼の責めとなっている。遊女の身であっても与兵衛が約束を交わした女を身請けし嫁にして、この店の身代継がして欲しい。」（急に物に憑かれたように）「どうしても婿を取るというならば、おかちの命はないものと思え！思い知ったか！思い知れ」（突然、辺りキョロキョロと見回し、身悶えして）あー、ああー、しんどいー！苦しい、助けて……。

　　　　　徳兵衛はおかちの様子に仰天する。

白稲荷法印　（少しもたじろがずに）汝はどこから来た？早く去れ！行者の法力は尽きんぞ！（再び錫杖をちりんちりんがらんがらんと振り鳴らし）去れ！去れ！この悪魔払いのための呪文を受けよ！急々如律令、急々如律令、急々如律令……。

与兵衛（不意に起き上がり）何を分かって去れ去れと言っている！この山伏野郎！止めやがれ！（奥座敷の白稲荷法印に掴みかかり、店の土間のところまで突き飛ばす。）

白稲荷法印　やあやあ、山伏の法力をしらんな！（すぐに起き上がって、座敷にかけ上がり、錫杖を振り鳴らしながら呪文を唱える。）

continues to chant.]

> YOHEI pushes him off the shop floor again. WHITE FOX runs up to the room again and repeats the incantation, "Namakusa manda masarada, namakusa manda masarada . . ."
>
> YOHEI and WHITE FOX repeat this sequence a few times, but finally YOHEI beats off WHITE FOX. WHITE FOX runs away for his life in the direction from which he came.

YOHEI [*Sitting down next to TOKUBEI, tucking up his kimono and threatening him loudly*]: Hey, Father, you heard what O-Kachi said in her delirium a moment ago. Would you send a dead soul to hell rather than let his son marry the woman he loves and succeed to the shop? Would you?

TOKUBEI: Be quiet! You are very noisy. You're disturbing the neighbours. Stop shouting and stop the nonsense! I, Tokubei, knew very well how to feed five or seven people without living off someone's legacy. On the contrary I suffered a great deal assuming the professional name of your father. I've never forgotten the anniversary of his death, and held his annual memorial service so that his soul won't go to hell and he may rest in peace. I will never pay a bride-price for the prostitute you love and take her in as your wife. I don't wish to see you bankrupt the Kawachi-ya in six months and abandon the late master's memorial service.

YOHEI: Then, no matter what O-Kachi wants, you will take a husband for O-Kachi and let her inherit the shop? That's what you want!

TOKUBEI: That's right! I'm doing it.

YOHEI: How dare you talk to me like that? You ungrateful old fool!

> YOHEI abruptly stands up, pushes TOKUBEI to the floor and stamps on his back.

KACHI [*astounded and throwing herself on YOHEI*]: Big Brother! Don't do such a terrible thing to our father! Please, stop it. It's dreadful!

TOKUBEI: O-Kachi! Leave him! Let him stamp on me as much as he wants! Let him do it!
[*TOKUBEI lets YOHEI keep assaulting him.*]

KACHI [*Unable to endure it*]: Big Brother! This is too much! You asked me to pretend to be possessed by your father's dead soul and to say all these things. You promised me that if I did, you would work hard, would be good to our father and mother and wouldn't con-

「女殺油地獄」

　　　　　　与兵衛は白稲荷法印をまた店の床に突き落とす。白稲荷法印は再び座敷
　　　　　にかけ上がり錫杖を振り鳴らして、「なまくさまんだばさらだ　なまくさま
　　　　　んだばさらだ」と呪文を繰り返す。
　　　　　　与兵衛と白稲荷法印はこうした取っ組み合いを繰り返すが、しまいに、
　　　　　白稲荷法印は与兵衛の暴力に負けて命からがらもと来た道へと逃げ去る。

与兵衛　（徳兵衛のそばに行き、膝捲りして座り、大きな声で凄んで）おい、親仁殿。
　　　おかちのさっきのうわ言が耳に入ったんか？死んだ人間を迷わせて地獄に落とし
　　　ても、この与兵衛が好いた女を女房にして店を継がせるのはいやだ、出来んと言
　　　うのか？
徳兵衛　ええい、やかましいわい！近所隣の手前もある。静かにせんかい。ふざけるの
　　　もええ加減にせえ！この徳兵衛は死んだ人の遺産継がんでも、五人、七人は十分
　　　に養うていく手段は心得ているが、死んだ人の年忌や命日を弔い、地獄へ落ちん
　　　よう、迷わせんよう思うて、名跡継いで苦労しとる。お前が好いた女郎を身請け
　　　して女房に持たせ、半年もたたんうちに所帯潰して親方の弔いも出来んようには
　　　させられん。

与兵衛　そしたら、どうしてもおかちに婿取ってこの家継がせる気いやな。

徳兵衛　おう、継がせる！
与兵衛　よう言うたなあ。この恩知らず！

　　　　　　与兵衛はいきなり立ち上がり、徳兵衛を俯せに倒して背中を足で踏み付
　　　　　ける。

おかち　（驚いて与兵衛にすがり）兄様、そんなひどいこと！止めてください！ああ、
　　　情けない。
徳兵衛　おかち、ほっとけ！こいつの腹の虫がおさまるまで思う存分踏ませとけ、踏ま
　　　せとけ！（動かずにじっとされるままにしている。）
おかち　（堪えかねて）兄様、あんまりです。兄様は『死霊が憑いたような振りをして
　　　これこのように言ってくれ。そうしてくれたら、以後は商売にも精出し、親たち
　　　に孝行尽くして決して逆らわん、これこの通り神仏に誓う。』と言われた。私は兄

tradict them any more. You swore it by all gods, goddesses and Buddha. I was so happy to hear it. So I pretended your dead father's spirit possessed me even though I was ill and it was so frightful. I knew it was very wrong, but I lied because I believed in you. [*While weeping, throwing herself on YOHEI in order to stop the violence*] But now you are kicking our father. How could you? Is this your filial piety, Big Brother? I shall never forgive you if our elderly father loses consciousness.

YOHEI [*freeing himself from KACHI by kicking her*]: You silly cow! Forgetting that I made you swear not to speak about it to anyone. Revealing our secret and saying those spiteful things to me! I shall teach you what agony the spirit of a living man can give you. Take this! [*YOHEI starts stamping on KACHI.*]

TOKUBEI: Are you going to kill your sick sister? Stop it, you beast! [*TOKUBEI clings onto YOHEI to stop him.*]

YOHEI [*kicking TOKUBEI*]: A moment ago you said, let me kick you as much as I like. All right then, I'll do it! Have this! How about this one? [*YOHEI starts stamping on TOKUBEI's face and head.*]

> *SAWA returns from the doctor from stage right. She drops the medicine bag in shock when she sees YOHEI assaulting TOKUBEI. Quickly she goes to YOHEI, grabs him by the topknot, then overturns him and hits him, sitting astride him.*

SAWA: Damn you! You beast! You shameless liar! We are not supposed to kick or stamp on anyone, even if a mean and vulgar fellow. Who do you think Tokubei-dono is? Isn't he your parent? Haven't you ever heard that your legs will rot and drop off if you use them to hurt your own parent? You ungrateful beast! Oh, it's dreadful! There are people who have bad eyesight, or deformed arms and legs from birth, but their hearts are in the right place. You were born healthy and normal. I don't know why you can't have a healthy normal human spirit. I've tried hard to do right by you, as I don't want to hear people say that you're no good because I've spoilt you out of pity that you lost your natural father. Your rotten nature, your evil mind, has been eating away at your mother's life. The other day you wheedled some money out of me saying that your uncle in Takatsuki needed it as he had embezzled his master's money. How dare you, how could you tell me such a terrible lie and deceive me like that? Just now on the way to get Kachi's medicine, I met your big brother Tahei and heard all about the incident in Nozaki. Tahei told me that your uncle wrote a letter to Tahei in which he says that he has found it hard to continue his service since the incident. He's decided to quit the service and come down to Osaka to restore his honour as a samurai. That's how your lie's come out. If I had

「女殺油地獄」

様のその言葉が嬉しゅうて、病みつかれたこの姿で怖い怖い恐ろしい死霊の憑いたふりして嘘ついた。（乱暴を止めさせようと泣きながら、与兵衛にくらいついて）それなのに父様を踏んだり蹴ったりして。それが兄様の孝行ですか。年寄った父様が目回されるようなことにでもなったら私は許しません！

与兵衛　（おかちを足で振りほどいて）このくそ女めが。誰にも言わんと誓いを立ててまで口止めしたのに。べらべらしゃべった上にその憎まれ口。死霊よりこれこの生き霊の与える苦しみ覚えとけ！（今度はおかちを踏み付け始める。）

徳兵衛　おのれは、病み疲れた妹を踏んで殺す気か！この鬼畜生め！（与兵衛にしがみついて乱暴を止めさせようとする。）
与兵衛　（逆に徳兵衛を蹴飛ばして）腹の虫のおさまるまで踏めと言うたな。こうしたら気がすむわい！（与兵衛は徳兵衛を顔や頭の区別もないほどに踏み付ける。）

　　　　舞台下手、お沢が医者から帰ってくる。お沢は与兵衛の乱暴している姿に驚いて薬の袋を落とす。が、すぐに、与兵衛のところに行き、髷を掴んで横転させて、馬乗りになり目といわず鼻といわず拳で叩く。

お沢　やい、この人でなしの恥さらし！大嘘つき！どんな下衆下郎にでも、足で踏むとか蹴るとかはしないもの。徳兵衛殿を誰と心得る？お前の親ではないか。親にこのようなことをすれば、すぐにもその脛が腐って落ちるということ知らんのか。この罰当たりが！ああ、恐ろしい。生まれたときから目の不自由な者や手足の揃わん者もいる。けれど魂には何の遜色もない。それに引き替えお前は、五体満足に産んだはずなのに、何が不足で人間の性根持たぬ？父親が義理の仲ゆえ母の心がゆがんでお前に悪い性根を入れると言われるのが嫌さに、なにかにつけて気を遣い苦労をしてきた。お前の腐った性根、邪悪の剣がこの母の寿命を削る。先日もお前は高槻の伯父さんが御主君のお金を遣い込んだと言って私からお金をせしめていったが、ようもようもあんなひどい嘘で私をまんまと騙してくれたな。たった今、太兵衛に行き逢い、伯父からの手紙にお前の野崎での不祥事のため侍の面目が立たなくなり浪人して大阪に下るとあったこと聞いた。それでお前の嘘がばれたが、もし、あのとき母が軽率に親仁殿に話していて、後で嘘と知れていたなら、さては母子が口裏合わせて嘘ついたかと疑われ、夫婦の義理を欠くことになったところ。内でも外でもお前の噂でまともなことは一つも無い。その度毎にお前はおのれの母の身を一寸ずつ削いでいる。この極悪人！もう、半時もこの家

told your step-father about it then and later the truth had been revealed, he might have thought that you and I had agreed on a story. I would have failed in my duty as wife. I don't hear anything good about you in my family or in my neighbourhood. Every time I hear a foul rumour about you, my life is shaved away, piece by piece. You're truly evil! I won't have you here even half an hour! I disown you right now. Get out! Get out of this house! [*SAWA pushes YOHEI to the entrance, while crying.*]

YOHEI: You disown me? But I have nowhere to go if I'm kicked out of this house.

SAWA [*grabbing the sleeve of YOHEI's kimono and pushing him away*]: Go to your beloved prostitute!

KACHI [*clinging to SAWA*]: I don't want to inherit the shop by ousting Big Brother. Mother, please, please, be patient!

SAWA [*freeing herself from KACHI*]: Sweetheart, you don't know anything! Stay where you are! [*Seeing that YOHEI does not seem to be leaving*] Look, Tokubei-dono, why the hell are you just looking at Yohei absent-mindedly doing nothing? What are you hesitating about? Oh, how infuriating! I'll get him out of this house!

SAWA picks up a carrying pole beside her, raises it over her head and tries to hit YOHEI with it, but YOHEI takes it from her.

YOHEI: I'll hit you with this!

He starts hitting SAWA with the pole. When TOKUBEI sees this, he jumps onto YOHEI, takes the pole from him, holds him down and hits him with it several times in one burst.

TOKUBEI [*glaring at YOHEI with tearful eyes*]: Look, Yohei! Even a wooden doll has feelings if we give life to it. If you have the ears to listen, you must hear what I say. Although I, Tokubei, am your father, I let you kick me because you were the son of my late master to whom I was much indebted. But just now you were hitting the woman who gave birth to you. It was unforgivable and made me shiver. You mustn't think it was I who hit you! Think that your late father returned from the other world to punish you. We've invented a story that we are taking a husband for O-Kachi and letting them succeed to the shop. Oh, how regrettable! We hoped that you would reform yourself when you heard your sister was going to inherit the shop. Don't worry! We'll marry your sister off. I thought that there must be some predestined connection between you and me: two strangers becoming father and son by chance. And that engendered in me strong feelings for you,

「女殺油地獄」

に置くことできん！ただいま限りお前を勘当する！出て行け！出て行きやがれ！出やがれ！（泣きながら、与兵衛を叩き出す。）

与兵衛　勘当？この家出されたら何処にも行くとこない。
お沢　（与兵衛の袖を掴んで引き）お前の好いた女郎のとこでも行きやがれ！

おかち　（お沢に取りすがり）兄様を追い出して私がこの家継ぐのは嫌や！母様、どうか堪えて！
お沢　（おかちを振りほどき）何も知らんくせに、引っ込んでおれ！（出て行く気配をみせない与兵衛を見て）これ、徳兵衛殿、ぼんやりと見ているだけで……誰に遠慮される？ああ、歯痒い！こうして叩き出してやる！

　　　　　　お沢は傍にあった天秤棒を取り、振り上げて与兵衛を叩こうとするが、逆に与兵衛に引ったくられてしまう。

与兵衛　この棒でお前様を打つ！

　　　　　　与兵衛、お沢をぱんぱん打ち始める。それを見た徳兵衛は与兵衛に飛びかかって、天秤棒をもぎ取り息もつかせぬ勢いで七、八回打って、与兵衛を押さえ付ける。

徳兵衛　（涙目で睨んで）おい、与兵衛！木や泥で出来た人形でも魂入れれば性根はある。お前に聞く耳あるならよう聞いておけ！この徳兵衛はお前の父ではあるが、大恩ある親方の子のすること、主筋の子のすることと思い、手向かいもせずにお前に踏まれた。けど、己がお腹借りた産みの母を叩くとは、傍で見ているだけで勿体のうて体が震える。今、お前を打ったのはこの徳兵衛ではない。先代の徳兵衛殿が冥途から手を出してお打ちなされたのだ。おかちに入り婿取るというのは根も葉もない作り事だ！ああ、残念でならん。妹に名跡継がせては口惜しいと、一心発起してその腐った根性直してくれるかと考えての一工夫。心配するな！おかちは他所へ嫁入りさせる。他人同士が親子となるのもきっと前世からの深い縁と、かわいさは実の子以上。お前が疱瘡にかかった時、日親様[21]に願けるため、先祖代々からの浄土宗[22]を棄てて百日法華[20]にもなった。こんなにまでし

perhaps more than for my own son if I had one. When you had smallpox, I changed my sect to the Nichiren Sect for one hundred days[20] so that I was able to make a vow to the great priest, Nisshin-sama[21] to cure it, although the family from father to son had believed in the Pure Land Sect.[22] I cared about you very much and brought you up. I didn't employ anyone and carried heavy oil barrels all on my own. It was only to save up more money to leave you a larger shop. But the more I earned, the more you wasted. If you were a merchant, you would work hard while you were young and strong, and resolve to have a shop with a frontage five or six ken wide[23] some day. Instead you cling to a shop only one and half-ken wide, hit your mother and kick your step-father. Wherever you go, you tell lies and cause problems. If you carry on like this, you won't be able to build even a pillar for your shop. Instead sooner or later you will end up displaying your head on the prison gatepost. Why don't you understand us? Damn it! Oh, I feel dreadful! [*TOKUBEI starts sobbing in the middle of the speech.*]

SAWA: Oh, no, Tokubei-dono, I'm losing my patience with you. You're wasting your breath. It's like talking to a rock. He has no ears. Now, get out of this house! Right now! If you don't get out of the house immediately, I shall call all the senior townsmen and neighbours[24] to kick you out of here. [*SAWA takes the pole from TOKUBEI and pushes YOHEI with it.*]

YOHEI, who has been fearless and underestimating the situation, realises that SAWA is serious and is suddenly startled.

KACHI [*clinging to SAWA*]: Mother, if you expelled Big Brother, I would leave too.

SAWA [*ignoring KACHI*]: Hurry up! Go! Do you need to be pushed again? Then have this! [*She swings up the pole once more and pokes YOHEI with it.*]

YOHEI is finally pushed out of the shop leaving in the direction of the hanamichi.

CHORUS: The son has crossed the threshold of his home,
    Which becomes a river of tears.
    That divides the son from his family.
    Who wants to hit and oust one's own child?
    The parents sit on a mountain of needles and shed tears of blood.
    Hitting the son and letting their hearts bleed,
    They try to teach him wrong from right.
    Why do we deserve this sadness?

「女殺油地獄」

てお前を育て、大きなお店の主人にしてやろうと丁稚も使わず肩に棒を担いで稼いでも、稼いだ尻からお前が使うてしまう。今の若い盛りに商売に精出して、五間口[23]、六間口の店の主人になろうというような念願をかけるのが商人なのに、たった一間半の間口の店に思いをかけ、母に手向かいし父を踏み付けて行く先々で嘘をつく始末。そんな根性でいたら店の門柱どころか、そのうちに獄門柱の台の上でさらし首になってしまう。この親の気持が分からんか。ああ、情けない。悲しい……。（言葉の途中で泣き出してしまう。）

お沢　ああ、じれったい！徳兵衛殿、何を言うても無駄。石に謎をかけるようなもの。口で言って聞くような奴ではない。さあ、出て行け！早う出て行け！ぐずぐずしやがると町内の町役人の年寄りや五人組の人[24]みな呼んで追い出すぞ！（お沢、徳兵衛から天秤棒を掴み取って、棒の先で与兵衛を突く。）

　　　　これまで怖いもの知らずでたかを括っていた与兵衛は母が本気なのに気づいてぎょっとする。

おかち　（母にすがり付いて）母様、兄様を追い出したら私も出て行く。
お沢　（おかちの言葉に耳を貸さず）さっさと行け！天秤棒の突きが食い足らんか！（棒を振り上げて、尚も与兵衛を突く。）

　　　　店から突き出された与兵衛は花道を去って行く。

コーラス　越える敷居の細い溝
　　親子別れの涙川
　　子を叩く
　　親の心に針の山　流す涙に血が滲む
　　突いて叩いて　心を裂いて
　　せめて伝えん親心
　　何でこんなに悲しい思い
　　何で通じん　愛しい我が子

109

Why does our love not reach you, my son?
Where are you, the gods, goddesses and Buddha?
Have mercy on us, Kannon-san!
The son has crossed the threshold of his home.
The river of tears is now the river of farewells.
He will never cross back over.
Warriors in the festival banners weep in sympathy.

TOKUBEI [*having been watching YOHEI leave, suddenly bursting into tears*]: Look at his profile and his back! The more he grows up, the more he resembles the late master. My heart bleeds when I see him standing at the crossing. I feel as if I were expelling my own master instead of our Yohei. Oh, I am sad. . . [*He squats down by the entrance pillar of the shop and starts crying aloud.*]

    SAWA starts sobbing, too. She leans forward to catch sight of YOHEI leaving, but the colourful festival banners over the townhouses block her view of her son.

    Blackout.

「女殺油地獄」

　　どこにいたはる　神さん仏さん
　　救うて下さい　観音さん
　　越えた敷居の細い溝
　　二度と戻れぬ　別れの川よ
　　五月節句の絵幟の　武者たちも　もらい泣く

徳兵衛　（与兵衛の姿をじっと見送っていたが、声をあげて泣き出し）あいつのあの顔、背格好。大人になるにつれて亡くなられた旦那に生き写し。あれ、あの辻に立っている姿をみると与兵衛めを追い出すのではなく、旦那を追い出すような気がしてもったいない。ああ、悲しい……。（徳兵衛は人目も構わず膝を落して泣き出す。）

　　　　お沢も堪えていた涙を流し、そっと伸び上がって与兵衛を見送るが、五月の節句の絵幟に邪魔されて与兵衛の姿はもう見えない……。

　　　　暗転。

WOMAN-KILLER IN OIL HELL

ACT THREE

PART ONE

At the Teshima-ya

Two days after the previous scene. Evening of the 4th of May. It is the evening of the seasonal settlement day and also the eve of the Boys' Festival day, the Iris Festival.
There are decorative displays of mugwort and iris flowers in the eaves of the townhouses in celebration of the festival. Colourful banners mark the house roofs of the townspeople with sons in their family.
The oil shop and residence of TESHIMA-YA SHICHIZAEMON stands from centre stage to right. The shop is located diagonally opposite to the Kawachi-ya in ACT TWO, which is off-stage upstage left in this scene. The street of Motodenma-machi runs through the hanamichi to upstage left and the willow tree in ACT TWO stands downstage left. An alley stretches throughout downstage, across the main street.
The Teshima-ya is a town house similar to the Kawachi-ya. But different from the Kawachi-ya, the shop has wood flooring. In the shop the oil barrels are lined up both on the shelves and the floor. The earth-floor of the entrance hall becomes a narrow path to the back of the house off Stage Right. In the centre of the shop there is a small table where ladles and measures are placed. Above the table a large light with an octagonal shaped lampshade is suspended from the ceiling. The lamp is lit now and the shop appears to be doing a good trade.
Two tatami-matted rooms, which are raised about 40cm above ground level, are positioned next to the shop towards stage right. There is a doorway to the inner part of the house in the first room and a long noren is hung over the doorway. As in the Kawachi-ya, the first room is used as a counting room as well as the family's living room. There are a few pieces of furniture such as a low counter desk, a cabinet with a safe and drawers and so on in the first room. The fusuma sliding doors to the second room are now closed.

As it is the seasonal settlement day today, TESHIMA-YA SHICHIZAEMON is out to collect money on credit accounts from his clients. KICHI, seeing off the last customer of the day to the shop, takes in their shop noren, on which 'the Teshima-ya'[1] *has been dyed, and closes the shop. Then she starts tidying up the shop with her two daughters, KINU and KIYO. KINU sweeps the floor and KIYO helps her sister. When the shop is cleared, KICHI goes into the inner part of the*

「女殺油地獄」

下之巻

その一

豊島屋の場

　前場の二日後。五月四日の節季の日の夕刻。端午の節句（菖蒲祭り）の前夜。
　家々の庇には蓬、菖蒲が飾られている。男の子のいる家の屋根には絵幟が見える。

　舞台中ほどから下手に向かって油屋豊島屋七左衛門の家。河内屋とは本天満町の通りを挟んで筋向いの位置、本天満町の通りの下手側に立つ。前場と同じく今度は花道から舞台上手奥に向かって元天満町の通りが走っている。前場の柳の木がこの場では上手にある。通りを横切って細い路地が舞台手前を走っている。

　豊島屋も河内屋と同じような造りの町屋で、入ったところが油屋の店になっているが板の間である。入り口付近の土間は細くなり下手袖の家の裏へと続いている。店には油樽が所狭しと並んでいて、活気があり商売が繁盛している様子が伺える。豊島屋では店の真ん中に油を汲んだり量ったりする売り場の台が置いてあり、柄杓や枡などの道具類が見える。売り場の真上には、天井から八角形のかさのついた大きな灯りが下がっている。
　店から下手に向かい座敷、次の間がある。座敷の中ほどに奥向きへの出入り口があり、店に近いところは帳場になっている。帳場の後ろには引き出しや金庫などの納まった戸棚が見える。今、次の間との間の襖は閉まっている。

　店の主である豊島屋七左衛門は節季の掛取りに出て留守である。お吉が店に来た最後の客を見送り、「豊島屋」[1]と染め抜いた店の暖簾をはずし店内に入れて店を閉め、その後、帳場や店内を片付け始める。姉のお絹が板の間の床を掃いたりして母を手伝っている。お清も姉の後にくっついて見よう見まねで、手伝っている。すっかり店の片付けが済むとお吉は座敷に上がり奥から櫛笥と鏡箱を持って出て来る。お絹とお清も座敷に

house and brings out a comb box and a mirror box. KINU and KIYO go and sit by KICHI. KICHI starts preparing by putting up the mirror and laying out the combs and the combing wax.[2]

KICHI [*To the daughters*]: Thank you very much for your help, girls. Now it's time to comb your hair. Let me begin with big sister Kinu. Please sit in front of the mirror.

> *KINU joyfully goes in front of the mirror. KICHI rubs sweet-fragrant plum flower oil onto the comb and starts combing KINU's hair with evident pleasure. It is a happy time for the mother and the daughters.*

KICHI: We women must keep our appearance and hair tidy. And when we comb our hair, we must comb out the dirt of the soul, too. Because we live in our husband's house after marriage, and also because we are born and grow up in our parents' house. It's been said that we women don't have a home except for this mirror box. I don't know who said this, but the house becomes a woman's house once a year, on the night of the fifth of May. [*She finishes combing KINU and now KIYO sits in front of the mirror.*] Perhaps it's because men are all out to celebrate their festival day and women are left alone at home. In the old days January, May and September were thought to be unlucky months. People turned them into festival months to rid them of bad luck. Let's pray that nothing bad will happen on this celebratory day of May. [*When KICHI runs the comb through KIYO's hair, a tooth snaps off. She throws down the comb in fear.*] Oh, dear! One of the teeth has broken. [*Quickly picking up the comb and to herself anxiously*] Oh, what have I done! People say throwing out a comb is a sign of a parting, something to be avoided . . . I hope that it isn't an omen or something. . .

> *SHICHIZAEMON comes back along the hanamichi.*

SHICHIZAEMON [*opening the side door of the front entrance and coming in*]: I'm home.
KICHI: Oh, good, welcome home. You've finished the collection earlier than I thought.

> *KICHI quickly finishes combing KIYO's hair and puts away the things that have been spread out. Two daughters, who are happy with their clean hair, take the mirror box and the comb box away through the doorway of the living room.*

Trade was good today, too. The Sen-ya in Ryōgae-machi bought two shō of light oil[3] and one gō of plum flower oil.[4] The paper shop in Imabashi brought their credit account

「女殺油地獄」

上がり、お吉の傍に行く。お吉は鏡を立てたり、櫛笥から解き櫛や梳き櫛、梳き油[2]などを取り出して、髪梳きの用意を始める。

お吉　（娘達に）ごくろうさまでしたなあ。さあ、ここへ座って。姉からな。髪梳いてあげまひょ。

　　　　　お絹が嬉しそうに鏡の前に座る。お吉は解き櫛に香りの良い梅花油を揉み込んだりして、うきうきした調子でお絹の髪を梳き始める。母と娘達の幸せなひとときである。

お吉　女はね、髪や姿を整えるとき、一緒に心の垢も梳かんとあかんのよ。女が嫁行った先は夫の家。実家の住家も親の家。女には鏡の家と呼んでるこの鏡箱以外に家というものはあれへんの。でもね、誰が決めたか知らないけれど、五月五日の一夜だけは、この家も女の家と言われている。（お絹の髪梳きが終わり、お清が入れ替わりに鏡の前に座る。）男が揃ってお祭りに出かけて留守になるからかしらね。昔は一月、五月、九月は凶月といわれていたので、それらの月を祝い月に変えたそうよ。その祝い月といわれるこの五月の祝い日に何事も起こりませんようにお祈りしまひょな。（梳いていた櫛の歯が折れる。お吉は驚いて咄嗟に櫛をほうり出し）まあ、嫌だ。櫛の歯が一枚折れた。（すぐに慌てて投げ出した櫛を拾い、不安げに独り言で）ああ、どうしよう。投げ櫛は別れの櫛と言うて忌み嫌うのに……何かのお告げの印やないとええけど。

　　　　　花道から豊島屋七左衛門が帰ってくる。

七左衛門　（店の潜り戸を開けて入って）只今。戻りました。
お吉　あ、お帰りなさいませ。思ったより早う済ませられましたのね。

　　　　　吉は髪梳きを止めて、櫛箱や鏡箱を手早く片付ける。母親に髪をきれいにしてもらった姉妹は嬉しくてはしゃいだ様子で、二人して櫛箱と鏡箱を座敷の奥にしまいに行く。

店の商いも首尾よう終えました。両替町の銭屋は灯油[3]二升と梅花油[4]一合。今橋の紙屋は付帳の通帳持参で灯油一升買いに来られましたので店の当座帳に付けて

115

book with them and bought one shō of light oil. I've written it down in the account book on the counter. You must be exhausted. Wash your feet, and come up.[5] Why don't you have an early night? Then tomorrow you can get up early and make courtesy visits of the Iris Festival to our neighbours.

SHICHIZAEMON: No, no, I haven't finished yet. I must go to Ikeda-machi in Tenma from now.

KICHI: I can't believe what I'm hearing. Go out there now? You've done enough work for today. Ikeda-machi is at the north end of Osaka. You've collected the bills in the neighbourhood today. The rest can wait till after the festival.

SHICHIZAEMON: What are you saying, love? If we fail to collect money on the seasonal settlement day, we'll never get it. They promised to pay after sunset today. I must make a quick trip there. [*Taking the purse out of his kimono bosom, then removing the money belt from his waist and handing them to KICHI*] Here's five hundred and eighty *monme* in the new silver[6] in the money belt. Will you please put it away with the money in this purse in the cabinet safe and lock it up?

SHICHIZAEMON hands the money belt and the purse to KICHI. KICHI takes them and goes to the cabinet.

I'll be back soon. [*SHICHIZAEMON is about to go out hastily.*]

KICHI [*surprised and going to SHICHIZAEMON*]: Oh, darling, wait for a moment, please. If you must go right now, please at least have a cup of sake before you go. [*To the kitchen in the inner part of the house*] O-Kinu! Will you prepare sake for your father?

KICHI goes back to the shop cabinet and unlocks the safe with one of the keys that she carries in the obi, and starts sorting out the money in the money belt and the purse, and then putting the money in the safe.

SHICHIZAEMON [*to KINU, off-stage*]: O-Kinu, there's no need to warm up the sake. I don't want a side dish, either. Just bring me sake in the container with a bowl, sweetheart. The night is short and I'm in a hurry.

KINU brings the sake container and the bowl on a tray and sits down at the edge of the living room close to SHICHIZAEMON who is standing on the earth floor.

　　　　　　　　　「女殺油地獄」

　　おきました。お疲れになりましたでしょ。まず、足を洗って[5]、今夜はもうお休み
　　になってください。そして明日の朝早うから、菖蒲の節句の挨拶回りにお出にな
　　ってください。

七左衛門　いやいや、まだ休まれんのや。これから天満の池田町まで行かんとあかん。

お吉　まあ、あきれた、今からですか。もう今日はお止めになったら。池田町は大阪の
　　北の端。近所の売掛金さえ集まったら残りは節句が済んでからでも。

七左衛門　お前は何を言うのや。節季に集まらん金が節季を過ぎて集まったためしはな
　　い。今日暮れてから渡しますと確かに口約束してもろてるんや。ちょっと、ひと
　　っ走り行ってくる。（懐から財布を取り出し、身体から胴巻きを抜き取って）この
　　胴巻きに新銀五百八十匁[6]、それからこの財布のお金と、全部戸棚に入れて鍵か
　　けといてくれるか。

　　　　　　七左衛門はお吉に胴巻きと財布を渡す。
　　　　　　お吉は胴巻きと財布を受け取って戸棚のところに行く。

　　すぐに戻る。（早々に出かけようとする。）
お吉　（驚いて七左衛門のところに戻り）まあまあ、ちょっと待って下さい。それなら、
　　お酒を一杯飲んでからお出なさい。（奥の台所に向かって）お絹、父様のお酒の
　　用意してくれるか。

　　　　　　お吉は戸棚のところに戻り、帯に挟んでいた鍵束の鍵で戸棚の金庫を開
　　　　　　け、受け取った胴巻きと財布のお金をしまい始める。

七左衛門　（奥のお絹に）ああ、これこれお絹。燗はせんでもええで。酒の肴もいらん。
　　ちろりの酒と中椀を持ってきてくれんか。夜は短い。気もせく。

　　　　　　お絹は奥から酒の盆を持って出て、七左衛門のそばの座敷の端に座る。
　　　　　　七左衛門は土間に立ったままである。

　　　　　　　　　　　　　　　117

SHICHIZAEMON [*receiving the bowl*]: Oh, thank you, sweetheart. Will you pour from there?

KINU: Yes, Father. [*KINU tries to pour sake while sitting but SHICHIZAEMON is too tall to do so; she stands up and pours the sake.*]

SHICHIZAEMON still standing, receives sake in the bowl.

KICHI [*finishing putting the money in the cabinet safe and locking it up, turning around and noticing that her husband and daughter are standing, pouring and receiving sake*]: What on earth are you two doing? How inauspicious! Kinu is a mere child, so she can be innocent, but you should know that you mustn't pour and receive sake standing up. That's only for funerals. Whose burial service is it?

SHICHIZAEMON [*blamed by KICHI, sitting down on the edge of the living room and holding the bowl properly, joking*]: It was for 'passing' this seasonal settlement day, wasn't it? Anyway wish me good luck on my departure. There should be no remaining credit in this world at all! [*SHICHIZAEMON raises his bowl praying for good luck, empties it and goes off in a hurry.*]

KICHI goes out of the shop to see off SHICIZAEMON, then comes in and closes the side door.

While KICHI is out, KINU spreads out the futon and bedding and puts up a mosquito net with KIYU in the second room. Then KINU puts DEN, the smallest sister, to sleep on futon. KIYO sleeps next to DEN, too. The fusuma sliding doors between the two rooms are kept open.

Soon after KICHI goes into the shop, YOHEI enters the hanamichi. He is wearing the lined kimono that he was wearing in the previous scene. His kimono is out of season since it is now early summer. He carries an empty two-shō oil barrel and wears a short sword at his side.

KINU [*from inside the mosquito net*]: Mother, you must come and sleep with us, too.

KICHI: Oh, well done! You've managed to put up the mosquito net by yourselves. You put your little sister to sleep, too. How good of you! I thank you for that, O-Kinu. I see Kiyo is already asleep next to Den. Your father will be late tonight. It's already late. You should sleep, too. I'll see to the outside of the mosquito net.

KINU [*fighting off sleep*]: I'm not sleepy yet. [*While saying this, KINU falls asleep.*]

「女殺油地獄」

七左衛門　（お絹から中椀を受け取り）すまんな。お絹、そこから注いでくれるか。

お絹　はい、父様。（座ったまま酒を注ごうとするが背が低くて届かないので、立ちあがって注ぐ。）

　　　　　　七左衛門は土間に立って中椀に酒を注いでもらっている。

お吉　（戸棚の金庫にお金をしまい終えて鍵をかける。夫と娘が立ったままで酒を注いだり注がれたりしているのに気付き驚き）まあまあ、何事ですか、縁起の悪い。お絹は子供で分別がないとしても。立ち酒なんぞして。誰の野辺送りです……。

七左衛門　（たしなめられて座敷の端に腰をかけ、椀を持ち直して）掛け金を集めに行く門出の、墓ならぬ、はかが行くようにとの立ち酒や。この世に未回収の掛け金は残らん残らん。（七左衛門は縁起を祝って中椀をあげ、酒を飲み干して、再び集金に出て行く。）

　　　　　お吉は七左衛門を店の外まで出て見送った後、店に戻り表の潜り戸を閉める。
　　　　　その間に、お絹が座敷の次の間に夜具を敷き、背が足りないので苦労しながら蚊帳を吊る。お絹は末娘のおでんを寝かしつける。お清もおでんの隣に寝る。次の間の襖は開けたままである。

　　　　　入れ違いに花道から与兵衛がやって来る。与兵衛は前場と同じ季節はずれの袷の着物で脇差をさし、二升入りの空の油樽を下げている。

お絹　（蚊帳の中から）母様ももうお休みなさいませ。
お吉　まあ、よう一人で蚊帳まで吊れましたね。おでんも寝かせてくれて。お清ももう寝ているのですね。今夜は父様も遅くなられることでしょう。もう遅いからお前もお休み。蚊帳の外は私が気いつけますよって。

お絹　（眠いのを我慢しながら）いいえ、私はまだ眠うありません。（言いながら眠り始

KICHI goes inside the mosquito net to tidy up the bedding of the children, and then lies down next to the children.

CHORUS: Irises are in bloom.
The season for our summer kimono[7] has arrived.
Beautifully coloured banners flutter joyously over the roof tiles in the May breeze.
Tomorrow, the fifth of May, is the Boys' Festival Day.
Oh, yeah, dear, however . . .
Here's a fellow who won't be able to celebrate the day of the festival.
The fellow is Kawachi-ya Yohei.
His chances for clearing his debts by the settlement day look awfully slim.
His parents have disowned him, but he doesn't seem to have learned anything.
He is still the same old dissipated son of the oil shop.
Nothing has gone according to his plans.
In a lined kimono out-of-season,
Carrying an empty oil barrel in his hand,
Hiding a short sword at his side,
Up to his neck in debt…
Yet he's got something on his mind…
Something…on his mind…

YOHEI stops at the Teshima-ya and peers into the inside cautiously. An employment agent and usurer, WATA-YA KOHEI walks in briskly from the alley downstage left.

KOHEI [*noticing YOHEI*]: Why, isn't that Yohei standing there?
YOHEI: Yes, it is. Who is it? [*Turning around*]
KOHEI: Goodness! Yohei-san, I've been looking for you all over. When I went to your big brother's place in Junkei-machi, I was told to go to your parents' shop in Motoden-ma-machi, and when I went to your parents', they told me that they had renounced you and didn't know your whereabouts. Look, even if you are absent, the deed of your loan bears your father's seal. If you fail to pay me back one thousand *monme* in new silver tonight, I'll have to go to see the town officials first thing tomorrow morning. You know that?

「女殺油地獄」

　　める。）

　　　　　お吉は子供達の夜具を整えてやるために蚊帳の中に入り、自分も横になる。

コーラス　菖蒲咲き　春から夏への衣替え[7]
　　甍に泳ぐ　様々の絵幟の色美しく
　　明日は目出度い　端午の節句
　　あああ、けどなあ……
　　男子の祭りも　御祝いも　出来ん奴がここにおる
　　この節季　越すに越されぬ河内屋与兵衛
　　親に勘当されて尚　性根変わらん道楽者
　　手筈の合わん古袷
　　手にした二升の油樽は　空っぽのカランカラン
　　腰に脇差し込んで
　　抜き差しならん借金で
　　首の回らん　河内屋与兵衛
　　何やら思案のある様子……
　　何やら思案のある様子……

　　　　　与兵衛、豊島屋の店のところまで来て立ち止まり、そっと中を窺う。
　　　　　上手から上町の口入れ綿屋古兵衛が急ぎ足で来る。

綿屋古兵衛　（与兵衛に気付いて）おや、そこにいるのは与兵衛やないか。
与兵衛　おお、そうやが。誰や？（振り返る。）
綿屋古兵衛　与兵衛さん、捜しましたがな。順慶町のお前の兄さんの所へゆくと本天満町の親御さんの所に行けと言われる。親御さんの所へ行くと与兵衛は追い出した、ここには居らんと言われる。お前は留守でもお前の借金の証文についた判はお前の親仁殿の判。新銀一貫目、今夜中に返済してもらえんと、明日の朝には町役人に届け出んなんことになります。

121

YOHEI: What? Kohei-dono, aren't you playing a bit of a dirty trick there? Although the deed says one thousand *monme* in new silver, the amount I actually borrowed from you was only two hundred *monme*. More than that, you promised me that I could return it on the night of the settlement day.

KOHEI: That's right. I did say that. If you pay me back by dawn, before the strike of the sixth hour of dawn[8] tomorrow morning, your debt is two hundred *monme*. But if the morning sun of the fifth day of May shows its face before us, your due date will be gone, and your debt will become one thousand *monme* -silver. [*Wilily*] It'll be very good business for me if I get one thousand when I lend two hundred. But I would feel very sorry for your father if he had to pay me such an unreasonable amount. That's why I've been pressing you for payment so persistently. Now you must pay me back my money tonight, all right?

YOHEI: Kohei-dono, you don't need to be so thorough. Kawachi-ya Yohei is a man to be relied upon. I've got someone to count on. I will return the money by the first cockcrow for sure, so you'd better wait up with your sleepy eyes wide open.

KOHEI: All right then. [*Suddenly flattering*] Suppose you clear your debt today and need some money tomorrow, then you can borrow it from me again. No worries! Lending money is my business. Whenever you need a couple of thousand or something, you must come to me. Of course, I know that you're a man of words, Yohei-san! I'll see you later. [*KOHEI goes off the hanamichi.*]

YOHEI watches KOHEI until he is out of sight.

CHORUS: Like tormenting someone with floss silk and choking him to death,
He squeezes money from his borrower with cunning words.
That's the way for the usurer and the employment agent, Wata-ya Kohei.
Now the usurer's talked to Yohei, he is going home content!
However, where is someone you can count on?
It's all bravado and empty words, isn't it?
Having been renounced by your family, you've got no one!
You can be tardy in paying for the pleasure quarters.
But Kohei's two hundred won't wait!
It won't wait!

YOHEI: Two hundred. There must be lots of money where the rich live. I wonder if someone's dropped some money somewhere, it's a big world.

Looking dejected, KAWACHI-YA TOKUBEI comes down the street of Motoden-

「女殺油地獄」

与兵衛　何やて？古兵衛(こへえ)殿、そりゃ、やり方が汚いやないか。証文の表書きは新銀一貫目でも実際にわしが借りたのは二百目。それに今晩中に返したらええという約束やないか。

綿屋古兵衛　確かに。その通りだす。明日の明け六つ[8]までに返してくれはったらあんさんに貸したのは二百目。けど、明日、五月五日の朝のお日(ひ)さんがぬっと出てしもたら、期日が過ぎて一貫目の借金になりまっせ。（ずるそうに）二百目の金貸して一貫目になればこちらの得になります。けどな、お前の親仁殿に割の合わん銀、払わせるのが気の毒や。お前さんのこと思うて借金の催促、せっついてますんや。今夜中に必ず返して下さいや。

与兵衛　古兵衛殿、これはえらい念の入ったことやないか。この河内屋与兵衛は男やでえ。お前に借りた金、返す当てはある。一番鶏(いちばんどり)が鳴くまでに必ずお前の所に持って行ったる。眠とうても目え開けて待ってもらわなあかんなあ。

綿屋古兵衛　そうか。（持ち上げて）今日中に返してもろて、必要やったら明日またすぐに貸しますがな。こっちも商売、商売。一貫目や二貫目のお金やったらいつでも云うてや。あんさんの男気、分かってますよってに。（花道から去る。）

　　　　　与兵衛は帰ってゆく綿屋古兵衛をじっと見送る。

コーラス　真綿(まわた)で首を締めまわすよう　言葉でねっちり絞りおき
　　高利貸(こうりが)しの口入れ屋　綿屋(わたや)古兵衛が帰って行く
　　返す当てなど　何処にある
　　口先だけの　空元気
　　親にも兄にも見放され　一銭のお金も持ってない
　　茶屋茶屋(ちゃやちゃや)の払いは　一時逃れがきくけれど
　　どうにもならんのは　この　綿屋に借りた　銀二百目

与兵衛　二百目。あるところにはあるやろになあ。世間は広いよってに誰ぞ落としていそうなもんやがなあ。

　　　　　河内屋徳兵衛が沈んだ様子で、「河」の字[9]の入った店の提灯(ちょうちん)を提げて、

123

*ma-machi from the direction of the Kawachi-ya, off-stage upstage left. He is carrying a lantern on which the letter 'kawa'*⁹ *the logo of his shop is written.*

YOHEI, who has been looking at KOHEI exiting the hanamichi for a while, turns around and notices the lantern.

YOHEI: The lantern with the letter 'kawa.' It must be my father. [*He quickly hides himself behind the willow tree downstage left.*]

TOKUBEI [*without noticing YOHEI, opening the side door of the Teshima-ya and to the inside*]: Shichizaemon-dono, have you finished today? [*TOKUBEI enters the shop.*]

YOHEI peeps and eavesdrops on the conversation in the shop through the crack in the side door.

KICHI [*emerging from the mosquito net*]: Oh, it's Tokubei-dono. My husband hasn't finished collecting bills, and has gone out to the north end of Tenma. I'm sorry that I've been so busy, but I should have come to your place to give the greeting myself. Please come up. You must've been through a hard time on this seasonal settlement day because of your Yohei-dono.

TOKUBEI [*bowing slightly, going up to the first room and sitting*]: Indeed, I have. You keep yourself busy looking after your small daughters; meanwhile I keep myself busy with my grown-up son. Whatever it is, looking after one's own children is a parent's job, so I don't mind. Though, if only he was living with us, my mind would be more at ease. But as we've disowned our crook, we don't know what he'll do next in desperation; tomorrow he may borrow one thousand *monme*-silver by signing ten thousand in the deed on a forged seal, and put himself at risk of having his head displayed on a prison gate; he could do that…playing with fire without reflecting on the risk…But, when his natural mother was determined to disown him, as a step-father, I couldn't say much . . . it would look as if I was indulging my stepson, so I couldn't stop her. We've heard that he is at his big brother's in Junkei-machi. If you see him wandering around in this neighbourhood, with the help of Shichizaemon-dono, please tell him that his father has forgiven him, so he must apologise to his mother and beg forgiveness, and that he should just go home to make a new start, and become a different man. My wife's family background is samurai, and so she has a strong sense of duty by birth. She won't easily take back what she has said . . . unfortunately Yohei doesn't take after her. His late father was also a man of good conduct with a strong sense of duty. He was a truly compassionate person, too. I brought up his sons with all my heart, as I was so indebted to him.

「女殺油地獄」

　　　河内屋のある方角、上手奥から通りをやって来る。
　　　　与兵衛は花道から去る綿屋古兵衛をしばらく見ていたが、豊島屋の方に
　　　振り向き父親の提灯に気付く。

与兵衛　「河」という字のあの提灯提げてくるのはうちの親仁殿。(とっさに柳の陰に身
　　　を隠す。)
徳兵衛　(与兵衛に気付かず、豊島屋の潜り戸をそっと開けて) 七左衛門殿、もうおし
　　　まいか。(豊島屋の中に入る。)

　　　　与兵衛は豊島屋の潜り戸の隙間からそっと中の様子を覗く。

お吉　　(蚊帳から出て来て) ああ、これは徳兵衛殿。内の人はまだ集金が済まず、今天
　　　満の端まで行っております。仕事に紛れてこちらからご挨拶にも出かけませんの
　　　に、ようこそお出でになりました。どうぞ、お上がり下さい。お前様もこの節季
　　　は与兵衛殿のことで大層ご苦労なことでございましょう。

徳兵衛　(会釈してから座敷に上がり) いかにもさようでございます。あなたは幼い娘
　　　さん達の世話。私は成人した与兵衛の世話。いずれにしても子供の世話で苦労す
　　　るのは親の役目。だから苦労とは思いません。ただ、傍においている間はまだ気
　　　も楽。けど、あのような無法者を勘当すれば、自暴自棄になって何をしでかすか
　　　分かりません。明日にでも、自ら火に入るやも知れん危険も顧みず、謀判、偽判
　　　ついて、一貫目の銀に十貫目の証書を書くような獄門刑の重罪を犯すためしもあ
　　　ると思うのです……。けれど、産みの母が追い出すのを、継父の私が道楽息子に
　　　媚びへつらうようで……止めるわけにもゆきませんだ。人の噂では順慶町の兄
　　　のもとに身を寄せているとか。もし、この辺りをうろついて姿みせましたら、七
　　　左衛門殿とご夫婦で口を合わせて、父親は万事承知しているから母親に出来るだ
　　　け詫びして許してもらい、根性入れ替えて、もう一度家に戻るようご意見なされ
　　　て下さるようお頼みします。うちの女房のお沢一門はみな侍で、その慣わしか、
　　　一度決めたら後には退かん義理堅い生まれ付き。与兵衛はそうした親に似ぬ道楽
　　　者。与兵衛の実父である亡くなられた私の旦那も行い正しく義理も情けも心得た
　　　お方でした。私が二人の息子に心を尽くすのもみな恩ある旧主人への奉公のため。

KICHI offers TOKUBEI a tobacco tray. TOKUBEI takes out a tobacco pipe from his kimono bosom.

If I expelled Yohei now, it would upset my old master in his grave, who never scolded me nor talked to me in a harsh manner in his lifetime. . . . One unhappy parent is more than enough. O-Kichi-sama, please have sympathy with this old man. [*He lights the tobacco and pretends that it is the tobacco smoke that causes his tears.*]

KICHI [*weeping in sympathy*]: Indeed, I feel for you. My husband will be back soon. Why don't you stay and talk to him, too?

TOKUBEI: Thank you so much, but it's the eve of the Boys' Festival tonight. Every house is busy with preparations for tomorrow. I shouldn't be bothering you. Umm . . . [*taking money out of the bosom of his kimono and put it on the tatami floor*] here are three hundred *sen*-coppers . . . I've brought these behind Sawa's back. If Yohei comes here, will you please give these to him, saying that he should buy some summer undergarments since the hot season is just around the corner? Will you tell him the money is from Shichizaemon-dono? A customary gratuity or something? But never tell him it's from me. Will you please do that for me, O-Kichi-dono? [*TOKUBEI puts money in front of KICHI.*]

In the middle of TOKUBEI's speech SAWA walks down the street of Motoden-ma-machi from the direction of the Kawachi-ya.
YOHEI notices SAWA and quickly hides himself from her.

SAWA [*opening the side door of the Teshima-ya and addressing the interior*]: O-Kichi-sama, have you finished today?

TOKUBEI [*panicked*]: It'd be very awkward if I met her here. I must hide myself. O-Kichi-sama, will you please excuse me . . . [*TOKUBEI is getting into the mosquito net.*]

SAWA [*entering the Teshima-ya and noticing TOKUBEI half in the mosquito net*]: Now, now, Tokubei-dono, why are you hiding yourself from your wife?

Flustered, TOKUBEI comes out of the mosquito net.
KICHI is also panicked and forgets to greet SAWA, offering her a floor cushion.

YOHEI: Here comes our ladyship Mother Talkative. [*He goes to the side door and puts his ear to it.*] I must hear what she has to say for herself tonight.

「女殺油地獄」

　　　　　お吉は徳兵衛に煙草盆をすすめる。徳兵衛はキセルを懐から出す。

　　今、与兵衛を追い出したら、生きておられる間手ひどい言葉ひとつをかけられた
　事のない大恩ある親方に草葉の陰から恨まれることになる……。不運なのはこの
　徳兵衛一人で十分です。どうか、お察し下さい、お吉様。（煙草に火をつけて、煙
　にむせた振りをして涙を隠す。）
お吉　（貰い泣きして）まことに、お気持ちお察しいたします。家の人も間もなく帰ら
　れましょうほどに、会ってお話なされればよい。
徳兵衛　いえいえ、どこのお家も今宵は節句の前夜で忙しい。何につけてもお邪魔でし
　ょう。あの……、（懐からお金を出して）ここに三百銭、女房の目を盗んで懐に入
　れてきました。与兵衛の奴が来よりましたら、間もなく暑い季節になるから、さ
　っぱりとした下着でも買うようにと、私の名を出さずに七左衛門殿からのお心付
　けとでも何とでも云うて、このお金渡してやって下さい。お頼み申します。（お吉
　の前にお金を置く。）

　　　　　徳兵衛の台詞の途中で、お沢が河内屋のある上手奥から来る。
　　　　　与兵衛は再び素早く身を隠す。

お沢　（豊島屋の潜り戸を開けながら声をかけ）お吉さま、もうおしまいか。

徳兵衛　（慌てて）ああ、ここでお沢に会うてはまずい。身を隠したい。突然でご無礼、
　どうか御免なされて下さい。（急いで蚊帳の中に隠れようとする。）
お沢　（店に入り、半分蚊帳の中の徳兵衛を見つけて）これこれ、徳兵衛殿。自分の女
　房を見て隠れるとは何事です。

　　　　　徳兵衛はうろたえて蚊帳から出て来る。
　　　　　お吉はまごつき挨拶するのも忘れて沢に座ぶとんをすすめる。

与兵衛　さあ、うるさい母様のお出ましや。（入り口の潜り戸の方に回り、鍵の落とし
　穴に耳をつけて）今夜はどんなお話をなさるのか。

SAWA [*going up to the living room, while sitting*]: It looks like Shichizaemon-dono isn't back yet. Shutting up shop early, you came to visit your neighbour on the busy evening of the settlement day. I wonder what's brought you here. I suppose you're too old to have an affair with your neighbour's young wife. My guess is that you came here to moan about our Yohei. It's true that you are Yohei's step-father, but your sense of obligation is beyond the ordinary. As I, his natural mother, expelled my son, no one can criticise you. [*Noticing the money on the tatami floor*] There're three hundred *sen*-coppers on the floor . . . are they for our good-for-nothing son? You lead a frugal life and save up money only to give it to our hopeless son. I tell you that your precious money will only go down the gutter. You're simply spoiling him to death. I'm not soft like you. Now I've disowned him, he is no longer my son. Whether he wears a paper kimono and jumps into the river, or oils himself and jumps into the fire, whatever stupid acts he does, he can please himself. You only worry about your devilish son. What about your good wife and daughter left forgotten? Well, now, why don't you go home? Please, go. [*SAWA pulls the sleeve of TOKUBEI's kimono in order to get him out of the Teshima-ya immediately.*]

TOKUBEI [*freeing himself from SAWA*]: Wife, isn't it a little too cruel of you to say that? I don't think you are right in this. A person wasn't a parent when he or she was born. A child grows up and becomes an adult. Every parent was once a child. Children live on the mercy of their parents, and parents live on the filial piety of their children. I, Tokubei, have little luck in this world and have no employee. But I have two sons. When I die, I wanted my two sons to carry my coffin and to be given a good burial. I wanted it rather than a hundred mourners coming to see me off at my funeral. But my dream has gone now. I would prefer my coffin to be carried on the shoulders of some stranger,[10] as they do for some unknown fellow fallen dead in the street. [*Sobbing*]

SAWA: Tokubei-dono, Yohei isn't our only child. We also have Tahei and Kachi. O-Kachi is a girl but she's yours. Now, now, please go home. I'll come after you . . . [*She tries to push him out.*]

TOKUBEI [*recovering his spirit*]: You may be right. Then we must go home now. Let's go home together. Come on, O-Sawa.

> *When TOKUBEI pulls the sleeve of SAWA's kimono, a bundle of the celebratory chimaki*[11] *and five hundred sen-coppers fall from the bosom of SAWA's kimono, and are scattered on the wooden floor.*

SAWA [*panicked and trying to hide the things that she has dropped*]: Oh, oh, what shall I do? I feel terrible. I'm ashamed. Tokubei-sama, please forgive me . . . [*weeping*] this is from

「女殺油地獄」

お沢　（座敷に上がって、座わりながら）みれば七左衛門殿もまだ戻っておられぬ様子。家の店じまいもそこそこにして、この忙しい節季の夜に、いつでも行き来できる向かい同士に住んでいるというのに、何の用事でここに来られました？浮気する年でもなし。また与兵衛めの愚痴を言いにですか。いくら義理の仲といってもあなたはあまりにも義理が過ぎます。実の母のこの私が勘当したのです。あなたが人からとやかく言われる筋あいはありません。（座敷に置かれたお金に気付いて）この三百錢……。あ、あの阿呆にやるためですか！あの道楽にやるために普段不自由な思いをして、倹約してお金を貯めても、それは淵に棄てるのと同じこと。お前様のその甘やかしが返ってあれには毒。この母はそうではない。一旦勘当という言葉を口にした限り、紙の着物を着て川に入ろうが、油を塗って火に焼かれるような馬鹿な真似をしようが、みんなおのれの勝手。あんな極悪人に気を使って女房や娘はどうなってもいいと思われるか。さあさあ、早う家にお帰りください。（お沢は徳兵衛を早くこの場から立ち去らせようと、徳兵衛の着物の袖を引く。）

徳兵衛　（お沢の手を振り離して）ええ、嬶、あんまりや。それは違う。人間は生まれた時から親やあらへん。子供が年いって大人になるんや。親も元はみな子供。子は親の慈悲で立ち行き、親は子の孝行で立ち行く。この徳兵衛は幸運に恵まれず、現世で使用人はない。が、二人の男の子がある。死んで葬式出す時は百人もの野辺送りの人々より、この二人に棺の先輿、後輿担いでもらい立派なお葬式にしようと思てた。けど、子供がありながらそれももうならんようになってしもた。縁のない人に棺担いでもらうくらいやったら、いっそ行き倒れみたいに釈迦荷い[10]で葬られるほうがましや。（嗚咽する。）

お沢　徳兵衛殿、与兵衛ばかりが子供ではない。太兵衛もいるし、娘ながらおかちは実の子ではないか。さあさあ、早う先にお帰り……。（徳兵衛を押し出すようにする。）

徳兵衛　（気を取り直し）そやな、ほんなら、今夜は失礼しましょう。お前も一緒に帰ろ。おいで。

　　　　徳兵衛がお沢の袖を引いたはずみに、お沢の着物の懐から端午の節句のお祝いに食べる笹に包んだ粽一把[11]と五百錢がばらばらと店の床に落ちる。

お沢　（狼狽して、あわてて床のものを隠すようにして）ああ、どうしょう。情無い。恥ずかしい。徳兵衛様、どうか許して……。（泣いて）これは今日集金してきた売

the money collected in the credit sale today. I stole five hundred *sen*-coppers to give to Yohei. I feel dreadful that I've acted like a stranger to you after twenty years of marriage. [*Ashamed*] But, even if he were as foolish as one of Buddha's disciples, Shuri Handoku, who could not remember his own name, or as devilish as the Prince Ajase of India who killed his father, imprisoned his mother and ascended the throne, as appalling as those characters in the sermons of the Pure Land Sect, how could I not love my son whom I gave birth to? I blame myself and ask what evil deed in my previous life transferred to Yohei while he was in my womb. My love for Yohei may be more than that of Tokubei-dono. But I couldn't show my true feelings, because I was afraid that you would say that I was too imprudent and over-protective to my son and wasn't doing him any good. So I pretended that I had enough of him, and then hit and rejected him. I acted harshly. I lied because I wanted him to be loved by you, Tokubei-dono. It's all a result of my petty thinking, a woman's shallow brain . . . Please forgive me, Tokubei-dono. You even tried to give some money to your stepson behind my back. You're so gentle and kind-hearted. While talking to you cruelly, in my mind, I was raising your money above my head to express my gratitude. As you know, Yohei is fond of showing-off. As it's a celebratory month, I thought he would be pleased to have new pomade[12] and a mottoi[13] for his topknot to go out into the crowd. We celebrated the day of the Boy's Festival every year since he was born, but we won't be able to do it this year. I just wanted to celebrate the day for him . . . I knew it was a really reprehensible thing to do, but I came to ask O-Kichi-sama to give Yohei the celebratory chimaki and these *sen*-coppers. If a doctor told me to make a concoction of my own liver because it was the best and the last medicine to cure my son's stupidity, I would gladly be torn apart. I have never falsified an account, even half a *sen*-copper, all my life. But I was confused by my feelings towards my son, stole money from our shop, and now my wrong doing has been revealed. Oh, I'm so ashamed of myself. [*Sobbing*]

TOKUBEI [*Also sobbing*]: You do not need to be ashamed of yourself at all. It's natural.

KICHI [*weeping in sympathy*]: I understand your feelings too as a mother of three children. It's natural that we want the best for the future of our children.

CHORUS: Parents sob and cry for their children.

Weeping in sympathy, the light of the mosquito incense has gone out.

Even the busy mosquitoes are humming in sorrow this evening.

TOKUBEI [*Stops sobbing*]: We have been very inconsiderate on the eve of a festival day. Please forgive our shameful behaviour. O-Sawa, why don't you hand those *sen*-coppers to O-Kichi-dono so that she will find a chance to pass them to Yohei? Now we must go home.

　　　　　　　「女殺油地獄」

　掛金。あの与兵衛にやりたいばっかりに私が五百銭盗みました。二十年も連れ添うた仲なのに、こんな水臭いことした自分が情けない。（恥じて）たとえあの与兵衛の極悪人が浄土宗のお説教に出てくる周利槃特のように、自分の名前も覚えられないほどの阿呆でも、父を殺し母を幽閉して王位についたあの阿闍世太子のような鬼子でも、産んだ母の私が何で子供が憎かろう。私の胎内に宿っていたどんな前世の悪縁であんな子を産むことになってしまったのかと、逆にわが身を責めている。あの子が不憫で……、かわいいと思う心は父親の徳兵衛様以上。けれど、私がそういう様子をみせたなら義理の父の徳兵衛さんから、母があまりに分別がない、庇い過ぎる、それでは益々与兵衛の性根が治らない、と非難されると思い、わざと憎む振りをして、与兵衛めを打ち叩き、追い出すの、勘当の、と言い、酷う辛う当たりました。あれもみんな継父のお前様にあの子をかわいがってもらいたかったから。女の浅知恵……。どうか、許して下さい、徳兵衛殿。この私に隠れてあいつにお金を遣って下さるあなたの優しさ、志、言葉ではつっけんどん、邪険には言いましたが、心の中ではもったいなくて有り難くて三度おし頂いておりました。隠しも致しません。あいつはどちらかといえば派手好み。とりわけ祝い月のこと、鬢付け油[12]や元結[13]も新しいものにして人中に出かけたかろう。生まれてこの方、節句毎の祝いを欠かしたことがないのに今回ばかりはそれが出来ない。あの子の身のお祝いをしてやりたいばっかりに……、このように恥じを晒してお吉様にお願いして、あいつに粽やお金を渡してもらおうとやって来ました。あの阿呆の根性を治す特効薬には母親の生き胆を煎じて飲ませるのがよいとお医者様が仰るなら、この身はやつ裂きにされても構いませぬ。けれど、これまで夫のお金をびた一文ごまかしたことのない私が、子を思う心に迷い、分別を失い、盗みをしてそれが露見してしまいました。恥ずかしゅうてなりません。（嗚咽する。）

徳兵衛　（同じく嗚咽して）何も恥ずかしいことなんかない。もっともなこと。
お沢　（貰い泣きして）私も三人の子を持つ母の身。母として我が子の行く末を思うのはみな同じこと。
コーラス　子を思う　親の泣く声　叫ぶ声
　　貰い泣いたか　蚊遣りの線香　火も消えて
　　今夜は　蚊もようさん　鳴いている
徳兵衛　（泣き止んで）ああ、祝い日の前夜に気のきかんことを。泣き喚いた失礼許して下さい。さあ、お沢、そのお金もお吉殿にお願いして与兵衛に渡してもらうと良いではないか。ささ、お暇しよう。

SAWA [*sobbing*]: No, I can't! I betrayed your trust and stole the money. I can't possibly give these to Yohei.

TOKUBEI: Yes, you can. I don't mind what you did, honestly, I don't. So why don't we leave them with O-Kichi-dono?

SAWA: No, no, I can't, I can't.

KICHI [*weeping in sympathy with TOKUBEI and SAWA's loyalty to each other, then conceiving a good idea*]: I understand how O-Sawa-sama feels. O-Sawa-sama, you think that you cannot possibly give that money to Yohei-dono from you. Now then, in that case how about this? You leave it on the floor as it is. I shall find someone suitable to pick it up.

SAWA [*relieved and delighted*]: Oh, what a merciful idea! With your mercy, please give this chimaki to some dog, too. [*Sobbing*]

> *Moved by KICHI's kindness, TOKUBEI sobs, too. SAWA and TOKUBEI thank KICHI, console each other and leave the Teshima-ya.*
>
> *YOHEI quickly hides himself behind the willow tree before SAWA and TOKUBEI come out of the shop.*
>
> *KICHI picks up the sen-coppers and chimaki,*[10] *turning her back to the shop entrance.*
>
> *YOHEI watches his parents walking back to their shop, nods to himself as if he has made up his mind about something and puts the short sword at his side into the bosom of his kimono. He slips into the Teshima-ya through the side door, and then quietly leaves the latch on the door.*

YOHEI [*taking a deep breath and with a forced smile*]: Has Shichizaemon-dono gone somewhere? I guess he must've collected all the credit accounts by now.

KICHI [*startled and turning around*]: Goodness! You made me jump! Dear, dear, why, it's Yohei-dono! What a lucky boy you are! You came at the right moment. Look, here are eight hundred *sen*-coppers and a bundle of chimaki, which have just fallen from Heaven for you. You'd better have them. You've been renounced, and are unfortunate at the moment but this is your lucky sign, because you're receiving money on the settlement day when money is most treasured. I'm sure these will bring you better luck from now on. [*She holds out the sen-coppers and chimaki to YOHEI.*]

YOHEI [*going up to the living room and sitting, neither surprised, nor taking the sen-coppers and chimaki*]: Is this charity from my parents?

KICHI: You mustn't jump to conclusions! There's no reason that your parents would want me to hand you money after disowning you.

「女殺油地獄」

お沢　（泣いて）あなたのその情け深いお心も知らず裏切って盗んで持ってきたこのお金。どうして与兵衛にあげられましょう。
徳兵衛　いやいや、そんなことは構わん。どうか与兵衛に渡してもらおう。

お沢　いえいえ、それは出来ません。
お吉　（徳兵衛とお沢が互いに義理を立て続けるのに貰い泣きしていたが、思いついて）確かに、お沢様のお心お察しいたします。お沢様から遣ることが出来ないと仰やるのなら、どうです、ここにこう捨ててお置きになっては？私が誰ぞ適当な人に拾わせましょう。
お沢　（安堵して喜び）ああ、有難いこと。そのお情けのついでにこの粽もどこぞの適当な犬に食わせてやってください。（すすり泣く。）

　　　　　徳兵衛もお吉の情けに泣く。徳兵衛とお沢はお吉に礼を言って、互いを労わりながら寄り添い、ひっそりと潜り戸から帰って行く。
　　　　　与兵衛は徳兵衛とお沢の帰る気配に、急いで柳の木の陰に隠れる。

　　　　　お吉は店の入り口に背を向けて夫婦の託したお金と粽を拾い集める。

　　　　　与兵衛は二人を見送った後、何かを決心したかのように頷いてから、腰に差していた脇差を懐にしまい、そっと身を滑らすようにして豊島屋の潜り戸から入り、物音を立てないようにして潜り戸の閂をかける。

与兵衛　（一呼吸してから、愛想をつくって）七左衛門殿はどこぞへ行かれたのですか。売掛金ももう集められたでしょうに。
お吉　（驚いて振り返り）ああ、びっくりした。まあ、誰かと思ったら与兵衛殿。何とあなたは幸せ者。ちょうどよいところに来られた。ここにある八百銭と粽、今、天からあなたにあげよと降ってきました。貰うておきなされ。いくら勘当された身でも、節季にその日の宝とされるお金が入るのは運のいい印。これであなたの運もいい方に向きますよ。（笑顔でお金と粽を与兵衛に差し出す。）

与兵衛　（少しも驚かず座敷に上がって座り、お金と粽を受け取ろうとしないで）これが親からの施しですか。
お吉　早合点されては困ります。あなたを勘当なされた親御さん達があなたにお金をあげて欲しいと言われる理由がない。

YOHEI: Don't lie to me, O-Kichi-dono. I've been standing outside your shop for some time, bitten by mosquitoes; I cried while hearing my parents grieving for my conduct.

KICHI: Oh, you've heard it all. Then you must've understood how much your parents are thinking about you. Even I, a mere neighbour, felt so sorry for them and couldn't stop weeping. Now here is the money. Don't waste even a *sen*-copper. Keep it on you and try to make more money with it . . . if you don't want to have the best carriage for your parents' funerals, you're not a man. If you ever betray your parents' love as deep as this, you will be damned by Buddha, all the gods and goddesses in Japan and heaven, and nothing good would come to you in the future. Now, as a start, why don't you take the money? [*KICHI holds out the money and chimaki to YOHEI once again.*]

YOHEI [*not taking it and meekly*]: What you've just said is right. I think so, too. From now on I'll reform myself and try my best to be a good and devoted son . . . Yet, well, I'm sorry to say this, but . . . the thing is, their mercy money isn't quite enough to help me out of the situation I'm in. Also the problem is . . . I can talk about it neither to my parents nor to my brother because of the way the things have developed. . . I guess that you must have the takings and the collection of money in your shop tonight. I only need two hundred *monme* in new silver. O-Kichi-dono, will you please lend me two hundred until my parents' disowning of me is forgiven!

KICHI: Now, now, it's exactly as the proverb says, "Hear what's said, to know what's in the mind." You've just given yourself away. Which part of you, do you say, has turned over a new leaf? You can't ask that of me whatever reasons you may have! I can see your way of doing things now. At first you borrow money, say by losing face in society, pay off all of your debts in the pleasure quarters with it, and then you slowly go back to those places . . . That is the plot, isn't it? [*Straightening herself up*] Certainly, we have five hundred *monme* in best silver and also some *sen*-coppers in the safe of our cabinet. But I won't lend you any money in my husband's absence whatever reason you may have. When I visited the Nozaki Kannon in April, I cleaned off the mud on your kimono. You have no idea how many days it took me after that to clear my husband's thoughts that I had committed adultery with you. [*Remembering*] Oh, it was awful! Awful! [*Disgusted*] Please leave here immediately with these *sen*-coppers before Shichizaemon-dono returns.

YOHEI [*edging up to KICHI*]: Then, why don't you commit adultery with me and lend me the money.

KICHI [*startled and backing away from YOHEI*]: What on earth are you saying? I said I wouldn't lend you any money. You are very persistent.

YOHEI: I won't be persistent. Please lend me money just this once. [*YOHEI edges up to KICHI again persistently.*]

「女殺油地獄」

世兵衛　隠されるな、お吉殿。先程からこちらの門口で蚊に食われながら長いこと親達の嘆き悲しむのを聞いて、私も泣いておりました。

お吉　そうですか、みな聞かれましたか。それなら、よう分かられたことでしょう。他人の私でさえお気の毒で涙が止まりませんでした。このお金は一文も無駄に出来ませんよ。これを肌身につけて一稼ぎして……、そして、お二人の葬式には立派な乗り物に乗って行ってもらおうという気持にならんようなら、一人前の男ではありません。ここまで深い親の情けに背かれるようなことされたら、天の神の罰、仏の罰、日本の神々の厳罰（げんばつ）が当たって将来良い事はありません。さあさあ、まず頂かれなさい。（と、再びお金と粽を差し出す。）

与兵衛　（受け取らず、しおらしげに）ほんまに、その通りです。よう分かりました。これからは心入れ替えて真人間になって、親孝行するつもりです。が……、肝心のお慈悲のお金がこれでは少し足りませんのや。と、云うて親や兄には言えないことの成り行き……。ここには売上金や集金の売掛金があるはず。新銀でたったの二百目ばかりのお金。お吉殿、親の勘当が解けるまでどうか、貸して下さらんか。

お吉　それそれ、「奥を聞こうより口を聞け」の諺（ことわざ）通り、あなたの本音がもう口をついて出てきました。それで、どの心が入れ替わった、治ったと云うのです。嘘でもお金を貸してくれとは言えないはず。世間の義理を欠いてもお金を借りて、ひとまず遊里の支払いをして、その後でまただんだんと遊里通いをしようという、そういう魂胆ですね……。（姿勢を正して）確かに、お金は戸棚の金庫に上銀が五百目余り、銭もあることはあります。けど、夫の留守には、どんなことがあっても一銭のお金も貸すことは出来まへん。この間、野崎参りの時、着物を洗うてあげたのでさえ、お前と不義（ふぎ）したと疑われてその疑いを晴らす言い訳をするのに何日かかったことやら。（思い出して）ああ、嫌嫌、嫌なこと。（厭わしそうに）七左衛門殿が帰らぬうちに、早うそのお銭持って、いんでください。

与兵衛　（お吉ににじり寄り）それじゃ、不義（ふぎ）の仲になって貸してくだされ。

お吉　（驚いて、与兵衛から逃げて）な、何を言われる！貸せないと言っているのに！くどい、くどい。
与兵衛　くどくは云わん。貸してくだされ。（尚もしつこくにじり寄る。）

135

KICHI [*fleeing from YOHEI*]: No! Stop it! I'll make a lot of noise if you ignore what I say simply because I'm a woman.

YOHEI: Well, however hopeless I may look, I'm still a man. At the moment I am terribly down after hearing my parents' grief over my conduct. I do not have any energy left to think of ignoring you or making light of you . . . Please listen to my story. On the twentieth of last month I borrowed two hundred *monme* in new silver by forging my father's seal, and the deadline is tonight.

KICHI is astounded and is about to speak to YOHEI.

[*Stopping her*] Please wait and listen to my story till the end. [*Taking the deed of the loan out of his kimono bosom and showing it to KICHI*] It says here 'one thousand *monme* in good silver' on the front, but in reality I borrowed two hundred only. However, if I fail to return two hundred by the end of tonight . . . I'll have to pay back one thousand as it says in the deed. Furthermore the problem is, if I fail to meet the deadline, the usurer will report to the senior townsmen and the neighbours in both Motodenma-machi and Junkei-machi, not to mention my parents and brother. No matter what one may do, tonight is the deadline for the payment, yet I still haven't found the money. Since things had come this far, I thought that the only thing left to me was to commit suicide. Look at this. I came out hiding a short sword in my kimono bosom. Then I heard my parents' grief and compassion for me a moment ago. It's made my mind falter. Also if I killed myself now, the trouble of my debt would go to them, then my father would be bankrupt and I would bring shame to my parents. When I think about the consequences, I can neither die nor live. . . I'm at my wits' end. I am asking you a favour by placing my trust in you. If you haven't got money, it can't be helped, but you've just said that you have some in your safe. You could save my life with a mere two hundred. I shall remember your kindness forever until I reach the end of the land of the dead. Please, O-Kichi-sama. Please lend me two hundred *monme* in new silver. I beg you!

CHORUS: "Yohei's eyes look trustworthy,
His words sound sincere,
But all the lies and wrong conducts in his past . . .
He could well be on his usual form…"
Oh, no! No!
Gentle-hearted Kichi's merciful Buddhist mind is unyielding tonight!

KICHI [*having listened to YOHEI's speech half in doubt and exhaling deeply*]: Phew! What a plausible lie! I nearly believed it. If you want to embellish your story with more lies, just

「女殺油地獄」

お吉　（再び逃げて）嫌！止めて下さい。女と思って嬲ってかかると大きな声を出しますよ。

与兵衛　はて、こう見えても与兵衛も男。二人の親の言葉が心の底に染み込んで悲しい思いをしている時に、嬲るの侮るのなどと、そんなところにまで気は回りません。……何を隠しましょう。先月の二十日に親仁の謀判ついて上銀二百目、今夜を期限として借りましたんや。

　　　　　　吉は驚いて事の次第を尋ねようとする。

（止めて）まあまあ、最後まで話しを聞いて下され。（借用証書を懐から出してお吉に見せて）これ、この手形の表書きには上銀一貫目と書いてありますが、借りたお金は二百目だけ。けど、明日になれば……、証文通りに一貫目で返す約束になっている。その上、悲しいことに、もし明日までに返さなければ、親、兄のところは言うまでも無く、本天満町、順慶町、両方の町年寄と五人組にも借金をした先方から届けが出るはず。今日の明日の今になっても、まだお金の算段が泣いても笑てもつきません。もうこの上は自害するしかない、と覚悟して、これこの通り懐に脇差も持っている。この脇差は差して出たけれど、ただ今の両親の嘆き、私のことを不憫に思われる心を聞いて、気持ちが揺らいだ。それに、私が死んだら借金の難儀は親仁の方へ行く。そうなると親仁が破産してしまう。それでは親不孝の上塗りをすることになる。そのこと考えたら死ぬにも死ねず、生きてもおられず……、どうしようもなくて、あなたを見込んでお願いしている。お金がないのなら仕方が無い。けど、そこにあると言われる。たったの二百目で私の命を助けて下さることが出来る。あなたへの恩、決して冥途の果てまで忘れません。お吉様、どうぞ、銀二百目、貸して下され。

コーラス　縋る与兵衛の　目の色　言の葉
　　誠らしくは　あるけれど……
　　今日までの　素行の悪さ　嘘の数々
　　今度もまた　例の調子やらしれぬ……
　　ああ！ああ！
　　お吉の中の菩薩の心　今夜はどうして　戸を閉ざす

お吉　（与兵衛の言葉を半信半疑で聞いていたが、深く息を吐いて）ふぅーっ。もっともらしいその嘘。また騙されそうになりました。尾鰭をつけて云いたければ、な

WOMAN-KILLER IN OIL HELL

keep going. But as I've already said, I won't lend you any money, I won't.

YOHEI: You don't believe me even if I swear on my honour as a man! I don't know what to do any more . . . [*thinking out a plan*] I see, I see, in that case, it can't be helped. Then [*pointing to the oil barrel on the shop floor which he has brought with him*] . . . Will you please sell me two shō of oil on credit in this barrel?

KICHI [*a little relieved*]: It's our business. We oil retailers can't make a living without lending and borrowing. Of course, I will pour two shō in your barrel for you.

> *KICHI descends to the shop floor, picks up Yohei's oil barrel and goes to the oil counter. She skilfully ladles oil from a large barrel to a masu measure[14] and then pours it into YOHEI's barrel.*
>
> *YOHEI quietly descends to the shop floor, while KICHI is measuring and pouring oil. He secretly takes the sword out of the sheath and goes behind KICHI.*

KICHI [*not noticing YOHEI's movement and recovering her usual gentleness*]: Just celebrate the festival day tomorrow and don't think of anything else. Talk it over with my husband some other time. If we think that we have enough money, we may be able to help you by lending some. You know, even if a woman has been married to a man for fifty or sixty years, she isn't supposed to use money for herself. It's a rule that we women have to follow. Please don't think ill of me.

> *The shop lamp hanging from the ceiling over the table sways in a sudden gust of wind.*
>
> *YOHEY's short sword reflects the lamp light and shines.*

KICHI [*seeing something sparkling on the surface of the oil, startled and turning round*]: Something's just glittered . . . What, what was it, Yohei-sama?

YOHEI [*holding the sword behind him*]: Nothing!

KICHI: Look at you! Your eyes are set. You look terrifying! Hold out your right hand in front of you!

YOHEI [*shifting the sword to his left hand*]: Here! Have a look! I haven't got anything.

KICHI [*shaking with fear*]: You are frightening me. Don't you come any nearer . . .

> *KICHI is nearly paralysed with terror and her legs fail her. She staggers backwards to the entrance of the shop and tries to open the side door frantically. She does not realise the latch has been left on. YOHEI follows her. She gives up on getting out of the side*

「女殺油地獄」

んぼでも言うとよい。けど、貸さんというたら、貸しまへん。
与兵衛　これほど男の名誉にかけて誓っても信じて貰えませんか。はあ、どうしたものか。（考えを巡らして）うん、うん、そうか……仕方がない。それなら、（提げてきた空の油樽を示して）この樽に油二升掛売りして下さらんか。

お吉　（やや安堵して）それは商売上のこと。油商同士がお互いに油の貸し借りをしないでは生計（せいけい）が立ちゆきまへん。勿論、詰めて進ぜまひょう。

　　　　お吉は店に降りて、与兵衛の油樽を取り、売り場の台へ行き、商売の手馴れた様子で柄杓で油を枡[14]に汲んで量って、樽に注ぎ始める。

　　　　お吉が油を詰めている間に、与兵衛も店に降り、気付かれないように脇差を抜いて、そっとお吉の後ろに立つ。

お吉　（何も気付かずに、いつもの優しさを取り戻して）節句はお祝いしてお済ましなさい。うちの人にも打ち明けて折り入って相談されるとよい。有るお金だったらお役に立てないものでもなし。五十年、六十年連れ添った夫婦の仲でも思い通りに出来ないのが女の習い。決して私のこと恨みに思われんようにね。

　　　　売り場の天井から吊られた灯火（とうか）が風で揺れる。

　　　　与兵衛の刀が揺れる灯火の明かりを受けてキラリとひかる。

お吉　（油の表面に反射した光を見て、仰天して振り返り）何かがきらっと光りました……今のは何？ 与兵衛様！
与兵衛　（刀を後ろに隠して）いや、何でもありません！
お吉　そのように、きっと目も据わって！恐ろしい顔をして！その、右の手、前にお出しなさい！
与兵衛　（刀を左手に持ち替えて）ほれ、見て下さい。何も持っておりません。
お吉　（わなわなと震えて）ええ、あなたは気味が悪い。決してそばに寄らんように……。

　　　　お吉は恐怖で腰が抜けたようになって、後ずさりして店の入り口へ行き、必死で潜り戸を開けようとするが、閂がおりているのに気付かない。与兵衛はお吉を付け回す。お吉は、今度は店の中を逃げ回る。

139

door and flees around the shop.

YOHEI [*chasing KICHI*]: Why are you looking around so restlessly? What are you frightened of? [*He keeps chasing KICHI.*]

KICHI [*fleeing from YOHEI and crying out loud*]: Someone! Help me! Help me! [*KICHI turns over several oil barrels to stop YOHEI coming near her.*]

The oil slowly flows out of the barrels overturned on the earth floor.

YOHEI [*jumping onto KICHI and seizing her by the lapels of her kimono to silence her*]: Stop shouting, woman! [*YOHEI stabs KICHI's throat with the sword.*]

Blood gushes out of KICHI and splashes YOHEI in red. The oil from the barrels has been covering the shop floor and the space becomes like a sea of oil.

KICHI [*writhing with agony, slipping in oil and thrashing her arms and legs around*]: Promise . . . I . . . I won't shout any more, if . . . if I am killed now, my small children will be at a loss . . . I, I can't bear the thought . . . I don't want to die . . . take our silver as much as you want . . . Please spare my life! Please don't kill me, Yohei-dono. Please! I don't want to die.

YOHEI: Of course you don't! I'm sure you don't want to die . . . it's natural. As you care about your daughters, I, too, care about my father who loves me. I need to repay my debt and save my honour as a man. Please give in and leave this world quietly. Someone might hear me if I say it aloud, so I'll chant a prayer to Buddha in my mind . . . [*as if muttering*] Namu Amidabutsu, may her soul rest in place . . . Namu Amidabutsu, may her soul rest in peace . . .

Slipping in oil, YOHEI draws KICHI towards himself, then stabs and slashes her from right to left and left to right several times, as if he is possessed. KICHI keeps writhing in agony. The oil shop is transformed into a battlefield of blood and oil.

Then a gust of night wind makes the banners for the Boys' Day outside flutter loudly. It snuffs out the lamplight on the ceiling. The shop floor gets very dark.

YOHEI tries to stand firmly on the floor without slipping in the oil and blood. By this time he is soaked in blood and his face is like that of a red ogre. Slipping and falling in a hell of oil, he continues slashing KICHI as if he has truly gone mad.

「女殺油地獄」

与兵衛　（お吉を追いながら）何をキョロキョロしている……。何が恐ろしい……。（お吉を付け回す。）
お吉　（逃げ回り、喚いて）誰か！誰か来て！誰か！（油樽を幾つかひっくり返す。）

　　　　　吉のひっくり返した油樽からゆっくりと油が流れ出す。

与兵衛　（お吉の口を塞ぐために、咄嗟に飛び掛って胸座(むなぐら)を締め付けて）大きな声を出すな、女め！（お吉の喉笛(のどぶえ)を脇差でぐいと刺す。）

　　　　　お吉の喉から返り血が迸(ほとばし)り、与兵衛を赤く染める。
　　　　　油樽から流れ出る油で店は次第に油の海となってゆく。

お吉　（苦しみ悶えて、油で滑りながら手足をバタバタさせて）そんなら、もう大声は出さない……今、今、私が死んだら幼い三人の子が途方に暮れる……それが辛い……死にとうない……銀も好きなだけ持って行ったらいい……。た、助けて、助けて下さい、与兵衛殿。助けて……お願い、お願いします。

与兵衛　おお、そうやろ。死にともないはず……尤もなこと。そなたが、娘がかわいいように、わしもわしを可愛がる親仁が愛しい。借金返して男の面目立てねばならん。諦めて死んで下され。声を出して言うたら人が聞く。心の中で念仏唱えます……（呟くように）南無阿弥陀、南無阿弥陀仏……。

　　　　　与兵衛は油で滑りながら、苦しみもがくお吉を引き寄せて、何かに憑(つ)かれた様に、右から左へとお吉のお腹を刺してはえぐり、刀を抜いては切る。お吉は苦しさにひたすらもがき続ける。店内は血と油の入り混じった修羅場(しゅらば)と化す。
　　　　　店の外の幟(のぼり)が夜の風に煽(あお)られ大きく音を立ててはためく。そのあおり風で店内の灯火が消えて土間が真っ暗になる。
　　　　　ぶち撒かれた油と流れる血にまみれて与兵衛は滑りながら足を踏みしめている。既に全身返り血を浴びて真っ赤で、顔面は赤鬼(あかおに)のようである。暗闇の中で油に滑って転倒しながら、与兵衛はなお狂ったようにお吉に切

WOMAN-KILLER IN OIL HELL

CHORUS: The sound of the banners fluttering outside
    The night has come for Kichi on the wind from hell.
    The wind snuffs out the shop light.
    The dark mind slips into the darkness on the shop floor.
    The mother's blood flows out into the sea of oil.

    The red faced ogre stamps and stumbles on the mother.
    He tosses his head with its cruel horn.

    "Oh, it's painful! It's tormenting!
    I'm in a wood of swords, blood and oil hell.
    Irises under the eaves can ward off all the disease.
    But they know not how to stop the evil destiny of a previous life."

    Three innocent girls!
    What sweet dreams are you dreaming?
    Are you dreaming of the mirror house your mother talked about?
    Can you find a sword of the Iris Festival in your house?
    A sword to fight for your gentle mother

    "Oh, it's painful! It's tormenting!"
    A drop of dew falls from a leaf of iris.
    The light of a mother's life now goes out.

> *KICHI dies. YOHEI looks into her face. For the first time he realises the seriousness of the crime he has committed and is deeply disturbed. He shivers. His knees knock. Then, as if trying to control the beating of his heart, he slowly picks up the bunch of keys hanging from KICHI's obi and goes up to the living room. When he passes by the mosquito net in the next room, he notices KICHI's girls sleeping soundly. He looks at them for a moment.*

CHORUS: Murderer! Murderer! You killed our mother!
    Give her life back! Give our mother back to us!
    Yohei the Murderer!

「女殺油地獄」

　　　りかかる。

コーラス　はためく門の幟の音
　　お吉迎えの冥途の夜風
　　風に売り場の火も消えて
　　床も心も闇の中
　　油の海　流れる血潮

　　赤面赤鬼　女踏み倒し　我踏み滑り
　　邪険の角を振り立てる

　　「ああ　苦しい　ああ　切ない
　　この身切り裂く剣の林　血と油の地獄絵のよう
　　軒にさしたる菖蒲の花々　千々の病を防ぐというが
　　前世の因業　防げない」

　　三人の幼い娘
　　どんな夢見てすやすや眠る
　　娘の夢は母の話した鏡の家か
　　その家に端午の節句の菖蒲刀無いか
　　優しい母様守る刀無いか

　　「ああ　苦しい　ああ　切ない」
　　菖蒲の葉の露の玉　流れるよう
　　お吉の命の露の魂　今流れ去る

　　　　吉の息が絶える。与兵衛はお吉の死に顔を覗き込み、初めて自分の犯した行為の重大さに気付き動揺してがくがく膝を震わす。それから高鳴る胸の動悸を押さえ込むかのように、ゆっくりとお吉の帯からぶら下がっている鍵の束を取り、座敷に上がって行く。座敷まで来たとき、次の間の蚊帳の中ですやすやと眠っている子供達に気付きじっと見る。

コーラス　人殺し！　人殺し！　母様を殺したな！
　　母様返せ！母様返せ！
　　　与兵衛の人殺し！

The girls' soft breathing sounds like a curse to Yohei.
   Yohei the Red Ogre!
The girls' sweet, sleeping faces look like a scowl to Yohei.
   The Murderer! The Red Ogre!
He shivers with fear!

> *YOHEI goes to the cabinet and unlocks the safe door. The keys make a loud rattling metallic sound like a roll of thunder. YOHEI is frightened of the sound as if struck by lightning and pushes himself up against the cabinet. Careful of the noise, he takes out five hundred and eighty monme of new silver from SHICHIZAEMON's money belt which KICHI put away earlier and pushes the money deep into his kimono bosom. He tries to get out of the house quickly, but he cannot walk straight because of fear, the weight of the money, and the oil and blood on the floor.*

CHORUS: Killing the mother of the three, Yohei's got the money he needs.
   The money weighing in his bosom,
   With heavy steps of a criminal,
   Walking on thin ice, burning flames, and risking his life,
   Yohei, the thief and the murderer, is now running away.
YOHEI [*quietly lifting the latch and slipping out of the Teshima-ya*]: I'll drop the sword into the river from the Chinaberry Bridge[15] on the way. Hell in the next world is too far to worry about. I should think it's my lucky day because I've got this money . . .

> *He takes care not to be seen and runs off the hanamichi.*

> *Blackout.*

「女殺油地獄」

お吉殺した　与兵衛の耳に　子供の寝息　非難の叫び
　　赤鬼与兵衛！
かわいい子供の寝顔まで　自分を睨んでいるようで
　　赤鬼の人殺し！
恐ろしさに身が震う

　　　　与兵衛はお金のしまってある戸棚のところに行き錠を開ける。鍵がジャラジャラと大きな金属音を立てる。与兵衛は自分の立てた音に雷が落ちたかのように驚いて、戸棚にぴったりと身を付ける。それから、辺りの物音(ものおと)に気を配りながら戸棚の中にお吉がしまった七左衛門の胴巻き(どうま)から上銀五百八十目を取って、懐に深く捻じ込む。お金の重さと気が動転しているのとでよろめいて、まともに歩けない。

コーラス　三人の子の　母の命　奪って盗った　このお金
　ずっしり重い懐に　足もと重く　罪重く
　薄(はくひょう)氷踏んで　火炎(かえん)を踏んで　危険犯して　逃げる与兵衛の
　大盗人(おおぬすっと)の　人殺し(ひとごろ)！

与兵衛　（そっと閂(かんぬき)を抜いて、ゆっくりと豊島屋の潜り戸から出て）この脇差は途中で梅檀の木の橋[15]から川へ沈めよう。来世の地獄はまだみえぬ先。今はこの金手に入れて、幸運の到来の時や……。

　　　　与兵衛は人に見られないように注意しながら、花道から逃げて行く。

　　　　暗転。

PART TWO

SCENE ONE
At Shin-machi

The sixth of June.
The street of the Shin-machi, the Licensed Pleasure Quarter in Osaka. The place is crowded with visitors and courtesans beautifully dressed for the summer festival.
The Bizen-ya Brothel is upstage right. On the ground floor of the building, the courtesans' rooms are lined up, each with individual entrances hung with noren. The width of each frontage is one ken.

CHORUS: Spring scenery in Kyoto is better than that in Osaka.
But the summer festival in Osaka in June is better than that in Kyoto.
Four main streets of Shin-machi are filled with the beautiful courtesans, the never withering flowers.
Look at their gorgeous kimonos and the elaborate buildings of ageya.[1]
The place is one of the most famous landmarks in Japan,
As the mount of the love stories here is taller than Mount Fuji, the highest mountain in Japan.

Owners of the brothels like celebrating festival days.[2]
They do that nearly every day in a year.
For the charge for a festival day is higher.
And yet, they still complain about the festival days being three days short!
Oh, they are truly greedy sorts!
These festival days make courtesans' hearts sink.
For they impose a burden on their good clients.
Many clients want to cancel the appointments on a festival day.
Those who prefer coming on the festival days are the serious ones.

Someone hurries his palanquin to an ageya.
Someone hides his face with a fan when he visits a brothel.
Someone is careful about the booked time and not much fun to be with.
Someone swaggers in the quarter and browses around.

「女殺油地獄」

その二

(一) 新町の場

六月六日。
夏祭りで賑わう大阪は新町の廓筋。艶やかに着飾った遊女達の姿が美しい。

舞台下手奥に揚屋備前屋がある。備前屋の一階は入り口に暖簾のかかった慎ましやかな間口一間の局が並ぶ。

コーラス　難波の春景色は京に劣ります
　　けど　六月の夏祭りには　京が難波に劣ります
　　大阪新町の廓四筋は　散ること知らん美しい花々　遊女でいっぱいです
　　遊女の身なり　揚屋[1]のこった構えは　どうです
　　富士のお山に負けない高さの恋の山も　日本一の名所です

　　一年三百六十日の毎日を　紋日や祝い日[2]と言って高値をふっかけて
　　それでもまだ三日足りんと嘆く遊女屋の主の　何と欲の深いこと
　　儲けの大きい紋日が多いほど　客に散財させて厄介かける
　　揚屋の主人の好きな紋日は　女郎泣かせの客泣かせ
　　紋日の約束を　変更するお客もようさんいはる
　　紋日の頼みを好んで引き受けるお客さんは　一段といかめしげ

　　駕籠を急がせるのは　揚屋で遊ぶお客
　　扇で顔を隠して通うのは　色茶屋のお客
　　時間で決めての遊興は　型とおりでおもろないお客
　　肩で風切って歩くのは　ひやかしの客

Someone from the countryside wants to know courtesans' ranks.
A regular client enjoys pillow talk with his courtesan.
A courtesan's lover whispers to his courtesan to meet him after the drumbeat which marks the closing of the gates.
A courtesan invites her favourite at her own expense to be with her through the night.

Some trouble their family and their master by lavishing too much money on a courtesan.
Others use up all of their fortune.
We receive all sorts of clients here.
A selfish client makes a big fuss about the mix-up of his appointment.
The four streets of Shin-machi are always hustling and bustling.
People impersonate kabuki actors' voices, mimick birds' and animals' calls, joke, sing kouta and jōruri, and what not,
As if being quiet was a kind of sin.
People stroll from the West Gate to the East Gate and enjoy themselves.
Every night is a boisterous merrymaking.
All this is thanks to our peaceful times when all is right and affluent with the world.

Yamamoto Moriemon comes from the direction of the East Gate off-stage left.

CHORUS: That's Yohei's uncle Moriemon,
Swallowing his pride, inquiring after his nephew's whereabouts in the pleasure quarter.
Moriemon was astounded when he heard the news of Yohei.
He asked leave of absence from his master and came down to Osaka.
There is nothing to prove that Yohei has done it.
But the rumour says, "Yohei must have killed the wife of the oil shop and stolen their money."
Yohei had been living a dissipated life beyond anyone's endurance.
To make matters worse, he has not returned home and cannot be questioned.
MORIEMON [*to a passer-by*]: Excuse me please, sir. I'm looking for the Bizen-ya. I wonder if you've heard of it. They told me at the East Gate that it was around here.

The passer-by shakes his head and walks off.
MORIEMON walks farther and approaches the Bizen-ya. He gazes at the Bizen-ya and a few other brothels there, but cannot tell which one is the Bizen-ya, as all the brothels look very much alike.

「女殺油地獄」

　　「太夫さんか」「天神さんか」と女郎の位を聞くのは　田舎客
　　寝物語するのは　馴染みのお客
　　廓の大門閉める「太鼓の合図の後で」と囁くのは　女郎の真夫
　　自腹切って会う　振舞客とは　一晩しっぽりと

　　お金使うて親や親方に損かける客
　　自分の財産みな失くす客
　　いろんなお客さんいたはります
　　わがままいっぱいの困ったお客や　手はず違いが入り混じり
　　ごったがえしで行き交う新町の廓四筋
　　ちょっとでも　口きかんのは　恥みたいで
　　役者の声色　鳥獣の鳴き真似　小唄　浄瑠璃　冗談口
　　廓の西口から東口まで　口々に口ずさみ　行くも帰るも思いのまま
　　毎夜大勢繰り込んでの大騒ぎ
　　これもみんな　世の中が豊かでちゃーんと治まってるおかげとか

　　　　山本森右衛門が廓の東口のある方角の上手から来る。

コーラス　与兵衛の伯父の森右衛門
　　廓の中　恥をしのんで甥訪ね歩く
　　甥の素行の知らせに驚き
　　暫く主君にお暇願い　高槻から大阪に
　　確かな証拠はないとはいえ
　　「油屋の女房殺してお金盗ったは与兵衛ではないか」、とのもっぱらの噂
　　甥の目に余る放蕩振り
　　おまけに　詮議しようにも家に寄り付かず

山本森右衛門　（通りすがりの男に）お尋ね申す。備前屋を探しておるのだが。ご存知
　　ないか。先程、東口で聞いたところによるとこのあたりということだが……。

　　　　男は「分からない」といった様子で去って行く。
　　　　森右衛門はもう少し歩いて備前屋のあたりまで来る。備前屋の建物を見
　　　たり、二三軒他の揚屋の入り口を覗いたりするが、どれもよく似ているの
　　　でどの店が備前屋なのか分からない様子である。

At this point THE KAMURO OF SHIN-MACHI walks in from stage right, in the direction of the West Gate of the quarter. She carries bulky letters.

MORIEMON [*to KAMURO OF SHIN-MACHI in a stiff manner*]: Hello, miss, would you please answer my question? I should be grateful if you tell me which house is the Bizen-ya. Also have you ever heard of Matsukaze-dono, one of the courtesans of the house? If you have, will you please tell me where I could find her? I'm not familiar with the place, and I would be truly grateful if you could help me.

KAMURO OF SHIN-MACHI: Oh, my word! What a pompous way of talking! The Bizen-ya is this house. Matsukaze-sama's room is the one at the end, to the west. She must be with a client at the moment as her door is shut. Hey, O-samurai-sama, why don't you raise your left leg? [*MORIEMON raises his left leg.*] Next, why don't you raise your right leg? [*This time MORIEMON raises his right leg.*] Hah, hah, hah, hah! You've done very well. Thank you very much for your great performance! Hah, hah, hah, hah! [*Talking to MORIEMON pertly, KAMURO OF SHIN-MACHI goes off to the left while laughing joyfully.*]

MORIEMON [*laughing*]: What a lighthearted girl! Having been in this sort of place, she is used to socialising.

MORIEMON goes to the front of Matsukaze's room.
The room is lit and its front door is firmly shut.

The client in her room must be Yohei. He must've been hiding himself here. I'll catch him when he comes out.

Before long a man who hides his face in an amigasa hat comes out of MATSUKAZE's room. MORIEMON quickly grasps him from behind.

MATSUKAZE [*coming out after her client in amigasa*]: Who are you? Please stop acting hastily!

MORIEMON: Leave me alone! I'm not acting hastily. You wretch! Yohei, do you think you can avoid us as long as you hide yourself? [*Pulling off the man's amigasa and seeing his face*] Dear me, you aren't Yohei. I mistook you for my nephew. I apologise. Please, forgive my careless conduct.

MORIEMON makes a sincere apology by bowing down and rubbing his hands.
The client, who had been here incognito, nods and quickly goes off to the east, stage left,

「女殺油地獄」

　　　　ちょうどこの時、禿が廓の西口の方角、下手からくる。禿は両手にかさ
　　　ばった手紙を持っている。

山本森右衛門　（禿に、堅苦しく）これこれ、お尋ねしたい。備前屋と申す遊女屋は
　どちらかな。その家の松風殿と申す遊女、ご存知ならばお教え下され。私は当地
　不案内の身、お頼み申す。

禿　へえー、なんと大げさな物の言いよう。備前屋はこの家。その西の端の戸の閉まっ
　ている、今客のある局にいるのが松風様じゃ。これ、お侍様、左の足を上げなさ
　れ。（森右衛門は左足を上げる。）また、右の足も上げなされ。（森右衛門、今度は
　右足を上げる。）あははは、よう上げなさった。おおきに。ご苦労さん。（こまっ
　ちゃくれた様子で嬉しそうに笑いながら上手の方に去る。）

森右衛門　（笑って）場所柄だけに人馴れして、何と気の軽い奴。

　　　　森右衛門は松風の局の前に行く。
　　　　局の中に灯はともっているが、戸口はぴしゃりと閉まっている。

中にいる客はきっと与兵衛の奴。ここに隠れておるに違いない。出てきたところ
を捕らえてやる。

　　　　間もなく、松風の局から編み笠を被って顔を隠した客が出てくる。森右
　　　衛門はすかさずその客を後ろからしっかと抱きかかえて捕まえる。

松風　（編み笠の客の後から出て来て）となたか！軽率なことなさるな！
森右衛門　ほおって置いて下され。軽率でもなんでもない。おのれ、与兵衛、隠れてい
　たら会わずにすむと思うのか。（編み笠を引き千切り、客と顔を見合わせる）なん
　と、これは与兵衛ではない。人違いじゃ。まっぴら御免。面目ない。

　　　　森右衛門は腰をかがめ、揉み手をして平謝りする。忍びの色遊びの客は
　　　頷いただけで、編み笠で顔を隠して足早に東口の方、上手に去る。

151

hiding his face with amigasa.

MORIEMON [*bowing to MATSUKAZE lightly*]: Are you Matsukaze-dono of the Bizen-ya? We hear that you and Yohei are on intimate terms.

Matsukaze bows back to MORIEMON and nods.

I wonder if he came here yesterday or today. Don't worry, there's something I want to see him about. It's no good lying for him. Will you please tell me the truth?
MATSUKAZE: He was here a moment ago. But he's gone to Sonezaki saying that he had something urgent to attend to.
MORIEMON: What? Gone to Sonezaki! Damn it! I am one step behind! In that case I must set off for Sonezaki now. But before that, I have another question to ask. Sometime around the Boys' Festival in May or after that, well it's only sixth of June today, anyway, during that period did he use a lot of silver to pay here? Would you please answer me honestly?
MATSUKAZE [*offended by MORIRMON's insensitive question*]: I'm afraid I have no idea! We courtesans don't deal with money. Please ask the procuress of the house about it. [*She quickly goes back to her room and closes the door with a slam.*]
MORIEMON: Oh, I beg your pardon . . . Well, once I find Yohei, all will be revealed. I know the way to Sonezaki all right. Shall I take a run to Sonezaki then? (*MORIEMON tucks up the hem of his kimono and runs back towards the East Gate at full speed.*)

Blackout.

SCENE TWO
At Sonezaki

The same day of the previous scene.
The street of the Sonezaki Pleasure Quarter in the north of Osaka. The Corbicula River runs behind the buildings of ageya.
The Tennōji-ya Brothel, where KOGIKU lives, is seen upstage centre towards left. A house lantern, on which the name of 'the Tennōji-ya'[3] is written, is hung in front of the brothel. A couple of shōgi benches are put out on the right side f the building by the river.

「女殺油地獄」

森右衛門　（松風に会釈して）備前屋の松風殿か。河内屋与兵衛と深い仲と噂に聞いております。

　　　　　松風、会釈を返して頷く。

　昨日か今日、与兵衛はここに来ませぬか。安心されよ。ちと用事があって尋ねる者だ。隠されては与兵衛のためになりませぬ。本当の事を言って下さらんか。
松風　与兵衛様でしたら、少し前にお越しになって、どうでもこれからすぐに曽根崎まで行かねばならぬ用があると言ってお出になりました。
森右衛門　何と、曽根崎へ！しまった、一足遅かったか！それなら、私も曽根崎へ行かねばなるまい。ついでにもう一つお尋ねしたい。五月の節句の前か後か、六月に入ってから今日はまだ六日だが、とにかくその間に与兵衛がこちらでの支払いに銀をたくさん遣ったことはございませんか。これもどうか隠さず言って下さらぬか。
松風　（無粋な問いに気を悪くして）さあ、どうですか。お金のことは私には分かりません。どうか、遣り手にお尋ね下さい。（言い残して、すぐに局に入り戸口をぴしゃりと閉める。）
森右衛門　これは失礼致した……。まあ、それも、与兵衛に会えば分かること。曽根崎なら道もよく知っている。これから、一っ走りするか。（尻からげして、大急ぎでもと来た東口の方角に走出す。）

　　　　　暗転。

（二）　曽根崎の場

同日。
大阪北の廓、曽根崎新地の道筋。揚屋の家々の後ろを蜆川が流れている。

　舞台中央奥、上手よりに小菊のいる女郎屋天王寺屋があり、女郎屋の前に「天王寺屋」と書かれた門行灯[3]がかかっている。天王寺屋の下手側に床机が置かれている。

THE MAID of the Tennōji-ya is sweeping in front of the building.

CHORUS: (From a popular song "In Love")
'The night I wait for you is nay, nay, nay.
The west, the east, the south, in none of those directions must you go.
You must come to the north of Osaka where I wait for you through the night.'

Look over there, Yohei is coming; he comes in running.
Leaving his flower in Shin-machi, the murderer rushes to Sonezaki, desperate to see Kogiku, his other darling courtesan.
He's one of the familiar faces in this corner of the pleasure town.
Even the dogs on the streets do know him.

YOHEI comes from the hanamichi briskly. THE MAID notices him and goes in the building of the Tennōji-ya to inform KAME of his arrival.

KAME [*coming out of the Tennōji-ya with a pleasant smile*]: Oh, why, Yohei-sama, welcome home. I say to the client who comes here occasionally, "You're very welcome." But Yohei-sama, you are a frequenter and our place is like your home, so I say, "Welcome home," for a change. [*To THE MAID*] Call Kogiku-sama here, will you? [*To YOHEI*] We're terribly sorry about this, but at the moment all the rooms both upstairs and downstairs are occupied. Why don't you sit on the shōgi by the river and start today like a carpenters' drinking party? Now, now, please come this way . . .

KAME takes YOHEI to the shōgi by the Corbicula River and makes him sit down on it. THE MAID brings a tray of sake and side dishes and places it on the shōgi. KOGIKU comes out of the house led by KAMURO OF SONEZAKI by the hand.

KAME [*beckoning KOGIKU*]: Kogiku-sama, we are here, come this way.

KOGIKU goes to the shōgi led by KAMURO OF SONEZAKI and sits next to YOHEI with the sake tray between them.

KAME [*to THE MAID*]: Pour some oil in the lantern, will you? [*Remembering*] Oh, about the oil, I've heard that Takeshima Kōzaemon's Theatre is staging a play based on the recent

「女殺油地獄」

　　　　　　今、天王寺屋の下女が店の前を掃き清めている。

コーラス　（唄）［流行歌「思やこそ」より］
　　君を待つ夜は　よやよやよ
　　西も　東も　南も　嫌よ
　　とかく　待つ夜は　来た（北）が良い

　　ホレホレ、与兵衛が来る　小走りでやって来る
　　新町の花　後にして　曽根崎の別花　小菊に会いたい一心で
　　あの人殺しが　大急ぎで走って来る
　　花街のこのあたりでは知れた顔
　　通りの犬さえお馴染みさん

　　　　　　花道から与兵衛が急ぎ足でやって来る。店の前を掃いていた天王寺屋の
　　　　　下女が、与兵衛の来たのを家の中に知らせに入る。

かめ　（天王寺屋から出てきて、愛想よく）まあまあ、与兵衛様、御帰りなさいませ。
　　たまに来られるお客には「ようお出でなさいました。」と言いますけれど、与兵衛
　　様はお馴染み様で、ここがあなたの家のようなものですから、ちょっと趣向を変
　　えて「御帰りなさいませ」でお迎えしました。（下女に）小菊様をここへ。（与兵
　　衛に）すみません。中はあいにく一階も二階も座敷が塞がっております。まずは、
　　この川端の床几で大工酒盛りのようにお酒を飲んで始めてくだしゃんせ。さあさ
　　あこちらへ……。

　　　　　　かめは与兵衛を川の傍に置かれた床几の所へ連れて行って座らせる。下
　　　　　女が酒、肴の乗った盆を持って来て、床几に置く。小菊が禿に手を引かれ
　　　　　て家の中から出てくる。

かめ　（小菊を手まねきして）小菊様。さあさあ、こちらへ。

　　　　　　小菊は禿に手を引かれて床几の所に来て、酒の盆を挟んで座る。

かめ　（下女に）行灯に油を注いでおくれ。（思い出して）そうそう、油ついでに……、
　　この間あった油屋の女房殺しを酒屋に変えて竹島幸左衛門座で上演しているそう

155

murder of the wife of an oil shop. They've altered the oil shop to a liquor shop, and Sagawa Bunzō, who's well known for a villain's part, is taking the role of the murderer. There is much talk of Bunzō looking awfully fearsome. Have you seen the play, Yohei-sama? If you haven't, why don't you take Kogiku-sama to go with you? [*Noticing that sake cups are not on the tray*] Oh, dear, there's no sake cup on the tray . . . Anyone, quickly . . . bring a sake cup to Yohei-sama . . .

> THE MAID *brings a sake cup and hands it to* KAMURO OF SONEZAKI *who hands it to* KOGIKU. *Then* KOGIKU *gives it to* YOHEI *and starts pouring sake for him.*

YOHEI [*stopping* KAME *who is about to go on talking*]: Hey, hey, Widow! I think you've talked enough! It's my turn now! I've never had sake in such a messy place as this all my life. Though, it's all right for today. Oh, yes, I've got a good idea! Why don't you rent the house next door and build a special room for me. I'll pay for the timber, the carpenter and all the other expenses. Are you surprised? I'm really something, aren't I? What's this? Dear me, what's happened here! Who the hell's managed to slice up fish paste as thin as this . . . [*After his bluster,* YOHEI *swigs sake.*]

> KAME *goes in the house.*
> Served sake by KOGIKU, YOHEI *is content, enjoying drinking.*
> YAGORŌ *comes from the hanamichi hastily; he soon finds* YOHEI *and runs up to him.*

YAGORŌ: Oh, good! Yohei, you're here! I've got something to tell you . . . [*sitting next to* YOHEI] a samurai is looking for you.
YOHEI [*startled*]: What? A samurai is looking for me? What does he look like? [*All of a sudden he is panicked and looks around restlessly.*]
YAGORŌ: Why the hell are you looking around in a panic? Calm down. They say that he came to stay with your big brother yesterday.
YOHEI [*relieved*]: Goodness! You frightened me to death. It's my uncle Moriemon from Takatsuki. [*To himself*] But if he finds me now, things will get really troublesome. I must find a good excuse and leave here as soon as possible . . . [*Brooding while looking around and hitting on a good idea*] Oh dear...goodness! I remembered something very important. . . I left my purse in Shin-machi. There's a lot of money in it . . . I must run and fetch it. Brush! You must come with me!

「女殺油地獄」

でございますよ。殺し手はあの悪役で名高い佐川文蔵が扮しているとか。それはそれは憎らしいとの評判です。与兵衛様はまだご覧になっておられませんか。小菊様をお連れしてちょっと見に行かれてはどうですか。（杯が出ていないことに気付いて）あれ、お杯がまだ……、ちょっと、誰か、早うお杯をお持ちして……。

　　　　　下女、内から杯を持って来て禿に渡す。禿がそれを小菊に渡し、小菊が
　　　　　与兵衛に持たせて酌を始める。

与兵衛　（まだ喋ろうとするかめを止めて）おいおい、後家！ちょっと慎め！わしにももの言わせてくれんか。生まれてこの方こんなむさ苦しいところで酒飲んだことないぞ。まあ、今日はええことにするが。そうや、東隣の家を借り足して、一つこの与兵衛用の座敷を作ってくれ。材木、大工、諸々のお金は全部わしが出す。どや、たいしたもんやろ。何や、しみったれた、この蒲鉾の薄い切りようはどや……。（大口をたたいてから、酒のがぶ飲みをする。）

　　　　　かめは家の中に入る。
　　　　　与兵衛は好きな小菊に酌をしてもらって、悦に行って酒を飲んでいる。
　　　　　刷毛の弥五郎が花道から急ぎ足でやって来る。すぐに与兵衛を見つけて
　　　　　駆け寄る。

刷毛の弥五郎　与兵衛、ここに居たのか。お前に知らせることがあって来たんや……。
　（与兵衛の隣に座りながら）お前のことをお侍が探してる。
与兵衛　（ビクッとして）えっ！わしを？で、どんな侍じゃ？（急にうろたえて目をキョロキョロさせる。）
弥五郎　何をキョロキョロしてる。落ち着け！昨日からお前の兄さんの所へ来ている侍やそうや。
与兵衛　（安堵して）ああ、びっくりした。そりゃ、高槻の伯父の森右衛門や。（独白）けど、会うては厄介なことになる。なんぞ口実作って早うこの席外したいが……（辺りを見回しながら考え、良い口実を思いついて）あああ……大変なことを思い出した！新町に紙入れ忘れてきた。中に唸るほど金入ってるんや……。一っ走り行って取ってこう。刷毛、お前も来い！

157

KOGIKU [*stopping YOHEI*]: Come, come, Yohei-sama, why do you make such a fuss? Since you know where you've left your purse, you can go for it tomorrow.

YOHEI: No, no, I can't leave my purse. [*Smoothing over*] . . . see, I can't spend a good time with you when the bosom of my kimono is so light.

> *YOHEI ignores KOGIKU who tries to stop him and hastily goes off to stage right with YAGORŌ. KOGIKU sees them off and goes into the house. KAMURO OF SO-NEZAKI follows her.*
>
> *Before long, less than the time for a few sips of tea, MORIEMON comes from the hanamichi. He sees the house lantern of 'the Tennōji-ya' and goes straight to the Tennōji-ya.*

MORIEMON [*to the inner part of the house*]: Hello! Excuse me, please. I would like to see the procuress of this house. Will you please come here? I'm after Kawachi-ya Yohei. Is he upstairs or downstairs? Please excuse me, but I'm entering the house. [*He goes inside.*]

KAME [*off-stage, in the house*]: Come, come, O-samurai-sama. Yohei-sama's just gone. He said that he had left his purse in Shin-machi . . .

MORIEMON [*off-stage, in the house*]: What? He's gone! [*He comes out of the house.*]

KAME [*coming out after MORIEMON*]: I think . . . he should be still this side of the Umeda Bridge.

MORIEMON: Damn! Once again I am one step behind! Well, now then Procuress, will you please do me a favour? Will you send someone to Kawachi-ya Tokubei of Motoden-ma-machi immediately if our Yohei comes back here tomorrow? And please try to keep him here by serving sake or something till we come. Just a moment ago, on the way here, I dropped by Sakurai-ya Genbei's restaurant. They told me that Yohei paid them three *ryō*-gold coins and eight hundred *sen*-coppers on the night of the fourth of May. I would like to know how much he paid you. It's no good hiding it. You must tell me the truth.

KAME: Yohei-sama came and paid us three ryō-gold coins and ten hundred *sen*-coppers, too, on the same night.

MORIEMON: Do you remember what he was wearing then?

KAME: He was wearing a lined wide-sleeved cotton kimono . . . I think it was light indigo blue . . . but I'm not so sure . . .

MORIEMON: Thank you very much. You've been very helpful. Please go back to the house.

> *MORIEMON goes off the hanamichi to Shin-machi.*

Blackout.

「女殺油地獄」

小菊 （与兵衛を止めて）何を騒々しいこと。有り場所の分かっている紙入れ。明日にでも取りに行けば良いではないか。
与兵衛 いや、そうもゆかん。（取りつくろって）……懐が軽いとお前とゆっくり遊ぶことも出来んやないか。

　　　　与兵衛は小菊が引き止めるのを振り払い、刷毛の弥五郎と共に急ぎ早に下手に去る。与兵衛を見送った後、小菊は家の中に入る。禿がその後に付いて家の中に入る。
　　　　熱いお茶を四、五服飲むほどの間も置かず、与兵衛を追う森右衛門が花道から来る。天王寺屋の屋号のかかれた門行灯を見て、真直ぐに店に向かう。

森右衛門 （天王寺屋の中に向かって）おかみにお会いしたい。ここへ出てきてくれぬか。河内屋与兵衛の後を追って参った。二階に居るのか、下座敷か？通らせてもらうぞ。（天王寺屋の中に入る。）
かめの声 これこれ、お侍様。与兵衛様は新町に紙入れを忘れたと言われて、たった今お帰りになりました……。
森右衛門の声 何だと！帰った！（店から出て来る。）
かめ （森右衛門の後から出て来て）まだ、梅田橋を越すか越さないくらいで……。

森右衛門 しまった！また、後手に回った！それなら、すまぬが、明日にでも与兵衛が来たら、酒でも飲ませてここに引きとめ、すぐに本天満町の河内屋徳兵衛の所まで必ず知らせるよう頼む。たった今、来がけに与兵衛の行き付けの茶屋桜井屋源兵衛の所に立ち寄り問い合わせたところ、五月四日の夜、金三両と銭を八百目受け取ったという。こちらにはいくら支払ったか教えて欲しい。隠してはお前方の為にはならぬ。有りのままに申せ。

かめ 私の方でも五月四日の夜に入って、金三両、それと銭を一貫目払われました。

森右衛門 それで、その時、与兵衛は何を着て参った？
かめ 広袖の木綿の袷で……色は確か薄い藍色だった……と思いますが、はっきりとは覚えておりませぬ。
森右衛門 そうか。分かった。もうよいから店に戻ってくれ。

　　　　森右衛門は花道を新町へと引き返して行く。

　　　　暗転。

SCENE THREE
At the Teshima-ya

The eve of the thirty-fifth day of the death of KICHI.[4]
The stage setting is the same as the Teshima-ya oil shop in PART ONE of ACT THREE. But a new altar[5] *for KICHI is added in the living room. A small vase full of flowers and a bowl with burning incense sticks are placed besides the altar.*
The fellow believers of the True Pure Land Sect are holding a memorial service for KICHI and saying prayers for the dead.

FELLOW BELIEVERS: (From the prayer for the dead) We pray to Buddha for transforming her from a woman to a man; a woman vowed to pass away peacefully.[6] Ganishi kudoku byōdō se issai, Dōhotsu bodaishin ōjō anraku-koku shaku-no myōi. Here is the prayer on the eve of the thirty-fifth day of the dead.

THE FELLOW BELIEVERS finish the prayers for the dead. The eldest believer among them, the paper merchant GORŌKURŌ, turns around to SHICHIZAEMON.

GORŌKURŌ [*to SHICHIZAEMON*]: We feel that it happened only a couple of days ago, but time has passed very fast and tonight is already the eve of a memorial service for the thirty-fifth day of the death of O-Kichi-dono. Her life ended at the age of twenty-seven due to an unexpected misfortune. However, she was extremely good-natured, more than anyone else; and always acted out of gratitude to Saint Shinran, the founder of the True Pure Land Sect. Regrettably in this world she was sent to her death by a sword, but I'm certain that O-Kichi-dono will be spared from all hardships and given an easy and peaceful death in the other world. That was her long cherished wish and the Original Vow of Amida. You should be pious ever more, read Buddha's mind and take the death of O-Kichi-dono as his guidance. Don't be misled by worldly things and every time you pray, do so from the bottom of your heart. Try not to grieve over the death of your wife. Is that all right with you, Shichizaemon-dono? The murderer will soon be caught. At the moment the most important thing for you is to look after your daughters. I'm sure that O-Kichi-dono wants the same in the other world.

SHICHIZAEMON [*moved by GORŌKURŌ's compassionate words and in tears*]: I think so, too. I try to forget Kichi's misfortune and to take it as Amida's guidance. Every day I try to be more pious and repeat my prayers in gratitude. But Den, my youngest daughter, was only two and still wants her mother's milk. It was too pitiful to leave her without a

「女殺油地獄」

（三）豊島屋の場

　吉の三十五日のお逮夜[4]。
　下の巻の（一）豊島屋の場と同じ舞台装置。座敷にはお吉の新しい仏壇[5]が置かれている。仏壇のそばに花が飾られ、線香が焚かれている。
　今、お吉の仏壇に向かい、信者の長老の帳紙屋五郎九郎を中心に浄土真宗の信者仲間が死者の三十五日のお逮夜の供養の読経をしている。

信者仲間　〔回向文〕変成男子の願[6]を立て　女人成仏誓いたり　願以此功徳平等　施一切、　同発菩提心往生安楽国　釈　妙意　三十五日のお逮夜の志。

　　　　　信者一同、経を終える。信者仲間の長老帳紙屋五郎九郎が七左衛門のほうに向き直る。他の信者も同様に七左衛門のほうに向き直る。

帳紙屋五郎九郎　（七左衛門に）昨日今日の事のように思われましたが、早くも三十五日の法事のお逮夜になりました。二十七歳を一生として思いがけない災難による死に方をされたが、ふだんの気立ての良さは人に勝り、宗祖親鸞上人の御恩徳に対する報恩の心も深かったお吉殿のこと、この世でこそ剣難の苦しみはあったが、来世では数々の業苦を逃れて、本願通りの衆生済度、極楽往生は疑いのないことと思われます。仏のご催心に目覚めて一層信心をあつくし、この度のお吉殿の死を仏の導きと考えて、世俗のことにあくせく迷わず一度の念仏も心からお唱えなされ。決してお嘆きなされませんように、な、七左殿。殺し手もそのうちに分かるでしょう。今は何よりも娘さんの世話が第一。亡くなられたお吉殿もそうしてもらいたいと思われておられることでしょう。

七左衛門　（気遣いに有難く涙を浮かべて）まことにその通りでございましょう。お吉の不幸は忘れて、これも如来様の御導きと、日々信心を深くして仏のお示しと繰り返し喜び、お称名を欠かさぬよう心がけております。けれども末のおでんはまだ二歳。乳がのうては、と不憫に思い、お吉が殺された翌日にお金を付けて他所

mother; so on the day after the incident I sent her away with some money to be fostered. Kinu, the eldest daughter, understood her mother's death when I talked to her. But then she stays by her mother's altar all the time and keeps the incense and flowers for Kichi. The middle one is the worst, though. She cries for her mother from morning till night every day. I don't know what to do with her. [*He hides his face from the others by turning to the wall behind him and sobbing secretly.*]

FELLOW BELIEVERS [*crying in sympathy*]: No one can blame her. Any child would be like that.

At this moment a mouse runs across the beams of the ceiling and drops sooty dust. A piece of old paper drops off the beam with the dust. Soon the mouse is quiet.

FELLOW BELIEVERS: Look over there, Shichizaemon-dono! Something's just fallen from the beam.

SHICHIZAEMON: Indeed . . . I wonder what it is. [*Picking up the paper and looking at it*] What? It says, "Number one . . . ten *monme* and fifteen in silver . . . each one's share for Nozaki visit. . . date: the first of May" [*He sends the paper around the fellow believers.*]

BELIEVER 1 [*receiving and examining the paper*]: This looks like an invoice from someone to someone else . . . [*Handing it to BELIEVER 2*]

BELIEVER 2 [*receiving and examining the paper*]: There are blots like bloodstains here and there on the paper . . . [*Handing it to BELIEVER 3*]

BELIEVER 3 [*receiving and examining the paper*]: This is a strange article. [*Handing it to BELIEVER 4*]

BELIEVER 4 [*receiving and examining the paper*]: Indeed, it is. [*Handing it to BELIEVER 5*]

BELIEVER 5 [*receiving and examining the paper*]: I think I may have seen the handwriting on the paper somewhere. [*Handing the paper back to BELIEVER 4*]

BELIEVER 4 [*receiving and re-examining the paper*]: I think, I've seen it somewhere, too. [*Handing the paper back to BELIEVER 3*]

BELIEVER 3 [*receiving and re-examining the paper*]: Goodness! I think this is Kawachi-ya Yohei's handwriting. [*Handing the paper back to BELIEVER 2 and 1*]

BELIEVER 2 & 1 [*receiving and re-examining the paper together*]: You're right. We think so, too. It's Yohei's. [*Handing back the paper to SHICHIZAEMON*]

SHICHIZAEMON [*examining the paper again*]: Indeed! This is Yohei's handwriting! We visited the Nozaki Kannon on the eleventh of April. O-Kichi told me that Yohei and his friends, Zenbei the Vermilion and Yagorō the Brush, were also visiting Nozaki on the same day. This bloodstained paper must be the invoice for each one's expenses on that

「女殺油地獄」

に貰うてもらいました。上の娘のお絹はよく言い聞かせると納得して、香花(こうはな)の切れないよう仏壇についてばかりいます。が、中娘めが朝から晩まで母様母様と言って泣きよります。これには困りました。（泣き顔を見られないようさっと後ろの壁に顔を背けて、声を殺してすすり泣く。）

信者仲間　（貰い泣きして）いかにも、そうでありましょう。無理もない。

　　　　　天井の桁(けた)や梁(はり)をネズミが走り、煤(すす)まみれの埃(ほこり)を蹴(け)散らす。この時、何か書き付けてある古い紙が埃と一緒に落ちる。その後、すぐにネズミは静かになる。

信者仲間　七左殿、それ、そこに何か落ちてきました。

七左衛門　ほんに、これは……。（落ちてきた紙を拾い上げて見る。）何……？「一、銀十匁一分五厘　野崎の割り当て　五月一日」と書いてある。（紙を仲間衆に回す。）

信者仲間1　（紙を受け取り）これは、誰から誰への宛名のない請求書……。（紙を信者仲間2に渡す。）
信者仲間2　（紙を受け取り）何やら所々血に汚れたような……。（紙を信者仲間3に渡す。）
信者仲間3　（紙を受け取り）不思議な物。（紙を信者仲間4に渡す。）
信者仲間4　（紙を受け取り）ほんに、不思議な物。（紙を信者仲間5に渡す。）
信者仲間5　（紙を受け取り）これは何処かで見たことのある筆跡(ひっせき)だが。（紙を信者仲間4に渡す。）
信者仲間4　（再び紙を見て）私もどうやら見覚えのある手。（紙を信者仲間3に渡す。）
信者仲間3　（再び紙を見て）ああっ！これは河内屋の与兵衛の手！（紙を信者仲間2＋1に渡す。）
信者仲間2＋1　（再び紙を見て）ほんに、そうや。与兵衛の筆跡。（紙を七左衛門に渡す。）
七左衛門　（再び紙を見て）ほんに！与兵衛の手だ！四月十一日に私ら夫婦が野崎参りをいたしました日、皆朱の善兵衛、刷毛の五郎、河内屋与兵衛も三人連れで参詣していたと死んだお吉が話していた。この血に汚れた請求書はその時の費用の割り当て。お吉殺した犯人も、ほぼこれで分かりました。三十五日のお逮夜に見事

day. Now, I think I know who murdered Kichi. A mouse dropped this on the eve of the thirty-fifth day of Kichi's death. It must be a message from the dead to tell me who murdered her. Thanks to merciful Buddha! May Kichi's soul rest in peace! Namu Amidabutsu . . . [*SHICHIZAEMON prostrates himself before the altar with joy.*]

> *All THE FELLOW BELIEVERS thank and pray to Buddha.*
> *YOHEI enters from the hanamichi.*

YOHEI: Tonight is the eve of the thirty-fifth day of Kichi's death. I hate to go in that shop but I must. Once I attend the service, people should stop talking of me as her killer. . . [*He goes to the Teshima-ya and enters with an innocent look, more than ever arrogant.*] Good evening everyone. It's Kawachi-ya Yohei here. Time has flown and tonight is already the eve of the thirty-fifth day of the death of O-Kichi-sama. I came to attend her memorial service. I'm so sorry to hear that they haven't caught her murderer yet. But I'm sure everything will be sorted out before long.

SHICHIZAEMON [*extremely agitated as YOHEI has suddenly turned up, he tucks up the hem of his kimono and grabs a long pole kept on the lintel for self protection.*]: Oi! Yohei! How dare you, you murdered my wife! Did you come here to be caught? You won't be able to run away any more! [*He raises the pole over his head aiming at YOHEI.*]

YOHEI: Come, come, Shichizaemon-dono. Please don't be reckless. Where's the proof that says I've done it?

SHICHIZAEMON: Shut up! Here I have the note of the invoice of 'ten *monme* and fifteen in silver, each one's share for Nozaki visit.' It's in your handwriting. Moreover it is smeared with blood. Do you need any more proof than this? Dear fellow believers, please catch this man!

> *SHICHIZAEMON raises the pole to YOHEI. THE FELLOW BELIEVERS surround YOHEI.*

YOHEI [*flinching for a second but pretending to be calm*]: It's a big world and there must be similar handwriting to mine. Also the expenses for the Nozaki visit were all on me. I don't know anything about the note or the invoice.

> *SHICHIZAEMON throws the pole over YOHEI, but YOHEI sweeps him aside.*

にネズミがこれを落とすというのも死者の知らせに違いない。これも仏の御慈悲……。南無阿弥陀仏。(有難さに仏に平伏し、喜ぶ。)

　　　　　信者仲間も仏に祈る。
　　　　　与兵衛が花道からやって来る。

与兵衛　今夜はお吉の三十五日のお逮夜。あの豊島屋に入って行くのもぞっとしないが、今夜顔を出しておくのは、自分が殺したと人に言われないため……。(豊島屋まで来て、何食わぬ顔をして、一段と横柄な態度ですっと店の中に入る。)河内屋の与兵衛です。お吉様のお参りに上がりました。早いもので今夜はもうお吉様の三十五日のお逮夜でございますなあ。殺した奴もまだ知れず、まことに御気の毒なことでございます。けれど、それもすぐに分かりましょう。

七左衛門　(突然の与兵衛の姿に、とっさに尻からげをして、長押から寄り棒を取り)おい、与兵衛！女房お吉をようも殺したな！お前はここへ縛られに来たのか！逃げようと思っても逃げられんぞ！(寄り棒を与兵衛に向かって振り上げる。)

与兵衛　まあまあ、まあまあ、七左衛門殿。乱暴なことは止めて下さい。それで、俺が殺したという証拠はどこに？
七左衛門　黙れ！ここに野崎参りの割り当て、銀十匁一分五厘という書付がある。これは、お前の筆跡。それにところどころ血が付いている。これより他にまだ証拠がいるのか？仲間の皆様、どうかこいつを捕らえて下さい。

　　　　　七左衛門は与兵衛に向かって寄り棒を構える。信者仲間の衆は与兵衛を取り囲む。

与兵衛　(一瞬たじろぐが、平静を装って)この広い世の中に似た筆跡の人がないわけでもなし。それに野崎参りの出費はみんな俺の奢りです。割り当ても何もそんなことは知りまへん。

　　　　　七左衛門は与兵衛に打ってかかろうとするが、与兵衛がその寄り棒を払う。

Stop doing things unbecoming to your age! You fool! [*Also intimidating THE FELLOW BELIEVERS*] Well, you lot are the same, what the hell have you been doing, getting excited and surrounding me?

SHICHIZAEMON and THE FELLOW BELIEVERS try to catch YOHEI, saying things such as "Take this!" or "You murderer!" But YOHEI is used to fighting, and so they are thrown, kicked or stamped on by him instead. YOHEI takes the pole from SHICHIZAEMON and gives a full swing with it. THE FELLOW BELIEVERS retreat in fear. YOHEI tries to run away during this. But THE FELLOW BELIEVERS come back and quickly encircle him, saying, "Catch him! Don't lose him!" The chase continues in the small shop.

Soon after YOHEI enters the Teshima-ya, led by MORIEMON, THE TOWN MAGISTRATE, THE TOWN MAGISTRATE'S Men and THE TOWN MEGISTRATE'S MEN come through the hanamichi. TAHEI comes after them carrying the kimono that YOHEI wore on the fourth of May. They come to the Teshima-ya and stand outside for a while to watch the events inside.

Finally YOHEI escapes from the chase and slips out of the shop.
THE MAGISTRATE'S MEN surround YOHEI. One of THE MEN seizes YOHEI by the kimono lapels, saying, "You aren't going anywhere! You're caught."

MORIEMON: The town magistrate and his people have been standing here and listening to the conversation inside for some time. Don't give any more unmanly excuses. You can neither hide nor run away. Rumour has it that it was your work. Nine out of ten people in the town think so. Have you ever considered how I have been taking this as your uncle? If it were at all possible, I wanted to let you run away to a remote land, but if not, I wanted you to commit suicide before your evil deed would be known to the magistrate. I tried my best to prevent you from disgracing yourself any further. I went to the places in Shinmachi and Sonezaki where you usually go, to find you. But I was always one step behind. I think that your luck ran out at that point. Tahei, will you bring the lined kimono in here?

TAHEI, who has been shedding tears at the sight of his younger brother behind THE TOWN MAGISTRATE and his MEN, comes forwards with YOHEI's kimono and stands by MORIEMON.

「女殺油地獄」

ええ年して、阿呆な真似しやがるな！（仲間の衆にも凄んで）お前らまで同じように取り囲んで騒いで、何しやがる！

　　　　七左衛門と仲間の衆は「こうしてやる！」「こいつ！」などと口々に言って与兵衛に掴み掛かるが、喧嘩馴れのした与兵衛に逆に投げられたり、蹴られたり、踏み付けられたりする。与兵衛は七左衛門から寄り棒を引ったくり、力任せに一振りする。皆は「わっ！」と逃げる。与兵衛はその隙を窺って、逃げようとするが、「そりゃ、逃すな！」と、すぐにまた皆に回りを取り囲まれてしまう。狭い土間で追いかけたり追いかけられたりが続く。

　　　　与兵衛が豊島屋に入ると同時に、花道から伯父の森右衛門に案内されて、町奉行、奉行配下の与力や役人達が来る。太兵衛も五月四日に与兵衛の着ていた着物を持って一行の後から来る。一行は豊島屋まで来て、しばらくの間、店の外から中の様子を窺っている。

　　　　与兵衛が信者仲間をかわし、スルリと店の外に出て来る。
　　　　与力や役人達が与兵衛を取り囲み、役人の一人が「どっこい、捕らえた！」と与兵衛の胸倉を掴んで取り押さえる。

森右衛門　先ほどから、町奉行所の御役人の皆様方がここで家の中のことは全て聞いておられた。決して未練がましく言い逃れはするな。もう、逃げ隠れは出来ん。世間の噂では十人のうち九人までがお前の仕業だと言っている。この伯父がそれをどんな気持で聞いていたか、お前には分からんのか。お前の悪事が露見しないうちに、遠い国へ逃すか、それが出来ない時には自害を勧め、お前の恥じを隠してやろうと、新町、曽根崎と、お前の行く先々を尋ねても、後手後手になって出会えんかったのが、お前の運の尽き。太兵衛、ここへその袷を持ってきてくれぬか。

　　　　町奉行所の役人達の後で、弟の姿に涙していた太兵衛が袷の着物を持って伯父の傍に行く。

MORIEMON: This is the kimono that you wore on the night of the fourth of May. It has some smudged and hardened spots here and there, and that has aroused the town magistrate's suspicion. We are going to examine the substance on your kimono in front of the magistrate now. Look, Yohei, this is the moment of your life or death. Someone! Please bring sake here! We need sake! Please bring it to us!

> *TOWNSPEOPLE OF MOTODENMA-MACHI have been gathering and watching the events from a distance for some time. A few among them bring sake in a container or in a saucepan. One of THE MAGISTRATE'S MEN takes it and pours sake over the kimono. The substance on the kimono dissolves in sake and the blood red liquid runs down.*
> *MORIEMON and TAHEI look at each other speechless.*

YOHEI [*seeing the blood running in front of his eyes, giving in and speaking loudly*]: I led a life of debauchery throughout my life, but I hadn't stolen even a sheet of paper or half a *sen*-copper. It didn't bother me at all that the bills for restaurants and brothels were six months or one year in arrears. However, I forged my father's seal and borrowed two hundred *monme* in silver on the deed of the loan for one thousand. I had to pay it back before the end of the fourth of May otherwise my father would be in deep trouble. I couldn't bear the thought that he would be put in such a terrible position . . . [*Crying*] I was only concerned about myself and my family . . . I completely forgot about the pain and the agony of the person whom I killed. I also forgot about the trouble and the grief of her family . . . Twenty years of disobedience to my parents and wrong doing had grown into a devil in me and blinded me. I, Kawachi-ya Yohei, murdered O-Kichi-dono and stole the money in the shop . . . Namu Amidabutsu. Save us, merciful Buddha. May O-Kichi-dono's soul rest in peace! Please forgive me Amida Buddha and save my sinful soul too. Namu Amidabutsu.

> *Before YOHEI finishes his speech, THE MAGISTRATE'S MEN tie him up with a rope. THE TOWN MAGISTRATE and HIS MEN take YOHEI through the hanamichi among the big crowd.*
> *MORIEMON and TAHEI see off YOHEI in tears.*

CHORUS: Yohei forged his father's seal for a mere two hundred *monme* in silver.
Driven to the edge, he killed a good woman, Kichi, who had given him sisterly love.

「女殺油地獄」

森右衛門　この袷は五月四日の夜にお前が外に着て出たもの。所々に沁みが見え、こわばっているのを町奉行からご不審があった。今すぐお役人の前でこの沁みの痕跡の真偽を調べる。よいか、与兵衛、お前の生死の瀬戸際であるぞ。誰か、酒だ！酒！酒を持ってきて下され。

　　　　　遠巻きに取り囲むようにして見ていた町の衆が、ちろりや燗鍋に入れた酒を持って出る。役人の一人がそれを受け取り、袷に酒をサラサラとかける。袷の沁みが流れ出て酒が血の朱色に染まる。

　　　　　森右衛門と太兵衛は顔を見合わせるばかりで口が利けない。

与兵衛　（目の前で鮮血が流れるのを見て覚悟を決め、大きな声で）一生遊蕩をしてきたが、一枚の紙も半銭も、盗みということだけはしたことが無かった。茶屋や遊女屋の払いは一年や半年遅れても苦にならんかった。けど、銀二百目を借金するため、「新銀一貫目」とある証文に親父の謀判突いてしもた。未済で五月四日の一夜を過ぎると、親の難儀、逃れられんことになる。その親不孝の罪だけはもったいのうて出来んかった……。（泣いて）そう思うことばかりに目が向き、人を殺せば、殺された人、その家族の嘆き苦しみ、難儀があるのをみな忘れてしまっていた……。二十年来の親不孝や悪業の数々が人間の知恵や善性を失わせる魔王となって私の心をくらませました。お吉殿を殺して金を盗ったのはこの河内屋与兵衛でございます……。南無阿弥陀仏。阿弥陀様、どうか、迷うた罪深い私を、お吉殿をお救いされると共にお救い下さい。南無阿弥陀仏。

　　　　　役人の一人が与兵衛の言葉の終わらぬうちに、与兵衛を三寸縄に縛り上げる。人だかりが一際大きくなる中、与兵衛は花道を役人に引っ立てられて行く。
　　　　　森右衛門と太兵衛は与兵衛の後姿を涙しながら見送る。

コーラス　銀二百目のために　謀判突いて　にっちもさっちもいかんようになり
　あの優しい姉様のようなお吉様殺した与兵衛は

WOMAN-KILLER IN OIL HELL

He was executed on the grounds near the Temple of a Thousand Days.[7]
Hereafter, may the lesson that Yohei the fool learnt remain with us along with his infamous name.

Blackout.

THE END

「女殺油地獄」

千日寺[7]の近くの処刑場で　処刑されました。
そして、あの阿呆の与兵衛の残した戒めが
その悪名と一緒に　その後も　長いこと　世に残ることになりました。

　　　暗転。

　　　　　　　　　　（幕）

Woman-Killer in Oil Hell

Notes
CHARACTERS
1. The present day Fushimi-chō, Chūō ward of Osaka city
2. *ryōrijyaya* in Japanese, where clients were served drinks and meals, and entertained by courtesans.
3. An area in the present day North ward of Osaka city which used to be known as a pleasure quarter. The Corbicula River (*Shijimi-gawa*) ran across the south of the area.
4. The name of the area around Aizu Valley in Fukushima Prefecture in the northern-east region of Honshū. Aizu produces high-quality white wax for a candle.
5. *kaishu* in Japanese: red lacquered goods
6. *shiro-inari-hōin* in Japanese: *inari* is the god of the harvest and the fox is his messenger.
7. *kuchiire-ya* in Japanese; in the play KOHEI is a loan shark.
8. *kamuro* is an apprentice girl, between around six to fourteen years old, who would attend a high-ranking courtesan. Originally it meant a hair style of trimming hair to an even short length.
9. One of three licensed pleasure quarters of the Edo period (1603 – 1867). It was located on the west of the present day Shinmachi-bashi, Nishi ward of Osaka city. The other two quarters were Yoshiwara in Edo (present-day Tokyo) and Shimabara in Kyoto.
10. A tightly braided hat made of a straw, rush etc. worn to hide a face. Brothels lent out *amigasa* to their clients.
11. *Jōdoshin-shū* in Japanese: founded by Shinran (1173 – 1262), the disciple of Hōnen (1133 – 1212), the founder of *Jōdo-shū*. It preaches that the power of Amida Buddha will save our soul and give us a peaceful death through absolute piety.

ACT ONE
1. The common name of the Jigen Temple in Nozaki in present-day Daitō city of Osaka prefecture, it also refers to the Statue of Eleven-faced Kannon, the principal image of the temple.
2. An elevated walkway running from the stage to the rear of kabuki theatre through the audience: it is part of the stage and mainly used as an entrance and an exit for an actor. The main hanamichi (*hon hanamkichi*) is situated towards the stage right.

「女殺油地獄」

女殺油地獄

註
登場人物
1 現在の大阪市中央区伏見町。
2 客に酒色の遊びをさせる店。

3 曽根崎は大阪市北区の一地区。もと遊里があり南側を蜆川が流れていた。

4 福島県会津盆地を中心とする地域名。会津蝋燭は会津地方で出来る上質の蝋燭。純白で絵模様がある。
5 漆塗りの一種で全部を朱塗りにする。
6 法印は山伏や祈祷師の総称。

7 奉公人などの周旋を生業とする人や店のこと。両替屋で高利貸しでもある。
8 英語版でも kamuro とする。上級の遊女に仕えて見習いをした六、七歳から十三、四歳までの少女のことを指す。元の意は、髪を短く切りそろえて垂らした子供の髪型、その髪型の子供のこと。
9 大阪市西区新町橋の西にあった。十七世紀前半に幕府からこの土地を賜り開かれた公に許可された遊郭で、江戸の吉原、京都の島原とともに三大遊郭として栄えた。

10 英語版では an amigasa hat とする。菅、すげ、いぐさなどで編んで作った笠。遊郭で貸し出した。
11 鎌倉初期に浄土宗の開祖法然（1133－1212）の弟子の親鸞（1173－1262）が開いた浄土宗の一派。阿弥陀仏の力で救われる絶対他力を主張し、信心だけで往生できるとする。

上之巻
1 大阪府大東市野崎にある曹洞宗慈眼寺の通称。またその本尊十一面観音のこと。

2 歌舞伎の劇場で観客席を貫いた舞台と連なる道。俳優の登退場の通路、舞台の一部として用いられる。下手よりの常設のものを本花道、上手側に設けるものを仮花道という。

Occasionally the temporary hanamichi (*kari hanamichi*) is built towards the stage left.
3   A large sunshade made of reed
4   An outdoor bench without a backrest. It is also called *endai*.
5   *yakatabune* in Japanese: a river boat with a roof-shaped top. It was used to go boating on a river.
6   The principal image of the Seiganto Temple of the Nachi Mountain in Nachikatsuura of Wakayama prefecture
7   The head temple of the Shōtoku Sect of Buddhism, built by Prince Shōtoku in the early 7th century in Ikaruga-chō, Nara prefecture, the oldest existing wooden structure in the world.
8   A long sash worn with traditional Japanese kimono

9   *-san*, *-sama*, *-dono*: suffixes to indicate the speaker's or writer's politeness towards the person (See Notes No. 19&20 of ACT ONE, **Lovers' Suicides at Imamiya**)

10 Old measurement for volume: one *shō* is about 1.8 litres. (See No. 5 (3) of **Measuring System in the Edo Period**)
11 It is a travelling game. One person of the company carries the load first and when they come across a monk, the person trades off the load to another person.
12 'O' of O-Kichi is a prefix that expresses politeness; often used for the first name of a woman's or a girl's name in the Edo period.
13 *irogawari* in Japanese: a kimono dyed in a different colour around the lower back
14 (See No. 4 of **Measuring System in the Edo Period** for monetary system.)
15 *ame-zaiku* in Japanese: it has the meaning of something which appears good on the surface but has no substance.
16 *zōri* is a pair of slip-on sandals with flat soles made of a straw, a rush or a bamboo peels.
17 *kamishimo* is a set of *kataginu*, a shoulder-piece, and *hakama*, loose-legged pleated trousers, in the same colour; it was worn as formal and ceremonial attire for samurai and ceremonial attire for townspeople. (See Notes No. 13 of ACT THREE, **Drumbeats over the Horikawa**)
18 *haori* is a short coat wearing over a kimono
19 *chō* is a measurement of distance: one *chō* is about one hundred and nine meters. (See No. 5 (1) of **Measuring System in the Edo Period**)

3 　葦の茎で編んで作った日よけ。
4 　細長い板に足をつけた簡単な腰掛け。
5 　屋形船。屋根の形をした屋形をつけた船。江戸時代以降川遊びなどに用いられた。
6 　和歌山県那智勝浦町北東部にある那智山青岸渡寺の本尊のこと。
7 　奈良県生駒郡斑鳩町にある聖徳宗の総本山。聖徳太子により建てられたといわれている。一度消失するが漸次再建される。現存する世界最古の木造建築。
8 　英語版でも *obi* とする。着物の上から腰のあたりに巻いて結びつける細い布。着物を体にまとい付け、装飾も兼ねる。
9 　「－さん」、「－さま（様）」、「－どの（殿）」などは接尾語で人の名前や職業名などに付けて親愛の情や尊敬の念を表す。（「**今宮の心中**」上之巻第二場・註19と註20参照。）
10　五升入る樽。升は尺貫法の量の測り方。一升は約1.8リットル。（「**江戸時代のものの数え方**」5の（3）参照）
11　数人の同行者が坊主に出会うごとに荷物の持ち主を交替すること。
12　「お吉さま」の「お－」は接頭語で話し手、書き手の対象に対する丁寧・尊敬を表す。
13　腰のあたりのみ色変わりに染めた着物。
14　江戸時代の貨幣については（「**江戸時代のものの数え方**」4参照）。
15　竹などの管の一端に飴を付け、他方から吹いてふくらませて動物などの形に作ったもの。立派そうに見えても実体のないもの。
16　英語版でも *zōri* とする。鼻緒の付いた平底の履物。藁・藺（いぐさ）・竹皮などで編んだもの。
17　英語版でも *kamishimo* とする。肩衣（袖なしの上衣）と袴を組み合わせたもの。江戸時代、武士の公服で庶民の礼服。（「**堀川波鼓**」下の巻　註13参照）
18　英語版でも *haori* とする。長い着物の上に着る短い外衣。
19　距離の単位。（「**江戸時代のものの数え方**」5（1）参照）

ACT TWO

1. There were five *sekku*, seasonal festival days on which the important annual events were held according to the lunar calendar. They were *jinjitsu* the seventh day of January, *jōshi* the third day of March (Doll's Festival), *tango* the fifth day of May, *shichiseki* the seventh day of July and *chōyō* the ninth day of September (the Chrysanthemum Festival). The fifth of May was called *Tango-no Sekku*, the Iris Festival Day. The celebrants put up picture banners and decorated the eaves of the houses with mugwort and irises to ward off the evil spirits. They ate *chimaki*, steamed rice dumpling wrapped in bamboo leaves, and *kashiwa mochi*, steamed rice cake wrapped in an oak leaf. They also took an iris-leaf bath. In the Edo period this became the Boys' Festival Day and in samurai households armour and banners were decorated. Townspeople imitated the practice and decorated warrior dolls. At present the festival is known as Children's Day and a national holiday.
2. A large shop curtain on which often the shop name or logo is dyed. *Kanji* (Chinese characters) of Kawachi-ya is 河内屋. It is hung outside a restaurant or shop to indicate that it is open for business. *Noren* is also used as a dividing curtain for rooms.
3. A mattress made of straws covered in rush facing. In general the length of *tatami* is one *ken* and its width half a *ken*. One *ken* is about 1.8 meters. *Tatami* is placed on the floor of a Japanese room.
4. It is a sliding door with timber frame and paper or cloth screen used as a room partition.
5. A folding screen
6. People gave twelve *sen*-coppers when they made an offer of money to a shrine. The name of the group derives from this.
7. *hannya-shingyo* in Japanese: the sutra of Mahayana
8. It is the group of the believers of the mountain asceticism. They make a visit to the peaks of the Kinpusen in Yoshino of Nara prefecture, where the Great Ascetic En is worshiped as the principal image of the sacred mountain.
9. The present day Kawazu-cho, Higashi-Sumiyoshi ward of Osaka city
10. The ascetic who trained in the Katsuragi Mountain in Nara around the seventh or the eighth century: the founder of mountain mysticism.
11. The present day Minami-Senba, Chūō ward in Osaka city
12. The merchants settled all the accounts for sales and purchases before *bon* (15th of July), *kure* (at the end of year) and *sekku* in the Edo period. *Sekki* is a terminal settlement day and the deadline for the settlement.

「女殺油地獄」

中之巻

1 陰暦では年に五つ節句、人日（1月7日）、上巳（3月3日　桃の節句）、端午（5月5日　端午の節句）、七夕（7月7日）、重陽（9月9日）があった。端午の節句には鐘馗や武者などの絵が描かれた絵幟がたてられ、古くは菖蒲や蓬を軒にさして邪気を払う風があった。江戸時代以降、男子の節句とされ、武家で甲冑、幟を飾ったのに倣い町人も武者人形などを飾り、鯉のぼりをたてるようになった。また、粽、柏餅などを食べ、菖蒲湯を立てた。現在は「こどもの日」として国民の休日。

2 商店で屋号などを染め抜いて店先に掲げる布。また、部屋の入り口や仕切にたらす短い布。ここでは「河内屋」と染めてある。英語版でも *noren* とする。

3 畳の敷かれた部屋。英語版では *tatami-matted* とした。

4 英語版では a *fusuma* sliding door とする。

5 英語版では a *byōbu* screen とする。
6 普通賽銭が十二銭だったところから、十二の銅でこの名前をつけた。

7 般若心経。大乗仏教の経典。般若経の精要を説く。
8 奈良県吉野の金峰山にある蔵王権現（円の行者の尊像）に参詣する信者の組合。

9 現在の大阪市東住吉区桑津町。
10 奈良時代の人。修験道の祖。

11 現在の大阪市中央区南船場。
12 商店が仕入れ、売り上げ、貸借関係の総勘定、清算を行った時期。江戸時代は盆、暮、節句の前などが節季であった。

13 A samurai form of suicide involving ritual disembodiment. From around the twelfth century it was regarded as an honourable death for samurai.
14 Following the development of commerce, merchants and craftsmen in the same trade formed a union and granted licenses in order to monopolise their trade. The Tokugawa government put tax on it under the name of offertory while giving official protection.
15 Present-day Tokyo: Tokugawa Ieyasu (1542-1616) opened *bakufu* the central government in Edo in 1603. From then to 1867, *bakufu* was located in Edo. In 1868 it was named Tokyo.
16 Since the arrival of the Portuguese in 1571, Nagasaki developed as the port for international trade; it was the only place kept open during the period of national isolation. It is located in the north of Kyūshū which is far away from Osaka.
17 *Yakushi nyorai* in Japanese: Bhaisajyaguru (Skr.), the healing Buddha
18 *Amida butsu* in Japanese: Amitabha (Skr.), infinite light
19 *Sekkyō jōruri* in Japanese: a style of narrative prevailing from the end of the middle ages to the early-modern times. It was derived from a Buddhist sermon.
20 To join the Nichiren Sect for one hundred days in the hope that disease would be cured by making a vow to Nisshin. Hokke sect is a different name of the Nichiren Sect, *Nichiren-shū* in Japanese, and was founded by Nichiren (1222-1282). The Nichiren Sect and the Pure Land Sect were opposed to each other.
21 Nisshin (1407-88) is a priest of the Nichiren Sect.
22 *Jyōdo-shū* in Japanese: One of the schools of the national Buddhism. Founded by Honen (1133-1212). It preaches salvation by faith and a peaceful death in the Pure Land of Unending Delight, the Buddhist Paradise.
23 A measurement of length: one *ken* is 1.8 meters, which is the same as the length of one *tatami*. (See No. 5 (1) of **Measuring System in the Edo Period**)
24 *goningumi* in Japanese: a five-household neighhourhood unit. A neighbourhood watch system for the peasants and the townspeople created by the Tokugawa government: one unit consisting of five households had collective responsibility for fire or crimes in their neighbourhood. The senior townsmen undertook civil administration of the area where they lived under the town magistrate.

ACT THREE
PART ONE
1 *kanji* (Chinese characters) of Teshima-ya is 豊島屋.
2 *suki-abura* in Japanese: combing wax made of sesame oil, Japanese wax and per-

「女殺油地獄」

13　英語版では hara-kiri とする。

14　江戸時代に商人・職人らが共同の利益を確保するために結合した同業組合。初めは私的なものであったが幕府や諸藩は冥加金(みょうがきん)を取り立て、これを保護公認した。

15　現在の東京の旧名。1603 年に徳川家康が幕府を開いた。1868 年に東京と改名される。

16　1571 年にポルトガル船が寄港して以来、貿易港として発展した。江戸時代は国内唯一の開港場であった。

17　東方浄瑠璃世界の教主。病気を治す力を持つ。

18　西方の極楽世界を主宰するという仏。

19　中世末から近世に行われた語り物のひとつで、仏教の説教から発する。大道芸、門付芸として発達する。

20　他宗の者が病の治癒などを祈るために一時的に法華宗信者になること。法華宗は日蓮宗の俗称で、日蓮(にちれん)（1222 〜 1282）によって開かれた。

21　日親（1407 〜 1488）は日蓮宗の僧。

22　日本の国仏教の一派で法然(ほうねん)（1133 〜 1212）を開祖とする。自力教を排して、他力念仏によって極楽浄土に往生することを目的とする。日蓮宗とは犬猿の仲であった。

23　長さの単位。一間は 1.8 メートル。（「**江戸時代のものの数え方**」5（1）参照）

24　江戸幕府が百姓や町々の地主・家主に命じて作らせた隣保組織。近所の五戸を一組として、火災や犯罪などの連帯責任を負わせたもの。町役人の年寄りは町奉行の指揮を受けつつ民政に携わった。

下之巻
その一
1　暖簾(のれん)に「豊島屋(てしまや)」と染めてあるもの。
2　髪を梳くときに用いる練り油。胡麻油に生蝋(きろう)を加え香料を加えたもの。

fume

3   *tomoshi-abura* in Japanese: rapeseed oil was much used.
4   *baika-abura* in Japanese: oil fragranced with a plum flower, a clove and a white sandalwood etc.
5   The footwear of the Edo period was mainly *geta* (wooden clogs) and *zōri* (see Notes No. 16 of ACT ONE). It was customary to wash the feet in the entrance hall before stepping into the living area of the house after a long walk.
6   New silver valued more than old silver. When someone borrowed money in old silver and returned in new silver, they repaid a few times of the original amount.
7   *koromo-gae* in Japanese: to change kimono in accordance with the seasons. By the Edo period there were a great variety of kimonos. As a result the Tokugawa government asked the samurai to change kimono four times a year when they went to work. Samurai wore *awase* (lined kimono) from April 1 to May 4, *katabira* (unlined kimono) from May 5 to end of August, *awase* from September 1 to 8, and *wataire* (padded kimono) from September 9 to end of March in the old calendar. Townspeople followed this custom.
8   *ake-mutsu* in Japanese. (See No. 1 of **Measuring System in the Edo Period**)

9   *kanji* (Chinese characters) of 'kawa' is 河 . The letter 河 is drawn on the lantern.
10   *shaka-ninai* in Japanese: a literal translation for the word is shouldering-Buddha. When the statues of Buddha were moved, they were carried over people's shoulders backwards. If someone fell dead in the street, he or she was carried over the shoulders of *hinin*, who belonged to none of the hierarchy of samurai, farmers, artisans and merchants of the Edo period, and was considered an outcast.
11   A rice-dumpling wrapped in bamboo leaves. It was eaten on the Boys' Festival Day.

12   *bintsuke-abura* in Japanese: the fragranced wax made of Japanese wax, rapeseed oil etc.
13   a thin cord to bind the top-knot, mostly made of paper
14   *masu* is a square wooden measure container for liquid or grains.
15   *Senda-no-ki no hashi* in Japanese: the bridge between Kitahama, the north end of the merchant town area, and Nakanoshima in Osaka.

PART TWO

1   *Ageya* is a place in a pleasure quarter where a client called out a courtesan from the courtesan house in order to dine and to be entertained by her.

「女殺油地獄」

3　灯火用の菜種油。
4　丁子、白檀、梅の花などの香りを付けた髪油。

5　江戸時代の履物は下駄、草履などで足が汚れたので長い間外に出ていた者は足洗う習慣があった。

6　新銀は旧銀の幾倍もの価値があった。上銀は新銀と同じ意。

7　着物の種類が増えたことから、江戸幕府は公式に年四回の衣替えの出仕を制度化した。武家の制服は旧暦の４月１日〜５月４日は袷（裏つきの着物）、５月５日〜８月末日は帷子（裏無しの単仕立ての着物）、９月１日〜８日は袷、９月９日〜３月末日は綿入れ（表布と裏布の間に綿を入れた着物）とした。町人はこれに習った。

8　日の出の半時間ほど前、東の空が明るくなり始める頃を「明け六つ」と言った。（「**江戸時代のものの数え方**」1参照）
9　提灯に店の名前を入れてある。
10　行き倒れは検死後、身元不明の場合、非人が死体を後ろ向きに背負って埋葬地まで運んだという。仏像を背負う形と同様なのでいう。

11　粽は端午の節句に食べた米粉などを笹や眞菰の葉で包んで蒸したもの。古くは茅の葉で包んだのでこの名がある。
12　菜種油などと晒木蝋に香料を混ぜて製した固練りの油。主に日本髪の後れ毛を止め、髪の形を固めるのに用いる。
13　髪を頭の頂に束ねたところ、もとどりを結ぶ細い紐。近世は紙捻が用いられた。
14　物の容量を量る木製の器。
15　現在の北浜から中ノ島にかかる橋。ふつう「せんだん」と読む。

その二
1　遊里で遊女屋（置屋）から上級遊女を呼んで遊ぶ場所。

2   *mon-bi* or *iwai-bi* in Japanese: the seasonal festival days and so forth. Courtesans had to take clients and the clients had to pay more on these special days.
3   *kanji* for 'Tennoji-ya' is 天王寺屋.
4   *o-taiya* in Japanese: one of the Buddhist memorial services held for the dead.
5   *butsudan* in Japanese: a piece of furniture where memorial tablets and a statue of Buddha are placed. Normally it is a wooden cabinet with double doors at the front.
6   The Hokke sutra said that women had five obstacles which prevented them from dying in peace. So a woman would wish to be reborn as a man in order to have an easy death and enter the paradise of the west.
7   The common name of the old Hōzen-ji Temple, one of the temples of the Pure Land Sect. The name was derived that the temple chanted a prayer to Buddha for one thousand days. There was an execution ground on the north side of the temple and a crematorium on the south. The present day Hōzen-ji Temple is located in Nanba, Chūō ward of Osaka city.

「女殺油地獄」

2　江戸時代官許の遊郭で五節句など特に定めた日。この日、遊女は客をとらねばならず、客も揚げ代をはずむ習慣であった。

3　家名・屋号などを書いて門口に掛け目印とする行灯。

4　忌日の前夜。死者の追善供養のために行う仏教の行事、三十五日の前夜。

5　位牌や仏像を安置するための仏具。主として木製の箱型で正面は両開き。

6　女子は五種の障りがあるため、男子に成り変えて極楽往生を願う願。（法華経）

7　浄土宗の寺で古い法善寺。千日念仏を行ったことから千日寺と呼ばれた。寺の北に刑場、南に火葬場があった。現在の法善寺は大阪市中央区難波１丁目にある。

DRUMBEATS OVER THE HORIKAWA
A Play in Three Acts

Original Jōruri
Horikawa Nami no Tsuzumi
By
Chikamatsu Monzaemon

Adaptation & translation
By
Masako Yuasa

「堀川波鼓」
三幕四場

原作

近松門左衛門

翻案・英訳

湯浅雅子

Performance Poster（公演ポスター）
Tsuzumi-Drumbeats over the Horikawa（「堀川波鼓」）
Hull in March 2006（2006年3月ハル大学）

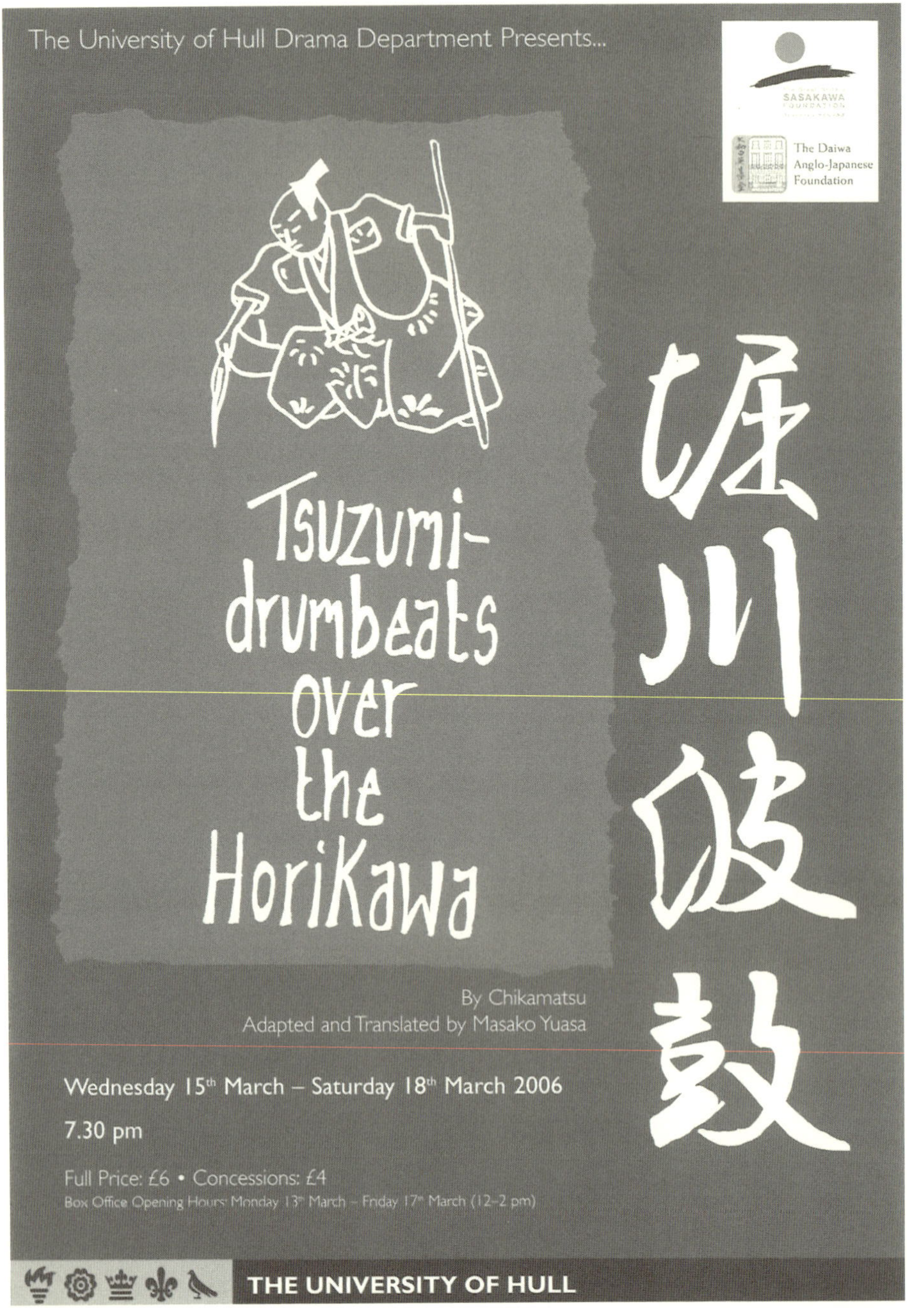

Stage Photos （舞台写真）
Tsuzumi-Drumbeats over the Horikawa （「堀川波鼓」）
Hull & Japan Tour, Tokyo in 2006（2006年 ハル大学＆日本ツアー・東京）

ACT ONE
(From the left)Fuji and Tane
上之巻
（左から）ふじとたね
Photograph by Mike Park（撮影 マイク・パーク）

SCENE TWO OF ACT TWO
Fuji and Tane
中之巻
ふじとたね
Photograph by the Theatre Museum at Waseda（撮影 早稲田大学演劇博物館）

ACT THREE
Fuji, Genemon(on the floor), Bunroku, Yura and Hikokurō
下之巻
ふじ、源右衛門（床の上）、文六、ゆら、彦九郎
Photograph by the Theatre Museum at Waseda（撮影早稲田大学演劇博物館）

Original Design for *Tsuzumi-Drumbeats over the Horikawa*   ACT ONE
「堀川波鼓」舞台図原案　上之巻
Tane's parents' house　　たねの実家

SCREEN　スクリーン

BLACK CURTAIN　　　　　　　　　　　　　　　　BLACK CURTAIN　暗幕

踏み台　木の廊下（座敷と同じ高さ）　　　　　　　　　　　　踏み台
STEP　　　　　　　　　　　　　　　　　　　　　　　　STEP

CORRIDOR
(WOODEN &
RAISED)

LANTERN　行灯

網代垣
AJIRO SCREEN

座敷
TATAMI-MATTED ROOM
（раised area 床を上げてあるところ）

WELL
井戸

WASHTUB
盥

踏み石
FOOTBOARD/STEPPING STONE

サイドステージ　役者待機ベンチ（床几）　脇舞台
ACTORS' WAITING BENCH　SIDE STAGE

脇舞台　ACTORS' WAITING BENCH　SIDE STAGE

木戸
WOODEN
GATE

庭
GARDEN
(MAIN STAGE 本舞台)

Tree
松の木

*THIS STRUCTURE IS USED THROUGHOUT
THE PLAY.
全幕通してこの舞台構造を用いる

花道　THE HANAMICHI

AUDIENCE
客席

DESIGN by YUASA
Feb. 2005

Original Design for *Tsuzumi-Drumbeats over the Horikawa*   ACT THREE
「堀川波鼓」舞台図原案　下之巻
Genemon's house　源右衛門の家

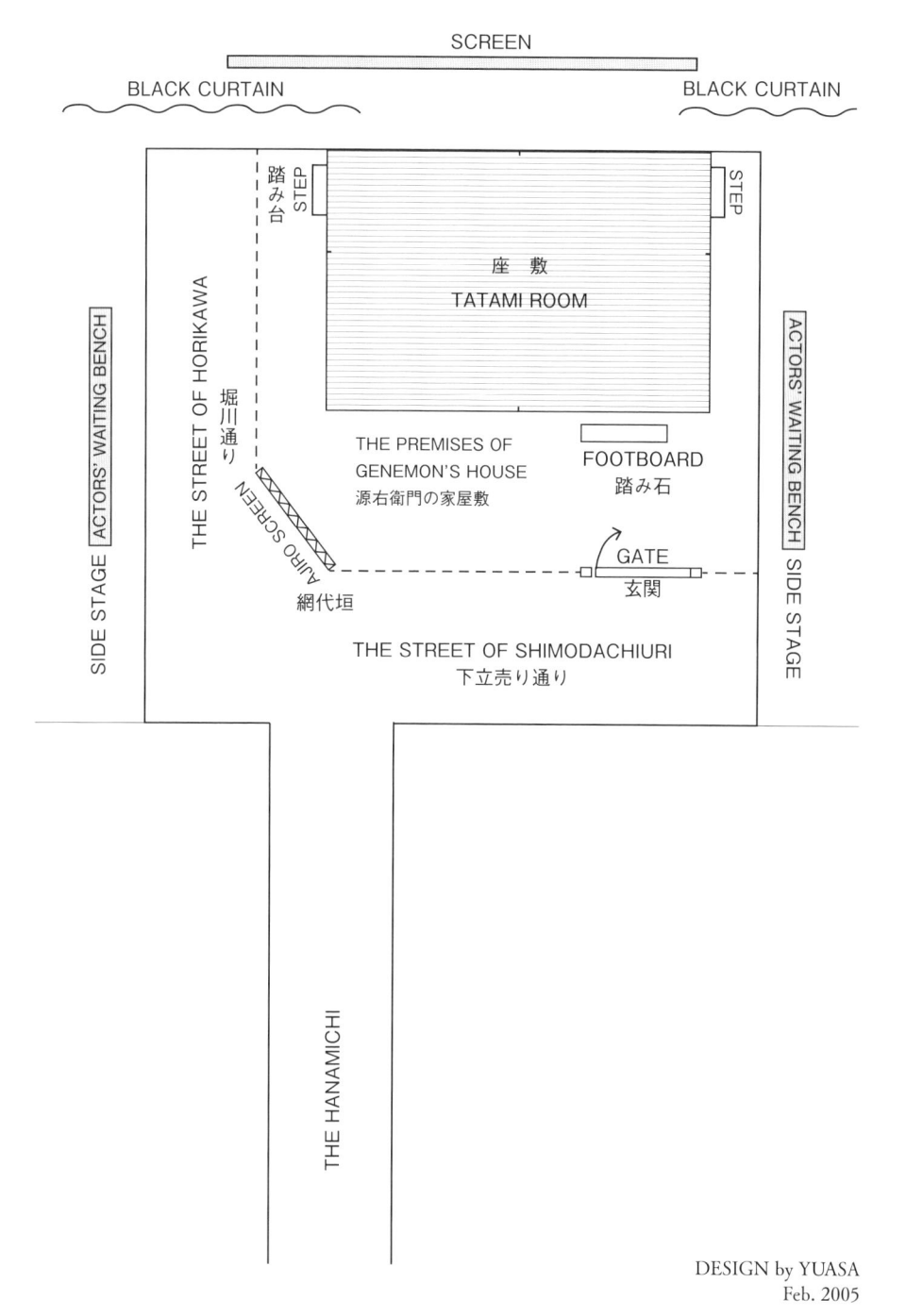

SCREEN

BLACK CURTAIN　　　　　　　　　　　　　　　　　BLACK CURTAIN

踏み台 STEP　　　　　　　　　　　　　　　　　　　　STEP

座敷
TATAMI ROOM

SIDE STAGE | ACTORS' WAITING BENCH

THE STREET OF HORIKAWA
堀川通り

THE PREMISES OF GENEMON'S HOUSE
源右衛門の家屋敷

FOOTBOARD
踏み石

AJIRO SCREEN
網代垣

GATE
玄関

ACTORS' WAITING BENCH | SIDE STAGE

THE STREET OF SHIMODACHIURI
下立売り通り

THE HANAMICHI

DESIGN by YUASA
Feb. 2005

DRUMBEATS OVER THE HORIKAWA

The original *jōruri* was first performed at the Takemoto-za in February 1707. The proprietor of the theatre was Takeda Izumo. The *jōruri* reciter was Takemono Chikugonojō who was fifty-seven years old at that time. The *jōruri* was written by Chikamatsu Monzaemon when he was fifty-five.

Reference: 'Horikawa Nami no Tsuzumi,' *Nihon Koten Bungaku Zenshū Chikamatsu Monzaemon Shū 2*, edited and translated into current Japanese with notes by Torigoe Bunzō. Published by Shōgakukan in 1998. (Page 485-582)

The adaptation was first staged at the Donald Roy Theatre at the University of Hull from 15th to 18th March 2006, with the following cast and crew.

OGURA HIKOKURŌ	Adam Widdrington
TANE	Milly Brann
BUNROKU	Claire Emmott
NARUYAMA FUJI	Chloe Davies
MASAYAMA YURA	Nikki Williams
MIYAJI GENEMON	Phil McDonnell
ISOBE YUKAEMON	Richard Cottyn
CHORUS 1	Adel Hulsmeier
CHORUS 2	Alice Bartlett

The other characters were performed by the members of the cast.

Direction and original design	Masako Yuasa
Design	Hannah McGranaghan and Steven Bell
Lighting	Andy Davidson
Sound	Phillipa Herrick
Costume	Pauline Chambers
Props	Fran Bradley
Stage managers	Laura Parkes and Luke Dominy
Production Manager	Shannon Collins (Hull), Richard Tall (Japan tour)

The production toured to Japan as the first Japan tour of the Chikamatsu Project. The performances on the tour were held at the Seika Small Theatre (Seika Shō Gekijō) in Osaka on 30th and 31st March, and at the Ono Memorial Auditorium (Ono Kinen Kōdō) of Waseda University in Tokyo on 4th and 5th April.

「堀川波鼓」

　1707年2月竹本座初演。座本竹田出雲。太夫竹本筑後掾、五十七歳。作者近松門左衛門、五十五歳。

参考資料　日本古典文学全集『近松門左衛門集②』「堀川波鼓」（485 〜 582頁）
　　　　　鳥越文蔵　編・校注・訳　小学館　1998年5月1日出版。

　湯浅版初演は2006年3月15日〜 18日に英国国立ハル大学ドナルド・ロイ劇場で以下のスタッフ、キャストで上演した。

小倉彦九郎	アダム・ウィドリントン
たね	ミリ・ブラン
文六	クレア・エモット
成山ふじ	クロエ・デイヴィス
政山ゆら	ニッキ・ウィリアムズ
宮地源右衛門	フィル・マクドネル
磯部床右衛門	リチャード・コティン
コーラス　1	アデル・フルスミア
コーラス　2	アリス・バートレット

　その他の登場人物は出演俳優皆で演じた。

演出・舞台原案	湯浅雅子
舞台装置	ハナ・マクグラナガン、スティーブン・ベル
照明	アンディー・デイヴィッドソン
音響	フィリッパ・ヘリック
衣装	ポーリーン・チェンバー
小道具	フラン・ブラッドリー
ステージ・マネジャー	ローラ・パークス、リューク・ドミニイ
プロダクション・マネジャー	シャノン・コリンズ（ハル大学）
	リチャード・トール（日本ツアー）

　この公演で近松プロジェクトは第一回日本ツアーを行った。ツアーの公演日程は2006年3月30日、31日に精華小劇場（大阪）、4月4日、5日に早稲田大学小野記念講堂（東京）。

The adaptation for the performances in 2006 has been revised with companion notes for the publication.

ACTS AND SCENES

(The Play is in Three Acts with Four Scenes.)

ACT ONE
At Tane's parents' house
In Inaba district in the fief of Tottori in the early spring of 1706

ACT TWO
    SCENE ONE   The Lord of Tottori's homecoming
                         May
    SCENE TWO   At Ogura Hikokurō's residence
                         In Inaba district in the fief of Tottori
                         The day of Hikokurō's homecoming on the 27th of May

ACT THREE
At Miyaji Genemon's house
In Shimo-dachiuri of Horikawa, Kyoto
The opening day of the Gion Festival on the 7th of June

CHARACTERS

OGURA HIKOKURŌ A retainer of Inaba district in the fief of Tottori,[1] a steward of the Tottori castle
OGURA TANE   HIKOKURŌ's wife and NARUYAMA CYŪDAYŪ's elder daughter
OGURA BUNROKU HIKOKURŌ and TANE's adopted son, TANE and FUJI's younger brother
NARUYAMA FUJI   TANE's younger sister who works in the residence of TAMURA ORINOSUKE, a high-ranking retainer of Tottori fief.
MASAYAMA YURA HIKOKURŌ's younger sister and the wife of MASAYAMA SAN-GOBEI who is a retainer of Tottori fief and an equerry at the Tot-

「堀川波鼓」

　この本に掲載した翻案戯曲は出版のために初演台本を一部改訂し、註を付けたものである。

劇の構成

　（三幕四場）

上之巻
　　たねの実家の場
　　　　一七〇六年早春、鳥取藩因幡の国。

中之巻
　　第一場　お国入りの場
　　　　　　五月。
　　第二場　小倉彦九郎屋敷の場
　　　　　　五月二十七日、小倉彦九郎国入りの日、鳥取藩因幡の国。

下之巻
　　源右衛門宅の場
　　　　六月七日祇園祭初日、京都堀川下立売。

登場人物

小倉彦九郎　　　　鳥取藩因幡の国[1]の藩士。台所役人。

小倉たね　　　　　彦九郎の妻。成山忠太夫の長女。

小倉文六　　　　　たねの弟。現在は彦九郎とたねの養子。

成山ふじ　　　　　たねの妹。家中田村折之助宅に奉公している。

政山ゆら　　　　　彦九郎の妹。鳥取藩因幡の国の藩士で馬廻役人の政山三五平の妻。

193

tori castle
MIYAJI GENEMON BUNROKU's tsuzumi[3] teacher from Shimo-dachiuri of Horikawa Street in Kyoto[2]
ISOBE YUKAEMON A retainer of Tottori fief, HIKOKURŌ's colleague
KAKUZŌ   TAMURA ORINOSUKE's servant[4]
UME   NARUYAMA CYŪDAYŪ's maid
RIN   TANE's maid
THE MESSENGER OF MASAYAMA SANGOBEI

THE FIRST WOMAN STONE-SELLER[5]
THE SECOND WOMAN STONE-SELLER whose name is FUJI
THE YOUNG MAN WITH LOOSE HAIR   a young man whose hair is loose
THE YOUNG MAN FROM HANAMICHI   A friend of THE YOUNGN MAN WITH LOOSE HAIR
THE YOUNG RETAINER   GENEMON's *tsuzumi* pupil from a provincial fief
THE YOUNG RETAINER'S FOLLOWERS: A few young samurai, the travelling-chest carriers and a footwear carrier and so forth
THE MENDICANT PRIEST[6]
GENEMON'S SERVANT
SUMI   GENEMON'S maid
GENEMON'S WIFE
TOWNSPEOPLE of Shimo-dachiuri of Horikawa Street in Kyoto

CHORUSES: CHORUS 1, CHORUS 2 and CHORUS 3
         The speeches of the CHORUS in SCENE ONE of ACT TWO are not written for a separate chorus. They were spoken by members of the cast in the first production.

「堀川波鼓」

宮地源右衛門(みやじげんえもん)　　　京都堀川下立売(ほりかわしもだちうり)[2]に住む鼓(つづみ)[3]の師匠。文六の鼓の先生。

磯部床右衛門(いそべゆかえもん)　　　鳥取藩因幡の国の藩士。彦九郎の同僚。
角蔵(かくぞう)　　　田村折之助屋敷の中間(ちゅうげん)。[4]
うめ　　　成山忠太夫屋敷の下女。
りん　　　たねの下女。
政山三五平の使いの者

石売りの女１[5]
石売りの女２（ふじ）
さばき髪の若い男
花道から来た若い男

若侍
若侍のお供（若党、奴、草履取(ぞうりとり)等）

托鉢の僧[6]
宮地源右衛門の家の下人(げにん)
すみ　　　宮地源右衛門宅の下女。
宮地源右衛門の女房
京都堀川下立売(ほりかわしもだちうり)の町の衆

コーラス（コーラス１、コーラス２、コーラス３）
　　　　　　中の巻第一場のコーラスはコーラス１、コーラス２、コーラス３に書き分けていない。初演では出演者全員で演じた。

DRUMBEATS OVER THE HORIKAWA

ACT ONE

At Tane's Parents' House

On a warm and sunny afternoon in the early spring of 1706.
OGURA TANE's father, NARUYAMA CYŪDAYŪ's house in the fief of Tottori of Inaba district.

A sitting room with a tokonoma alcove[1] in the centre of the stage. The floor of the house is raised about 16 inches from the ground, as is common in a traditional Japanese house. Corridors stretch offstage from each side of the room. One Upstage Right leads to the kitchen and the utility area of the house, and the other, Upstage Left, leads to the inner part of the house. Also an external corridor surrounds the room.
A large country-style garden dominates Downstage Centre. In the garden there is a well near the corridor Upstage Right. A pine tree with shapely branches stands Downstage Left. A wooden gate close to the hanamichi is the entrance of the house.

There are a few wooden buckets and a wooden washtub filled with laundry around the well. Having kimono sleeves pulled back by the tasuki,[2] a band of cloth, TANE and FUJI are happily starching and stretching the washed pieces of kimonos[3] by the well. Their refined appearance is notable in a regional fief like Tottori.

A Nō song 'Matsukaze'[4] is heard from the start of the play.

CHORUS 1: Long time ago, there was a famous poet and court noble called Lord Yukihira of Ariwara[5] who was banished from court to the Suma Seacoast[6] for three years. This is a story about him at that time.

CHORUS 2: Lord Yukihira spent his time boating by day and admiring the moon on the waves at night. Being far away from his home Kyoto, Yukihira-sama felt so isolated and lonely, these were the only things to relieve the sorrow of his exiled days.

CHORUS 3: One day Yukihira-sama saw two beautiful local girls on the shore drawing brine to make salt. They were sisters. He named the elder sister *Matsukaze*, Pining Wind, and the younger sister *Murasame*, Autumn Rain. And the beautiful local sisters became his attendants at night.

「堀川波鼓」

上之巻

たねの実家の場

一七〇六年早春、うららかな春の陽光が庭いっぱいに広がる暖かな午後。
鳥取藩因幡の国、小倉たねの実家の成山忠太夫屋敷。

舞台中央に成山家の床の間[1]付きの座敷があり、座敷の上手奥に奥座敷への廊下、下手奥に厨房、勝手口への廊下がのびている。座敷を囲むように縁側がある。

舞台手前は田舎風の広い庭になっていて、上手前に枝ぶりの良い松の木が一本、下手奥、庭の角に井戸、下手前花道近くにこの家敷の入り口の木戸がある。

井戸の周りには洗濯物の浸かった盥や桶が置かれている。その傍でたねとふじの姉妹が仲良く襷[2]がけで洗い終えた布に糊を付けて張り物[3]をしている。姉妹は因幡のような地方の藩には珍しいほど、垢抜けしていて美しい。

幕開きから謡曲「松風」[4]が鼓の音とともに聞こえている。

コーラス1　その昔、かの歌人在原行平卿[5]が須磨[6]にお流されになって三年余りその地で暮らされた頃のお話です。

コーラス2　行平卿は都を遠く離れた淋しい日々を、舟遊びをしたり、美しい月を愛でたりして、気持ちを紛らせて過ごしておられました。

コーラス3　そんな日々の夜伽のお相手に、美しい海女の乙女姉妹を選ばれまして、姉を松風、妹を村雨と土地に相応しい名前をつけて呼ばれました。

CHORUS 1: As time passed, the sisters' coarse kimonos full of the smell of the sea were exchanged for delicate thin silk kimonos of a sweet scent. Those were the sisters' happiest moments. The time came when Yukihira-sama was forgiven and returned to the court. He promised them he would come back. The sisters believed his words and waited for him ever since, driving Matsukaze insane with grief.

CHORUS 2: That was the story about a change of clothing by the sisters drawing brine.

CHORUS 3: Meanwhile this is the story about an incident happened to the wife of a samurai retainer. Her husband has been away attending on the lord of Tottori, in his Edo Residence at that time.

CHORUS 1: It's a warm and sunny afternoon in the early spring today. Tane is at her father's house and is washing, starching and stretching the pieces of kimonos, one of the seasonal jobs for the wives of the low-ranking retainers.

CHORUS 2: Fuji, Tane's younger sister, works in Tamura Orinosuke's residence, one of the high-ranking retainers in Tottori. Today she has a day off and has come home. And as her elder sister is doing a seasonal washing, she is helping her.

CHORUS 3: Two sisters are washing kimono cloth with their kimono sleeves tucked with the taski band. They are stunningly beautiful as the people of Inaba say.

TANE: Fuji, my darling little sister, you must do your best at your work and please your master Tamura-sama and his family, so that you will be able to stay in their service. You must never take a husband. Look at me. Hikokurō and I were childhood friends and we grew to become very much in love with each other. I was so happy at my wedding and my feelings then were beyond description. Yet, as Hikokurō is a low ranking retainer, he has to follow his lord when he attends the Shogun in Edo every other year.[7] When his lord stays here in Tottori, Hikokurō goes to the castle every day. You think then it's all right, but it's not. Being a steward at the castle, he has to stay overnight for at least ten days a month. As a result, for some time there hasn't been a night when we talked and spent freely as a married couple. My husband is very much a man with a samurai spirit. He often told me in his dependable manner, "I must fulfil my mission by working hard like this; otherwise I am not going to make my way in life as a samurai." But when he departed for Edo last June, he looked in my eyes and said, "We won't be able to see each other until next May when I return with my lord on his homecoming. Be well and look after the house of Ogura while I am away. Keep everything safe and sound." I haven't forgotten the look on his face. It's floating in the air all the time. I think, since then I have lost my heart to him. I'm longing for his return every moment. (*TANE goes to the pine tree in the garden, hangs one end of kinubari kimono-cloth-pegs[8] to it and ties it to the pine tree with the linen cord attached to the peg. She does this with all her feelings to HI-*

「堀川波鼓」

コーラス1　月日が経つうちに潮の匂いのしみ込んだ海女の乙女の粗末な着物は、そこはかとなく芳しい香りの立つ薄絹に変わってゆきました。やがて行平卿が都に戻る時が来ました。卿は姉妹に必ず帰ると約束されて行かれ、姉妹はその言葉を信じて待ち続けました。卿が戻られないので姉の松風は悲しみで狂ってしまいました。

コーラス2　それは謡の塩焼く海女が衣(ころもか)を替えたお話。

コーラス3　これは、夫が江戸詰めで留守の妻の身に起こったお話。

コーラス1　うららかな春の日差しの眩(まぶ)しい今日、たねは実家に戻って夫の留守仕事のひとつの着物の洗い張り。

コーラス2　いつもは家中田村家(かちゅうたむらけ)でお屋敷勤(やしきづと)めをしている妹ふじが、今日は久々のお里帰り。姉様たねが実家に戻って着物の洗い張りをしているのを見て、急遽(きゅうきょ)そのお手伝い。

コーラス3　襷(たすき)がけで布を絞る二人の姉妹は因幡の国の国中の評判通りで、ほんに水もしたたる美しさ。

たね　おふじ。お前はご主人の田村様のお気に召すよう精出して、いつまでもご奉公できるようにしたがいい。決して夫なんぞは持たれぬように。私をご覧なさい。夫彦九郎とは幼馴染。好いて好かれた仲であったから、嫁入りの時の嬉しさは例えようもなかった。けれど、下級武士の悲しさ。彦九郎殿は隔年のお江戸勤め[7]。お国元(くにもと)におられる時は毎日のお城詰めで、台所役人というお役目ゆえ、月のうちの十日は泊り番。それだから、いつの頃からか夫婦らしゅうゆっくりと語らい合える夜もない。夫は侍気質(さむらいかたぎ)でいつも『このようにしてお勤めをまっとうせねば立身出世も叶わぬ身だ。』と頼もしい様子で言われていた。けれど、去年六月にお江戸に発たれる時には、『また来年五月にご主君のお国入りのお供をして戻るまでは互いの顔が見られぬ。無事でいてくれ。つつがなく留守(つと)を務めてくれ。』と言われた。そのときの夫のあの顔つきがいつもちらちらとこの目に浮かんで、片時も忘れたことがない。あれから私はずーっと夫に恋をしているようで、いつお帰りか、いつお帰りかとあの人の帰りを待っているのです。（言いながら、衣張(きぬば)り[8]を松の木に掛けて、細い麻紐を夫への想いを込めるかのように、きゅっと結ぶ。）

KOKURŌ.)

FUJI [*looking at TANE and laughing at her*]: Sister, you are asking too much. Being single, I have put up with lonely days without a man. Especially in my master's house, because they are very strict about such matters, we are not allowed to stay overnight even at our parents'. If you were me, you would die. People will laugh at you if you keep saying such things and pining for your husband. (*FUJI laughs in a loud voice while sticking the shinshi-bamboo-needles[9] to stretch the washed kimono cloth hanging from the kinubari kimono-cloth-pegs.*)

There is the sound of a tsuzumi drum.

TANE: Shush! O-Fuji! Shush! Don't talk loud! Bunroku is taking a tsuzumi-drum lesson in the inner drawing room. (*TANE looks in the direction of the inner drawing room while sticking the shinshi-bamboo-neeales*)

FUJI stops laughing and looks in the direction of the inner room, too.
The drumming of tsuzumi gets louder.
The passionate sound of tsuzumi makes TANE think of Hikokurō more. She hangs HIKOKURŌ's kimono on a pine branch to air it[10] and looks at it absentmindedly.
There is a shout "Yah!" indicating the ending of a Nō song.

CHORUS 1 [*sharing TANE's emotion*]: This is the kimono he left me as a token of his memory, yet it only gives me grief…

CHORUS 2: "I could have already forgotten him if he hadn't left me his kimono." I now see what this old poet meant.

CHORUS 3: My feelings for you are deepened day by day because of your kimono.

TANE [*suddenly to Hikokurō's kimono hung from the pine tree*]: Oh, how delightful! My husband has come home. Let's go and welcome him. [*TANE runs to the pine tree.*]

FUJI [*embarrassed*]: Dear, dear, Sister. You are out of mind. That thing over there is a pine tree in the garden. Your husband is still in Edo. Have you gone mad?

TANE: Fuji, my dear! What a silly thing you say! I haven't lost my mind. It is just a way of killing time in my husband's absence. I was only playing at comparing the pine tree to my pining feelings for my husband to cheer me up. It has been chanted in a Nō song 'Matsukaze.' "If the lover knew his sweetheart was pining for him, as unchanging as the evergreen pine tree of Mt Inaba, he would come back to her immediately." [*TANE laughs*

「堀川波鼓」

ふじ　（たねの様子をみて笑って）姉様、それはお前、贅沢というもの。私のように夫の無い身でさえ、淋しい毎日を辛抱していますのに。ことに私の奉公先の田村様のお屋敷では、行儀のことは厳しゅう申されて、親里に一泊することさえ叶いませぬ。姉様なら死んでしまわれます。そのようなことを言って夫を恋しがっておられるのを人が聞いたら笑いますよ。（伸子[9]を打ちながら、大きな声で笑う。）

　　　　　　鼓の音が聞こえる。

たね　しーっ！おふじ。しーっ！大きな声を出されるな。今日は奥の座敷で文六が鼓のお稽古をしています。（伸子をうちながら、奥座敷の方を覗き見る。）

　　　　　　ふじも笑うのを止めて奥の様子を窺う。
　　　　　　鼓の音が少し高くなる。
　　　　　　たねは鼓の調子に誘われて彦九郎のことを想い、上の空で松の木に彦九郎の着物[10]をかけてうっとりと眺める。
　　　　　　謡曲「松風」が終わり近くになったことを示す掛け声が「やあ」と聞こえる。

コーラス１　（たねと想いを重ねて）思い出のこの衣が今ではあだ……。

コーラス２　「これが無ければ忘れる時もあるものを」と昔の歌に詠まれるのも道理。

コーラス３　この衣ゆえになおもあなた様への想いは深まるばかり。
たね　（突然、松の木に吊るした夫の着物に）まあ、嬉しい。旦那様がお帰りになった。さあ、お迎えに参りましょう。（松の木に走り寄る。）
ふじ　（恥じて、とがめるように）これ、姉様。お前様は正気でない。あれはお庭の松の木。兄様はまだお江戸ではないか。気でも違われたか。
たね　まあ、何を馬鹿なことを。おふじ、私は気など違ってはおらぬ。恋しい夫のお留守の退屈しのぎに、せめてもの慰めに松を夫になぞらえて待っているだけ。ここは因幡の国。ほら、謡曲にも「松と聞けば帰ってくる」と謡われているではないか。（いたずらっぽく笑う）

201

mischievously.]

> The sisters start taking in the dried washing and folding it joyously.
> The sound of tsuzumi becomes louder and reaches a crescendo.
> 'Matsukaze' is heard in the background once again.

CHORUS 1: "We have been living apart like this, but if I heard that you were 'pining' for my return like the 'pine' tree of Inaba Mountain, I would come back to you immediately," It was the old poem about the pine tree in the deep mountain of Inaba.

CHORUS 2: And another story tells of the 'pine tree' on the Suma Seacoast where noble Yukihira once lived. [*As being Pining Wind, a character in a Nō play, Matsukaze*]: If he ever returned here, I would wait by the pine tree. The branches bent by the blustering sea-wind are like my mind yearning for Yukihira-sama, pining to be near him….

CHORUS 3 [*as Autumn Rain, a character in a Nō play, Matsukaze*]: If it happened, it would be like the good old days. Oh, the wind is losing its mind with sorrow as it blows towards the pine tree…

> The Nō song, 'Matsukaze' goes low and gradually dies down.

CHORUS 1: To return to Inaba in Tottori and Tane. This is the story of a retainer's wife who consoles herself with the sound of the *tsuzumi* drum and waits for her husband's homecoming.

CHORUS 2: People say that the lord of Tottori will return before long. It's a bright and warm spring day today. The air is sweet and fresh. It's a lovely day for washing the husband's summer kimonos.

CHORUS 3: The kimonos are drying well in the spring sun. They have done as many jobs as the number of joints in the bamboo clothes pole.

CHORUS 1, 2 and 3 [*together*]: They're delighted!

TANE [*in high spirits*]: Oh, how nice! We've done so much today. Now I want to enjoy the Nō song 'Matsukaze' while waiting for my husband's homecoming.

> FUJI carries the washed laundry and aired kimonos to the utility room off Upstage Right.
> The sound of tsuzumi drum stops. BUNROKU comes from the inner drawing room.

「堀川波鼓」

　　　　　姉妹は楽しげに洗い張りを終えて、乾いた着物の布を取り入れてたたみ始める。
　　　　　鼓の音が一段と高く聞こえる。
　　　　　謡曲「松風」が再び聞こえ始める。

コーラス1　「こうして別れているけれど、因幡の国の山の峰に生える松のように、あなたがいまも私を待っていると人が言うのを聞いたなら、すぐに帰ります」とうたうあの頼もしい御歌（おうた）。それは、因幡の遠い山の松のこと。

コーラス2　そして、これは懐かしの君の住まれた須磨の浦の松のこと。（謡曲「松風」の登場人物松風になって）恋しい行平卿（ゆきひら）がここにお帰りになるのなら、私も松の木陰で待ちましょう。風に吹かれ、曲げられた磯馴れ（そな）の松のように行平様を思う私の心。

コーラス3　（謡曲「松風」の登場人物村雨になって）もしも恋しい行平卿（ゆきひら）がここにお帰りになったら、懐かしいあのころのよう。ああ、風が狂ったように松に吹き付ける……。

　　　　　謡曲「松風」の音が低くなり、徐々に消えてゆく。

コーラス1　さてさて、再びここは鳥取藩因幡の国。夫の留守の淋しさを鼓に心を慰める妻たねの夫彦九郎を待つお話。

コーラス2　夫が江戸から戻るのも、もうすぐという風のたより。今日は風も涼しく、夫の薄絹の夏袴（なつばかま）を洗って張るも春ののどか。

コーラス2　洗った着物もやさしい春の光にすっかり乾いて、物干し竿の竹の節の数ほど沢山の仕事を終えました。
コーラス1、2、3　（一緒に）おお、嬉し。
たね　（はしゃいで）ああ、嬉しいこと。今日は沢山いい仕事が出来ました。江戸にいる夫を待ちながら、これからじっくり「松風」を聞くといたしましょう。

　　　　　ふじは洗い張りや虫干しの終わった着物を持って下手厨房の方に入る。
　　　　　鼓の音が止み、文六が上手の奥の間から出てくる。

203

BUNROKU: Mother! My tsuzumi lesson is over. You remember that I've talked about my *tsuzumi* teacher, Mr Miyaji Genemon, before? He is here today. I think this is a good opportunity for you to meet him.

TANE: Oh, Bunroku. Is the lesson over? I've been thinking of greeting your teacher, too; only it took us longer to finish the laundry than I thought.

TANE takes off the tasuki band and adjusts her appearance. She then steps up to the sitting room.

BUNROKU leads his tsuzumi teacher MIYAJI GENEMON to the sitting room. FUJI also comes back to the room. GENEMON is given the seat of honour on the left in front of the tokonoma alcove. The others then sit down, TANE first, followed by BUNROKU and FUJI.

GENEMON [*sitting up straight and courteously*]: How do you do? It is a pleasure to meet you. I am Miyaji Genemon. I live on Shimo-dachiuri Street in Horikawa, Kyoto. I teach the tsuzumi hand drum to the retainers of Tottori. It seems that my wish to work officially for the fief of Tottori is likely to be fulfilled. So I've come down to stay here for a few months or even a year. I have not yet had the pleasure of meeting your husband, Ogura Hikokurō-dono yet. But your son, Bunroku-dono, wanted to learn the *tsuzumi* with me and we've become master and pupil recently. Your son is quite gifted. You must be proud of him.

TANE [*nodding with a smile and in the delicate and gentle manner of a refined woman*]: When I say that I am Bunroku's mother, it sounds as if Hikokurō and I are quite old. But actually Bunroku is my younger brother whom my husband decided to adopt. We only earn a small salary as low ranking retainers, so at present Bunroku lives with a good retainer's family to be educated and taught manners. His grandfather thought if Bunroku learned how to play the tsuzumi, then with luck and ability the lord of Tottori might consider giving him a post to serve him directly. So in the absence of his father he asked you to teach Bunroku tsuzumi. We would be grateful if Bunroku could welcome his father by playing the tsuzumi when he returns with the lord in May. I hope that you will be a kind tsuzumi teacher to my son.

CHORUS 1: How very charming Tane looks! And how creditable she sounds!

CHORUS 2: People would never think that she was born and bred in a provincial place like Tottori.

CHORUS 3: I think that she is equal in elegance to any woman in Kyoto.

「堀川波鼓」

文六　母上。鼓のお稽古がおわりました。かねてからお話いたしておりました私の鼓のお師匠様の宮地源右衛門先生がおいでです。良い機会ですので、お近づきになられては如何ですか。

たね　あれ、文六。お稽古が終わりましたか。私も先ほどからご挨拶をと思っていたのですが、洗い張りで遅くなってしまいました。

　　　　　たねは襷をはずし、身繕いしながら座敷に上がる。
　　　　　文六が源右衛門を表座敷に案内する。
　　　　　ふじも下手から戻り、源右衛門を上座にして、たね、文六、ふじの順に座る。

宮地源右衛門　（膝を直して、丁寧に）お初にお目にかかります。京都堀川下立売に住まいする宮地源右衛門でございます。因幡鳥取藩内の方々に鼓の指南を致しております。ゆくゆくは藩へのご奉公の望みも叶いそうでございますので、時々、京都から当地に下っては一年、半年、五ヶ月、三ヶ月と逗留いたしております。御主人の小倉彦九郎殿にはまだお目にかかったことはございません。最近、御子息の文六殿が鼓の稽古を望まれましたので師弟のとりきめを交わしましたが、なかなか御器用でおられます。お母上もさぞ満足されておられることでございましょう。

たね　（にっこりと会釈して、しっとりと柔らかな物腰で）文六の母と申しますと、夫彦九郎も私も年寄りのように聞こえますが、もともと文六は私の実の弟でございますのを、夫が養子にいたされました。私共は僅かの御扶持をいただく下級者でございますので、現在はご家中のある方のところに預け置いて、行儀作法や学問を習わせております。お師匠様にご指導を仰いで、鼓の一曲も打てるようにして、ゆくゆくは殿様直々の御奉公に出したいとの念願で、夫の留守中ではございますが、これの祖父がご指南をお頼み申し上げました。この五月には夫もお殿様のお供をして国元に帰ってまいります。その折には一曲も打って、父御に聞かせることが出来ますようによろしくお指導をお頼み申し上げます。

コーラス１　たねの物腰の何と艶やかで立派なことよ。
コーラス２　このような地方藩鳥取育ちには見えませぬ。

コーラス３　京のどの奥方にも引けを取らぬほどでございますなあ。

205

DRUMBEATS OVER THE HORIKAWA

FUJI [*in the same delicate and quiet manner as TANE and with the dignity of a samurai gained from her work*]: How do you do? I am Tane's younger sister Fuji. I work in the house of one of the Tottori clansmen, Tamura Orinosuke. I am delighted to hear that you have been so good to our Bunroku. My elder sister's husband, Ogura Hikokurō, is a low ranking retainer, so their residence is smaller and has fewer rooms than here. As Hikokurō-sama is in Edo this year, we do all sorts of house hold chores including the laundry here at our parents' house. But I think that it must be inconvenient for you to do your teaching here. I am sure you will be invited to Ogura's house when Hikokurō-sama comes home. [*Finishing her greeting to GENEMON and turning in the direction of the kitchen*] Maid! Will you please prepare *sake* for our guest? Where is our father? Is he still out? [*Turning around to GENEMON*] Our maid has just arrived from the country. We are inconvenienced even in entertaining a guest. It's most embarrassing.

CHORUS 1: The expression of her eye when she speaks is beautiful.

CHORUS 2: She is as elegant as her sister.

GENEMON: Oh, no, no. I am fine. Please do not worry about me.

The maid of Naruyama's house, UME, comes in from Upstage Right. She brings a tray of sake and a side dish.

TANE: Oh, thank you, Ume. How considerate of you. As our father has retired from work, we have nothing special to serve you. But how about enjoying a cup of sake? [*TANE picks up sake cup and offers it to GENEMON.*]

GENEMON: Well, thank you very much. You must be busy with a lot of other things to attend to. How very generous of you! After you, please.

TANE: You are our guest. Please, you must drink first.

GENEMON: In that case, Bunroku-dono, you must drink first. [*He offers the cup to BUNROKU.*]

TANE [*stopping GENEMON and in the manner of an experienced drinker*]: I think it's better if I drink first to check the temperature of sake. As Bunroku's mother, it's my responsibility. [*She receives the sake cup from GENEMON, drinks it all up in one and holds out the empty cup to BUNROKU and serves sake.*]

BUNROKU [*receiving the cup*]: I have not tasted sake much… [*Drinking very little*] Please, teacher. [*He returns the sake cup to GENEMON and fills the cup with sake.*]

GENEMON [*receiving the cup, drinking it up in one and smacking his lips over it*]: Well, well, this is good, very tasty. I don't drink heavily, but as I like sake very much, I always have some when I am out visiting. I must say your sake is not inferior to that in Kyoto. As

「堀川波鼓」

ふじ　（同じく、もの柔らかに、屋敷勤めで身についた武家の風格を備えて）お初にお目にかかります。この者の妹で、ふじと申します。藩中の田村様方にお勤めに上がっております。文六に目をかけていただきまして嬉しゅう存じております。姉の夫小倉彦九郎殿は、今はお江戸勤めで留守にしております。また、下級武士で屋敷の部屋数も少なく手狭でございますので、留守中の洗濯などその他万端にいたるまで、このように親のところでいたしております。文六の鼓の稽古までここでいたしましては何事も御不自由でございましょう。彦九郎殿が戻られましたら、自宅の方にもご招待されることと思います。（挨拶を終えて、下手台所の方に向かって）これ、お杯でも用意してくれぬか。父様はお留守なのか。（源右衛門に）下女が田舎から出て来て間がございません。お客様が一人来られても、まあまあ、不都合なことばかりで、まあ、ほんに恥ずかしいことでございます。

コーラス１　恥ずかしいと云って会釈する妹ふじの目元の美しさ。
コーラス２　姉にひけをとらぬ美しさ。
源右衛門　いえいえ、どうぞ、お気遣いなされませぬよう。

　　　　　下女のうめが下手から酒と肴を取り揃えた盆を持って出る。

たね　まあまあ、これはよう気が付きました。父はもうお殿様へのご奉公を退いた浪人者でございます。ろくなお肴もございませんが、お慰みにお一ついかがでございますか。（酒杯を源右衛門にすすめる。）
源右衛門　色々とお忙しく御用もおありでござりましょうに。これは誠に有難いことでございます。まず、そちらより。
たね　いえいえ、あなた様から。どうぞ、ご遠慮なされずに。
源右衛門　それでは、先ず、文六殿から。（杯を取り、文六に差し出す。）

たね　（源右衛門を手で遮って、酒好きな様子で）それでは、母の役目で私がお酒の燗の具合を見ることに致しましょう。（源右衛門から杯を受け取って、ぐーっと飲み干す。その後、その杯を文六に渡して、酒を注ぐ。）

文六　（杯を受けて）私はまだお酒をいただいたことがないのですが……。（少しだけ飲んで）失礼ながら。（源右衛門に杯を返して、酒を注ぐ。）
源右衛門　（注がれた酒を飲みほし、舌鼓を打って）たっ、たっ、これはまた、見事なお酒でございますなあ。私もあまり深酒はいたしませんが、お酒は好きなほうでございますので、方々の土地で色々なお酒を吟味しております。けれど、このお

you know, *sake* made in Kyoto is well-known for its flavour because of the good water there. [*In ringing tone*] The colour, the smell and the taste, everything is perfect, which leads me to admire the generous hospitality of the mistress of the house.

CHORUS 3: It can be tasteless to overpraise drink or to be too courteous as a guest.

GENEMON: Now, let me return the cup to Bunroku-dono. [*He offers the cup to BUNROKU.*]

TANE: Now, let me stop Genemon-sama there. I would like to receive the cup in place of my son, and take the role of a drinking-partner for you. [*TANE takes the cup from GENEMON and is served sake by BUNROKU. Then she drinks it up in one joyously. To GENEMON, while returning the cup onto the sake tray*]: It appears that you are very fond of our sake. Why don't you have another one?

GENEMON [*taking the cup in no time*]: Oh, how very kind. In that case I must have another one. [*GENEMON holds out the cup to TANE.*]

TANE fills the cup with sake to the brim.
GENEMON drinks it up and then holding the cup to BUNROKU.

BUNROKU [*receives the cup, and once again drinks very little*]: Now, this time, I would like to pass the cup to my aunt. [*He is about to pass the cup to FUJI.*]

TANE [*stopping BUNROKU*]: No, no, where are your manners? I understand you don't drink much, but even so it's not agreeable thing to do. You are supposed to empty your cup at least once. All right, then, I'll be your drinking-partner. [*Receiving the sake cup from BUNROKU, waiting it to be filled and drinking it up all in one*]: How wonderful! I am so happy that I had the chance to be my son's drinking-partner. Now I propose that I continue the role in place of your father in Edo to perfect this auspicious moment. Well, Genemon-sama, you must become a drinking-partner of a drinking-partner. [*TANE gives the cup to GENEMON.*]

GENEMON [*receiving the cup*]: It seems the mistress of the house is very fond of sake. This might sound too impudent and impolite, but I would like to accept your challenge.

TANE fills the cup with sake.
GENEMON drinks it up once again and returns the cup to TANE.
TANE receives the cup delightedly.

FUJI [*worrying that TANE has started drinking heavily*]: No, no, please, not. My sister cannot

「堀川波鼓」

酒には水が良いので美味いと言われる京の酒も及びません。（ほめちぎって）色といい、香りといい、また風味も良くて、この家のご主人のお心まで慕わしく思われるようでございます。

コーラス3　酒の挨拶や客ぶりの良いのも過ぎてはかえって災い。

源右衛門　では、文六殿に御返杯いたしましょう。（杯を文六に差し出す。）

たね　ここはこの母がその杯を止めまして、お師匠様の相手をして杯をお受け致しましょう。（たねは文六に代わって源右衛門から杯を受け取り、文六に酒を注がせて美味しそうに飲み干し、盆に杯をもとしながら）このお酒がお気に召しましたのなら、もう一つ召し上がって下さい。

源右衛門　（たねが杯を盆に置くか置かないうちに、杯を取り）それではなにはさておき頂きましょう。（杯を差し出す。）

　　　　　たねが源右衛門の差し出した杯になみなみと酒を注ぐ。
　　　　　源右衛門はそれをぐっと飲み干して、文六に戻す。

文六　（杯を受け取り、また少しだけ杯に口をつけて）恐れながら、これは叔母様に差し上げましょう。（ふじに杯を渡そうとする。）

たね　（文六を止めて）まあまあ、いくらお酒は飲まないといってもそれではあんまり愛想がない。一つ、飲み干しなさい。母が相手を致しましょう。（たねは文六から杯を受け取り、酒をなみなみと注がせて、一気に飲み干す。）母の身で我が子の酒の相手が出来るとは、何とめでたい事。そのめでたさのその上に、江戸におられるそなたの父御の名代(てでごみょうだい)にもう一杯いただきましょう。源右衛門殿、酒の相手のその相手をお願いいたします。（言いながら、源右衛門に杯を差し出す。）

源右衛門　（杯を受け取って）どうやら、奥方はお酒を嗜(たしな)まれるとお見受けいたしました。馴れ馴れしくて失礼であるかも知れませぬが、されば、お手前、拝見いたしましょう。

　　　　　たねが杯に酒を満たす。
　　　　　源右衛門はそれをまたぐっと飲み干して、たねに返す。
　　　　　たねが嬉しそうに杯を受け取る。

ふじ　（たねが止(と)め処(ど)なくお酒を飲み始めたのを心配して）いえいえ、姉はそんなにお

drink much. Furthermore she has been a little under the weather recently. [*In a cautioning tone*] Sister, would you like to stop drinking now? Will you, please?

TANE [*stubbornly, putting with the attitude of a heavy drinker*]: Oh, dear! What nonsense you tell! We haven't put anything special for a side dish. So, drinking with the guest is the best side dish that we can serve. [*In the direction of the kitchen in high spirits*] Ume! Will you please bring more sake?

GENEMON [*also in high spirits*]: Now then how about drinking to this song. [*He claps his hands imitating a tsuzumi drum.*]

> *UME brings in more sake.*
> *TANE and GENEMON carry on drinking.*

> *The sun begins to set.*
> *The temple bell rings in the distance.*

> *TAMURA ORINOSUKE's servant, KAKUZŌ, enters on the hanamichi.*

KAKUZŌ [*at the outside the gate, loudly*]: O-Fuji-sama, I've come to pick you up. It is time to go back. Soon our house gate will be closed.

FUJI [*noticing KAKUZŌ*]: Oh, it's Kakuzō. Thank you for coming. How good of you. Sister, I am going back to Tamura's. [*To GENEMON*] It is not well-mannered in front of our guest, but I must leave now. Please excuse me. When one serves a retainer, one must expect such things. I hope that we'll meet again.

> *FUJI bows to GENEMON, says goodbye to TANE and BUNROKU and exits with KAKUZŌ on the hanamichi.*

BUNROKU [*speaking very much like an adult*]: I must go back to my master, Ōkura-sama's place earlier than usual, for he is inviting some guests this evening. Teacher, please stay here until my grandfather Chyūdayū is back.

GENEMON: Then, for the time being, I'm quite happy to do so. However, I don't think that it is appropriate to be alone with your mother in the same room. I should wait in the inner room where we had our *tsuzumi* lesson. [*He bows to TANE and exits to the inner drawing room, Upstage Left.*]

> *BUNROKU sees GENEMON off and then walks towards the gate. TANE follows*

　　　　酒はいただけませぬ……、ことに、近頃は時候のせいか、気分もあまり優れぬ様
　　　　子でございます。（傍らから嗜めて）姉様、お酒はもうお控えなさいませ。
たね　（酒飲みの常で、かえって意地っ張りになって）まあ、何をいうのです。これと
　　　いう酒の肴もないのだから、一緒に飲んでお相手をして差し上げるのが、何より
　　　のご馳走ではありませんか。（下手に向かって、上機嫌で）うめや。もっとお酒を
　　　お持ちしてくれぬか。
源右衛門　（同じく上機嫌で）それでは、この曲を肴にもう一献。（手鼓を打ち始め
　　　る。）

　　　　　　うめが酒のお代わりを持って来る。
　　　　　　たねと源右衛門はさしつさされつ酒を飲む。

　　　　　　日が陰り夕方になる。
　　　　　　遠く鐘の音が聞こえる。

　　　　　　田村家の中間角蔵が花道から来る。

角蔵　（表門のところまできて大きな声で）おふじ様、お迎えに上がりました。お帰り
　　　のお時間です。お屋敷の御門が閉まります。
ふじ　（角蔵に気づいて）おお、角蔵か。お迎えご苦労様です。姉上、それでは私はお
　　　屋敷に戻ります。（源右衛門に）お客様には無礼なことではございますが、儘なら
　　　ぬお屋敷勤めの身、どうかお許し下さい。また、お目にかかれることと存じます。

　　　　　　ふじは源右衛門に挨拶をして、たねや文六に別れを告げて角蔵とともに
　　　　　　花道から退場する。

文六　（大人びた口調で）私も今宵は御主人大蔵様のお屋敷にお客様がお見えになると
　　　のことですので、これで失礼致します。お師匠様は祖父成山忠太夫が戻ります
　　　までしばらくここにおいで下さい。
源右衛門　それでは、ともかく、そうすることにいたそう。しかしながら、そなたのお
　　　母上と差し向かいでここに居るのもどうかと思うゆえ、先ほどのお座敷で待たせ
　　　ていただこう。（たねに会釈をしてから、上手の奥座敷のほうに退く。）

　　　　　　文六は源右衛門が奥に行くのを見送ってから、表門に向かう。たねも文

him.

TANE: Bunroku, will you drop by my house and ask your grandfather to come back? I want to go home, too. Also please tell my maid Rin, to come and pick me up.
BUNROKU: All right, mother. I will. [*BUNROKU exits on the hanamichi.*]

The ringing of a temple bell is heard again in the distance.
It is evening and the time when the people of the castle town of Tottori close their house gates.

After seeing off BUNROKU, TANE closes the gate, goes back to the sitting room and lights the andon lamp stand[11] *in the corner of the room. Then she takes a mirror box from the shelves by the tokonoma alcove and goes to sit near the garden. She opens the box and takes out a mirror and a comb. She looks at her face glowing with sake and combs her hair. TANE is feeling slightly heavy in the head having drunk too much. But she looks very attractive. Her appearance suggests her loneliness and longing for her husband's return.*

ISOBE YUKAEMON, one of HIKOKURŌ's colleagues, enters from Downstage Right. He is on his own. YUKAEMON has been allowed to stay in Tottori owing to his illness. He opens the wicket gate and enters the garden quietly.

YUKAEMON: Good evening!
TANE [*frightened by the unexpected visitor, putting away the mirror box and quickly adjusting her appearance*]: My father Chyūdayū has been out since this morning. He hasn't returned yet. Please excuse me. [*She tries to go to the inner part of the house to hide from the visitor.*]
YUKAEMON [*rushing onto the sitting room and holding TANE tightly from behind*]: Please wait, O-Tane-dono. I came here knowing that Chyūdayū-dono was out. I didn't come for him. I came to see you. I came, because I am deeply in love with you. I wanted to get here much earlier, but I had to wait until dusk to avoid people's eyes. I, Isobe Yukaemon, knew well that my salary would rise if I went to Edo with our lord this year. But I chose to throw away success in my samurai life. Instead I played sick and asked permission to stay in Tottori. I have done this all for you, to be with you. I've just said that I played sick, but the truth of the matter is that I didn't, because I was and am truly a poor lovesick samurai. Tane-dono, I am madly in love with you, I...I want you. I am a

「堀川波鼓」

　　　　　　六を送って出る。

たね　文六、家に寄って祖父様にお帰りなされるように申してくれぬか。私も早う家に
　　　戻りたい。りんを迎えによこしておくれ。
文六　承知いたしました。（花道から退場する。）

　　　　　　鐘の音が再び聞こえる。
　　　　　　藩中の家々で門口を閉める夕暮れ時。

　　　　　　たねは文六を見送り、門を閉め、座敷に戻り行灯[11]に灯を入れる。それ
　　　　　　から、床の間の違い棚から鏡箱を取り出して庭の近くに持って行って座り、
　　　　　　鏡箱から鏡と櫛を取り出す。たねは酔ってほてった顔を鏡に映し、酒で少
　　　　　　し重くなった頭の髪の乱れを直す。たねの姿はなまめかしく、夫の留守の
　　　　　　淋しさ、人恋しさが滲み出ている。

　　　　　　彦九郎の同僚、磯辺床右衛門が上手から供も連れずに一人で登場する。
　　　　　　床右衛門は病気を理由に今年は江戸詰めを免れて国元に居る。彼は閉めて
　　　　　　ある表門の潜り戸をそっと開けて入って来る。

床右衛門　お見舞い申す。
たね　（驚いて、急いで鏡箱をもとの場所に戻す。身繕いしながら）父忠太夫は今朝か
　　　ら出かけてまだ戻りませぬ。（奥に入ろうとする。）

床右衛門　（座敷に走って上がり、たねを後ろから抱きすくめて）お待ちくだされ、お
　　　たね殿。忠太夫殿がお留守であるのを承知で来ております。お祖父様には用は無
　　　い。あなた様に焦がれて来ましたのじゃ。心は急いても人目があってこの夕刻に
　　　なるまで来られなんだ。この磯辺床右衛門、今年お江戸勤めをしたなら、俸禄が
　　　増すのは分かっておりました。その武士の立身出世も振り捨てて、仮病と偽りお
　　　殿様にお願いして国元に留まりましたのも、みなそなた恋しさゆえ。今、仮病と
　　　偽ったと申しましたが、仮病ではござりませぬ。おたね様ゆえ、この磯辺の焦が
　　　れ船、漕いで焦がれて、止まらぬ恋路、そなた故の恋の病に身も心も苦しんでお
　　　りまする。おたね様、どうか仮の情けのお薬を私に一服下され。頼みまする。と

213

wrecked, sinking ship loaded with love destined for you. I'm sailing when it's hailing and I'm rowing when the wind's blowing on storm-tossed seas until my illness is cured by the sweet breeze of your love, and moored to you, the most beautiful woman, in heaven. O-Tane-sama, my soul and body are in hell without you, please, please help me out of this. Give me a spoonful of the honey of your love. I beg you. Please have mercy on me. Let me have you this once. [*He tries to hold TANE tightly in his arms against her will.*]

TANE [*breaking away from YUKAEMON, helped in a drunken moment*]: Stop it! Go away! You, horrible creature! [*Trembling with fear, but keeping her dignity*] You are a beast wearing the skin of a samurai! I thought you were one of my husband's close friends. How dare you make advances towards your friend's wife! What sort of man are you to leave the path of virtue like this? That's not all. If this act is revealed among the Tottori clansmen, people will criticise you behind your back. What's more, if the lord hears of this, he will deprive you of your rank and fortune. You must know this. Be very careful about what you do. I am Ogura Hikokurō's wife, the wife of a retainer of Tottori. If you keep up this rudeness, I won't be responsible for whatever punishment may come your way later. [*Bitterly*] I won't talk about what happened tonight to anyone; so, quickly, you must leave!

YUKAEMON: No, I won't. I've already given much thought to the blame and disgrace I'm letting myself in for. But I've made up my mind. If you don't do as I ask, I will stab you and myself right on this spot to make it look like love suicide which, I hear, is coming into fashion into Kyoto and Osaka. Then our grand love affair will be known throughout Inaba and we will become a public disgrace. I am ready for that. [*Drawing out the sword he wears at his side, YUKAEMON seizes TANE by the kimono collar and draws her towards him.*] Now will you satisfy my desire?

TANE shivers with fear.

CHORUS 1: Oh, I'm frightened! The blade is cold!
CHORUS 2: If I don't grant his wish, he is going to kill us both. I do not want to die in vain. People will falsely accuse of me of committing love suicide with this man. Oh, what shall I do? I don't want to die.
CHORUS 3: I can't let it happen. What can I do? I know. I must deceive this man with sweet words. It's the only way for me to save my chastity and my life.
TANE [*acting as if she were truly moved by YUKAEMON's words and deeply in love with him*]: You've just said very sweet things to me. Are they true?
YUKAEMON: I swear. It is the truth among truths. Even if I were denounced by our lord

「堀川波鼓」

うか、どうか、御情けをお頼み申す。（床右衛門は嫌がるたねを一層強く抱こうとする。）

たね　（酒に酔っている勢いで、床右衛門を振りほどき）ええい、厭らしい！わずらわしい！（恐ろしさに震えながらも、威厳を保って）やい！侍の皮を被った畜生め！お前は、我が夫彦九郎殿とは親密な間柄。その朋輩の女房に言い寄るとは、何と人の道に外れたことをされるのじゃ。そればかりではござらぬ。このことが藩内に知れたら皆に後ろ指差されることになる。また、もしも、お殿様のお耳に入ったなら、お前の扶持も身分もお取りあげ。それを知らぬわけではあるまい。いやしくも私は小倉彦九郎の女房、武士の妻。その私に無礼を働き、後で何があっても知りませぬぞ。（苦々しく）今日のことは誰にも申さぬゆえ、さあ、さあ、早くお帰りなされ。

床右衛門　いいや、帰りませぬ。人のそしりも、我が身の恥辱もよく考えた上でのこと。万一、私の頼み承知していただけぬ時には、お前とここで刺し違え、京、大阪で流行っているという心中をして、二人の仲を因幡中に広め、共に恥を晒す覚悟を決めて出て来たのじゃ。（床右衛門は腰の刀を抜き、たねの胸倉を掴んで引き寄せて喉に刀を当てる。）さあ、私の頼み、聞いてくださるか。

　　　　　　　たねは恐怖で身を震わせる。

コーラス1　ああっ、恐ろしい！刀が冷たい！
コーラス2　本懐を遂げぬときには、この男は本気で私を殺して自分も死ぬ気でいる。今、ここでこの男に殺されては犬死。その上、無実の心中の罪まで着せられてしまう。どうしよう。助かりたい。
コーラス3　もうこのうえは、この男を誑かして、この場を逃れるしか女の身を守り、生き延びる術はない。
たね　（床右衛門の言葉に気持ちを動かされたかのように、惚れた素振りをしてしみじみと）今、お前様の言われたことは誠か。
床右衛門　おお、誠も誠。殿様に御勘当を受け、卑しい雑兵に首を討たれるようなこと

215

and had my head cut off by a nameless footman, I wouldn't regret it. There isn't any shred of deceit in my love for you.

TANE [*pretending joy*]: Oh, how happy I am! How can I think lightly of your true love for me? But, we are in my parents' house. If my father comes home at this moment, it will be the end of our love. So first, why don't you go home tonight? Then you can visit me at my house secretly, say tomorrow night. How about that? [*Seductively*] If you go now, I will do whatever you want me to do for you tomorrow. Do you understand? [*TANE gently taps YUKAEMON on the shoulder.*]

YUKAEMON [*completely deceived and touched by TANE's words, and sheathing his sword*]: Oh, thank you! I'm deeply grateful. Look, this may sound impulsive, but since you feel that way, how about giving me a token of your love here and now? Please, O-Tane-dono, I beg you! Please let me love you here a little . . . [*He presses himself hard against TANE again.*]

TANE [*breaking away from him*]: Please! Behave yourself! Stop it! Oh, no, stop it! Stop! Don't!

Suddenly the sound of a tsuzumi drum is heard breaking off in the inner part of the house. Then GENEMON's voice singing a Nō song[12] follows.

CHORUS [*over GENEMON's singing*]:
> Adultery is sinful. It is a painful torture.
> Adultery is sinful. It is a painful torture.
> Your lover waits for you on the top of a mountain of swords.
> You climb the mountain to be with your lover.
> But the sharp blades of the mountain mercilessly pierce your flesh.
> Brutal rocks fall and crush your bones.
> How fearful! How dreadful!
> Adultery is the worst sin to commit.

TANE [*pretending to be shocked and upset*]: Oh, how terrible! Awful! Someone has been listening to our conversation. [*Threatening YUKAEMON*] Now, you must leave quickly!

YUKAERMON [*extremely shocked and speaking loudly to the inner room*]: What you've heard is not true! It was a joke! Understand? I was only joking.

YUKAEMON runs away hurriedly.

TANE [*flustered*]: Oh, what shall I do now? The guest from Kyoto in the inner room must

になっても構わん。そなたを想う心に偽りはない。

たね 　（嬉しい振りをして）まあ、何と嬉しいお心。お前様のそんなお気持ちをなんであだや疎かに出来よう。けれど、ここは親の家。今、父が戻られたらどうしようもない。ひとまず、今夜のところは帰られて、明日の夜にでも私の家にそっと忍んで来て下され。（誘うように）そうして下さったら、私も、もっとうちとけて、お前の想いが叶うよういたします。ええな。（床右衛門の肩を軽くたたく。）

床右衛門 　（ころりと騙されて、ほろりとなり、刀を鞘におさめて）おお、忝ない！有難い！そういうことなら、厚かましいかもしれぬが、いっそ、ここで少しだけあなたのお情けをいただかせて下さらぬか！のう、おたねどの、後生じゃ、なあ、ほんの少しばかりを……。（再びたねに抱きつく。）

たね 　（床右衛門から逃げて）聞き分けのないことを。およし下さい！あれ、ああ、嫌、止めて！

　　　　突然、襖の向こうの奥の座敷から鼓の音が聞こえて、源右衛門が大きな声で謡曲[12]をうなり始める。

コーラス 　（源右衛門の声に被さるように）
　邪淫の罪は身を責めて
　邪淫の罪は身を責めて
　剣の山の頂に　恋しい人の姿あり
　嬉や嬉やと　登り行けば
　剣の山の剣が身を貫き
　大岩が身を砕く
　ああ　恐ろしや　恐ろしや
　恐ろしき罪は　邪淫なり。

たね 　（驚いたふりをして）あれ、恐ろしい！恐ろしい！人が聞いていた。（床右衛門を脅して）さあさあ、早く帰って下され！

床右衛門 　（びっくりして、鼓の音の聞こえる方向にむかって、卑屈に）今までの話はみんな嘘！冗談！冗談ですぞ！

　　　　床右衛門はほうほうのていで走って表へ逃げてゆく。

たね 　（うろたえて）どうしよう。奥の座敷の京都からの客は今の話を聞いていた。あ

have heard our conversation. How dreadful! He doesn't know that I was lying to Yukaemon to save my honour. I'm in trouble. He must misunderstand my true intention and despises me. And I don't think that it will stop there. He goes from house to house teaching tsuzumi. Sooner or later all the clansmen will be talking about what happened here tonight. It will become a big scandal. Oh, how dreadful. [*Trying to calm the furious beating of her heart*] What, what shall I do? [*Having an idea, callling in the direction of the kitchen Upstage Right*] Ume! Are you there?

UME [*coming in from the direction of the kitchen, looking very sleepy*]: Did you call me, Mistress?

TANE: Yes, I did. I'm sorry to give you more work, but please warm up more sake and bring it for me. And, it's getting late. Lock the house gate and then go to bed.

UME: Yes, Mistress.

> *UME steps down to the garden and locks the gate and exits to the kitchen.*
> *TANE looks at the garden absentmindedly.*

UME [*comes back with a tray of sake and places it by TANE*]: Here you are. Now, Mistress, I'll go to bed. Good night.

TANE: Oh, thank you very much, Ume. You've done a lot today. Have a good night.

> *UME goes back to her room next to the kitchen, spreads the futon and lies down.*
> *TANE sips sake and sobs.*

CHORUS 1: Hikokurō-sama!
CHORUS 3: I miss you.
CHORUS 1: I wish I could see you here.
CHORUS 3: And you could hold me tight.
CHORUS 1: My darling husband!
CHORUS 3: How I miss the warmth of your gentle arms.

> *The garden is lit under a hazy spring moon. The house is cloaked in a strange tranquillity. A cuckoo calls.*

> *GENEMON slips out of the inner part of the house. He tries to leave by the external corridor stealthily.*

あ、恥ずかしい。身を守るために床右衛門を嘘で誑していたことなど知るよしもない。困ったことになった。私のことを誤解して蔑むだけでは済むまい。源右衛門殿は藩中の色々なところに出入りする人だから、そのうちに今夜のことは人々の口の端に上り、大変なことになる。（不安で胸が早鐘のように高鳴るのを押さえて）ああ、どうしよう……。（思いついて、下手の台所に）うめ！うめや！

うめ　（下手から眠そうに出てきて）呼ばれたか。

たね　お酒の燗をして、ここに持って来てくれぬか。それと、もう遅いから表の戸締りをして、お前はお休み。
うめ　へえ。

　　　　　うめは庭に下りて門の戸締りをしてから厨房のある下手に退く。
　　　　　たねは放心して庭を眺めている。

うめ　（燗酒を用意して持って来て）では、お嬢様、わしはこれで寝ますで。お休みなさりませ。
たね　ごくろうでした。お休みなさい。

　　　　　うめは台所の横の部屋に布団を敷いて寝る。
　　　　　たねは酒を飲みながら静かに泣く。

コーラス1　彦九郎様。
コーラス2　恋しい。
コーラス3　会いたい。
コーラス1　抱かれたい。
コーラス2　愛しいお前の。
コーラス3　胸が恋しい。

　　　　　庭は朧月に照らされ、不思議な静寂があたりを包む。
　　　　　ホトトギスの声。

　　　　　源右衛門が奥座敷からそおっと出て来て、縁先から去ろうとする。

TANE [*Noticing him*]: Oh, it's Genemon-sama. Where are you going?

GENEMON: Well, I felt uncomfortable staying in a house where a lady is on her own. I would like to go. [*He is moving quickly to exit.*]

TANE [*Holding onto GENEMON's kimono sleeve*]: You've heard our conversation. No, no. You have misunderstood me. What I said to that man wasn't true. You must believe what I say. I am married to Ogura Hikokurō. I respect and love my dear husband. Why should I say and do a terrible thing like that when I am married to a good man! I lied to that man so that I could escape from him. You must understand the situation I had been put in. Genemon-dono, will you please keep silent? I beg you. [*TANE puts for hands together in prayer to GENEMON while sobbing.*]

GENEMON [*with reluctance*]: I might have heard your conversation. At the same time I might not have heard your conversation. You were both talking loudly near the room I was in. I was embarrassed by the content of your talk, so I sang a Nō song to distract my attention. But I don't think the matter is a simple and easy one. I won't tell anyone, yet we say the tip of a gimlet tends to be out of a bag. If someone hears it somewhere else and talks about it, that won't be my fault. [*GENEMON tries to leave shaking off TANE who is clinging to his kimono sleeve.*]

TANE [*still clinging to GENEMON*]: What you've just said is too heartless! I am a young woman and you are a young man, too. Even if what I said to that man a moment ago were true, you should be kind enough to keep it a secret as a man of compassion. Oh, if I let you go like this, my mind won't be at ease. [*Conceiving an idea*] Yes, that's a good idea. We must exchange cups of sake and swear not to let the matter out. [*TANE takes out a tea bowl for a tea ceremony*[13] *from the shelves of the tokonoma, fills up the bowl and drinks it up in one. Then she refills the bowl, drinks half and offers the rest to GENEMON.*]

GENEMOM [*at first hesitating and a moment later*]: Well, it's very unusual. That's 'kissed-sake.'[14] Are you offering it to me? [*He gives in and takes the bowl, raises it once and drinks it in one.*]

TANE [*by this time quite drunk and holding GENEMON firmly by the hand*]: Well, Genemon-dono, you've just accepted 'kissed-sake' from a married woman. That means you have committed a sin, too. We're in the same boat now. You can't talk about the incident tonight to anyone any more, can you? [*She draws near GENEMON.*]

GENEMON [*Realising that he has been set up*]: No! I don't know about it. I didn't mean it at all. [*He tries to flee from TANE.*]

TANE [*holding onto GENEMON unconsciously*]: How could you be so cold-hearted? [*By alcohol, becoming suddenly aroused*] Really! What an irritating man you are!

「堀川波鼓」

たね　（気づいて）あれ、源右衛門様。どこへ行かれます。
源右衛門　いや、ご婦人ばかりのところはどうも気が引けますゆえ、退出いたそうと思います。（そそくさと去ろうとする。）
たね　（源右衛門の着物の袖を捉えて）今の話を聞かれましたか。最前、私があの男に言ったことは本心ではありませぬ。信じて下され。彦九郎と言う大切な夫のいる身。そのような不届きな、空恐ろしいことを本気で言うわけがございませぬ。あれはあの場を逃れるためにだまして言っただけのこと。どうかお分かり下さい、源右衛門殿。決して他言なされて下さるな。ひとえにお願い申します。（源右衛門に手を合わせて、泣き出す。）

源右衛門　（仕方なく）いや、聞いたでもなし聞かぬでもなし。あまり近くでのお話で、私も聞きにくく、謡をうたって紛らわしておりました。と、申しましてもこれは安からぬ大事。私は、他言はいたしませぬ。けれど、錐は袋に入れても先が外に出ると申します。外からどなたかに知れて取り沙汰されても、それは私の知らぬところでございます。（袖を掴んで頼むたねを振り切って行こうとする。）

たね　（尚も縋り付いて）それはあまりに冷たいお言葉。あなた様も若き殿御。私も若い女の身。もし仮に、私が最前、あの男に言ったことが真実であっても、他言せぬのが人の世の情けというもの。こんな風にお前様をお帰ししては、私の心が落ち着きませぬ。（思いついて）そうじゃ、この上は、他言せぬという誓いの杯を取り交わしてから……。（棚から濃茶茶碗[13]を取り、たっぷりと酒を注いでぐーっと飲み干す。次に、もう一杯注ぎ、半分飲んで、源右衛門に差し出す。）

源右衛門　（一瞬、間をおいて）これは珍しい。「付け差し」[14]でございますか。（誘われるように杯を受け取り、押し戴いてから一気に飲み干す。）

たね　（すっかり酒に酔ってしまって、源右衛門の手をしっかりと握って）さあ、源右衛門殿。夫ある者からの情のしるしの「付け差し」を受けられたからには、お前も私と同罪じゃ。この上はもう誰にも話すことは出来ませぬぞ。（源右衛門に詰め寄る。）
源右衛門（仕組まれたことに気付いて）いや、それは知らぬ。そのようなつもりではなかった。（急いで、たねから逃げようとする。）
たね　（思わず源右衛門に抱きついて）ええ、それは、あんまり情け知らずな言いよう。（酒のせいで抑制が効かなくなって）お前様は、まあ、なんと、歯がゆいお人じゃ。

DRUMBEATS OVER THE HORIKAWA

TANE puts her arms around GENEMON, and then starts undoing his obi sash belt and his kimono impatiently. This arouses GENEMON and makes him frantic, too. GENEMON is a man who likes drinking and women. In addition, what has happened in the house has inflamed his sexual desire. Now the two want each other fervently. They make love to each other greedily until they satisfy their sexual appetites.

TANE [*in the arms of GENEMON, exhausted and gratified in her lust*]: After this, I don't think you'll want to tell anyone any more.

GENEMOM [*similarly exhausted*]: Of course not. It's not someone else's problem any more, but mine too. How could I not keep it a secret from others?

TANE and GENEMON fall asleep from the drink and the fatigue of making love. The sliding doors around the room are left open.

The night has advanced and a profound tranquillity is wrapped around the house. A night bird sings.

Suddenly someone knocks on the house gate.
TANE wakes up by the sound of knocks and sits up with a start. Being sober, she looks around and realises that she has been sleeping with GENEMON.

TANE [*shocked*]: What? This is…oh, no, what shall I do? I've done a terrible thing! I remember tricking Genemon with 'kissed-sake'. But I don't remember anything after that…I think…I was very drunk. Fuji always told me that I must stop drinking, but I've never listened to her. Now I've slept with a man who isn't my husband and disgraced myself. How shameful! Adultery is the worst sin for a woman to commit. It's been said that adulterers are the most dishonourable people both in this world and the next. I have besmeared the honour of my family. How awful! I wish I were dreaming this. [*She sobs.*]

GENEMON is woken up by TANE's sobbing. He is also sober. He looks around for a moment and recalls what he has done. GENEMON and TANE look at each other. They tremble with fear of having committed adultery.

GENEMON: What a shameful thing I have done! [*He looks down with shame and embarrass-*

「堀川波鼓」

　　　　たねは両手を源右衛門の腰に回して性急に源右衛門の帯を解き始める。
　　　女のたねに帯を解かれ、つい最前の出来事も手伝い、もともと酒好き女好
　　　きの源右衛門の欲情に火が付く。二人は、激しく求め合い、肉欲に溺れ込
　　　み、互いを執拗に貪り合い、愛し合って果てる。

たね　（源右衛門の腕の中で、肉欲に満たされて疲れた声で）こうなった上は、お前も、
　　　もう、最前のことは、他言はなさるまい。
源右衛門　（同じく疲れた声で）おお、おお、勿論のこと。他人事ではない、今はわが
　　　身のできごと。この事を隠さんでなんとしよう。

　　　　たねと源右衛門は酒の酔いと肉欲の疲れで、縁側の障子を開けたまま眠
　　　ってしまう。

　　　　夜が更けて、辺りは一層の静寂に包まれる。
　　　　夜鳥の声。

　　　　突然、表の門を叩く音がする。
　　　　たねはその音で目を覚まして、はっと身を起こす。酒の酔いが醒め、帯
　　　を解いて源右衛門と共に寝ている自分の姿に気付く。

たね　（仰天して）ああ、これは……。どうしよう、大変なことをしてしまった。床右
　　　衛門と不義をしたと世間に噂されることを口止めするために、源右衛門に「付け
　　　差し」を仕掛けてお酒を飲ませたことまでは覚えている。けれどその後は、酒に
　　　酔ってしまって何をしたのか全く覚えていない。妹のふじが常から、酒は止める
　　　ようにと言っているのに、それを聞きもせず、夫で無い見知らぬ男の肌に触れて
　　　この身を汚してしまった！何と浅ましい！淫乱は女の罪の第一のもの。あの世
　　　はいうに及ばず、この世の恥。親兄弟の名まで台無しにしてしまった。ああ、悲し
　　　い！どうか、夢であって欲しい！（むせび泣く。）

　　　　たねの泣き声で源右衛門が目を覚ます。たね同様に、すっかり酔いの覚
　　　めた様子である。酒に酔った勢いで男として道に外れた行為に及んだこと
　　　に気付き、はっとして、たねと目を合わす。二人は犯した姦通という罪の
　　　重さに慄く。

源右衛門　何と、恥ずかしいことを……。（恥ときまり悪さで俯く）

ment.]

TANE [*sobbing*]: Oh, I'm ashamed of myself.

> *The knocks on the front gate get louder.*

TANE [*frightened*]: If my father saw this, I wouldn't be able to live. What shall I do?

> *TANE is very upset and frantically looks for a place to hide but unable to find a suitable place. Completely flustered, she slips into UME's futon.*

UME [*astonished, rushing from the futon in her underclothes, screaming loudly*]: Ooh! How terriii-ble! A dirty robber got into my futon and tried to play havoc with my fair skin.

> *UME rushes into the sitting room and knocks over the andon lamp stand. Suddenly the room becomes dark which upsets UME more than ever.*

> *The knocks at the gate continue. A voice "Open the gate!" comes with the knocking sound.*

> *TANE and GENEMON are terrified every time they hear it. Finally after a brief whispered exchange, they walk to the gate together. TANE goes first, hiding GENEMON behind her.*

TANE: Is that you, Father? Will you please come in? [*She unlatches the wicket gate.*]
YUKAEMON [*covering his face outside, suddenly reaching out the hands through the wicket gate and grabbing the kimono sleeves of TANE and GENEMON*]: Caught you! I've got the proof of the adulterers!
TANE [*trying to free her kimono sleeve*]: Get off! Let go of me! Stop it! Stop!

> *TANE shuts the wicket gate and tries to free their kimono sleeves. But YUKAEMON is like a dog with a bone and does not release the sleeves. GENEMON takes out the short sword at his side and promptly cut off the sleeves caught by YUKAEMON. He then quickly opens the wicket gate and runs away like a rabbit.*
> *YUKAEMON tucks the cut-off fabrics into his kimono bosom. He then forces open the wicket gate, which TANE has been trying to keep shut, and enters the garden. TANE*

「堀川波鼓」

たね　（泣きながら）ああ、恥ずかしい。

　　　　表門を叩く音が一層大きく荒々しくなる。

たね　（怯えて）このありさまを父様に見られたらもう生きてはいられぬ。どうしよう。

　　　　たねは動顛して家の中をあちらこちら隠れ場所を探して回る。が、隠れる場所が見付からない。困りはてて、うめの寝ている布団のなかに潜り込む。

うめ　（びっくりして、下着のままで布団から飛び出し、大声で）おお、悲しい！嘆かわしい！おらの寝床に盗人が入ってきて、おらの雪の肌を荒らしおる！

　　　　うめは家の中を走り回り、座敷の行灯を足でひっかけて倒す。行灯の灯が消えて、座敷が真っ暗になる。うめは一層逆上して家中を走り回る。

　　　　表で「門を開けよ！」「門を開けよ！」の声と門を叩く音が続く。

　　　　たねと源右衛門は門を叩く音がする度に震え上がる。そのうちに二人は小声でなにやら相談し、たねが源右衛門を自分の体で隠して先に立ち、門のところに行く。

たね　父様か？さあ、お入り。（表門の潜り戸の掛け金をはずして開ける。）
床右衛門　（顔を隠して、外から手だけ伸ばし、たねと源右衛門の着物の袂を掴んで）さあ、どうだ。不義者の証拠を掴んだぞ。

たね　（袂を振りほどこうとしながら）あれ、何をする！止めて下され！

　　　　たねはすぐに潜り戸を閉じて、源右衛門とともに掴まれた袂を振りほどこうとするが、床右衛門は二人の袂を離そうとしない。とっさに源右衛門は腰の脇差を抜き、袂の掴まれているところを切り離し、潜り戸を引き開け、一目散に逃げ去る。
　　　　床右衛門は切り離された袂を懐に捻じ込んでから、たねが閉めようとする戸を無理やりに開けて中に入ってくる。たねは素早く暗闇に身を隠す。

quickly hides herself in the darker corner of the garden.

YUKAEMON: Tane-dono! Aren't you being unkind to me? You let others undo the cord of your undergarment, yet you won't allow me to do so. Why? Now, if you want me to be quiet about tonight, you must let me have you right now. Please allow me to make love to you. I am dying for love of you. Tane-dono, please help me. Please . . .

YUKAEMON is upset and jealous as TANE refused him and slept with GENEMON. He becomes like a mad man, goes onto the dark sitting room and searches for TANE. He bumps into UME who has been running around the house in her underclothes. She accidentally falls into his arms. Scared out of her wits, UME runs into her futon and hides under the cover.

YUKAEMON [*mistaking UME for TANE*]: Oh, how kind of her! [*He follows UME into the futon and climbs over her.*]
UME [*hating it and struggling*]: Ahhhh! Nooo!

TANE's maid RIN comes on the hanamichi with a lantern. She sees that the wicket gate of the house is left open and the house is unlit. Thinking that it is very odd, she carefully steps into the dark premises.

RIN [*lighting the sitting room with her lantern*]: O-Tane-sama! Your Rin is here to pick you up.

The house is faintly lit by RIN's lantern.

YUKAEMON [*realising that the woman he is holding is not TANE but UME in the dim shadow*]: Ah! You're the maid of the house. Damn! How stupid! It's a terrible mistake! I nearly broke my fast with this vulgar peasant woman.

YUKAEMON runs away from the house without looking at UME twice.

The scenery of the early spring night lit under RIN's lantern and the hazy moon is so beautiful that it looks like a picture in a dream.

Blackout.

「堀川波鼓」

床右衛門　たね殿、つれないではないか。他の男には下紐を解かせるくせに、この私にはそれを許してくださらんのか。今夜のことを内緒にしておいて欲しいのなら、今すぐに私の思いを遂げさせて下され。私にもお前を抱かせて欲しい！お願いでござる、お情けを。たねとの、お情けを……。

　　　　嫉妬で頭に血が上ってしまい、気が狂ったようになった床右衛門は、行灯が消えて真っ暗な座敷に上がってたねを探し回る。そのうちに、下着のままで逃げ回っていた下女のうめと行き当たり、抱き合う形になる。仰天したうめは自分の布団に逃げ込んで、布団を頭から被る。

床右衛門　（うめをたねと思いこんで）これは、忝ない。（うめの後から布団に潜り込み、うめの上から伸し掛かる。）
うめ　（嫌がって暴れて）ああ、あれ。

　　　　花道からたねの家の下女りんが提灯を提げて登場する。りんは屋敷の表門の潜り戸が開いていて、家の中が真っ暗なので、不審に思い、用心しながら屋敷の内に入る。

りん　（提灯の灯で暗い座敷を照らして）おたね様。りんがお迎えに参りました。

　　　　真っ暗だった家の中が、提灯の灯に照らされて、ぼんやりと明るくなる。

床右衛門　（火影にすかし、自分の抱いている女が、たねではなくて下女のうめであることに気付いて）あっ！お前はこの家の下女！ええい、もったいない！忌ま忌ましい！あやうく、こんな鰯のような女で精進落としをするところであった。

　　　　床右衛門は言い捨てて、後も振り返らずに逃げてゆく。

　　　　りんが掲げる提灯のあかりにぼんやりと映し出された春の夜の情景が夢現のように美しい。

　　　　暗転。

ACT TWO

SCENE ONE
The Lord of Tottori's Homecoming

The Tōkaidō Road[1] in May.
The returning procession[2] of the lord of Tottori

CHORUS: (*a road-horseman's song*)[3] "What handsome horses they are! They carry two beautiful clothes boxes at their sides,[4] seven layered futons and the round-backed chairs[5] on their back. Pages[6] are sitting at ease on the futon…"

People in the lord daimio's procession are humming a jubilant tune and parading through the Tōkai-dō Road of one hundred ri.[7]

The first group in the procession are the spear carriers. Plain spears, sickle spears, cross-shaped spears, all spears are on the move! So many different spears!

People say the best decoration for a warrior's helmet is red yak hair from China, the best colour for kimono is light pink and the tastiest fish is sea bream. This may sound repetitive, but certainly it appears the best among us people is a samurai.

Look at those spear sheaths in the amazing shapes! One looks like a Tenmoku tea-bowl for ground tea[8] from which a footman drank sake this morning, and the other is like the hair-style of a *kamuro*.[9]

Wave the spears!
Fall the snow on Mt. Fuji!

Leaving the snow-capped Fuji Mountain and Mt. Asama[10] behind, the long spear procession goes on. The beautiful decoration made of the cock plumes falls on the sheaths. And the parade is rolling through the Nakayama Pass in Sayo.[11]

On the west of the Osaka Barrier[12] people hear about the beautiful strong horses bred in the stables of Mochizuki [13] in Shinano.

「堀川波鼓」

中之巻

第一場
国入りの場

　一七〇六年五月の東海道[1]。
　鳥取藩主国入りの大名行列[2]。

コーラス　（馬子唄[3]）『さても、見事なお葛籠馬[4]よ。七枚重ねの布団に曲泉の椅子[5]置いて、布団敷き詰め、小姓[6]衆乗せて…』

　あれあれ、お大名の行列が東海道百里[7]を華やかに鼻歌交じりで通ってゆく。

　お行列の先を行くのは素鑓、鎌鑓、十文字鑓。

　甲の頭に唐渡来の紅色の飾り、着物は紅梅色、食べる魚は鯛。今更言うのも管鑓の、くどいことではあるけれど、「ほんになあ、人は武士が一番よ」と言ってしまうほどの立派なお行列。
　奴が今朝ほど朝酒飲んだ、天目茶碗[8]の槍鞘に、禿[9]の形の禿鞘。

　鑓を振れ振れ、富士のお山に白雪降れ降れ。

　白雪の富士、浅間の山[10]を後に見て、長い道中、長々と続く素鑓。槍鞘にかかるは鶏毛の飾り。お行列はそろそろ佐夜の中山[11]さしかかる。

　逢坂の関[12]より西に知らぬ者の無い、その名も知れた、信濃の国の望月の駒[13]。

There is the sound of the horses' bits, ringing *shan-shan rin-rin sharirin-sharirin*.

The horses of the procession move on to the Hikimano[14] field, the Pulling Horses Field, in Hamamatsu.

Shan-shan rin-rin sharirin-sharirin.
Shan-shan rin-rin sharirin-sharirin.

Riding along to this sound are the leaders of six samurai groups[15]: they are the inspectors,[16] the chief footmen,[17] the messengers[18] and the flag carriers.[19]

All the flags on the flag tops are railing in the sky peacefully.
The four seas surrounding our country are calm and the winds in the air are lulled.
How thankful! We live in a wonderful time of peace.

Doctors, scholars, wise or ignorant, rich or poor, whoever they are and whatever they are, everyone is amazed by the splendid succession of the procession of the daimio lord.

Next in the parade are the poles for the marquees and a succession of lacquered travelling chests.[20] Then, they are followed by a large numbers of the archers with bows of *shigetō* rattan,[21] *nurigome* lacquered rattan,[22] *sobaguro* plain wood and bamboo covered wood.[23]

They are followed by the arrow carriers and the arrow boxes: *utsubo*[24] and *yashi*,[25] and the double-covered daimio's armour, the armour boxes[26] and the armour stand.

It seems just a little while ago when the Tottori daimio and his retainers made a journey to the Shogunate capital Edo to attend the shogun for a year. Happily the year in Edo has passed without any trouble.

There are seven essential objects for a daimio's procession; they are spears, *naginata* halberds, long-handled sedge-hats for decoration,[27] long-handled parasols[28] a commander's battle flag,[29] lacquered travelling chests *and o-torige*,[30] a chestnut shaped large feather balls. The fief of Tottori's *O-torige* is renowned for its handsomeness.

「堀川波鼓」

轡の音も、シャンシャン、リンリン、シャリリン、シャリリン。

さてもさてさて、お行列の引き馬が、浜松の引馬野[14]を進みます。

シャンシャン、リンリン、シャリリン、シャリリン。
シャンシャン、リンリン、シャリリン、シャリリン。

轡の音に、心の拍子を合わせ、乗り掛け馬に乗って通るは、六番頭[15]、使い番[16]、侍大将[17]、奏者番[18]に旗大将[19]。

その後先に続いてたなびく旗竿のよう、時世は治まり、四方の海は波静か、天空の風も凪いで、長刀続く。

医者よ、儒者よ、物知りよ。物知りと物知らず、皆が見事な行列に舌を巻いておりまする。

幕串、挟箱[20]がひっきりなしに続いた後、持ち弓方の数は多く、重藤の弓[21]、塗籠の弓[22]、白木の弓、側黒の弓[23]。

靫[24]、矢籠[25]、矢箱。二重の覆いを被せた大将の兜、具足櫃[26]に甲立て。

ついこの間、国を出て東に向かったばかりと思った江戸詰めだが、お国を留守に無事一年、江戸の勤めも終えました。

大名行列の七つのお道具は、槍、長刀、台笠[27]、立傘[28]、馬印[29]、挟み箱に大鳥毛[30]。中でも大鳥毛は鳥取藩自慢の槍印でもありまする。

The parade of the Tottori daimio and his clansmen has all these seven essentials[31]. The daimio's horses are exuberant and neighing loudly because they are reminded of their northern homeland when the fierce north wind blows. And last in the procession is a pair of spears.

The people in the procession must be celebrating the completion of a year's station in Edo and of the safe procession to Tottori.

The chief retainer, has been waiting in the Tottori castle in the absence of his daimio. He must be delighted at the safe homecoming of his lord.

The lord served his duty in Edo while his retainers in Tottori took care of the country. Today is a happy reunion. Let's celebrate it with newly brewed sake.

The song for the celebratory banquet has to be [*singing*] 'The sound of the pine trees on the beach goes zazanza, zazanza, zazanza, zazanza'

May their homeland last hundreds of thousands of years like the evergreen pine trees of their mountains! We all wish that the Tottori fief in Inaba will prosper forever.

Blackout.

「堀川波鼓」

七つ道具[31]を無事揃え、お召しの駒、乗り換えの駒は、北風に己の故郷を懐かしみ、ヒヒヒーンといななく元気よさ。行列の最後を括る一対の槍。

お国に帰るは一年ぶり。無事の長旅、お勤め終えて、さぞかしめでたいことでありましょう。

お国元のご家老様もさぞかし嬉しいことでありましょう。

主君は立派にお江戸勤め。国元のご家臣衆も皆無事のお留守番。今日はめでたいお国入り。さあさ、新樽の酒でお祝いしようよ。

宴に謡うは『浜の松の音は、ざざんざ、ざざんざ、ざざんざ、ざざんざ』

松の緑の常磐のように、万代も続けと願う故郷へのお国入り。鳥取の因幡のお国は久しく永く栄えることでありましょう。

　　　暗転。

SCENE TWO

At Ogura Hikokurō's Residence

The day of HIKOKURŌ's homecoming on the 27th of May.
At OGURA HIKOKURŌ's residence in Inaba district in the fief of Tottori

A large room with a tokonoma alcove in the centre of the stage. As in ACT ONE, the floor is raised and upstage corridors stretch offstage from each side of the room. The one Upstage Right leads to the kitchen, the utility area and the tradesman's entrance and the other Upstage Left leads to the inner part of the house.

The main entrance of the house is a wooden gate which stands at the foot of the hanamichi. The layout of the OGURA house resembles the NARUYAMA house in ACT ONE, but the OGURA house has a small front garden and not as fine as the NARUYAMA house.

HIKOKURŌ's swords are placed on the sword holder in the tokonoma alcove. Objects such as HIKOKURŌ's travelling outfit, lacquered travelling chests and gifts from the other retainers are placed in front of the alcove. Several rolls of Eastern linen[1] are seen among the gifts.

The house is buzzing with excitement for the master's return after a year absence. TANE, BUNROKU and FUJI are welcoming HIKOKURŌ in the room. They sit in order of HIKOKURŌ at the head, Stage Left.

TANE: Welcome home. We are delighted that the master of the house has returned to Tottori safe and sound. All the people of Ogura have been looking forward to this day. We heard that the lord greatly increased your salary on departure from Edo. I would like to offer my congratulations on your promotion.

BUNROKU: Father, welcome home. I've been looking forward to your return with Mother and Aunt every day. I am delighted to see you at home in good health. I heard that the lord increased your salary for your distinguished work over the last several years and the rise is not to be compared with that of other retainers'. As a result you have more young samurai and menservants in the house of Ogura. Very many congratulations on your achievement.

FUJI: Brother, welcome home. I am delighted that you've come back to Tottori safely. Also many congratulations on your outstanding success.

「堀川波鼓」

第二場

小倉彦九郎屋敷の場

　一七〇六年五月二十七日、小倉彦九郎国入りの日。
　鳥取藩因幡の国、小倉彦九郎屋敷。

　舞台中央に床の間付の座敷がある。上乃巻と同じように、小倉の家も座敷から上下両方向に廊下が延びており、下手廊下側には厨房や納戸や勝手口などがあり、上手廊下側は家の奥になる。

　屋敷の玄関口である木製の門が下手花道付近にある。屋敷の間取りはたねの実家の丸山の家と良く似ているが、この家には広い前庭がなく、家屋も丸山の屋敷ほど立派ではない。
　座敷の床の間横の刀置きには彦九郎の刀が置かれ、その前に葛籠、旅の荷物、藩中の人々からの国入りのお土産などが置かれている。土産物の中には真苧[1]の反物がある。

　今、小倉家は一年ぶりの彦九郎の国入りで、華やいで賑やかな雰囲気である。
　座敷には、彦九郎を上座に、たね、文六、ふじの姿がある。

たね　お帰りなさいませ。御無事で御国入りなされましたことをお喜び申し上げます。家のもの皆一同に、今日の日をお待ち申しておりました。また、お江戸ご出立の折には殿様より多くの御加増を賜られたとのこと、まことにおめでとうございます。

文六　父上、お帰りなさいませ。母上や叔母上共々、お帰りになられる日を毎日、心待ちにしておりました。お元気なお顔を見ることが出来まして、分六、嬉しゅうございます。父上のここ数年の立派なお勤めに対し、他の藩士の方々とは比べ物にならないほどの御加増をいただかれて、若党、下男の数も増したとお聞きしました。誠におめでとうございます。

ふじ　兄上、お帰りなさいませ。御無事でこの鳥取にお帰りになられましたこと、心からお喜び申し上げます。また、この度の群を抜いた御出世、誠におめでとうござ

HIKOKURŌ: Thank you for your hearty welcome. I am home now. Let me thank all of you for having taken good care of the house of Ogura in my absence. I was indeed given a generous salary increase by my lord when we were setting out from Edo. I wanted to let you know about it as soon as possible and see your happy faces. I was thinking about it all the way through the journey. Now I am pleased that all of you are happy and looking well. And Bunroku seems to have grown up so much in one year.

A messenger of MASAYAMA SANGOBEI, the equerry at Tottori Castle, comes at the gate. He is bringing a homecoming gift.

MESSENGER: Good morning! I came to deliver a homecoming gift for the mistress of the house on behalf of my master, Masayama Sangobei.

FUJI goes to the MESSENGER to receive the gift.

MESSENGER: This is my master's homecoming present to O-Tane-sama. Here are his words to Ogura-sama, [*handing a gift to FUJI, clearing his throat and in a manner of passing along a message*] "You safely attended the lord throughout his journey and by now are happily reunited with your family. I congratulate you. I am in the same situation and much pleased to see my family after a year away from home. I looked for a suitable present for O-Tane-sama but it was not an easy task as most of the things we brought back from Edo were too familiar to us. So this time I chose something new. It is called Eastern linen. It looks home-spun and ordinary, but is in fact pliant and luxurious. On the journey home I heard that O-Tane-sama had been weaving a special kimono lining for special occasions during her husband's absence. I checked on the matter when I got home, and found that it was indeed the talk of Tottori. I think that this is the most suitable present for her as it will be useful for her when her time comes." [*Clearing his throat once again*] That's all from my master. I must go now. Please excuse me. [*The MESSENGER leaves.*]

FUJI pretends to be calm and thanks the MESSENGER.
HIKOKURŌ and BUNROKU are talking about something happily during this speech. TANE tries to keep her composure.
FUJI returns to the room, places the roll of Eastern linen on the pile of other gifts in front of the alcove and sits at the place where she was.

「堀川波鼓」

います。
彦九郎　ただいま戻りました。皆も一年の間のお留守番、ご苦労でした。我が殿より思いがけなく多分の御加増をいただき、大変有難く、そのことを一刻も早くそなた達に報告して、喜ぶ顔を見るのが楽しみで戻ってきました。皆、元気そうで何より。文六は一年見ない間にたいそう大人になったようだ。

　　　　彦九郎の妹ゆらの婿馬廻役政山三五平の家の使いの者が、お国入りの土産を持って表門まで来る。

三五平の使いの者　ごめん下さいませ。主人政山三五平からの使いで、奥様にお国入りのお土産をお届けにまいりました。

　　　　ふじが土産を受け取りに出る。

三五平の使いの者　これは、主人からこちらのおたね様へのお土産の品でございます。（土産をふじに手渡し、咳払いをして、伝言の口調で）『先ずは道中何事もなく殿様のお供をなされ、ご家族ともご対面を果たされまして、誠におめでとう御座います。当方も同様で、久方ぶりに家族の顔を見る事が出来まして、嬉しく思っております。さて、おたね様へのお土産を何にするか思案いたしましたが、あまり代わり映えのしない品ばかりでございます。これは関東麻の真苧と呼ばれる布で、あまり、見目の良いものではございせんが、お留守の間、おたね様が真苧……トコ（間男）を繙んでおられると、道すがら噂されておりました。家にもどり確かめたところ、藩中でもそのような評判でございますので、この品を進上いたします。』との、主人の言葉でございます。（再び咳払いをして）では、私はこれにて、ごめん下さい。（言い終えて去る。）

　　　　ふじは平静を装って礼を言う。
　　　　この間、彦九郎は文六となにやら楽しげに話をしている。たねは平静を装っている。
　　　　ふじは座敷に戻って真苧を土産の置いてある所に置いてからもと居た場所に座る。

RIN comes in the corridor Upstage Right. She carries more rolls of Eastern linen.

RIN: Messengers from Kawakami-sama and Yoshimura-sama came to the tradesman's entrance and delivered these as a homecoming present for the mistress of the house. [*She puts the rolls of linen onto the gift pile and goes back to the kitchen.*]

FUJI and BUNROKU are embarrassed by the rolls of Eastern linen and look at each other. TANE looks anxiously at HIKOKURŌ, wondering. But HIKOKURŌ seems unaware of the insinuating remark about the Eastern linen at all.

HIKOKURŌ [*satisfied*]: Now we must open our travelling chests and send our greetings to the other retainers. Oh! I've nearly forgotten to make a courtesy call to my father-in-law. I must do it now before anything else. Tane, will you please bring me a pair of *hakama* trousers for that.

TANE: Yes, darling, in a moment. [*She goes off Upstage Left.*]

BUNROKU carries HIKOKURŌ's lacquered travelling chests to the utility room, Upstage Right.

FUJI [*going to HIKOKURŌ soon after TANE and BUNROKU exit*]: Hikokurō-sama, how terribly cold and cruel you have been! I sent two letters to Edo, but you didn't reply. Why didn't you? I've written down my feelings for you in this letter once more. I thought and thought and wrote this. You must accept what I say whether you like it or not. [*She pushes the letter into the bosom of HIKOKURŌ's kimono.*]

HIKOKURŌ [making a face]: Fuji-dono, have you lost your mind? Certainly, when I was thinking of marrying your elder sister, marriage to you was also suggested. However, I chose Tane to be my wife. Perhaps it was because you and I were not fated to marry. Tane and I have been happily married for ten odd years. Furthermore as we had not been blessed with a child, we adopted your younger brother Bunroku. Now, you start telling me that you are terribly in love with me and that I must divorce Tane and marry you. I have no ears for such a silly story! And I do not wish to read this sort of thing! [*He throws away FUJI's letter and walks out of the house.*]

TANE was looking at the two from the back room. She comes straight at the letter,

「堀川波鼓」

　　　　　　下手奥から、下女のりんが、真苧の反物を幾つか運んで来る。

りん　只今、川上様、吉村様からのお使いが見えて、奥様へのお土産にとこれらをお持ちになりました。（言い終えてから、土産の所に反物を置いて下手に退く。）

　　　　　　ふじと文六は土産の真苧の反物に困惑して顔を見合わせる。
　　　　　　たねは自分の姦通を彦九郎が知っているのではないかと不安げに彦九郎の顔を窺う。しかし、彦九郎は「真苧」のあてつけに、一向に気付かない様子である。

彦九郎（満足げに）さてさて、我々も早く荷物を解いて、藩中の方々に土産の品を遣わすことにいたそう。おっと、忘れていた。まず先に、舅殿のところにご挨拶に参らねばならん。たね、袴を出してくれ。

たね　はい、ただいま。（袴を取りに上手に退く。）

　　　　　　文六は葛籠を抱えて下手に去る。

ふじ　（たねと文六の姿が座敷から見えなくなるとすぐに彦九郎に近寄り）彦九郎様。お前様はつれないお方です。私が二度もお江戸にまで出した手紙の返事を何故下さらなかったのでございます。私の気持ちはこれこの文に、もう一度、詳しく書きました。このふじが考えて考え抜いた上で書いた文でございます。否でも応でも承知していただかねばなりませぬ。（封をした手紙を彦九郎の懐中に押し込む。）
彦九郎（苦い顔をして）ふじ殿、そなたは気でも違われたか？確かに、そなたの姉たねを嫁に迎えるころ、そなたとの縁談もあった。しかし、縁がなかったからこそ、姉のたねと夫婦になり、既に十幾年という年月を重ねている。その上、夫婦が子宝に恵まれぬゆえ、そなた達姉妹の弟である文六を養子に置く仲にまでになっている。それを、どのように恋い慕われようが、たねを離別してそなたと添おうとは、この彦九郎、申しかねる。このような手紙は手にも取らん！（手紙を投げ捨てて、外に出て行ってしまう。）

　　　　　　二人の様子を奥から見ていたたねが、つかつかと出てきて手紙を拾って

picks it up and puts it into the bosom of her kimono.

FUJI [*rushing to retrieve the letter and clinging to TANE*]: It is an important private letter. No one else should read it.

TANE kicks FUJI to the floor without saying a word. Then she goes to get a hemp-palm broom and attacks FUJI with it.

FUJI: Ow! Ah, that hurts. Help me! Help!

BUNROKU and RIN hear FUJI's cries and rush into the room from Upstage Right.

RIN: O-Tane-sama! Oh, please stop! O-Tane-sama!
BUNROKU [*protecting FUJI*]: Mother, I do not know what has happened between you and Aunt, but please forgive her. [*He wrenches the broom from TANE.*]
TANE [*this time picking up a riding crop[2] from the pile of HIKOKURŌ's travelling items*]: I will rip your lying face with this! [*TANE hits FUJI with it several times.*]
FUJI [*crying and screaming*]: Ow! That hurts! She's killing me! Ouch! Help! Help me!
BUNROKU [*wrenching the riding crop from TANE and disgusted*]: Look, Mother! I don't know what Aunt has done. But, if you talked to her, she would understand. I am sure of it. You don't need to hit her like this. If Aunt collapses, what are you going to do?
TANE: Even if I beat her to death, I won't regret it. She deserves it. Your Aunt is in love with my husband. She set her heart on him and sent him love letters to Edo. I heard it with my own ears a moment ago. More than that, I've just got her latest letter to my husband. [*Taking out FUJI's letter*] Look at this! Do you think I'm just imagining it? [*Opening the letter and reading it*] How could you? It says here, "...divorce my sister, marry me ..." and she's even enclosed her nail clipping to make it a vow. This is not something I've made up. You must read this, too. [*Giving the letter to BUNROKU, then to FUJI*] I hate you! Oh, how I loathe you! [*Grabbing FUJI by the hair of tabusa,[3] winding it around the arm and kneeling on it*] You...you tried to steal my husband, my childhood friend, who, who means the world to me. I would even put him before my precious parents and child... How dare you! I waited for his return for a year. I adore him like people adore the stars and the moon. And at last I saw my dear husband's face this morning...I, I was so happy. I was just thinking that we would be able to live in the same house for a year until he departed for Edo once again... How dare you ask my husband to divorce me!

「堀川波鼓」

　　　　懐にしまい込む。

ふじ　（手紙を取り戻そうと、たねに取り付いて）それは大事な手紙。誰にも見せられませぬ。

　　　　たねはものも言わずにふじを蹴り倒してから、棕櫚箒を取ってきてふじを叩く。

ふじ　あれ！ああ、痛い！助けて！

　　　　文六とりんがふじの声を聞きつけて、下手から駆けつける。

りん　おたね様！お止め下さいませ。おたね様！
文六　（ふじを庇いながら）母上、何事があったか知りませぬが、どうぞご堪忍を。（たねから箒を奪い取る。）
たね　（今度は彦九郎の旅の荷物に付いていた、荒馬の鼻をねじる道具の「はなねじ[2]」を引き抜き）顔も頭も砕けてしまえ！（と、「はなねじ」でふじを続けさまに打つ。）
ふじ　（声を上げて泣き叫び）ああ！痛い、痛い、死んでしまう！痛い！助けて！
文六　（たねから「はなねじ」をもぎ取り、苦りきった様子で）これ、母様。何があったのかは存じませぬが、言葉でお叱りになればよいものを。このように荒々しく打ち叩くことはございません。叔母様が目でも回されたらどう言い訳なさるおつもりですか。
たね　いいや。打ち殺しても大事無い！このふじは、姉の夫に思いを寄せ執心して、江戸にまで手紙を出していたと、今、この耳で確かに聞いた。それにたった今、ふじが彦九郎殿に書いた文も拾いました。（懐から手紙を取り出し）これを見や！これが、嘘か？偽りか？（手紙の封を切って読んで）あろうことか、「姉を離別して暇をやり、私が代わってお前と夫婦になろう」などと、真実の心の証に自分の生爪剥がして入れたこの文。これが嘘偽りであるものか。読んでみるがいい！（手紙を文六に手渡す。）ええ、憎い！腹の立つ！（ふじの髻[3]を掴んで、髪の毛をぐるぐると手に絡ませてから、自分の膝に敷いて）親にも子にも替えられぬほど大切に思っている幼馴染の我が夫を、よくもお前は……。一年もの長いお留守の間、月よ星よと、この上なく愛しく思って待ち焦がれて、今朝、やっと、我が殿御のお顔が見られた……ああ、嬉しい、来年のお江戸勤めまでの一年は、一緒に寝起きが出来るものと喜んでいた矢先に……おのれは、よくも姉を離縁せよなどと、言ったな！その畜生面！生かしておくのも腹立たしい！（目鼻の区別もなく、ふじをうち叩く。）

241

You're no better than an animal. I hate to see you alive! [*She beats FUJI in a frenzy way.*]

FUJI [*breathing with difficulty and imploring*]: Sister! Please, please listen to me. There, there is a reason for this. Everyone, please calm her down… Oh, I, I'm losing my breath…

BUNROKU [*stopping TANE forcibly*]: Mother, first, you must listen to Aunt's story!

TANE [*stops hitting, coldly*]: If your story fails to convince me, I swear, I will take your life. Now tell us! [*She raises FUJI by the hair and pushes her away.*]

FUJI [*out of breath and choking*]: I'll tell you the reason right now, but only to you, alone. [*To BUNROKU and RIN*] Please go to the other room and leave us.

BUNROKU and RIN reluctantly go off Upstage Right.

TANE [*coldly*]: You have no need to act as if there were something significant in this. Now, let me hear your 'explanation.'

FUJI [*shedding a torrent of tears*]: Sister, I wrote to Hikokurō-sama and asked him to divorce you. It was all because I wanted to be good to you. I was trying my best to save your life… I do not think that you need me to tell you why. I think that you know very well…You're having a relationship with Bunroku's *tsuzumi* teacher, Miyaji Genemon, aren't you?

TANE [*quickly covering FUJI's mouth with her hand*]: Be quiet! That is a silly thing to say, and you shouldn't speak such things aloud. What have you seen? Where is the evidence for your accusation?

FUJI [*in control*]: What more do you need? I don't have to show you anything to prove it. Tell me who is the father of the four-month old child you are carrying? You sent Rin to buy some abortion drugs. Tell me who's taken them? Sister, you seem to think that no one has noticed your pregnancy. You're wrong! Everyone is talking about you. Just now we were given Eastern linen as a homecoming present. You know what that means. It was a message from his close friends. They tried to tell him that he'd been cuckolded. As a result of your shameful conduct, our parents', sisters and brothers' and your husband's pride as a samurai, all have been ruined. [*She cries aloud.*]

TANE [*having nothing to say and to herself*]: I always ignored your warning…and in the end I was caught out by my weakness for sake. [*She sheds tears quietly.*]

FUJI [*wiping her tears away*]: Oh, Sister! Your words have come half a year too late! Being a younger sister, I thought and thought about this. And I reached the conclusion that your honour as a samurai's wife couldn't be restored at any price. In this situation the most I could do was to save your life. I thought about how to do it. I thought, if you were divorced, if only you succeeded in getting a letter of divorce from your husband,

「堀川波鼓」

ふじ 　（息も絶え絶えに）姉様、これにはいろいろ訳がある。皆、どうか姉様を取り静めて……。ああ、息が切れる……。
文六 　（たねを強く制して）母上、先ずは、叔母様の言い訳をお聞きになって下さい。
たね 　（叩くのを止めて、冷たく）もしも、言い訳立たぬ時には、今度はお前の命をとる。言い訳あるならしてみよ！（ふじの髪を掴んで引き立て、突きのける。）
ふじ 　（苦しげに息をしながら）今、その言い訳を申します。けど、その言い訳は姉様と二人、差し向かいでなければ言えませぬ。（文六とりんに）どうか、皆は次の間へ。

　　　　　文六とりんは仕方なく下手に去る。

たね 　（腹立たしそうに）そのように、尤もらしく仔細ありげにしなくともよい。さあ、お前の言い訳、聞こう。
ふじ 　（はらはらと涙を流して）姉様、私が彦九郎様に手紙を出し、姉様を離別して下さいと言うてやったのは、みんな姉孝行のため、お前様の命を助けたいため……。その理由は、ここで私が言うまでも無い。身に覚えがございましょう。お前様は文六の鼓の師匠、宮地源右衛門と深い仲ではござりませぬか？

たね 　（急いでふじの口を押さえて）お黙りなさい！馬鹿馬鹿しい話とはいえ、易からぬ大事。何を見てそのようなことを言う。どこに証拠がある？

ふじ 　（静かに）何を言われる。証拠などさがすには及びませぬ。お前のそのお腹の四月になる子は誰の子じゃ？下女のりんに買いに遣られた堕ろし薬は誰が飲まれたのか。姉様は、人は気付いていない、と思われているようですが、藩中では皆お前の噂で持ちっきり。たった今も、家中の方々から「間男」の隠語である「真苧」の土産の数々。これも、みなお前の不義を彦九郎様に知らせんがための親しい方々からのご注進、とふじは見ました。あなた一人のために、親兄弟、夫の武士まで廃ってしまった。（声を上げて泣く。）

たね 　（返す言葉もなく、自分自身に）常日頃から注意を聞かずにいた……、酒が我が身の敵……。（泣く。）
ふじ 　（あふれ出る涙を抑えながら）ああ、姉様！その言葉が半年遅かった！妹として考えあぐねておりました。もはや、姉様の名誉は回復出来るものではない。ならば、せめて、命だけでも助けたい。色々様々思案して、もしお前様と彦九郎様との縁が切れて、暇状さえいただけたなら、たとえ大道の真ん中で子を産ませても大事ないはず、お前の命に障りはないはずと、浅はかな女の思案から、姉の夫

you wouldn't have to die. If you weren't the wife of a retainer, even if you delivered your child on the street, no one would blame you. So I decided to pretend to take a fancy to Hikokurō-sama. I know it was a woman's shallow thinking but I had to do something to try and help you, Sister. And that wasn't all. I also thought about our mother. I had to do something for her, too. Surely, you haven't forgotten her final words. Dear Mother called us to her deathbed and said, "I have taught you woman's duties since you were little girls. You've learned how to read and write, how to sew, to spin cotton into yarn and to reel silk. I believe that wherever you go that you won't disgrace yourself in these things. However most important of all is how to behave after you take a husband. You must care for your father-in-law in the same way you do to your own father, and see your brother-in-law as your own brother and your sister-in-law as your own sister. And if you are in a room with another man, whether your husband is there or not, you must never look straight at his face. You must keep this up, especially when your husband is away. You must treat every man in this way whether he is one of your servants, family or unrelated, young or old. If you cannot do this, your knowledge of the Nine Chinese Classics will be no use. Please take these words as your Analects of Confucius and never forget them." Her words have been with me ever since. She also told me privately, "Your elder sister Tane has taken after her father drinking since she was in her child's kimono.[4] Listen, Fuji. You must look after her for me." After that, Mother was out of breath and extremely exhausted. Even now I remember the expression on her face so well. Every morning and evening when I face her mortuary tablet and pray, I take her words as my sutra and repeat them. Sister, have you already forgotten what our mother said? You've made your little sister worry in this world and your mother ashamed in the other... [*FUJI throws herself down and cries aloud.*]

TANE [*choked with tears*]: I always liked *sake*, but now I know that it was fated to be my downfall before I was born into this world. It has poisoned my life. When I woke up that night and realised what I had done, I thought I must commit suicide. But I wanted to see my husband once more before I died. So I stayed on another day. When that day was over, I wanted to live until the next evening. I stayed on every day and disgraced myself to the world. I, I was possessed by an evil spirit...

    TANE and FUJI cling to each other, crying.

    Suddenly there is a noise outside the gate.
    HIKOKURŌ enters in a hurry on the hanamichi. YURA, HIKOKURŌ's younger sister, follows him. She is holding a naginata halberd.

「堀川波鼓」

に執心する浮気者の振りをしました。これもみな、姉様孝行のため。いいえ、それだけでなく、亡くなられた母様への孝行とも考えました。愛しい母様がご臨終の二日前にお前と私の二人を枕元に呼ばれ、遺言されたお言葉をよもや忘れはなさるまい。『そなた達二人には、幼い頃から女子の道を教えてきました。ですから、読み書き、縫針、糸くりの道などはどこに行っても恥をかくことはありますまい。けれど、女子の第一のたしなみは、夫を持ってからが肝心。舅は親、小姑はお前の兄、姉と考えて孝行をつくすように。夫以外の男とは、差し向かいになっても顔を上げて見てはならぬ。とりわけ、夫が留守の時には、男とあらばたとえ召使でも一門の者も他人もみな一様に、年寄り若者の区別無く、このたしなみが守れぬなら、たとえ四書五経を空で読めても何の役にもたちませぬ。この私の言葉をそなた達の論語と思うて、決して忘れることのないように。』この母様のお言葉が肝に残って忘れられませぬ。『姉は父御の血を引いて、後ろ紐の童の着物[4]を着ていた頃から酒を飲む。よいな、ふじ、この母になりかわり、姉に注意をしておくれ。』と、話されて、その後すぐに息が切れてやつれ顔になられた。あのときの母様のお顔がこの身に付きまとうて忘れられず、朝夕、お位牌に向かう時も、この遺言をお経と思い、一遍ずつは繰り返して唱えている。あの母様の言葉を姉様はもう忘れられたのか？この世の妹に心配をかけ、あの世においでの母様の屍を苦しませて……。（声をあげて泣き伏す。）

たね　（涙に咽んで）好きで飲んだ酒も、今思えば、この世に生を受ける前からの、悪い因縁の毒の酒。私の心を惑わした酒の酔いが覚めたとき、自害しようと思った。けれど、もう一度、夫の顔が見たいと思う一心から、今日までと延ばし、今日が終われば明日の暮れまでと、延ばし続けて、世間に恥を晒してきました。悪魔にこの身を魅入られてしまった……。

　　　　　姉妹は縋り合って泣く。

　　　　　表が急に騒がしくなる。花道を彦九郎が急ぎ足で帰ってくる。その後を、長刀を構えたゆらが追って来ている。

YURA: Brother! Please wait! Brother!

TANE [*wiping her tears away*]: It's noisy outside. I wonder what's going on.

FUJI [*also wiping her tears away*]: It sounds like a quarrel. Anyway you'd better go to the inner room, Sister. I'll go and see Bunroku. He must be anxious about us.

> *TANE goes to the inner room off Upstage Left. FUJI goes off Upstage Right. HIKOKURŌ comes in through the gate. YURA enters through the gate after him.*

YURA: Brother! I've been asking you to wait for me. I'm your younger sister, but at the same time I'm a retainer's wife, too. Even if you are my elder brother, you must acknowledge my right to justice. Brother, you must answer the question that I asked. Please let me have your answer.

HIKOKURŌ [*turning around, and glaring at YURA sharply*]: How dare you, you insolent woman! How dare you to tell your elder brother that I am ignoring justice! What is it that I'm ignoring? You must explain that to me. If you don't, I will twist off your arm that's holding your precious naginata halberd.

YURA [*laughing loudly*]: Ha-ha-ha! How admirable! But what a coward you are! As you wish, I shall tell you all about it. Your wife is committing adultery with your son's tsuzumi teacher, Miyaji Genemon. Wherever you go in Tottori, it's the talk of the clansmen. Some of your close friends felt obliged to inform you and sent the rolls of Eastern linen as a hint. But, you pretended not to notice anything, because you are a coward and will not take revenge on the adulterer. My husband told me that he could not have a wife who was the sister of such a weak samurai and divorced me for that reason. He said that I could return when you became a proper samurai. Listen, Brother, it's all up to you whether or not I become Sangonei's wife once again. [*YURA assumes a proper defensive posture with the naginata. She looks as if she will use it if HIKOKURŌ flinches.*]

HIKOKURŌ [*shocked with the utterly unexpected news and striking the palms of his hands unconciously*]: What did you say? You've made a very serious accusation. I haven't met Miyaji Genemon but I've heard of him. However, I do not think that Genemon has even been to my house. Do you have any proof?

YURA: Of course, we do. You don't think that a samurai like Sangobei would say something as serious as this without any evidence. Your good friend, Isobe Yukaemon, suspected Genemon and your wife. So he went to the Naruyama house on the evening of their secret meeting, pretending to inquire about the health of your wife in your absence. When

「堀川波鼓」

ゆら　兄様！お待ち下さい！兄様！
たね　（涙を拭きながら）何やら、表が騒がしい。
ふじ　（同じく涙を拭いて）どうやら喧嘩のようです。姉様、お前はひとまず奥へ、私は文六の様子を見てまいります。

　　　　　　たねは上手の奥の間へ、ふじは下手に去る。
　　　　　　彦九郎は屋敷内に入る。
　　　　　　ゆらも彦九郎を追って屋敷内に入る。

ゆら　兄様！お待ち下さいと申しておりますのに。そなたの妹とはいえど、私は政山三五平という武士の妻。いかに、兄様とはいえ、義の立たぬことをされるなら、このゆらが許しませぬ。兄様、さあ、お返事を。お返事をしてくだされ！

彦九郎　（ゆらを睨み返して）何を生意気な女郎めが。兄であるこの彦九郎に向かって、義の立たぬことをしているとは、無礼千万。私のしていることの何が義が立たぬのか、その仔細を言え。言わねば、その長刀を持ったお前の腕節共にねじ折るぞ。

ゆら　（高笑いして）は、は、はっ！何としおらしい腰抜け殿ではないか！では、その仔細をお聞かせしよう。そなたの内儀は息子文六の鼓の師匠である宮地源右衛門と密通していると、今、御家中はどこへ行ってもその話で持ちっきりじゃ。それ故、皆は、そのことをお前様に知らせんと、土産に「間男」の隠語である「真苧」を遣わした。『なのに、彦九郎は自分の妻と姦通した男を討たずに、聞かぬ振りをしている。そのような男の妹を妻にはしておけん』と、夫三五平は私に暇を出された。『兄の腰抜けが直ったら、戻って来い、元通りの夫婦になろう』との約束で別れてきました。これ、腰抜けの兄様。私を夫と添わせるか添わせないかは、そなたのお心一つですぞ。（ゆらは長刀を構えなおし、閃かせて、彦九郎が話を聞いて怯んだら、切ろうとの勢いである。）

彦九郎　（あまりに意外な話に、思わず両手を打って）何だと！これは重大なことを聞く。今、そなたの言った源右衛門という者、顔は見たことは無いが、名前は聞いて知っている。しかし、まだ、この屋敷内に来たことはない。何か、確たる証拠でもあるのか。

ゆら　三五平ほどの者が証拠も無しに、このように重大な事を言うとお思いか。兄様の朋輩であるあの磯辺床右衛門が、義姉上と宮地源右衛門の不義密通の気配を察し、二人が忍び逢う夜に、兄様のお留守見舞いを口実に成山の家を訪れ、不義の証拠にと、両人の着物の袖を切り取りました。その後、しばらく、床右衛門は切った

he found them together, he cut off their sleeves as evidence of their misconduct. For a while he kept them to himself, but the rumour about their adultery didn't die down. It was extremely difficult for him to keep quiet, but it was also hard for him to come and tell you. In the end he came to see my husband and told him that the matter needed urgent attention. [*Taking the sleeves out of her kimono bosom and throwing them at the feet of HIKOKURŌ.*] Look at them. Do you still doubt what I've said? [*YURA has changed her complexion with anger.*]

HIKOKURŌ [*picking up the sleeves*]: I don't know the man's sleeve but I do remember the woman's. Sister, follow me! I will clear your name right now.

> *HIKOKURŌ goes into the house in a hurry. YURA follows him.*
> *The conversation between HIKOKURŌ and YURA was loud enough to be heard in the house, but no one is around in the sitting room and the place is very quiet.*

HIKOKURŌ [*to the inner part of the house*]: Wife! Sister-in-law! Come here! Bunroku, my son! You must come here, too.

> *FUJI and BUNROKU come in from Upstage Right.*
> *A little later TANE comes from the inner room. She staggers slightly.*

CHORUS: Oh, I'm sad! I'm so miserable!
    It's my own entire fault.
    My undreamed of ill-fated destiny ruined my happiness.
    I was more than ready to be killed by my dear husband.
    Only, I wanted to be with him one last time.
    I wanted to look at his face and touch it one last time.
    It was all that I wanted.
    I lived from day to day and wished for his return.
    But my small wish goes unheard.
    It seems that our last night was the night before he left for Edo.
    That was our last true night together.
    What a fool I have been! I didn't think of the consequences of my misconduct until this moment of my death.
    I wish I could see my beloved husband's face once more.
    But, I cannot see it. I cannot see a thing!

「堀川波鼓」

　　袖をそのままにしていたのですが、藩中の二人の不義の噂がなかなかおさまらないので、隠しきれなくなったそうです。しかし、いくら同輩の近しい仲であるとはいえ、兄様に直接このことを知らせるわけにはゆかぬと考え、そなたの義弟にあたる我が夫にことの急を知らせてきたのです。（懐中から切り取られた袂を取り出し、彦九郎の足元に放り投げて）これをご覧下さい。これでも、お疑いか？（ゆらは怒りで顔色を変えている）。

彦九郎　（袖を拾い上げて）男の袖に見覚えはないが、女の着物の柄には覚えがある。妹、ただ今これから、お前の恥辱を雪いでやる。付いて来い！

　　　　彦九郎は足早に家の中に入る。ゆらもその後を追う。
　　　　彦九郎とゆらの遣り取りは家の中にまで聞こえていた。が、今、座敷はひっそりと静まり返っている。

彦九郎　（奥に向かって）女房ども！こちらに参れ。倅も参れ。

　　　　ふじと文六が下手より静かに出て来る。
　　　　少し遅れて、たねが上手から出て来る。たねは足元が少しふらついている。

コーラス　かなしや！情けなや！
　　身から出た錆ではあるものの、
　　思わぬ悪縁が身の破滅。
　　愛しい夫の刃にかかって、この命なくす覚悟はとうに出来ている。
　　ただ、もう一度、会いたい、顔みたいの一心で、
　　長いお留守を耐えてきた、
　　そのかいも無く、
　　去年のお江戸への出立の前夜が、夫との最後の契りになろうとは、
　　命落とすことになる、今の今まで考えなんだ、この身の愚か。
　　もう一度、愛しい夫の顔がみたい！
　　けれど、涙にくれて、もう目も開かぬ。

For the tears of my remorse flood my eyes and blind me.

> TANE, *head down, sits and sobs silently.*

HIKOKURŌ [*throwing the piece of TANE's kimono sleeve in front of her*]: Everyone must have heard what Yura said. Look at it, wife! Do you have anything to say?

> TANE *does not lift her head and stays silent.*

HIKOKURŌ [*looking at TANE and calmly*]: I see. It looks as if you have nothing to say. We know that the go-between of the adulterers is as guilty as they are. Fuji, do you know who was mediating between them?

FUJI [*mortified*]: What a question you ask of me? If I had known the person, we wouldn't have faced disgrace like this. [*She sheds tears of frustration.*]

HIKOKURŌ: In that case, I suppose that it could only be Tane's maid, Rin. [*To BUNROKU*] Will you call her here?

BUNROKU [*in the direction of the kitchen, Upstage Right*]: Rin! Will you come here?

RIN [*off stage*]: Yes, sir! I'll be right away.

> RIN *has been listening to the conversation from behind the kitchen pillar. She comes out and kneels down at the edge of the room.*

RIN [*trembling with fear and with teeth chattering*]: No, never sir. It wasn't me, sir. I don't know anything. O-Tane-sama told me to go and get some abortion drug the other day, so I went out and bought three doses for her. It was seven *bu* for one dose, so I paid two *monme* and one *bu*. That was all. [*Frightened and incoherent*] But, sir... err...I didn't want to be thought that I'd bought an expensive drug, so, I, I cooked up the price.

HIKOKURŌ [*shocked*]: Then, Tane is carrying the man's child? [*Angrily*] Bunroku, I know you are still very young, but when you heard many Tottori clansmen were talking openly of your mother's adultery and pregnancy, why didn't you kill Genemon with your sword?

BUNROKU [*with regret*]: Father, we tried. But we only found it out this morning and when I sent out our men to Genemon's lodging, his landlord said that Genemon had already gone back to Kyoto a few days before.

HIKOKURŌ: I see. In that case it cannot be helped. You've done what you had to do. [*A short pause*] Now, please light the candle in the family altar room. [*To TANE*] Woman!

「堀川波鼓」

　　　　　　たねは俯いて、声も立てず泣いている。

彦九郎　（袖をたねの前に投げ出し）ゆらの言い分は皆も聞いたであろう。おい、女房！言い訳はないか。

　　　　　　たねは俯いたままである。

彦九郎　（たねの様子を見て、静かに）なるほど。返事がないようだ。さて、不義は間に立って仲立ちをする者も同罪。ふじ、そなた、誰が仲立ちをしていたのか知らぬか。
ふじ　（悔しげに）何を愚かなことを申されます。もしも、私がその者を知っておりましたなら、このように恥をみることはございませぬ。（情けなさに、さめざめと泣く。）
彦九郎　それでは、下女のりんが仲立ちであろう。（文六に）りんを呼べ！

文六　（下手に向かって）りん！ここへ！
りんの声　はい。只今そちらへ。

　　　　　　台所の柱の陰から座敷の様子を窺っていたりんが下手から出て来て、座敷の端に座る。

りん　（がちがちと身を震わせて）恐れ多いことでございます。私は何も存知ません。この間、おたね様が、誰にも内緒で子堕し薬を買って来るよう仰いましたので、一服が七分のお薬を三服、二匁一分[5]で買ってきただけでございます。（りんは恐怖で極度にうろたえて、しどろもどろになっている。）けれども、旦那様、あの……、高いものを買ってきたといわれて叱られるのではないかと思いましたので、お金のことは誤魔化しておきましたのでございます。
彦九郎　（はっと驚いて）それでは、たねは懐胎したのか……。（怒って）文六、お前はまだ若年とはいえ、たねのことがこれほど御家中で取り沙汰されているというのに、何故、源右衛門をすぐに討たなかったのだ。
文六　（口惜しそうに）いいえ、父上、我等も今朝、このことを知り、家来たちに言いつけて、源右衛門の逗留先に討手を遣わしたのですが、奴は二、三日前にすでに京都に帰ったと言われたのです。
彦九郎　そうか……、それでは仕方がない。やむを得ぬことであったな。（一瞬、間をおいてから）さて、仏間に灯をいれてくれ。女、立て！仏間へ来い。

You must come to the altar room.

TANE [*wiping her tears away*]: I wouldn't be able to say anything even if you continued to hate me to the end of this world and the next. Instead, you tell me to come to the family altar room. How generous of you. Perhaps, it is because you pity me as a childhood friend. I shall not ever forget your kindness. I have been very happy in our marriage. You have never disappointed me and I have loved you so much. No words can express my feelings for you. What happened with the other man was not done intentionally either to estrange or to sleight you, my darling husband. It was like a dreadful nightmare that turned out to be true when I woke. I foolishly put myself in the situation. There is someone else who has done a terrible thing to me, but if I start accusing him, I'll be a coward and lose the dignity of my death… I know that it's wrong to do this before my husband kills me with his sword. But, Hikokurō-sama, please, please forgive me. This is my excuse. This is all I wanted to do since that terrible night. Please have a look. Forgive me…
[*Breathing very feebly, TANE opens her kimono bosom with great difficulty.*]

> TANE's dagger is buried in her chest to the depth of the dagger guard. She has committed a premeditated suicide.
> HIKOKURŌ keeps calm at the sight of his wife's suicide. FUJI and BUNROKU are distraught and cry at first. But when they see HIKOKURŌ endure the matter bravely, they hold back their tears.
> Enduring the sorrow, HIKOKURŌ draws his sword quietly, holds TANE close to him, plunges the sword into her heart and kills her quickly. He does it gracefully in a manner of a samurai. He then places TANE's body on the floor, wipes off the blood on the blade and sheathes his sword. Next HIKOKURŌ puts on his travelling coat, picks up swords, the bamboo hat and a pair of waraji[6] sandals.

HIKOKURŌ: Listen, Bunroku. I am going to see the head clerk of the fief and ask for leave. Then I shall go to Kyoto and seek revenge. You must stay at the relatives' with Fuji until I come back.
BUNROKU: Father, please let me come to Kyoto with you.
FUJI & YURA: Brother, please let us come with you.
HIKOKURŌ [*angrily*]: Don't be ridiculous! I am going to take revenge on a mere townsman.[7] Do you want to humiliate me in public even more by coming to Kyoto to back me up? If any one of you tries to follow me, I will disown you right on the spot.
FUJI [*crying*]: It's so cold-hearted of you to say such a thing. I must avenge my sister's death.
BUNROKU: I must avenge my mother's death.

「堀川波鼓」

たね　（涙を拭って）未来の末の後の世まで憎まれても仕方のない私です。仏間に来いと言って下さるのは、さすがに、幼馴染の情のあるお仕打ち。未来永劫お忘れすることのない、あなたのそうしたお心をこの年月知って、言葉で言い尽くせないほど愛しく思っておりました。それまで大事な夫を疎遠疎略にする不義ではありませぬ。現実にあったこととは思えない、何か悪い夢の中で起こったような出来事が、気がつけば実際にこの身に起こっていた、そのような身の上になってしまいました。これにはひどいことをした憎い奴もおります。けれど、それを言えば、私が卑怯者に成り下がって未練の死となります。夫の刀にかかる前に、こうするのは良くないこととは存じております。彦九郎様、どうか、どうか、許してください！これが、私の言い訳です。あの夜以来、ずっと、こうしようと思っておりました。どうか、ご覧になって！許して……。（たねは息も絶え絶えに着物の胸を押し開ける。）

　　　　たねの胸元には九寸五分の長さの懐剣が鍔のところまで突き刺さっている。覚悟の自害である。
　　　　彦九郎は思いもよらないたねの姿に、身動きもしないで、毅然とした態度を保つ。ふじと文六は姉の自害の姿に泣き出すが、彦九郎の態度に気付いて嗚咽を堪える。
　　　　彦九郎は悲しみを堪えて、静かに刀を抜き、たねを引き寄せて、武士らしいあざやかな手つきで一度ぐっと刺し、次に返す刀でたねの止めを刺してやってから、死骸を押しやり、刀の血を拭って静かに鞘に納める。その後、今朝、脱いだばかりの旅装束を再び身につけ、大小の刀を腰に差し、笠、草鞋[6]などを手にする。

彦九郎　文六。私はこれから藩の番頭に訴えでて、お暇を申し願い、京都に上り、妻敵を討つ。その間、お前はふじを連れて親戚のところに身を寄せておれ。

文六　父上、私も一緒に行かせてください。
ふじ・ゆら　兄上、私たちもご一緒させて下さい。
彦九郎　（怒って）町人風情[7]一人を討つために、お前たちを召し連れて行くなどと……。この上、この私にまだ恥をかかせたいのか。お前達のうちの一人でも私についてきたら、すぐさま勘当する！
ふじ　（泣いて）それは、あまりにも情がない！私にとっては姉の敵。
文六　私には母の仇。

YURA: The man is my sister-in-law's enemy. I cannot leave him as he is.

FUJI, BUNROKU & YURA [*their hands pressed in prayer and in tears*]: Please, please let us come with you.

HIKOKURŌ [*finally unable to stay calm and in a pained voice*]: If you thought so much of Tane as your mother, sister and sister-in-law, why, why didn't you persuade her to wear the black robes of a nun and send her to a nunnery? If only you had, at least her and her child's lives would have been saved.

    HIKOKURŌ holds TANE's dead body tightly and weeps despite himself. BUNROKU, FUJI and YURA cling to TANE's body and weep.

    Blackout.

「堀川波鼓」

ゆら　この私には兄嫁の敵(がたき)。そ奴をこのまま見捨ててはおけませぬ。

ふじ・文六・ゆら　（泣きながら手を合わせて）どうか、一緒にお連れ下さい。

彦九郎（とうとう我慢しきれずに、辛く悲しそうな顔をして）それほどまでに、母、姉、兄嫁を大切に思う心があるのなら、何故、何故、たねが生きている間に墨染(すみぞ)めの衣を着せて尼にでもして、命を貰い受けてくれなかったのだ。

　　　　　彦九郎はたねの死骸を抱きしめて男泣きに泣く。
　　　　　文六、ふじ、ゆらの三人もたねの死骸(しがい)に取り付き泣く。

　　　　暗転。

ACT THREE

At Miyaji Genemon's House

Morning on the opening day of the Gion Festival[1] on the seventh of June. MIYAJI GENEMON's house at Shimo-dachiuri, Horikawa in Kyoto.

GENEMON's house stands Upstage Centre to Upstage Left. It is a typical two-storey tradesman's house in Kyoto. The floor of the house is raised like the houses in the previous ACTS. The sitting room of the house is seen on stage. There is a flight of stairs at the back of the room. The entrance of the house opens on to Shimo-dachiuri Street which lies east-west in front of the house across Downstage.

On the side of Stage Right Horikawa Street runs through the stage along the hanamichi, north to south. The Horikawa River is not seen onstage but it runs parallel to Horikawa Street. There is a small bridge over the river off Downstage Right. The west side of Genemon's house faces the Horikawa Street.

CHORUS 1: As we hear in the song of Kyoto, the main streets of the old capital have interesting names; starting from the east are Temple Street, Happiness Street, Wheat-gluten Bakers' Street, Wealth Street, Riding Grounds under the Willow Tree Street, Sakai Town Street, Between-streets Street, East Tōin Street.

CHORUS 2: Followed by Carriage Makers' Street, which reminds us of the noble people's ox-drawn carriages decorated with the five-strap bamboo blinds, then Karasuma Street, Money-exchange Street, Muromachi Street, Fabric Rack Street, New Town Street, Pan Makers' Street, West Tōin Street, Small Stream Street, Oil Lane and Waking-up Well Street, which joins this Horikawa Street.

CHORUS 3: When the fine sands on the riverbed of the Horikawa glisten in the sparkling waves of the river, it looks as if frost has spread in the summer night of Kyoto. Then the dawn comes to Shimo-dachiuri Street off Horikawa Street. Today is the opening of the Gion Festival of the Yasaka Shrine!

The music of the Gion Festival[2] is heard in the distance.
HIKOKURŌ, BUNROKU, FUJI and YURA are in their travel attire and enter on the hanamichi during the CHORUS.

「堀川波鼓」

下之巻

源右衛門宅の場

六月七日。祇園祭[1]の初日の早朝。
京都堀川下立売にある宮地源右衛門の家。

　舞台中央から上手に向かって源右衛門の家。家は典型的な京の二階屋の町屋。階下は居間と上手奥に二階への階段が見える。源右衛門の家の前、舞台手前を下立売の通りが東西に横切り、家の玄関はこの通りに面している。

　舞台下手には、花道から舞台奥へと続く堀川通りが南北に延びている。舞台上には見えないが、堀川がこの堀川通りと平行して流れていてその堀川には橋が架かっている。源右衛門の家の西側、家の下手側は、この堀川通りに面している。

コーラス1　うたに詠まれているように、京の都大路は東から
　　寺町、御幸町、麩屋町、富小路、柳馬場、堺町、間之町、東洞院と並びます。

コーラス2　それから、「高貴な方々が乗られた五つ緒の簾を配した牛車を思い出させる」車屋町、烏丸、両替町、室町、衣棚、新町、釜座、西洞院、小川、油小路、醒ヶ井、堀川と続きます。

コーラス3　堀川の岸の平らな砂原が、光に煌めく川の白波に照らされたら、夏の夜に霜が降りているように見えます。その堀川の下立売に、ほのぼのと夜も明けて、京は今日から八坂さんのお祭り、祇園祭の始まりどす。

　　　遠く祇園囃子[2]が聞こえ始める。
　　　彦九郎、文六、ふじ、ゆらの旅装の四人が、コーラスの台詞の間に花道から登場する。

257

CHORUS 1: Hikokurō, Bunroku, Fuji and Yura are arriving at their enemy's house. They stand at the crossroads near the house with their fists clenched and with good luck notes[3] tucked deep in their kimonos.
CHORUS 2: The *Naginata* Halberd Float, the tallest of the ceremonial floats and the first in the festival parade[4] is processing through the streets of Kyoto.
CHORUS 3: The four hope that the good fortune of the Halberd Float will aid the revenge,
CHORUS 1, 2, 3 [vigorously]: And that they can celebrate the triumph like the invincible Cock Float which comes next in the parade."

At first the four go to GENEMON's house to make sure that it is his, and then pair off to avoid attracting attention at the crossroads by the hanamichi.

CHORUS 1: The streets of the central part in Kyoto[5] are always busy. Yet this morning they are even busier.
CHORUS 2: For festival visitors are walking south in the morning mist where the float parade is taking place.
CHORUS 3: What's more, some residents are sprinkling water on the thresholds of their houses and others are sweeping their streets from the early morning.

The TOFU-SELLER goes across Shimo-dachiuri Street from east (Stage Left) to west (Stage Right).

TOFU-SELLER [*loudly*]: Tooofuuu! Toofuuu leeeees! [6] Nooo-need-tooo-cuuut! Tooofuuu! Toofuuu leeeees! Nooo-need-tooo-cuuut!
BUNROKU [*anxiously*]: It is inauspicious to hear the phrase "no-need-to-cut." It sounds as if the tofu-seller is saying that we could not cut down the enemy.
FUJI [*uneasily*]: Yes, indeed, it sounded like that to me. Namu-sanbō![7] Save us merciful Buddha! [*She goes to the foot of a bridge and prays to Buddha to ask for his help.*]

Two shabby looking female STONE-SELLERS come in from Stage Right. They are leading horses laden with Shirakawa Stones.

THE FIRST WOMAN STONE-SELLER: Listen O-Fuji, I didn't shoe my horse[8] this morning. I thought I'd finish early and go to the festival.

「堀川波鼓」

コーラス１　（彦九郎らを見て）彦九郎、文六、ふじ、ゆらの四人が仇敵の家にたどり着きました。仇討ちの門出を祝って結んだ力紙³を懐に拳を固め、今、四人は敵捜して、敵の家近くの四辻に立ってます。

コーラス２　祇園祭の山鉾巡行⁴の先頭行くのは背えのたかーい長刀鉾や。

コーラス３　「その長刀の切っ先で先ずは幸運を切り開き、

コーラス１、２、３（猛々しく）その次に来る、声を上げて時を打つ鶏鉾にあやかって勝鬨あげん！」

　　　　　四人は一旦、源右衛門の家の近くまで行って敵の家を確かめた後、人目に立つのを恐れて、堀川通りと下立売通りの交差している花道付近に戻り、通りを挟んで二人ずつに分かれて立つ。

コーラス１　常から上京⁵のあたりは仰山の人通りやけど、

コーラス２　今朝は朝霧の中を山鉾巡行のある南に下る祭り客や、

コーラス３　表に水をまく人、通りを掃く人などで、より一層の賑わいどす。

　　　　　豆腐売りが下立売通りを東（上手）から西（下手）に通る。

豆腐屋　（大きな声で）とーふー。おから⁶ー。きらずー。きらずー。

文六　（心配顔で）「きらずー」とは縁起が悪い。「敵を斬れず」に通じるではないか。

ふじ　（不安げに）確かに、そのようにも聞こえます。南無三宝⁷。（橋詰に寄り、手を合わせて唱えて仏に救いをもとめる。）

　　　　　賤しい身なりをした白川石の石売りの女二人が下手から橋を渡って石を馬に乗せて引いて来る。

石売りの女１　おふじ、わしゃ、今日は商いを早しもて、祭りにいこうと考えて、気がせいておったんで、馬に昏打たんと⁸来た。

THE SECOND WOMAN STONE-SELLER: Me neither. I overslept a little this morning and came out without shoeing my horse. I suppose no one could be bothered to shoe a horse this morning. Why don't we go straight home without shoeing them?

THE STONE-SELLERS laugh cheerily and exit, Stage Left.

CHORUS 2: Young people's casual chatter, the sounds of making breakfast from houses, women worry that chopping cucumbers will wake up their masters and husbands. In the morning all sorts of sounds echo in the Hiei Mountain[9] which stands on the north side of Kyoto.

CHORUS 3: Even so, this morning is terrible! It really is noisy!

CHORUS 1: Indeed. Dear, dear! This noise disturbs our peace of mind.

FUJI [*going close to the others and speaking under her breath*]: Everyone! What do you make of that? A little while ago a tofu-seller passed by saying, "no-need-to-cut." I felt that was inauspicious enough. Then, the women stone-sellers came and said, "Why don't we go straight home without shoeing our horses?" What disturbing remarks! One after another! I know that many people share the same names, but one of the women stone-sellers was called Fuji. When we feel as nervous as this, we are likely to fail. I think that the Sun Goddess is trying to tell us something. Tomorrow brings its own fortune. How about postponing today's vengeance?

The others seem to half agree with FUJI.
At this point a young man enters from the direction of the bridge over the Horikawa, Stage Right. His hair is loose[10] *and he has a tooth pick in the mouth.*
His friend, another young man, enters on the hanamichi.

THE YOUNG MAN FROM HANAMICHI: What has happened? Oh, dear! I didn't recognise you. Where are you going with your hair down like that first thing in the morning?

THE YOUNG MAN WITH LOOSE HAIR: Well, I was going to go to the festival in my best kimono. So I went to the barber's on the west end of the bridge to get the front of my head[11] shaved. Then, I don't know, what's wrong with him but the barber cut my head so many times while shaving it. His new razor was like a sword. He cut me all over my head! If he carries on like that, I don't know how many people he will cut by the end of the day. [*Pointing at the cuts on his head*] Look at these!

THE YOUNG MAN FROM HANAMICHI: Dear me! He's really cut you! Dear, dear! Hey, but if you go to the festival looking like that, you won't be attending the Gion Festival

「堀川波鼓」

石売りの女2　わしも同じや。今朝はちょっと寝過ごしてしもて、馬に沓打たんと来てしもた。今日はだーれも馬に沓打たんのと違うか。もうこのまま、打たんと、早よ家に帰ろやないか。

　　　　　　石売りの女達は大声で笑いながら上手に去る。

コーラス2　若者たちの何気ないお喋り。家々の朝食の支度。万事に気を揉んでは胡瓜揉み刻む音。そんな音まで全部、比叡の山[9]の峰々に響くと言われる京の朝。

コーラス3　それにしても、今朝の京都の、ああ、やかましいこと！
コーラス1　ああ、ああ、ほんに、心乱す音！音！音！
ふじ　（他の三人に寄って、小声で）皆様、どう思われますか。最前通った豆腐売りは『切らず、切らず』と言いながら、豆腐を売って行きました。それだけでも縁起が悪いと思うのに、次に通った石売りの女共は、『馬に沓打たんと来た』『もうこのまま、打たんと、早よ家に帰ろう』と言っておりました。何と気がかりなことばかり。おまけに、世間に同じ名は多々あるとはいえ、折も折り、石売りの女のひとりはふじと呼ばれておりました。このように味方の気後れがあっては、失敗するのは決まったこと。お天道様のお知らせです。明日という日もあることです。今日の敵討ちは延期にしては如何でしょう。

　　　　　　他の三人もふじの言うことに、半ば同意するような気配をみせる。
　　　　　　このとき、下手袖の堀川に架かる橋の方角からさばき髪[10]の若い男が口に楊子を加えてやって来る。
　　　　　　花道からはこの男の友達らしい別の若い男が来る。

花道から来た若い男　あれっ！なんや、誰かと思たらお前か。朝から髪も結わんと、何処へ行く。
さばき髪の若い男　祭りに行くのに、晴れ姿になろうと思て、橋の西詰めにある髪結い床へ月代[11]を剃ってもらいに行った。そしたら、床屋の親父、俺の頭を切ったわ、切ったわ。新しい剃刀の刃はまるで剣や。頭中、切りちゃくりよった。あの親父の腕にかかったら、何人でも切られてしまうぞ。（頭の切られたところを指して）これ、見てみい！

花道から来た若い男　ほんまに。切ったわ、切ったわ！お前、そんな頭で祭りの客に行ったら、祇園祭やのうて、軍神の血祭りやで！（笑う）

at the Yasaka Shrine. You'll be attending the Blood Festival of some War Shrine instead. [*Laughing*]
THE YOUNG MAN WITH LOOSE HAIR: That's right! [*Laughing*]

Two YOUNG MEN walk away in different directions.
The four people smile at one another.

HIKOKURŌ [*encouraged*]: Did you hear what they said?
BUNROKU [*smiling*]: Yes, father. I did.
YURA [*cheered*]: Things are working out! Luck has turned in our favour.
HIKOKURŌ: Right. Let's take advantage of this mood. We shouldn't wait any longer. Everyone, are you ready? [*He braces himself by tightening his obi belt while trying to relieve the tension.*] We can hardly see the inside of the house from this position. Yet, it is no good complaining here. Two women should get inside the building through the living-room from the side on Horikawa Street. We, father and son, will use the front entrance on Shimo-dachiuri Street and kick down the inner doors. Yura and I haven't seen our enemy's face. We should be very careful not to mistake someone else for Genemon. We'll just tell him our intention straightforwardly and kill him swiftly. We must do this in a proper manner and succeed. We should not be hasty or do anything wrong or low in accomplishing our vengeance. Do you understand?
BUNROKU, FUJI and YURA: Yes, we do.
HIKOKURŌ: Are you all right?
BUNROKU, FUJI and YURA: Yes, we are.
HIKOKURŌ (*straighten the posture*): Good! Now, let's go!

When they are about to part in two directions, a group of retainers enter from the direction of Oil Lane, Stage Left.

BUNROKU (*looking at the direction of Stage Left*): Look over there! A group of retainers are coming this way from the direction of Oil Lane.

The group of retainers, a YOUNG RETAINER in his early twenties and HIS FOLLOWERS, walk to GENEMON's house at a smart pace. THE YOUNG RETAINER is in a formal kataginu shoulder wear of coarse linen[12] over the kimono and a pair of hakama trousers made of Indian vertical striped silk.[13] His rank as a retainer looks something around the three-hundred koku rice stipend.[14] HIS FOLLOWERS consist of

「堀川波鼓」

さばき髪の若い男　ほんまや。（笑う）

　　　　　二人は、笑いながらそれぞれの方向に分かれて去る。
　　　　　敵討ちの四人は顔をほころばせる。

彦九郎　（元気付いて）皆、今の話を聞いたか。
文六　（顔をほころばせて）はい、父上、聞きました。
ゆら　（勇み立って）してやった！凶の運勢が吉に変わりました。
彦九郎　よし。この運気に乗じて敵を討とう。もう一刻も延ばしてはならん。皆、用意はいいか。（帯を締めなおし、体の緊張をほぐして）家の中の様子がここからは良く分からん。しかし、ここで話をしていても埒がゆかん。女達二人は堀川通りに面した居間から障子を蹴破って素早く家に入れ。私たち親子は下立売側の門口から中戸を蹴破って押し入る。ゆらと私は敵の顔を知らぬ。人違いするな。素直に我々の意図を述べて、ものの見事に討ち取りたいもの。早まって、騙し討ち、卑怯などと言われるような事はするな。合点か。

文六・ゆら・ふじ　合点しました。
彦九郎　心得たか。
文六・ゆら・ふじ　心得ました。
彦九郎　（姿勢を正して）では、踏み込もう。

　　　　　四人がそれぞれの方向に別れようとしたとき、侍の一行が上手から来る。

文六　（上手を見て）あれ、ご覧ください。油小路の方角からこちらに向いて侍の一団が…。

　　　　　侍一行は、茶宇縞[13]の袴に捩肩衣[12]を着た禄高三百石取り[14]ほどの二十歳過ぎの若侍とその供の者で、源右衛門の家の玄関まで足早に来て止まる。
　　　　　供の者は若党三人、挟み箱持ち、奴二人、草履取りなどである。供の幾人かは蝋燭の形の槍鞘印の槍を持っている。供の一人は「銀十枚」[15]と書いた紙を貼り付けた進物台を提げている。

263

a few young samurai, travelling chest carriers, a footwear carrier and a servant. Some are holding spears covered with a candle-shaped sheath, their house crest. One of THE YOUNG SAMURAI carries a gift stand with a sheet of paper upon which 'Ten Silver Bars in Token of our Gratitude' is written.[15]

THE YOUNG SAMURAI [*speaking in a provincial accent, to the inside of the house*]: Hello! Excuse me, please?

GENEMON'S SERVANT [*from inside the house*]: Who is it, please?

GENEMON's SERVANT comes to the front entrance, sees the visitors and prostrates himself on the spot. THE YOUNG SAMURAI gives his speech and offers the gift stand to GENEMON'S SERVANT. He shakes his head when he speaks. GENEMON'S SERVANT receives the gift respectfully and goes into the house.

YURA: I wonder what the follower said to the servant…
FUJI: Which fief are they from?
BUNROKU [*scratching his head*]: Damn! They arrived when we were just about to go in and spoilt everything. What can we do now? [*He is extremely irritated.*]
HIKOKURŌ: It's not so, Bunroku. We shouldn't be discouraged by this. They are a samurai family or court nobles from some provincial country. I think they've come to give Genemon a gift of gratitude for his performance on the tsuzumi drum. As soon as they have spoken to Genemon and received a reply, they will leave. It won't take long. Let's wait.
FUJI: Oh, the servant is back.
GENEMON'S SERVANT [*coming out of the house*]: Please come in. [*GENEMON's SERVANT leads the way for the retainers into the inside of the house.*]

THE YOUNG RETAINER goes in first. His FOLLOWERS leave the spears popped against the eaves of the house before entering the house.

The four try to peep inside the house. But as the entrance door is shut, they can only eavesdrop.

At this point a MENDICANT PRIEST enters from the hanamichi and stops at the front entrance of GENEMON's house.

THE MENDICANT PRIEST [*the voice of the mendicancy*]: Bowl. Please fill the bowl. Bowl! Please fill the bowl.
GENEMON'S MAID, SUMI [*shouting from inside the house, off-stage*]: We're busy! Go away!

「堀川波鼓」

若党の一人　（田舎訛りで、内に向かって）もうし、ごめんなさって下さい。

源右衛門の家の下人の声　（家の中から）どなたさまでございましょう。

　　　　下人は門口まで出て来て、客が侍であるのを見て、その場に平伏する。若党の一人が頭を振り振り、口上を述べ、進物台を差し出す。下人はうやうやしく進物台を受け取り家に入る。

ゆら　あの侍は何と言ったのでしょう…。
ふじ　どこの藩の者やら…。
文六　（頭をかいて）ええいっ！丁度これからという時に、腰を折られた！どうしたものか！（苛々する。）
彦九郎　いやいや、挫けることはない。いずれは武家方、公家方で源右衛門が鼓でお囃子を勤めた礼の品を納めにきたのであろう。返事を貰って帰るだけで、そう長くはかかるまい。待ってみよう。

源右衛門の家の下人　（家の中から出てきて）どうぞ、こちらへ。（若侍一行を中に招き入れる。）

　　　　若侍が先に家に入る。お供の者たちも鑓を家の軒先に立てかけてから家に入って行く。
　　　　四人は外から家の中の様子を窺うが、戸が閉まっているので、人の動く音が聞こえるだけである。
　　　　このとき、花道から托鉢の層が登場し、源右衛門の家の前まで来て止まる。

托鉢の層　（托鉢の声）はっち！はっち！

源右衛門の家の下女すみの声　（家の中から怒鳴って）忙しい！早う行っておしまい！

Quickly!

THE MENDICANT PRIEST is giving up and about to leave.

HIKOKURŌ [*stopping THE PRIEST*]: Priest! Excuse me! It appears that your clerical robe has seen better days. [*Taking out one ryō-gold coin from his kimono bosom and offering it to THE PRIEST*] Here is my little offering for your good works. Please buy a new robe and leave the old one here. I shall give it to some beggar and make the poor fellow happy.

THE MENDICANT PRIEST [*scarcely believing his eyes*]: Oh, this must be Buddha's mercy! [*Receiving one ryō-gold coin, raising it up to express his gratitude, and overjoyed*] It is terribly kind of you. Thank you so much. I'll leave my old robe here. [*He takes off his clerical robe and clerical bamboo hat,*[16] *puts them down and goes off Stage Left.*]

HIKOKURŌ picks up the robe and the bamboo hat, dusts them down and goes behind the pillar of a street-gate. First he puts on the robe over his kimono, next pulls back the hood he's been wearing and puts on the bamboo hat. He then goes to the entrance of GENEMON's house and starts chanting the Kannon sutra[17] *loudly.*

HIKOKURŌ: Myōhōrengekyō, Kanzeon Bosatsu Kannon the Goddess of Mercy, Fumonbon in the twentieth. Nijimujini Bosatsu sokujyūzakihendan ugetsugasshō butsunisazegon Seson, Kanzeon Bosatsu Kannon the Goddess of Mercy, Igaienmyō Kanzeon Bosatsu Kannon the Goddess of Mercy…
SUMI [*loudly from inside of the house, off-stage*]: Stop that racket! Shut up! Go away!

SUMI rushes out of the house angrily.

HIKOKURŌ [*throwing out a feeler politely*]: Good morning, Miss. It seems that some guests have entered in your house recently. I wonder who they could be. Would you mind my asking that of you?
SUMI [*in a manner of a typically talkative maid, rapidly and glibly*]: He is a retainer from a far-off province where my master goes and teaches the tsuzumi. That handsome young retainer is my master's pupil. Recently his lord has increased his stipend, for he is a good tsuzumi player. He came to express his gratitude to my master. He gave ten bars of silver[18] to my master, one and one fourth of *ryō*-gold[19] to his mistress and three hundred *sen*-coppers each to every one of us, too. [*Boastfully*] So, everyone in this house has a

「堀川波鼓」

　　　　　僧は、托鉢を諦めて行こうとする。

彦九郎　（僧を呼び止めて）もし、お坊様。失礼ながら、お見受けしたところご僧衣の破れ綻びがひどいようでございます。（懐から一両小判を差し出して）このお金を御報謝いたします。どうぞ、新しい衣をお求め下され。今、着ておられるものはここに置いていかれるとよい。物乞いにでもくれて、喜ばせてやることにいたしましょうほどに。

托鉢の僧　（夢かと思う顔つきで）ああ、これは如来様のお慈悲か。（一両小判を受け取り、幾度も伏し戴いて）誠に有難いお志。有難うございます。では、仰せの通りにこのぼろはここに置いてゆくことに致しましょう。（古着を脱いで、被っていた托鉢笠[16]と一緒に置いて上手に去る。）

　　　　　彦九郎は僧衣と笠を拾い上げて埃をよく振るってから、辻にある門の片隅に行って着物の上から僧衣を羽織る。その後、被っている頭巾を後ろに引いて托鉢笠を阿弥陀に被り、源右衛門の家の門口に行き、家の中を覗いてから、大きな声で観音経[17]を唱え始める。

彦九郎　妙法蓮華経　観世音菩薩　普門品第二十五　爾時無尽意菩薩　即従座起偏袒右肩合掌向仏而作是言世尊観世音菩薩　以何因縁名観世音菩薩。

下女すみの声　（家の中から）ええい、やかましい！黙れ！あっちへ行け！

　　　　　すみが外に飛び出してくる。

彦九郎　（探りを入れて）もし、お女中様、朝早くからお客様のようでございますが。どなた様でございますか？

下女すみ　（いかにもお喋りの下女らしく、早口でべらべらと）あのお客は田舎のお侍で、うちの旦那様の鼓の弟子や。この度、お国のお殿様から鼓が上手なことでご加増があったそうや。これもみんな鼓のお師匠様のお陰と言われて、お礼にまいられたのや。それでな、旦那様には丁銀[18]十枚。奥様に一分金[19]五つ。わしらにまで、ずらりと一人頭、銭三百文ずつ下さって、みんなの懐が暖まった。お前が一日中、朝から晩まで喉の穴が痛うなるほど観音経を唱えても、三百文は貰えまい。

heavy purse now. I suppose that you wouldn't be able to earn three hundred *sen* even if you chanted the Kannon sutra all day. Why don't you give it up altogether and do something different instead. Something like ...clapping hands like playing the tsuzumi? That's right. It's a good idea! [*Smiling*] Start doing the palm-tsuzumi from now on. Got it? [*She goes back to the house hurriedly soon after the speech.*]

HOKOKURŌ [*nodding with a smile and going back to the others*]: Now we know what's going on in the house. And the maid said, "Start doing the palm-tsuzumi from now on." I think it's a lucky omen.

The four exchange words and encourage one another.
At this point THE YOUNG RETAINER comes out of the house alone. He has taken off his formal attire. He wears an amigasa braided hat and has a short sword[20] *at his side. He walks off Shimo-dachiuri Street to the east, Stage Left.*

YURA [*seeing off THE YOUNG RETAINER and in a low voice*]: He is going West Tōin Street south. The young retainer has left his followers in the house and their spears are outside. I think he has made it look as if he is with the others in the house and has secretly gone to see the festival floats.

FUJI [*also in a low voice*]: It means that several of his followers are stopping in the house. When we get in, they will fight for Genemon against us. The vengeance won't be easy. Oh, what shall we do?

BUNROKU [*losing patience*]: If we keep saying such things, we will never find the right moment to accomplish our vengeance. If those followers want to be there, let them. Our enemy is Genemon. If they assist Genemon in a fight, we shall kill them all. Let's see how our luck goes. We must get in now! [*He is about to rush in.*]

HIKOKURŌ [*stopping BUNROKU*]: Wait, Bunroku. I have an idea. [*HIKOKURŌ goes to the front of the house once again and calls into the house loudly.*] Hello! Excuse me! Is anybody there? I saw a young samurai leave this house a moment ago. He must have gone to see the festival parade. But I think that he started a fight a little up from San-jō on Muromachi Street.[21] He was surrounded by many people when I left. I just wanted to let you know.

THE FOLLOWERS of THE YOUNG RETAINER rush out of the house with their swords in their hands. Each and every one says, "This is a problem." "Where is San-jō on Muromachi Street? Is it north?" "Or is it west?" Rushing ahead of others, THE FOLLOWERS go off the hanamichi, in the opposite direction to which THE

「堀川波鼓」

お経なんかさらりと止めて、手鼓でも打ったほうがええ。今からでもええ、鼓、打ち。(言い終わると、急いで家の中に走って帰る。)

彦九郎 (にっこり頷いて、三人のところに戻り) これで、中の様子が分かった。『今からでもええ、鼓、打ち』とは、また縁起が良い。

　　　　四人は互いに言葉を交わして勇み立つ。
　　　この時、最前の若侍が裃を脱ぎ、編み笠を被り脇差[20]だけで、一人で家から出てくる。若侍は下立売の通りを東に向かって、上手に退場する。

ゆら (若侍を見送りながら、小声で) 西の洞院の通りを南に下って行きます。察するところ、あの若侍は供の者を家に残し、家の表には鑓を置いて、自分はここに居る体裁にしておいて、祇園祭の山鉾巡行を見物に行ったものと思われます。

ふじ (同じく小声で) 七、八人の下人どもが家の中にいるからには、なかなかたやすく源右衛門は討てません。どうしたものでございましょう。

文六 (我慢しきれなくて) そのようなことを言っていては、いつまでたっても本望を遂げる機会はありません。下郎どもがいるのなら、いるがいい。私たちの目指す敵は源右衛門只一人。もし、奴らが助太刀に入るなら撫で斬りにし、その後は運次第です! さあ、斬り込みましょう!(駆け出そうとする。)

彦九郎 (文六を制して) まて、文六。考えがある。(再び、源右衛門の家の前に行き、中に向かって大声で) 申し、どなたかおられぬか。先ほど、この家から出て行かれたお侍様は、山鉾見物にでも行かれたと思いますが、三条室町通り[21]を上がったところで喧嘩を始めて、大勢の人々に取り囲まれておられます。そのことお知らせ申しあげる。

　　　　供の者たちが刀を下げて家からばたばたと走り出してくる。口々に「これは大変!」「三条室町とは北か?」「西か?」などと言いながら刀を手に、先を争って、若侍の行ったのと反対の方向になる花道を走り去る。

269

YOUNG RETAINER went.

HIKOKURŌ: Every action we have taken has gone well. I think our luck is at its height. Our victory is near.

HIKOKURŌ takes off the old clerical robe and hands a small sword at his side to YURA as has been planned. BUNROKU hands his short sword to FUJI. Then HIKOKURŌ and BUNROKU put on a white headband and tuck up their sleeves with a white tasuki band signifying vengeance.
When YURA and FUJI receive the short sword, they swiftly click it against the sword guard, and wear it at their side. Then they put on the white headband and the tasuki band in the same way the men have done. They hitch up the hem of their kimonos to their knees with another cloth band, and then stamp like a man, preparing for the fight.

YURA [*muttering*]: Namu Shō Hachiman Daibosatsu.[22] The Great God of Samurai, please give us strength.

FUJI [*muttering*]: Namu Shō Hachiman Daibosatsu. The Great God of Samurai, please give us strength.

YURA and FUJI move to the side of the building on Horikawa Street, and HIKOKURŌ and BUNROKU approach the front entrance. Each group kicks down the shōji sliding doors or the inner doors, and breaks into the house one after another.
The servant and the maid in the house are frightened and run off, screaming "Oh, I'm scared," "I'm scared."

FUJI [*recognising GENEMON quickly and pointing at him*]: The man over there is Miyaji Genemon!

GENEMON, who is in the living room, does not understand what is going on for a second, but soon realises who the intruders are from FUJI's voice. He runs up the stairs halfway, sits there on guard, and glares down at his enemies with his fist clenched. FUJI and YURA stand apart at the foot of the stairs so as not to let GENEMON escape.

HIKOKURŌ [*in a clear voice loudly*]: I am Ogura Hikokuro. Genemon, I killed my wife with my sword on the twenty seventh last month when I found out her adultery with you. You are my wife's enemy. I won't let you run away. [*He draws his sword and brings it*

「堀川波鼓」

彦九郎　こちらの計画がことごとく当たる。さあ、今が運の盛り、戦勝の時が来た。

　　　　彦九郎は羽織っていた僧衣をふわりと脱ぎ捨てる。男二人は計画通り脇差をそれぞれが女二人に渡す。その後、男二人は、仇討ちの白い鉢巻を締めて襷をかける。

　　　　女二人は、受け取った刀の鍔を一度鳴らしてから、手早く腰にさす。それから男達と同じように鉢巻、襷がけをしてから、腰紐で裾からげして膝元まで足をだし、男勝りに小刻みに足を踏みしめる。

ゆら　（口の中で）南無正八幡大菩薩[22]。武運の神様！どうぞ神力で力をお与えください。
ふじ　（口の中で）南無正八幡大菩薩。武運の神様！どうぞ神力で力をお与えください。

　　　　ゆらとふじは堀川側に向かい、彦九郎と文六は正面の門口に行く。女二人は居間の障子を、男二人は中戸を蹴破り、ほぼ同時にばらばらと家に走って入る。
　　　　家の中の下人や下女は驚いて「怖い！」「怖い！」と口々に喚いて逃げてゆく。

ふじ　（いち早く源右衛門を見つけて指差し）あの男が宮地源右衛門です！

　　　　居間にいた源右衛門は不意の乱入に、一瞬ぼんやりするが、ふじの声で相手が誰か気付き、二階に上がる梯子段の中ほどまで行って腰をかけて、拳を固めて下からの敵を睨んで身構える。
　　　　ふじとゆらは源右衛門が逃げないように梯子段の左右に立ちはだかる。

彦九郎　（大きな声ではっきりと）私は小倉彦九郎だ。宮地源右衛門、我が妻たねはお前との不義が露見したため、先月二十七日に刺し殺した。妻の敵、逃さぬぞ。（言い捨てて、抜き打ちで切りつける。）

down on GENEMON.]
GENEMON [*dodging HIKOKURŌ's attack*]: Ha! You missed! Now! [*He runs upstairs.*]

> When HIKOKURŌ is about to climb up the stairs after GENEMON, GENE-MON'S WIFE attack HIKOKURŌ with the naginata halberd kept on the lintel [23] for self-protection in order to stop him. GENEMON's servants and maids try hard to stab HIKOKURŌ with a stick, a pole or a broom stick. Because of their interference HI-KOKURŌ is kept on the ground floor.
> During this GENEMON grabs one of the spears left against the eaves of his house by reaching through the small lattice window[24] on the mezzanine floor. Then he starts thrusting it downwards.

HIKOKURŌ [*sneering*]: Ha! How pathetic! The way you handle your spear, you might just be able to kill a mouse. You know how to hold a tsuzumi, but don't know how to grip the shaft of a spear. Do you truly think that you can kill me with your ornamental spear in that sad posture full of unguarded moments? If so, show me.

> GENEMON thrusts the spear as hard as he can. HIKOKURŌ cuts the shaft into two in a single motion with his sword.

GENEMON: Oh, very good! Oi, look! I'm not a samurai. How should I know how to hold a spear? [*Lifting up a go-board*] But thanks to my strong arms, I can play the tsuzumi and I can lift things like this. Here! Take this!

> GENEMON throws the go-board at HIKOKURŌ. Then he throws anything within reach such as a sugoroku board, a shogi board, a tobacco tray, a lighter, an iron kettle for the Tea Ceremony, a tea bowl, a pillow chest and so on. HIKOKURŌ is unable to go upstairs.
> YURA goes out of the house, climbs up the pillar of the street gate, steps onto the bolt of the gate and onto the eaves of GENEMON's house. Then she enters the house through the upstairs window and strikes at GENEMON with a small sword from behind.
> GENEMON dodges her and holds her down with a small byōbu screen.[25] They struggle with one another but GENEMON takes away the short sword from YURA.
> The sound of their fight distracts the people downstairs and HIKOKURŌ runs up the stairs.

「堀川波鼓」

源右衛門　（かわして）そうはいかん！えいっ！（階段に手をかけて二階に駆け上がる。）

　　　彦九郎が源右衛門を追って駆け上がろうとしたところを、源右衛門の妻が長押[23]にかけてあった長刀で二階に上げまいとして切りかかる。下人や下女たちも物かげから寄り棒、杖、箒などで突いてくるので彦九郎は二階に上がることが出来ない。

　　　この間に、源右衛門は中二階の虫籠窓[24]から外に手を伸ばして、先ほど若侍のお供が軒先に立てかけておいた鑓を取り、下に向かって突き始める。

彦九郎　（あざ笑って）何を、こしゃくな。鼠を突くのが精一杯のその手つき！おのれは鼓の胴は握れても、鑓の柄の握り方は知らんようだな。そのような隙だらけの構えの飾り鑓で私を斬れると思うのか。手並みを見せてみろ！

　　　源右衛門が力いっぱい突くと、彦九郎は鑓の柄の蛭巻のところを一太刀で真二つに切り落とす。

源右衛門　おこがましいわ！おい、こら！俺は、もともと武士ではないのだ。鑓の持ち方とは知らん。（碁盤を持ち上げて）しかし、この強い腕の力のお陰で、鼓の打ち方は覚えられた。この碁盤を受けてみろ！

　　　源右衛門は狙いをつけて碁盤を投げつける。続けて、双六盤、将棋盤、煙草盆、火入れ、茶の湯の風呂釜、茶碗、枕箱など手当たり次第、ばらばらと階下に向かって投げる。彦九郎は全く二階に上がることが出来ない。

　　　ゆらは表に出て、辻の門の門柱をよじ登り、門のかんぬきを踏み台にして、屋根の庇に這い上がって、二階から源右衛門の家に進入し、後ろから源右衛門に斬りつける。

　　　源右衛門は身をかわして、そこにあった四尺屏風[25]で反対にゆらを上から押さえつける。二人はもみ合いになり、源右衛門がゆらの脇差を取る。
　　　この隙に、彦九郎は階段を駆け上がる。

HIKOKURŌ [*shouting*]: You can't escape from us!

> HIKOKURŌ *and* GENEMON *clash swords at first, but* GENEMON *realises that he cannot match. He runs on to the roof and jumps down to the street.* HIKOKURŌ *chases and catches up with* GENEMON *at the bridge over the Horikawa. They cross swords again.* BUNROKU, FUMI *and* YURA *chases after* GENEMON, *too.*

> TOWNSPEOPLE *hear the sound of a sword-fight, come out of their houses on all sides. They are excited and shout,* "*There's a fight!*" "*It's a sword-fight!*" "*Close the east and the west gates of the street!*" "*Flog them to death!*"

FUJI [*to the* TOWNSPEOPLE, *loudly*]: This is vengeance with official permission. It's none of your business.

YURA [*threatening and loudly*]: No one must commit a rash act.

> FUJI *and* YURA *motion the* TOWNSPEOPLE *to stay back and stand separately in front of each street-gate to stop anyone who interferes with their vengeance.*
>
> *The last moment of the vengeance has come.* HIKOKURŌ *and* GENEMON *continue to fight with all their strength, while drawing deep breaths now and then.* HIKOKURO *takes into account the fact that* GENEMON *is a townsman and so he does not strike first from his side. He waits for* GENEMON *to strike him for few times, and then strikes back. A while later* HIKOKURŌ *anticipates the final moment of the fight. He walks towards the enemy very swiftly as if shooting an arrow, bringing his sword down on* GENEMON *across his left shoulder to the right arm.* GENEMON *falls heavily on his backside and then lies face down on the ground.*
>
> BUNROKU, FUJI *and* YURA *approach* GENEMON *and strike him with a sword in ritual vengeance one by one.*

BUNROKU: You are my mother's enemy! [*He stabs* GENEMON.]

FUJI: You are my sister's enemy! Take my sword! [*She stabs* GENEMON.]

YURA: You are my sister-in-law's enemy. Take the sword of my revenge. [*She stabs* GENEMON.]

> GENEMON *dies.*
>
> THE TOWNSPOEPLE *who have been watching the vengeance come close. They*

「堀川波鼓」

彦九郎　（源右衛門を追って）逃すものか！

　　　　彦九郎は源右衛門と斬り結ぶ。かなわないとみた源右衛門は二階の屋根から道に飛び降りて逃げる。彦九郎も飛び降りて、橋の上で追いつき、再び斬り結ぶ。文六、ふじ、ゆらも彦九郎の後に続く。

　　　　騒ぎを聞きつけて、四方から町の衆が出てくる。人々は興奮して口々に「喧嘩だ！」「切り合いだ！」「東と西の辻の門を閉めろ！」「叩き殺せ」などとわめきたてる。

ふじ　（大声で町の衆に）これはお上に届けをすませた敵討ちでございます。他の方々に関係はございません。
ゆら　（威嚇するように）どなたも軽はずみなことはなさいませぬように！

　　　　ふじとゆらは敵討ちの邪魔しないように町の衆を遠ざけて、通りの東の辻の門、西の辻の門の前に分かれて立つ。
　　　　敵討ちの最後の時となり、彦九郎と源右衛門は、息を休めながら、力の限り打ち合う。彦九郎は相手が町人であることを考慮して、自ら打ち込むことはせず、源右衛門が打ちかかってくるのを待ち、二、三度受けては払う。その後、これまでと見定めて、矢を射るように素早く、つつーっと前に進み、源右衛門の構えの中に入り、左の肩先から右手まで、ざくりと斬り下ろす。源右衛門は犬のように尻餅をついてから、ドスンとうつ伏せに倒れる。
　　　　文六、ふじ、ゆらの三人も敵討ちの常道として、一太刀ずつ、源右衛門を斬る。

文六　母の敵！（斬る。）
ふじ　ふじにとっては姉の敵！刀を受けよ！（同じく、斬る。）
ゆら　兄嫁の敵！恨みの刀を受けよ！　　（同じく、斬る。）

　　　　源右衛門は止めを刺されて死ぬ。
　　　　遠巻きに敵討ちを見ていた町の衆が寄ってくる。町の衆は四人を用心深

carefully encircle the four by holding a pole in their hands.

TOWNSMAN 1: We understand that you have taken revenge on your enemy. But we must ask you to hand over your swords for a while as it is the law.
TOWNSMAN 2: We are sorry but you cannot leave until the town magistrate of Kyoto[26] has passed judgement on your case.
TOWNSMAN 3: You must stay in our meeting hall until his arrival.

The four hand their swords to the TOWNSPOEPLE obediently. The TOWNSPEOPLE usher them out using their poles. They exit in the direction of the meeting hall Stage Right quietly.
Someone covers the body of GENEMON with a straw mat.

The Gion Festival music starts in the distance.

CHORUS 1: The four killed their enemy together. It was grand, superb and fair! People had never seen or heard of the vengeance as marvellous as that.
CHORUS 2: The Gion Festival music sounds as if it is proclaiming the grandeur of this vengeance to the world.
CHORUS 1, 2 & 3 [*together cheerily*]: Chan-giri, Shik-kiri, Kittari-ya!
Done it! Made it! Vendetta!
Chan-giri, Shik-kiri, Kittari-ya!
Done it! Made it! Vendetta!
Chan-giri, Shik-kiri, Kittari-ya!
Done it! Made it! Vendetta!
CHORUS 2: The music went on joyfully in the floats.
CHORUS 3: When this story was made as a *Bunraku* play, recited by the sweet-tongued *jōruri* chanters, and acted by those innocent puppets, it was very well received. That's all we know. [*CHORUS 3 bows to the audience, together with CHORUS 1 and 2.*]

Blackout.

THE END

「堀川波鼓」

　　　　く突き棒で囲む。

町の衆1　敵討ちとは言え、町内として念のために腰のものはお預かりいたします。

町の衆2　京都町奉行[26]からのお指図があるまでは余所へ逃がすことは出来まへん。

町の衆3　それまで町の会所に押し込めさして貰います。

　　　　四人はおとなしく刀を差し出し、町の衆の突き棒に囲まれたまま押されて、会所のあると思われる下手に静かに去る。

　　　　源右衛門の屍には町の衆の手で筵が被せられる。

　　　　祇園祭の山鉾のお囃子が聞こえてくる。

コーラス1　四人一緒に一度に止めを刺す、こんな見事な敵討ちは、これまで聞いたことがおへん。
コーラス2　この仇討ちの、立派さ、見事さ、潔さを、世間にぱーっと伝えるみたいに、祇園祭の山鉾のお囃子が囃し立てます。
コーラス1、2、3　（お囃子のように）チャンギリ、シッキリ、キッタリヤ。
　　討ったり、やったり、女敵討ち。
　　チャンギリ、シッキリ、キッタリヤ。
　　討ったり、やったり、女敵討ち。
　　チャンギリ、シッキリ、キッタリヤ。
　　討ったり、やったり、女敵討ち。
コーラス2　お囃子が楽しそうに続いておりました。
コーラス3　この敵討ちのお話をそのまんま、舌先三寸浄瑠璃の操り芝居にしましたところ、また大変な評判になったそうで御座います。（コーラス3、コーラス1、2と一緒に客席に向かってお辞儀をする。）

　　　　暗転。

　　　　　　　　　　　　　　　　　　　　（幕）

Drumbeats Over the Horikawa
Notes

CHARACTERS
1 The fief of Tottori had two regions, Inaba and Hōki. Inaba was the middle and east part of the present-day Tottori prefecture.
2 Kyoto is one of the prefectures of the Kinki Region and is located from the middle to the north part of the region. The city of Kyoto is located in the southern part of Kyoto prefecture. The Horikawa River flowed south through the central part of Kyoto city, and Shimodachiuri of Horikawa is in Kamigyō ward.
3 A Japanese hand drum: there are three different types of *tsuzumi*, which are a large *tsuzumi* and a small *tsuzumi* played in *Nō* and *kabuki,* and the third *tsuzumi* played in *Gagaku*. *Tsuzumi* usually means a small *tsuzumi*.
4 KAKUZŌ is *chūgen* in Japanese, literally meaning 'the middle.' *Chūgen* was an attendant of a samurai. His social rank was between *samurai* and *komono*, a low ranking servant.
5 A woman who sold the cut stone in Shirakawa village, which is located in Sakyō ward of Kyoto city at present. The stone is biotitic granite used for a tomb stone, a stone monument and a stone lantern.
6 *Takuhatsu* in Japanese. It means that a priest or a nun goes about asking for food or money while chanting sutra.

ACT ONE
1 The raised recess in a Japanese room in which a scroll, an ornament and flowers can be decorated.
2 A band of cloth to pull back the sleeves of kimono.
3 When people wash a kimono, they undo the seam of the kimono, then wash and starch it. The washed pieces of the kimono cloth are spread on the board or stretched with *shinshi* and dried. (See Notes No.9 of this ACT for *shinshi*)
4 One of the Nō songs rewritten in a style of a dream play by Zeami: it is performed as the third play in a formal performance. ***Matsukaze*** is a love story about Sir Ariwara no Yukihira and two sisters, Matsukaze and Murasame, who drew brine on the shore. The song was written based on a poem which Yukihira wrote when he was sent into exile to Suma. The poem is collected in *Collection of Ancient and Modern Japanese Poetry.* . (See Notes No.5 of this ACT for Yukihira.)

「堀川波鼓」

「堀川波鼓」
（註）

登場人物

1　鳥取藩は因幡、伯耆の二つの国を領有した大藩で、因幡の国は現在の鳥取県の中部および西部にあたる。

2　京都府は近畿地方中部から北部に位置する府。京都市は府の南部に位置する。堀川は京都市の市街地のほぼ中央を南流していた川。堀川下立売は現在の上京区にある。

3　中央が細くくびれた木製の胴の両端に皮をあてて紐で締めた打楽器。能楽、歌舞伎囃子などの大鼓、小鼓や雅楽の三の鼓などがあるが、狭義は小鼓だけを指す。ここでは小鼓。

4　昔は公家・寺院などに召し使われた男。身分は侍と小者（身分の低い奉公人）の間に位置する。江戸時代、武士に仕えて雑務に従った者の称。

5　白川石を売る女。白川石は京都市左京区北白川付近から切り出した黒雲母花崗岩の石材。組織が緻密で美しいので墓石、碑石、石灯籠などに用いられる。

6　僧尼が修行のため、経を唱えながら家の前に立ち、食べ物や金銭を鉢に受けて回ること。

上之巻

1　日本建築で座敷の正面上座の床を一段高くし、掛け軸、置物、花などを飾る所。

2　英語版でも tasuki とする。着物の袖や袂が邪魔にならないようにたくしあげるための紐。背中でななめ十文字に交差させ両肩にまわして結ぶ。

3　糊を付けた布を板張り又は伸子張りにして乾かすこと。布が縮んだりしわ寄ったりするのを防ぐ。（伸子については同巻・註9参照）

4　能の三番目物の一曲。世阿弥の改作。『古今集』に在原行平の詠んだ須磨流謫の歌があり、後世、これに取材した謡曲「松風」などが生まれた。謡曲「松風」はこの歌をもとに行平に恋慕する二人の海女の姉妹、松風と村雨の情熱を夢幻能の構成で書いたもの。（同巻・註5参照。）

5   Sir Ariwara no Yukihira (818-893) was a poet in the early Heian period. He was the son of Prince Abo and the elder brother of Sir Ariwara no Narihira (825-880), a poet who was thought to be the protagonist in *The Tales of Ise*.

6   It is the south area of Suma ward in Kobe city at present. The place is a scenic beach with white sands and a green pine grove, facing the Osaka Bay.

7   A daimio's (feudal lord's) alternative-year residence in Edo. It was one of the controls by the Tokugawa government for its feudal lords made in 1635. A feudal lord ought to live in his residence in his fief and that of Edo every other year. It cost much and put a fief in financial difficulty, but at the same time it helped the development of the traffic and the cultural exchange of the fiefs.

8   *Kinubari* in Japanese: it is a wide wooden peg/clip to hold the end of silk cloth to hang and dry.

9   *Shinshi* in Japanese: it is a thin bamboo stick with a needle on each end. It is used to stop the cloth creasing from dying or drying.

10 TANE is airing HIKOKURŌ's kimono as a preparation of welcoming his home-coming. It is similar to 'summer airing.'

11 *Andon* in Japanese: a paper-covered lamp stand. The frame of *andon* is made of timber or bamboo and an oil saucer with a wick is set in the lamp.

12 The writing of this part is an alteration of a Nō song, *Ominameshi*, which is performed as the fourth song in a formal performance. It is a story about Ono no Yorikaze and his wife. When a priest was travelling through the Man Mountain, the couple appeared and told him that they had been tortured by an evil spirit for committing adultery.

13 It is a tea bowl with a large bottom used for serving strong tea in the tea ceremony. Strong tea, *koicha* in Japanese, is dark green and has some sweetness in its taste.

14 It is a way of serving tea or tobacco, which indicates affection to the person receiving it.

ACT TWO
SCENE ONE

1   One of the five main roads in the Edo period. *Tōkaidō* means 'east sea road.' It stretches from Edo, present-day Tokyo, to Kyoto along the sea coast of the Pacific Ocean.

2   It is the procession of a daimio or feudal lord. A daimio was expected to keep the

「堀川波鼓」

5 在原行平(ありわらのゆきひら)（818～893年）は平安前期の歌人。阿保親王(あぼしんのう)（792～842）の子。『伊勢物語』の主人公と言われる在原業平(ありわらのなりひら)（825～880）の兄。

6 現在の神戸市須磨区南部の地域。大阪湾に面する白砂青松(はくしゃせいしょう)の海岸で景勝地。

7 参勤交代のこと。江戸幕府の大名統制の一つ。原則として一年交代で、諸大名を江戸と領地に居住させた制度。1635年に制度化した。往復や江戸屋敷の経費は大名財政を圧迫したが、交通の発達や文化の全国的な交流をうながすなど各方面に影響を与えた。

8 絹布を洗い張りするとき、その両端につけて引っ張ってしわをのばすための木の棒。

9 伸子(しんし)は両端に針が付いた竹製の細い棒。反物を洗ったり染めたりするときに、布の幅の両端にかけ渡してぴんと張らせて縮まないようにする。(同巻・註3参照)

10 留守にしていた夫を迎える準備に夫の着物に風を通しているのであろう。夏の土用(どよう)（「**今宮の心中**」中之巻第一場・註14参照）や秋の晴天の日などに書画、衣装、調度品などを陰干しして風を通し虫の害やかびを防ぐ「虫干し」に似ている。

11 木、竹などの枠に紙を貼り、中に油皿を置いて火をともす照明具。

12 謡曲「女郎花(おみなめし)」を多少改筆した文章。「女郎花(おみなめし)」は能の一。四番目物。旅の僧が山城(やましろ)の男山(おとこやま)の麓に来かかると、小野頼風(おののよりかぜ)夫婦の霊が現れ、邪淫(じゃいん)の悪鬼に責められていることを語る。

13 濃茶(こいちゃ)は臼で引いた粉茶である抹茶(まっちゃ)の一つで、濃緑色で甘みがある。濃茶茶碗は濃茶をたてるのに用いる底の広い大型の茶碗。

14 口を付けて飲みさした杯や煙管(きせる)などを相手に差すこと。情の深さを示すしぐさとされた。

中之巻
第一場

1 江戸時代の五街道の一つで、江戸から京都に至る太平洋沿いの道路。五十三の宿場があった。海道(かいどう)は海沿いに通じる道、海辺の道路の意。

2 江戸時代、大名が参勤交代などの公式の外出に際し、格式に応じた既定の人

numbers of the followers and the equipage appropriate to his samurai status.

3   A folk song. A road-horse man (a man who carries a load on the horse) or a horse dealer sang it when they pulled the horse.
4   The clothes box is called *Tsuzura* in Japanese. It is a box-shaped woven basket originally made from the plant, Menispermaceae. In the Edo period people put these boxes on the sides of a horse to carry people or clothes.

5   *kyokuroku* in Japanese: the back of the chair is a semi-circular shape and its legs are mostly crossed.
6   *Koshō* in Japanese. Their job was to take care of noblemen in their home life.
7   One *ri* is about 3927ms. (See No. 5 (1) of **Measuring System in the Edo Period**)

8   It is a type of tea bowl for the tea ceremony; the rim of the bowl is a little compressed and its bottom rim is small and low. A priest who studied in the temple on the Tenmoku Mountain in Sekkō region of China in the Kamakura period brought this type of tea bowl back to Japan. The name of the tea bowl derives from this.
9   A hair style of trimming hair to an even short length. *Kamuro* also means a girl who has this hair style. (See Notes No. 9 of CHARACTERS, **Woman-Killer in Oil Hell**)
10 An active volcano of 2568 meters high, located between Gunma and Nagano prefectures. It erupted in 1783 and killed many people.
11 It is the pass between Hisaka and Kanaya in Tōtōmi country, the western area of the present-day Shizuoka prefecture.
12 The barrier was built on the Ousaka Mountain. It was one of the important barriers in the Edo period and an entrance to Kyoto.
13 The farms in Mochizuki were well known for raising fine horses from the old days. They were located in Shinano country, the present-day Nagano prefecture.
14 It was one of the post towns in Hamamatsu in present-day Shizuoka prefecture.
15 *Ban-gashira* in Japanese: the followers of a daimio were divided into six groups. *Ban-gashira* was the chief of each group.
16 *Tsukai-ban* in Japanese, who visited places to make an inspection in peace time and worked as a message runner in war time.
17 *Ashigaru Taishō* in Japanese, they lead one group of the foot soldiers.
18 *Sōshu-ban* in Japanese. Originally they conveyed a message to the emperor or the empress in the court. After the Muromachi period (1336-1573) they did it between a daimio and the superiors.

3 民謡。馬子(馬をひいて人や荷を運ぶことを業とした人)や博労(牛馬の売買・仲買を業とする人)が馬をひきながら唄った。
4 江戸時代、馬の背の両側に葛籠を付けた馬。葛籠の中に人を乗せたり、旅の荷物を入れて運んだりした。葛籠はツヅラフジで編んだ、衣服などを入れる箱の形をしたかご。後には竹・ヒノキなどの薄板で編み、上に紙を貼って柿渋・漆などを塗った。
5 背の寄りかかりを半円形に曲げ、脚をX字形に交差させたものが多い。

6 貴人のそば近くに仕えて、身の回りの雑用を務める役。
7 尺貫法の単位。一里は三十六丁で3927メートル。(**江戸時代のものの数え方** 5(1)参照)
8 抹茶茶碗の一種。すり鉢状で口縁はわずかにくびれ、高台は低く小さい。鎌倉時代に中国浙江省の天目山の寺院で学んだ留学僧が持ち帰ったところからこの名が付いた。

9 髪を短く切りそろえて垂らした子供の髪型。(「**女殺油地獄**」登場人物・註9参照)

10 標高2568メートルの群馬・長野両県にまたがる活火山。1783年の大爆発では多数の死者を出した。
11 東海道遠江の国(現在の静岡県西部)の日坂と金谷の境にある峠。

12 逢坂山にあった関所。東海道の京都の入り口にあたる要所。

13 「望月」は信濃の国(現在の長野県)北佐久郡望月町の御牧場。

14 浜松(現在の静岡県南西部の市)にある宿場の名前。
15 大名の供人を六組、即ち六番に分けたときの番頭。

16 平時は諸方を出張視察し、戦時には伝令使となる役。

17 足軽大将は足軽一組を預り指揮する者。
18 本来は朝廷で事を奏上する(天子に申し上げる)役目を云ったが、室町時代(1336〜1573)以後、君主に奏上を取り次いだり、上使に取り次いだりする役。

19   *Hata-taishō* in Japanese, who held the regimental colours and were under the control of the senior councillor of the Tokugawa government.

20   *Hasami-bako* in Japanese: a packing case carried on the back with the attached pole.

21   *Shigeto-no-yumi* in Japanese: a bow covered with a Japanese wisteria vine. It was used by a *shogun* or a *taishō,* a leader of the followers.

22   *Nurigome-no-yumi* in Japanese: a bow covered with a Japanese wisteria vine and lacquered over.

23   *Sobaguro-no yumi* in Japanese: a bow, putting timber between two pieces of bamboo, and only the timber is painted in black.

24&25   A case to protect the bow from the rain or damage: it was carried on the back or at the waist.

26   *Gusokubitsu* in Japanese. It is a chest for an armour.

27   *Dai-gasa* in Japanese. It was a hat kept in a sack on top of a pole, carried by a footman in a daimio's procession.

28   *Tate-gasa* in Japanese. It was a parasol with a long handle. It was kept in a sack made of velvet or thick woollen cloth.

29   *Umajirushi* in Japanese.

30   It was a globe-shaped object made of feathers of a hawk or a fowl, used as a decoration for *umajirushi,* a commander's battle flag, or a spear sheath.

31   They were spears, halberds, *dai-gasa, tate-gasa, umajirushi, hasami-bako* and *ō-to-rige.*

SCENE TWO

1   A cloth made of hemp or a false nettle, *mao* in Japanese. As the word for adulterer in Japanese is *maotoko* which can be shortened *mao*. As they share the same sound, homonymy, it was used as a colloquial term for an adulterer.

2   *Hananeji* in Japanese. It is a stick about 50cm long with a loop on top. The loop was used to tame a horse by putting it on the horse nose and twisting it. It was also used as a stick for self-protection.

3   A bundle of the hair tied with a paper cord on the top of the head in Japanese hair style.

4   A child's kimono has a cord at the back. It is pulled to the front and tied to stop the kimono coming loose.

5   (See No. 4 of **Measuring System in the Edo Period**)

6   *Waraji* in Japanese: a pair of straw sandals worn by tying up two straps at the toe to the ankle.

「堀川波鼓」

19　幕府で老中の支配下にあり、軍旗を掌る役。

20　衣服や小物を入れる箱に棒を挿して担ぐもの。

21　藤を巻いた弓。将軍や大将の持ち弓であった。

22　藤を隙間なく巻いて漆を塗った弓。

23　弓は二片の竹の間にはさみ、これを膠で結合してつくるが、竹のところを塗らず、側木だけを黒く塗った弓。

24　矢が雨に濡れたり折れたりするのを防ぐために、矢を入れて腰や背に負う道具。

25　24と同じ。

26　鎧を入れる櫃。櫃はふたが上方に開く大形の箱。

27　大名行列などのときに、袋に入れ長い棒の先につけて小者に持たせたかぶり笠。

28　びろうどまたは羅紗などの袋に入れた長い柄の傘。

29　戦陣で用いた標識の一つで、大将の側に立ててその所在を示すもの。

30　鷹または鶏などの羽を栗の毬状に大きく作り、馬印や槍の鞘にしたもの。

31　槍、長刀、台笠、立傘、馬印、挟み箱、大鳥毛の七つ。

第二場

1　麻または苧（カラムシ）の茎の繊維から作った糸で織った布。「間男」＝「間男」＝「麻苧」の音通から姦通の隠語。

2　暴れ馬を制するための道具。先端にひもを輪にしてつけた50センチさほどの棒で、その輪を馬の鼻にかけてねじって制する。護身用にもした。

3　髪を頭の頂に束ねたところ。

4　「後ろ紐」は着物の後ろに縫い付け、前に回して結ぶようにした紐。この紐着きの着物を着ている幼い時。

5　銭二文一分。(**江戸時代のものの数え方**　4参照)

6　藁で編んだ草履状の履物。足の形に編み、つま先の二本の緒を左右に付いた乳（輪）に通して足に結び付けて履く。

7   *Fuzei* in Japanese; a suffix, meaning 'someone unimportant' here.

ACT THREE

1   A festival of the Yasaka Shrine in Kyoto: it was held from the sixth to the fourteenth in the lunar month of June. At present it starts on the first of July, and lasts about a month. The peak of the festival is on the seventeenth of July with a parade of the festival floats and the passage of a portable festival shrine. The true record of vendetta was carried out on the seventh of the luner month of June.
2   Festival music: people play flutes, drums and hand bells in the festival floats.
3   A piece of paper praying for success.
4   It is an event in advance of the start of *mikoshi-togyo*, the passage of a portable festival shrine of the Yasaka Shrine on the evening of the seventeenth of July; townspeople of Naka-gyō and Shimo-gyō tow the floats belonging to their area through the central part of Kyoto in the morning of the day. In the play it was happening on the seventh of the lunar month of June.
5   The area in the north part from San-jō Street to the Imperial Palace.
6   *O-kara*, in Japanese: the bean curd lees produced after making tofu.
7   The translation of the phrase is 'I believe in the three Treasures of Buddha, laws and priests.' (See Notes No. 29 of SCENE TWO of ACT ONE, **Lovers' Suicides at Imamiya**)
8   Putting *waraji* on a horse. (See Notes No. 6 of SCENE TWO of ACT TWO of this play for *waraji*)
9   It is a mountain standing on the boundary of Kyoto and Shiga prefectures. It is regarded as a sacred mountain from ancient times. There is the Enryaku-ji Temple, the head temple of Tendai Sect, on the mountain.
10 Normally people had their hair done in Japanese style in the Edo period. Therefore seeing someone with his hair loose is a very unusual sight.
11 *Sakayaki* in Japanese: it is the shaved front part of the head of men. The custom started in the middle age.
12 *Kataginu* in Japanese: it is a stiff sleeveless ceremonial robe for a samurai, worn over *kosode*, a kimono with short sleeves. *Moji-kataginu* mentioned here is the one made of twisted linen cloth. (See Notes No. 17 of ACT ONE, **Woman-Killer in Oil Hell**)
13 A silk cloth with a pinstripe made in India.
14 An old measurement for volume. It was used for measuring rice. 1 *koku* = 180.39

7 ここでは接尾語。自らを謙遜したり他を卑しめたりするときに用いる。ここでは「…のようなつまらない者」の意。

下之巻
1 京都八坂神社の祭礼。もとは陰暦六月七日～十四日まで。現在は七月十七日の山鉾巡行・神輿渡御を中心に、七月一日の吉符入り（神事の打ち合わせ）からほぼ一ヶ月行われる。実記の敵討ちは六月七日。

2 祭囃子の一つで山鉾の上などで笛・太鼓・鉦で囃されるもの。
3 力が強くなるようにと祈願に使う紙。
4 七月十七日の夕刻に行われる八坂神社の神輿渡御に先だって、中京、下京の町衆が各町に伝わる山や鉾を曳行する行事であり、同日の午前中に市街中心部である四条通りや河原町通りを巡行する。

5 京都市北部の三条通り以北の御所を中心とするあたり。
6 豆腐を作る時の豆乳を搾った後の大豆の搾りかす。殻の意。
7 仏・法・僧の三宝に帰依する意。三宝に呼びかけて、仏の助けを求める語。（「**今宮の心中**」上之巻第二場・註29参照）

8 馬に草鞋を履かせること。

9 京都府と滋賀県の境、京都市の北東の方にある山。古来信仰の山として知られ天台宗総本山延暦寺がある。

10 髪を結っていないこと。

11 中世末期以降、成人男子が前額部から頭上にかけて髪をそり上げたこと。また、その部分をいう。
12 麻糸を捻って目を粗く織った布で出来た肩衣。肩衣は武士の公服。袖のない上着で小袖の上から着る。（「**女殺油地獄**」上之巻・註17参照）

13 インド産の縦縞小模様の絹布。
14 「石」は尺貫法の体積の単位。主に穀物を量るのに用いる。1石は180.39ℓ。（**江**

lit. In the Edo period a samurai's annual stipend was paid by rice or gold. (See No. 5 (3) of **Measuring System in the Edo Period**)

15 It means that ten *chō-gin* coins. (See Notes No. 18 of this ACT)
16 A cone-shaped hat made of bamboo worn by a mendicant.
17 Twenty-five pieces of the Hokke sutra. A common name of '*Kanzeon bosatsu fumonbon*'.
18 *Chō-gin* in Japanese: it is one of the silver coins of the Edo period. It was an oblong-shaped and counted one *mai*, two *mai*... One *mai* valued about forty-three *monme* silver. Ten *mai* of *chō-gin* was a little more than seven *ryō*-gold. *Monme* is a unit of silver. 1 *ryō*-gold is 50-80*monme* silver. (See No. 4 of **Measuring System in the Edo Period**)
19 One *bu* gold of the Genroku time was a quarter of one *ryō*-gold. Five of one *bu* gold is one *ryō* and one *bu*. (See No. 4 of **Measuring System in the Edo Period**)
20 *Wakizashi* in Japanese: a samurai keeps a set of a large sword and a small sword at his waist. *Wakizashi* is the small one.
21 Sanjō Muromachi Street is in the direction of south west of Genemon's house.
22 Hachiman-*jin* (Yawata-*no-kami*) is an ancient Japanese god for the fortunes of war. It was called Hachiman-*dai-bosatsu* in a synthesis of Buddhism and Shintoism.

23 *Nageshi* in Japanese: it is a horizontal piece of timber from the frame of a Japanese-style building.
24 *Mushiko* in Japanese: a fine latticed window, looking like an insect cage. It can be found on the wall of the mezzanine floor of a traditional townsman's house in Kyoto.
25 A small screen of 1.2 meters height. (See Notes No. 5 of ACT TWO, **Woman-Killer in Oil Hell**)
26 One of the posts of the Tokugawa Government: the duty of the Kyoto Town Magistrate was to keep a control over the town of Kyoto. He handled lawsuits, kept control over the temples and shrines in the neighbouring eight countries, and guarded the royal palace.

「堀川波鼓」

戸時代のものの数え方 5（3）参照）江戸時代には一人一日玄米五合を標準とし、この一年分を米または金で給与した。禄高は主君から家臣に給与した年間に与えられる俸禄の額。

15　丁銀十枚のこと。（同巻・註18参照）
16　竹などで作られたすり鉢型の托鉢僧の被る笠。
17　法華経第25品、観世音菩薩普門品（かんぜおんぼさつふもんぼん）の通称。
18　江戸時代の銀貨の一つ。海鼠形（なまこ）で一枚、二枚と数える。一枚は四十三匁相当で銀十枚は金七両強。**（江戸時代のものの数え方　4参照）**

19　元禄一分判金。金貨は小判一枚を一両とし、一両（りょう）＝四分（ぶ）＝十六朱（しゅ）の四進法で数えたので、一分金五つは一両一分。**（江戸時代のものの数え方　4参照）**
20　武士が腰に差す大小二刀の内の小刀の称。

21　源右衛門の家から南西の方角にあたる。
22　八幡神（やわたのかみ）は日本で信仰される神で清和源氏をはじめ全国の武士から武運の神（武神）「弓矢八幡」として崇敬（すうけい）された。神仏習合時代に八幡大菩薩とも呼ばれた。
23　日本建築で柱から柱へと水平に打ち付けた材。
24　京町屋の中二階にみられる虫籠（むしかご）のように細かな組格子（くみごうし）のある窓。
25　丈が四尺（1.2メートル）ある小型の屏風（びょうぶ）。（「女殺油地獄」中之巻・註5参照）
26　江戸幕府の職名。京都の町の支配、近隣の八つの国の公事訴訟や寺社支配、禁裏（きんり）御所の警護などを任務とした。

LOVERS' SUICIDES AT IMAMIYA
A Play in Three Acts

Original Jōruri
Imamiya no Shinjū
By
Chikamatsu Monzaemon

Adaptation and translation
By
Masako Yuasa

「今宮の心中」
三幕八場

原作

近松門左衛門

翻案・英訳

湯浅雅子

Performance poster （公演ポスター）
Lovers' Suicides at Imamiya（「今宮の心中」）
Japan Tour in 2008（2008年日本ツアー）

Stage Photos （舞台写真）
Lovers' Suicides at Imamiya （「今宮の心中」）
Hull & Japan Tour, Tokyo in 2008（2008年ハル大学&日本ツアー・東京）

SCENE TWO of ACT ONE (In the boat, from the left) Sukegorō, Shizue, Teihō and Yoshibei (On the bank) Boatman and Kyūza　上之巻第二場　（船中　左から）介五郎　静江　貞法　由兵衛（川岸）船頭　久三　Photograph by Mike Park（撮影 マイク・パーク）

SCENE THREE of ACT TWO Jirobei 中之巻第三場　二郎兵衛　Photograph by Futoshi Sakauchi（撮影 坂内太）

SCENE ONE of ACT THREE　Jirobei and Kisa 下之巻第一場　二郎兵衛ときさ　Photograph by Futoshi Sakauchi（撮影 坂内太）

Original Design for *Lovers' Suicides at Imamiya*　Ground Design
「今宮の心中」舞台図原案　舞台基本プラン

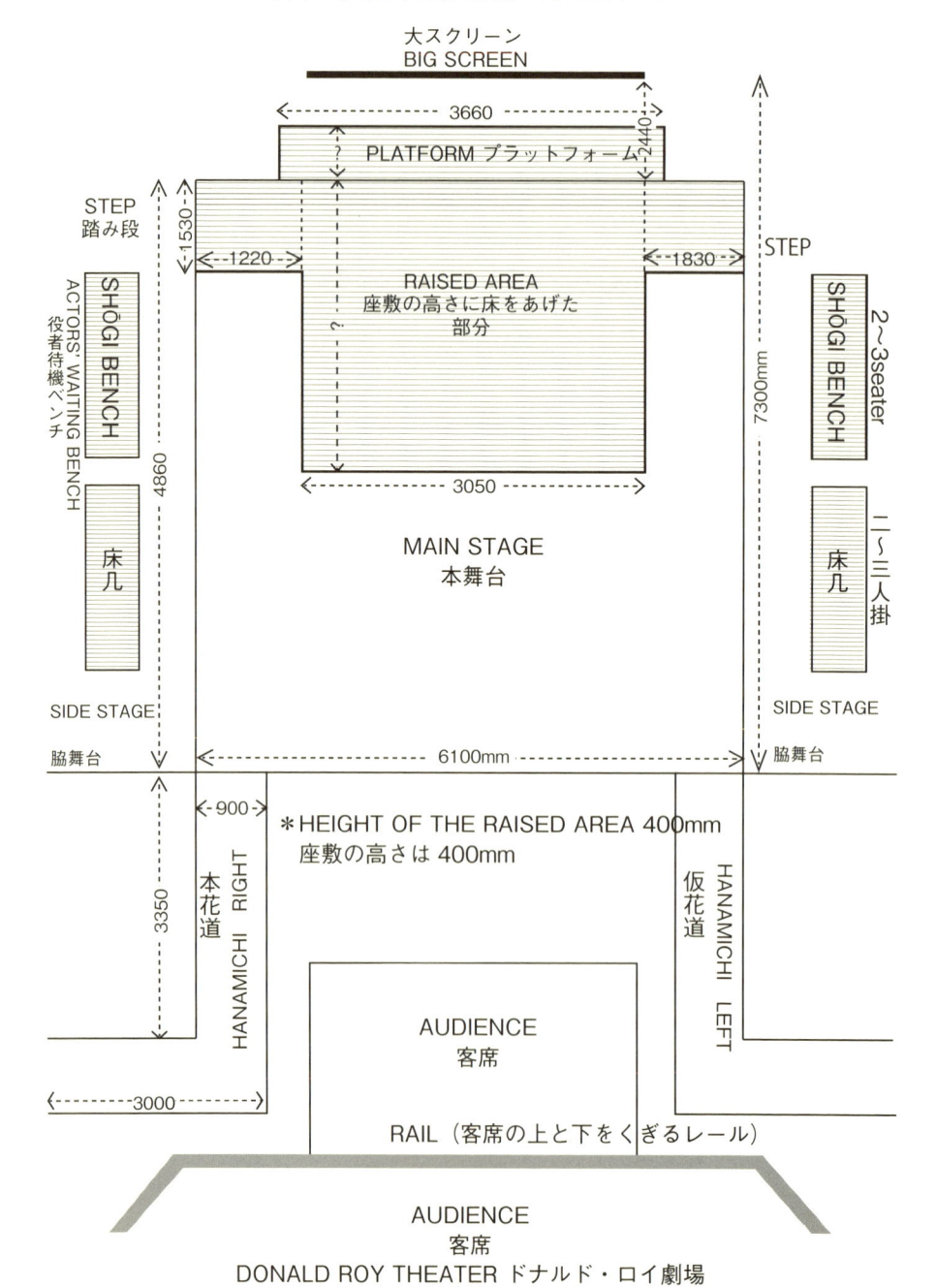

大スクリーン
BIG SCREEN

PLATFORM　プラットフォーム
3660
2440
1530
1220
1830

RAISED AREA
座敷の高さに床をあげた部分
3050

STEP
踏み段

STEP

SHŌGI BENCH
ACTORS' WAITING BENCH
役者待機ベンチ

床几

SHŌGI BENCH
2〜3seater
二〜三人掛
床几

4860
7300mm

MAIN STAGE
本舞台

SIDE STAGE
脇舞台

SIDE STAGE
脇舞台

6100mm

900
* HEIGHT OF THE RAISED AREA 400mm
座敷の高さは400mm

3350

本花道
HANAMICHI RIGHT

仮花道
HANAMICHI LEFT

AUDIENCE
客席

3000

RAIL（客席の上と下をくぎるレール）

AUDIENCE
客席
DONALD ROY THEATER　ドナルド・ロイ劇場

DESIGN by YUASA
Dec. 2007

Original Design for *Lovers' Suicides at Imamiya*　ACT ONE
「今宮の心中」舞台図原案　上之巻

大スクリーン
BIG SCREEN

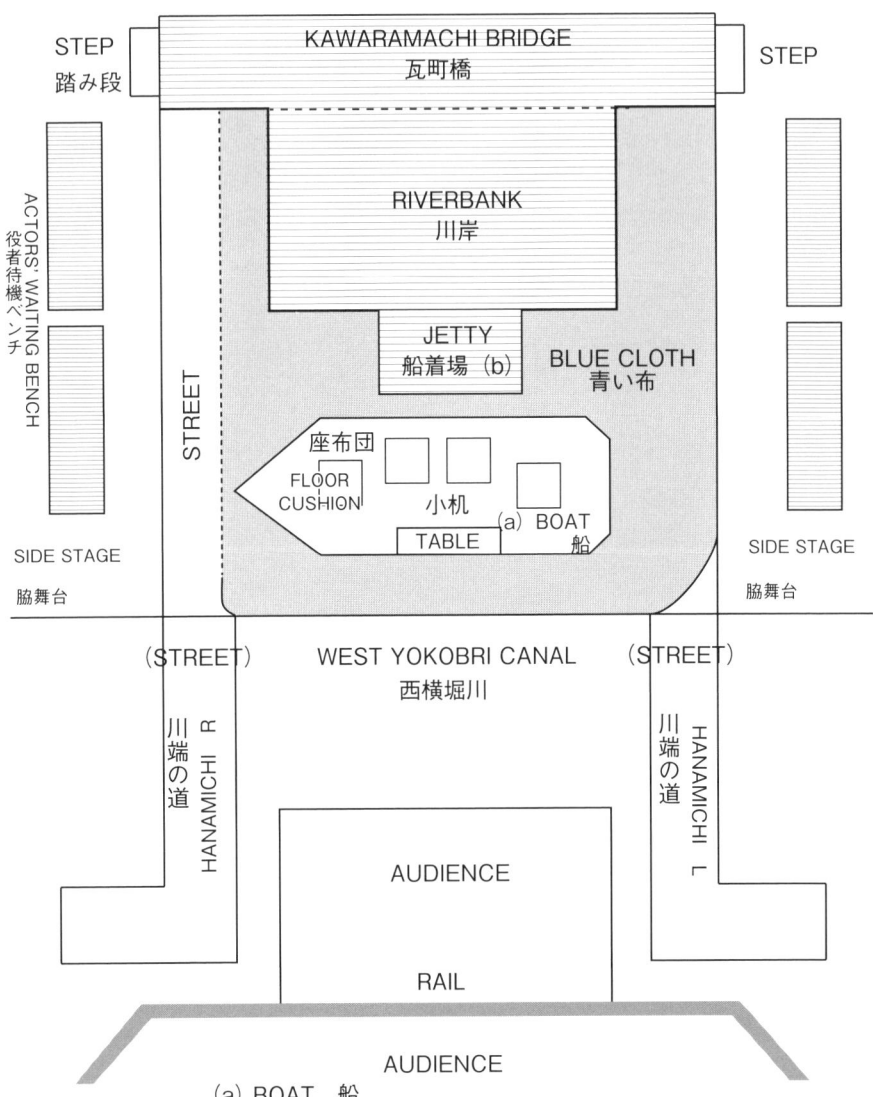

KAWARAMACHI BRIDGE
瓦町橋

STEP
踏み段

STEP

ACTORS' WAITING BENCH
役者待機ベンチ

RIVERBANK
川岸

JETTY
船着場 (b)

BLUE CLOTH
青い布

STREET

座布団
FLOOR CUSHION

小机
TABLE

(a) BOAT
船

SIDE STAGE
脇舞台

SIDE STAGE
脇舞台

(STREET)　WEST YOKOBRI CANAL　(STREET)
西横堀川

川端の道
HANAMICHI R

川端の道
HANAMICHI L

AUDIENCE

RAIL

AUDIENCE

(a) BOAT　船
(b) JETTY（wooden decking: height 200mm）
　　船着場（木製・川岸の半分の高さ）

DESIGN by YUASA
Dec. 2003

295

LOVERS' SUICIDES AT IMAMIYA

The original *jōruri* was first performed at the Takemoto-za in 1711. The proprietor of the theatre was Takeda Izumo. The *jōruri* reciter was Takemono Chikugonojō who was sixty-one years old at that time. The *jōruri* was written by Chikamatsu Monzaemon when he was fifty-nine.

Reference

'Imamiya no Shinjū,' *Nihon Koten Bungaku Zenshū Chikamatsu Monzaemon Shū 2,* edited by Torigoe Bunzō, translated into current Japanese with notes by Yamane Taneo. Published by Shōgakukan in 1998. (Page 287-330)

The adaptation was first staged at the Donald Roy Theatre at the University of Hull from 4th to 8th March 2008, with the following cast and crew.

HISHIYA SHIRŌEMON	Andrew Dawson
TEIHŌ	Harriet Howse
SHIZUE	Sarah Williams
SUKEGORŌ	Emily Lee
JIROBEI	Ian Bruce
KISA	Cookie Sami
YOSHIBEI	Jim Townsend
KYŪZA	Kyle Stealey
TARŌ SABURŌ	Rob Keeves
CHŌBEI	Rob Keeves
SHIBUYA BOKUAN	Jim Townsend
TAKE	Emily Lee
CHORUS	Anna Mitchell

The other characters were performed by the members of the cast.

Direction and original design	Masako Yuasa
Set Design	Naomi Jones
Set Construction	Aaron Carrington
Lighting	Jessica Hazlewood
Sound	Harry Lockyear
Costume	Pauline Chambers, Paul Goodman
Props	Tom Saunders and Jo Stevens
Stage manager	Laura Parkes
Production Manager	Richard Tall

「今宮の心中」

　初演　1711年竹本座。座本武田出雲。太夫竹本筑後掾、六十一歳。作者近松門左衛門、五十九歳の作品。

参考資料　日本古典文学全集『近松門左衛門集②』「今宮の心中」（287〜330頁）
　　　　　鳥越文蔵　編、山根為雄　校注・訳　小学館　1998年5月1日出版。

　湯浅版初演は2008年3月3日〜8日　英国ハル大学ドナルド・ロイ劇場で以下のスタッフ、キャストで上演した。

菱屋四郎右衛門	アンドリュー・ドーソン
貞法	ハリエット・ホース
静江	サラ・ウィリアムズ
介五郎	エミリー・リー
二郎兵衛	イアン・ブルース
きさ	クッキー・サミ
由兵衛	ジム・タウンズエンド
久三	カイル・スティーリー
太郎三郎	ロブ・キーヴズ
長兵衛	ロブ・キーヴズ
渋谷卜庵	ジム・タウンズエンド
竹	エミリー・リー
コーラス	アナ・ミッチェル

　その他の登場人物は出演俳優全員で演じた。

演出・舞台原案	湯浅雅子
舞台装置デザイン	ナオミ・ジョーンズ
舞台装置作り	アーロン・カーリントン
照明	ジェシカ・ハイゼルウッド
音響	ハリー・ロックイヤー
衣装	ポーリーン・チェンバー、ポール・グッドマン
小道具	トム・サンダース、ジョー・スティーヴンス
ステージ・マネジャー	ローラ・パークス
プロダクション・マネジャー	リチャード・トール

The production toured to Japan as the second Japan tour of the Chikamatsu Project. The performances were held at the Seika Small Theatre (Seika Shō Gekijō) in Osaka on 30th and 31st May, and at the Ono Memorial Auditorium of Waseda University (Waseda Daigaku Ono Kinen Kōdō) in Tokyo on 5th and 6th June. The production was also performed at the Greenside at the Edinburgh International Fringe Festival from 18th to 23rd August in 2008.

The adaptation for the performances in 2008 has been revised with companion notes for the present publication.

ACTS AND SCENES

(The Play is in Three Acts with Eight Scenes.)

ACT ONE   The town of Osaka, a fine day in May, 1711
   SCENE 1   On a small pleasure boat
   SCENE 2   At the Kawara-machi Bridge
   SCENE 3   On the Kawara-machi Bridge

ACT TWO   At the Hishi-ya on the 23rd of May
   SCENE 1   Lovers' quarrel
   SCENE 2   Moxa Treatment
   SCENE 3   Lecture

ACT THREE   On the 24th of May
   SCENE 1   Lovers' journey
   SCENE 2   The Forest of the Imamiya Ebisu Shrine

CHARACTERS

HISHIYA SHIRŌEMON, a kimono maker,[1] the owner and the master of the Hishi-ya,[2] in Honmach, Osaka[3]
TEIHŌ, aged 73, SHIRŌEMON's mother and the old mistress of the Hishi-ya
SHIZUE, SHIRŌEMON's wife and the mistress of the Hishi-ya
SUKEGORŌ, SHIRŌEMON and SHIZUE's son

「今宮の心中」

　この公演で近松プロジェクトは二回目の日本ツアーを行った。ツアーでの公演日程は2008年5月30日、31日　精華小劇場（大阪）、2008年6月5日、6日　早稲田大学小野記念講堂（東京）であった。同年8月18日〜23日に英国エディンバラのグリーンサイド劇場で公演してエディンバラ演劇祭フリンジに参加した。

　この本に掲載した翻案戯曲は出版のために初演台本を一部改訂したものである。

劇の構成

　（三幕八場）

　上之巻　　大阪市中　一七十一年　五月の晴れた日
　　第一場　遊山船
　　第二場　瓦町橋の畔(ほとり)
　　第三場　瓦町橋の橋上

　中之巻　　菱屋内の場　五月二十三日
　　第一場　痴話喧嘩
　　第二場　灸据え
　　第三場　説教

　下之巻　　五月二十四日
　　第一場　道行
　　第二場　今宮の戎の森

登場人物

菱屋(ひしや)[2]四郎右衛門(しろうえもん)　　大阪本町[3]の新物の仕立屋(しんぶつ)[1]、菱屋の主人。

（菱屋(ひしや)）貞法(ていほう)　　七十三歳　四郎右衛門の母で隠居(いんきょ)、お上様(かみ)。
（菱屋）静江(しずえ)　　四郎右衛門の内儀（妻）、お家様(いえ)。
（菱屋）介五郎(すけごろう)　　四郎右衛門の息子。

JIROBEI, aged 21, a junior shop assistant[4] at the Hishi-ya
KISA, aged 26, a seamstress at the Hishiya
YOSHIBEI, a former senior shop assistant at the Hishi-ya, now independent and running his own shop
KYŪZA, a man servant of the Hishi-ya[5]
CHŌBEI, a senior shop assistant at the Hishi-ya
GONBEI, a shop assistant at the Hishi-ya
TAKE, a maid of the Hishi-ya

TARŌ SABURŌ of Sanda Village,[6] Kisa's father
SHIBUYA BOKUAN, SHIRŌEMON's doctor
THE BOATMAN
THE retired SAMURAI
THE YAKKO with a moustache, a man servant of the SAMURAI[7]

CHORUSES (CHORUS 1, CHORUS 2 and CHORUS 3)
  The speeches of the CHORUS in SCENE ONE of ACT ONE and ACT THREE are not written for a separate chorus. They were spoken by members of the cast in the first production.

「今宮の心中」

二郎兵衛（じろべえ）　　　菱屋の下手代(しもてだい)[4]。二十一歳。
きさ　　　　　　　　　　　菱屋の針子(はりこ)。二十六歳。
由兵衛（よしべえ）　　　　元菱屋の重手代(おもてだい)。今は独立して店を構えている。

久三（きゅうざ）[5]　　　菱屋の下男(げなん)。
長兵衛（ちょうべえ）　　　同　重手代(おもてだい)。
権兵衛（ごんべえ）　　　　同　手代。
竹（たけ）　　　　　　　　同　下女。

三田村(さんだむら)[6]の太郎三郎(たろうさぶろう)　　きさの父親。
渋谷卜庵（しぶやぼくあん）　菱屋四郎右衛門の医者。
船頭（せんどう）
浪人侍（ろうにんざむらい）
髭奴（ひげやっこ）[7]

コーラス（コーラス1、コーラス2、コーラス3）
　上の巻・第一場と下の巻のコーラスはコーラス1、コーラス2、コーラス3に書き分けていない。初演では出演俳優皆で演じた。

LOVERS' SUICIDES AT IMAMIYA

ACT ONE

The town of Osaka,
A fine day in May, 1711

Upstage Centre the Kawara-machi Bridge[1] spanning the West Yokobori Canal.[2] There is a jetty at the foot of the bridge Centre Stage. Two hanamichi, the hanamichi Right (the main hanamichi) and the hanamichi Left (the temporary hanamichi), stretch through the auditorium in parallel from the main stage; they are the streets running either side of the West Yokobori Canal.

SCENE ONE
On a small pleasure boat

The town of Osaka where the streets, rivers and canals are lively.
The sound of a samisen is heard.

CHORUS [*joyfully*]: Heeey, hey, hey, heeey!
You can see flowers and admire the moon in whichever city you may wander.
But the most amusing and the rarest pleasure is boating on the rivers and canals in Osaka in summer.

From the shop masters to the shop assistants, man servants and maids, the old and the young, all together,
Let's get on the boat.[3]
The summer breeze crossing the water is as cool and refreshing as in autumn.
I swear that it's true.

Starting from the Hon-machi Bridge Canal and rowing down the Tenma River,[4]
In the Tenma Vegetable Market[5] on the north bank, the first melons of the summer season are lined up.
Buy a melon, cool it well and cut it in half.
The halves look so much alike, like a rabit-ear iris and a blue flag one.
There's a purple-blue hat on the water,

「今宮の心中」

上之巻

大阪市中
一七十一年、五月の晴れた日

　舞台奥に西横堀川[2]にかかる瓦町橋[1]。その橋の下の方、舞台中央手前に船着場。本舞台から下手花道と上手花道の二つの花道が延びている。花道は西横堀川を両側から挟む川端の道である。

第一場
遊山船

　　　　人々が行き交い、通りや川筋は活気に満ちている。
　　　　三味線の音。

コーラス　えーい　えいえい　えいえい　えーい！
　月見花見はどこでも同じ
　諸国名物数あるなかで
　類まれなるお遊びは　夏の難波の船遊び

　主も手代も　下男も下女も　老いも若きも　皆々で
　さあさ　乗ろうよ　川御座船[3]に
　袂　抜ける川風は　涼し爽やか　秋のよう
　嘘やおまへん　ほんまのほんま！

　本町橋から漕ぎ出し　天満川[4]下れば
　北に天満の青物市[5]　並ぶは夏の初真桑

　真桑　買って冷やして　二つに割れば
　これがほんまのうりふたつ　いずれが菖蒲か杜若
　杜若色の水の紫花帽子
　水面に映る花影は　どこぞのお内儀　涼やかにお買い物

303

It's the reflection of someone's wife enjoying her shopping.
A water carrier scoops up the reflection of the purple-blue hat and pours it into the barrel.

Doshōbon, the Buddhist monk with a shaven head,
Shakes his head and a tin ladle, pats his patient and mouths a few words.
Blessed! With one stroke of the ladle the monk has cured the patient.

A tea boat[6] carries sake brewed in Itami.[7]
Where are the sake cask and all that good food destined for?
A village woman married to someone in Osaka and visiting her family is on board.
A funeral boat bearing a coffin sails past.

The boat shows us all the sights of the world at once.
"How about a cup of sake to drink with these sights?"
Someone plays the samisen softly on the rolling boat,
While someone else runs the oil mill in the riverside warehouse.[8]
So many people, so many different lives.

> On the bridge a fan seller who carries many fan-shaped boxes is displaying and selling fans, saying, "Fan yourself! Fan yourself!" Another peddler sells various tobacco pouches which are made of leather, woven fabric or papers. A pipe seller is also passing, crying "Anyone for pipes?"

We hear peddlers' voices from the bridge,
Selling fans, round fans, tobacco pouches, pipes and what have you.
The loudest cry among them is from a peddler who sells a magazine called Moshiho-gusa, 'Salt Seaweed.'[9] It's writing about kabuki actors' performances in Osaka, comparing them to the famous points and bridges in Osaka.

"Ogino Yaegaki, that beautiful young female impersonator, should be compared to the Kamei Bridge."[10]
Why is that?
"Because it is the only bridge to Ebisu Island, where the Tenmangū Shrine stops on its annual tour. There is nothing before and nothing after it. No actor as good as he has ever

「今宮の心中」

水汲みが来て　紫の花帽子の水汲みあげて　売り歩くたごの棒

坊主頭の道正　坊
頭振り振り　金柄杓振り振り　病人撫で撫で
ムニャ　ムニャ　ムニャ
あら有難や　一撫でで　病本復　いたみいる

伊丹のお酒[7]が　茶舟[6]で下る
酒樽　肴は　いずれのご祝儀
在所嫁御の里帰り
上荷で送るお葬式

世の有様の様々を　一時に垣間見る　水の難波の舟遊び
常ならん景色を酒の肴に　「まあ、おひとつ」と杯勧めます
船に揺られて三味線弾く者
岸の浜納屋[8]で油臼引く者
世はそれぞれでございます

　　　橋の上を扇売りが扇の形の箱をいくつも担ぎ、扇の紙を見せながら「あおぎいー、あおぎいー。」の売り声で扇を売っている。その他、団扇売り、皮、織物、紙などでできた煙草入れを売る煙草入れ売り、煙管売りも通る。

橋の上には物売る者の物売りの声
扇に団扇、煙管に煙草入れ
中でも一際高い売り声は
難波芝居の歌舞伎役者のありさま書いた役者評判記、『藻塩草』[9]売る者の声
難波の橋々、名所にたとえて　役者評判伝えます

「伊勢の海女ではないけれど　その浜荻の荻野八重桐は　亀井橋[10]に譬えましょう」
はて、その心は？
「橋の先は天神のお旅所で　後にも先にも続くものなし」

305

existed before or will ever exist again."

"Sodejima Genji should be compared to the street of Shin-Utsubo."[11]
Why do you say that?
"Because it's the street for salted fish; his charm flavours like salt, as it permeates and his acting has a lot of guts, too!"

"Arashi Sanjūro should be compared to Katsuo-za-bashi, the Bonito Bridge."[12]
Why is that?
"Because dried bonito flakes are best for making good soup stock. Whatever play he is in, he is the tastiest leading actor."

"Ichimura Tamagashiwa should be compared to Umeda Bridge."[13]
Why is that?
"When you cross the bridge, you arrive at Sonezaki, the new pleasure quarter. If you go on, you reach the crematorium of Umeda. He can perform in both a love story and a sad story."

"The leading actor Yamamura Utazaemon poses for dramatic effect, parting his legs widely. It reminds us of Hyakken-bori, the landing stage of the One Hundred Ken Width."[14]
Then the peddler says, "Now, I've told you half of what's in the magazine."

While listening to his story, rowing through the Itachi Canal,[15]
We have reached the spot where we can see the rear of the tall Midō temple.[16]
Now we come to Araya-bashi,[17] the Washing-up Bridge.
Let's wash up the lunch dishes.
We brew fresh tea in an iron teapot at the Bingo-Bridge.[18]
Shall we moor our boat?
We've arrived at the Kawara-machi Bridge.

「今宮の心中」

「袖島源治は　干物の問屋町の新靫」[11]
その心は？
「塩物町では塩がしたたります。塩、即ち愛嬌が零れ落ち、しかも芸には骨がある。」

さて、嵐三十郎を鰹座橋[12]と仰るその心は？
「何の料理に使うても　仕出しがうまい。押し出しのきく立役者。」

市村玉柏が梅田橋[13]と言うのは？
「梅田橋、渡れば色町曽根崎新地、その色町を越えれば梅田の火葬場。濡れ事も憂い事もよううつる。」

「姿りりしい立ち役の山村歌左衛門がかっと見得切って両足広げたその大股、広い荷揚げ場の百間掘[14]を思い出す。」
「さて、ここまでが表半分」と『藻塩草』売りの声

男の話聞くうちに
裏の御堂[16]が高々と見える立売堀[15]を漕ぎまわり
お弁当済めば　お碗もお箸もサッと洗うは荒屋橋[17]。
後は香り立つ出花のお茶を入れた茶瓶の備後橋[18]。
さあさあ、岸に船寄せまひょ。
瓦町橋に着きました。

SCENE TWO
At the Kawara-machi Bridge

The same scenery as Scene One. Late afternoon.

A boatman is guiding a small pleasure boat to the jetty, helped by KYŪZA, the man servant of the Hishi-ya, a kimono maker in Hon-machi.

TEIHŌ, SHIZUE, SUKEGORŌ and YOSHIBEI are in the boat. TEIHŌ, HISHIYA SHIRŌEMON's mother and the old mistress of the Hishi-ya, is a hale old woman. SHIRŌEMON's wife, SHIZUE, the mistress of the Hishi-ya, is a typical Osaka merchant's wife. SUKEGORŌ is a young man with a peaceful manner.

Sake and dishes of food are in front of the people on board who are happily eating and talking. YOSHIBEI, a former senior shop assistant of the Hishi-ya, is now independent and runs his own shop. Today he is entertaining his old master HISHI-YA SHIRŌEMON's family by taking them boating on the rivers running through the town of Osaka to express his long standing gratitude to the Hishi-ya.

SUKEGOROŌ: Yoshibei has played the host and treated us to good sake and food all day today. It has been lovely and I have enjoyed it so much. But I think the sun will soon be setting. Yoshibei, you must be tired by now. Grandmother, Mother, how about getting off here?

TEIHŌ: I think that it's a good idea. Thank you so much for your hearty welcome today, Yoshibei. It's been a wonderful treat for us. I enjoyed boating on the rivers very much today. You've become independent of the Hishi-ya and run your own shop. You've gained credit in your business, too. It is a great pleasure to see one of our former employees making something of him and inviting us, his former master's family, out like this. You've achieved a great deal. But, Yoshibei, life can sometimes be a little difficult when you are single. I think that you need to marry a respectable woman and settle down. (*Asking for agreement*) Don't you think so, Shizue-san?[19]

SHIZUE: Yes, I do, Mother. [*To YOSHIBEI*] Yoshibei, why don't you take a wife? Have you got someone in mind?

YOSHIBEI [*nodding his head at SHIZUE's words, pleased and inflated with pride*]: Thank you for your kind words, Old Mistress, Mistress and Sukegorō-sama.[20] I am delighted to hear that all of you have enjoyed yourselves very much today. What's more, you are even concerned about my future wife. I am so grateful. You care so much about me. Yes, as a matter of fact, it is just as the mistress has said. I have someone in mind, but this woman is not so easy to win over. Indeed she is hard work. But soon the time will come to ask

「今宮の心中」

第二場
瓦町橋の畔

　　　　前場と同じ場所。遅い午後。
　　　一艘の御座舟（屋形船）が瓦町橋の船着場に着いたところである。船頭が大阪本町の仕立屋菱屋の下男の久三に手伝わせて御座船を岸に着けている。
　　　船には菱屋の隠居貞法、内儀の静江、息子の介五郎、菱屋の元手代の由兵衛の姿がある。貞法は矍鑠とした老女。静江は典型的な大阪のお店の内儀。介五郎は温和な感じの若者。
　　　人々の前には重箱、酒などが並んでいて、皆楽しげに飲んだり食べたりしている。今日は既に独り立ちした由兵衛が日頃のお礼にと、主にあたる菱屋の人々を大阪市中の川遊びでもてなしているのである。

介五郎　今日は一日、由兵衛がこの御座船の亭主になって私たちにご馳走をしてくれて、誠に有難いことでありました。そろそろ日の暮れも近いようす。由兵衛、お前もさぞくたびれたことでありましょう。祖母様、母様、この辺りで岸に上がるのが良いと思われますが。

貞法　（矍鑠として）そうですな。そうしましょうか。由兵衛、お前の心のこもった手厚いもてなしの御馳走で今日は一日、たいそうええ気晴らしをさせて貰いました。お礼を言います。元菱屋の奉公人だった者が店を一軒構え、商いの信用も得て私たち親方一家をもてなしてくれるまでになったことは、私たちの喜びでもあるし、お前の手柄でもあります。けどなあ、由兵衛、お前も女房がなければ日々の生活も落ち着かんことでありましょう。早う堅気の女房を貰うて落ち着かんといけません。（同意を求めて）静江さん[19]、あなたもそう思いませんか？

静江　ほんに、そうだすなあ。（由兵衛に）由兵衛は何故女房を貰いませんのや？どこぞに心に決めたお人でもありますんか？

由兵衛　（嬉しそうに得意顔で頷いて）今日はお上様、お家様、介五郎様[20]に心おきのう遊んでいただきまして誠に有難うございました。また、其の上に私の女房の心配までしていただきまして、誠に忝ないことでございます。お家様の仰せの通りでございます。少し心に思う人が居るには居るのですが、この女が簡単に行きそうで行きにくい。ちょっと難しいのです。いずれはお上様、お家様方のお口添えをお願い申し上げる時が来ると思うております。

309

the old mistress and the mistress to put in a good word for me with her.

TTEIHŌ: Well, if you think that a good word from us would persuade the woman you love, why shouldn't we act as a go-between? Now, tell us, who is she?

SHIZUE: Whoever is she?

YOSHIBEI [*smiling a satisfied smile as things have gone as he planned*]: Oh, I'm so grateful to you. I'll pray three times to express my gratitude. [*Praying with his hands pressed together*] Once I gave you her name, you'd know very well who she was, but let's not reveal it for now. [*Beating time with his hand light-heartedly*] Now, now, how about having a proper drinking party? [*Offering sake to SUKEGORŌ*] Sukegorō-sama, you should be the first as the captain of the boat. Please have another cup. Now then, what shall I offer for a side dish? Let me see... [*Looking at a goze*[21] *in a boat passing-by*] Hey, Goze-dono! Will you please play us your music?

> *The goze plays the samisen and sings a song.*
> *A quiet moment passes as the music plays.*
> *YOSHIBEI serves more sake to SUKEGORŌ.*

SUKEGORŌ [*receiving sake, merrily*]: Mother, it's a pity that Jirobei has gone back home to Hōryūji, isn't it?[22] If he were with us, he would recite a jōruri[23] about a lovers' suicide pact.

SHIZUE: Yes, indeed. And if O-Kisa[24] were here, she would sing us her favourite utasaimon.[25]

SUKEGORŌ: Oh, yes, she would. It really is a shame.

YOSHIBEI [*spirits suddenly dampened*]: I see. Jirobei told me that he was going home for his mother's memorial service,[26] but I didn't know that O-Kisa had gone with him, too.

SHIZUE: Oh, no. Don't be silly! Kisa has got a cold and a terrible headache, so she's gone to her sister's in Hyakkan-machi.[27] You know that Kisa's sister there is her guarantor.

YOSHIBEI [*hardly listening to SHIZUE*]: I think, compared to my time, the Hishi-ya has become soft on its employees. Jirobei has just been promoted from an apprentice to a junior shop assistant. When the shop is so terribly busy, he has taken leave and gone to Hōryūji in Nara to attend his mother's memorial service. Hōryūji is a good ten ri[28] away from Osaka. I am much displeased with him. It's especially bad that he is not in the shop when Kisa is ill and gone to her sister's. Really what a wicked thing to do!

> *YOSHIBEI is upset. He kicks at the side of the ship and stamps the sake cup to*

貞法　はて、私たちの口添えで済むことならば、仲を取り持たんで何としましょう。その、お前の思うお人の名は何と言うんです？
静江　一体、何処のどなたですのんや？
由兵衛　（思惑通りに話しが進み、にんまりして）ほんに忝ないことでございます。この通り、お言葉の有難さに三度拝みます。（手を合わせて拝む。）その女の名を申しあげたらすぐにお分りになります。けど、今のところは名前は言わずにおきまして（陽気に手拍子を打ちながら）「しゃんしゃんしゃん」と、さあさあ、これからが本酒、本酒。（介五郎に酒を勧めて）先ずはご亭主からということで、介五郎様からもう一杯。酒の肴は……っと。（通りがかった船の瞽女[21]に、頭を下げて）瞽女殿、一節お願い致します。

　　　　　船から瞽女の三味線を弾き、歌う声が聞こえる。
　　　　　ゆったりとした空気が辺りを包む。
　　　　　由兵衛が介五郎に酒を注ぐ。

介五郎　（盃を受けながら愉快そうに）母様、二郎兵衛が里の法隆寺[22]から戻っていたら、あれの好きな浄瑠璃[23]の心中物を語らせますのになあ。
静江　ほんにそうですなあ。それと、せめてここにおきさ[24]でも居てくれたらあれの得意の歌祭文[25]を聞かせてくれますのに。
介五郎　ほんに残念なことでございます。
由兵衛　（急に興ざめて）そうでおますか。二郎兵衛は母親の年忌[26]で在所に参ると申しましたが、おきさも一緒に行ったのでございますか？
静江　まあ、何を言いますのや。とんでもない。きさは風邪を引いて頭痛がすると言うてあれの姉の家に行ってますのや。百貫町[27]に住んでいるきさの身元引受人の姉のことはお前も聞いてますやろ。
由兵衛　（静江の話をろくに聞きもしないで）お店も私がご奉公しておりました頃とは違い、ずいぶんだらしのうなりましたなあ。まだ歳も若いくせに二郎兵衛めは、丁稚から上がったばかりの下手代の分際で己の母親の年忌でございますと言うて、この忙しいのに十里[28]も離れた法隆寺へ帰りよるとは、気に入らんことでございます。ことにきさが患うて宿下がりしている時に同じように店を出おって。ほんまにろくなことはしよりまへん。

　　　　　由兵衛は自分独り勝手に嫉妬に心を苛立たせて、むやみやたらと腹を立

pieces in anger. The HISHI-YA family listen attentively to the goze's singing and the samisen; they are unaware of YOSHIBEI's mood and behaviour.
The sun is setting and darkness falling.

TEIHŌ [*noticing the change of the light and to SHIZUE and SUKRGORŌ*]: Oh, it's getting darker. I think we'd better leave the boat....

The people prepare to get off the boat.

YOSHIBEI [*very confident*]: Please do not worry about the darkness at your feet. I've thought of this and brought a lantern. [*He takes out the lantern proudly, but it has no candle.*] Namu-sanbō![29] Goodness! I haven't brought a candle. [*To KYŪZA on the shore*] Kyūza! Will you please come here?

KYŪZA approaches the boat.

YOSHIBEI: You know that O-Kisa's sister's house is on Hyakkan-machi Street, which is a few chō[30] down from here. I'm sorry to trouble you, but would you mind running over there and saying that I've told you to ask her to lend us a candle? And if O-Kisa looks well enough, ask her to come with you, too. While you are at it, have a good look around the house and see if anyone else is there. Have you got that? Now go quickly.

KYŪZA: Yes, sir. I'll be back soon.

KYŪZA runs down the Hyakkan-machi Street through the hanamichi Right.

The sound of a samisen in the distance.
JIROBEI enters from the hanamichi Left. He is walking along the other side of the West Yokobori Canal.

CHORUS 1: Look over there! Jirobei is coming. He's only recently celebrated his coming of age and become a junior shop assistant. So inexperienced!
CHORUS 2: There's a quilted kimono[31] that looks like an ordinary one. He is that sort. He's pretending nothing special is going on between him and Kisa, one of the experienced kimono seamstresses of the Hishi-ya. But the truth is that he's been having an intimate

「今宮の心中」

　　　　て船端を蹴り、杯を踏み割る。他の人々は瞽女の歌と三味線に聞き入っ
　　　　ていて、そんな由兵衛には全く気付かない。
　　　　　日が落ち始めて辺りが暗くなってくる。

貞法　（静江と介五郎に）日が暮れてきました。このあたりで、そろそろお暇すること
　　にしましょうか。

　　　　　貞法の言葉に促されて、人々は下船の支度を始める。

由兵衛　（自信たっぷりに）ご心配はご無用でございます。暗うなっても足元が危ない
　　ことはございません。こういうこともあろうかとこの由兵衛、ちゃーんと提灯の
　　用意をいたしております。（提灯を出して、蝋燭のないことに気付き）南無三宝[29]、
　　しもた！蝋燭、忘れてきた！（岸にいる久三に）久三！ちょっと来てくれ。

　　　　　川岸にいた久三が由兵衛のところに来る。

由兵衛　この前の百貫町の通りを四、五町[30]行ったらおきさの保証人の姉の家があるの
　　ん、お前も知っているやろ。ご苦労やけとな、一っ走りそこへ行って、「由兵衛か
　　ら言付かってきました。蝋燭を一本貸して下さらんか。」と、言うて蝋燭借りてき
　　てくれんか。ついでに、おきさの病気がようなってるようやったら、ちょっとこ
　　こまで来てくださらんかと頼んで一緒に連れてきてくれ。ああ、そのついでにな、
　　家の中に他に誰もおらへんか、よう見回して来てくれ。分かったか？分かったら、
　　早行って来てくれるか！
久三　へえ、分かりました。すぐ、行て参じます。

　　　　　久三は下手花道を百貫町に向かって走り去る。

　　　　　遠くに誰かの弾く三味線の音。
　　　　　二郎兵衛が上手花道、船着場の対岸の川端の道を来る。

コーラス1　あれっ、あそこに来るのは、ついこの間前髪取って下手代に成ったばっか
　　りの出来立てのほやほや、菱屋の新米手代の二郎兵衛。
コーラス2　綿入れの南京綿[31]のように上辺はなーんでもないように装っているけれど、
　　あの二郎兵衛、実は店の姉さん針子のきさとは深あーい仲。

relationship with her.

CHORUS 3: It was a tall lie that he was going back to his home country for the anniversary of his mother's death. Instead he's been hiding out at his friend's in West Yokobori. He waits for dusk and goes to meet up with Kisa who pretends to be ill and is staying with her sister.

CHORUS 1: Look at Jirobei's face smiling with glee!

CHORUS 2: Oh, oh, careful! You'll drool!

JIROBEI [*in a merry mood*]: At last the sun has returned to its home in the west. [*Smiling gleefully*] My gentle and beautiful Kisa must be looking forward to meeting me. Please be patient a little longer, Sweetheart! I'll be there soon. [*Noticing the people of the HISHI-YA on the boat*] What! I can see dimly people sitting under the roof of the boat moored on the other shore...they look like the mistresses and the young master of my shop...and... the man in the bows is Yoshibei who's got his own shop in Andōji-machi! Oh, dear! I'll be in trouble if I am caught walking out like this in Osaka. I must hide myself.

KYŪZA comes back down the hanamichi Right hastily carrying a lantern which bears HISHI-YA's family crest. KISA is behind him, half running.

JIROBEI [*noticing at the lantern*]: That's Hishi-ya's lantern...and Kyūza is carrying it...then, what? The woman coming after him is Kisa! [*Suddenly anxious*] There must be some reason for this.

JIROBEI gets upset as he views this unexpected encounter. He hides himself behind one of the timber warehouses along the canal and watches the event from there. He wants to know what is happening to KISA.

The evening wind drops and it is airless in the shade of the warehouse.

YOSHIBEI takes the lantern from KYŪZA and hangs it on the boat.

KISA [*approaching the boat, sitting on the ground and bowing to the people on the boat*]: Good evening, Mistresses and Young Master. Kyūza told me on the way here that you all enjoyed a day out on the boat today. I am very delighted to hear it. [*In desperation*] Umm, I haven't recovered from my illness, but I came here because...I'm so sorry to spoil your evening with my personal affairs, but Old Mistress, and Mistress, there's something that I must ask of you. [*Looking pained*] It's been awful...my cold has got worse...I'm feeling terrible... [*Sighing*].

「今宮の心中」

コーラス3　母親の年忌に在所に帰ったなんぞは嘘八百の八百八橋。実は西横堀の友だちのところに隠れていて、日が暮れて人目につかんようになるのを待っては、これも病気と嘘ついて姉の家に帰っているきさと逢瀬の重ね着三昧。

コーラス1　ほれほれ、二郎兵衛のあのゆるんだ顔見てみ。
コーラス2　ああ、ああ、気いつけな涎（よだれ）こぼれるでえ。
二郎兵衛　（上機嫌で）やっとお日さんが、西の宿にいんでくれはった。（にやけて）あの優しい美しいきさが首を長うしてこの私を待ってくれてるんやろなあ。待っててやあ、おきさ。すぐ行くでえ。（御座船の人々に気付き）あれ、あの向こう岸の御座船の屋形の下にぼんやりと見えるのは、菱屋のお上様、お家様、若旦那様やないか。それに舳先（へさき）におるのは安堂寺町（あんどうじまち）に店構えよった由兵衛。おっと、こんなとこ見つかったらえらいこっちゃ。隠れよ。

　　　　下手花道から久三が菱屋の紋入りの提灯を手に早足で戻って来る。きさがその後を小走りに来る。

二郎兵衛　（提灯の紋に気付いて）おやっ、あれは菱屋の提灯……。提げているのは久三……。あれっ、その後を来るのはおきさやないか。（俄に心配そうになって）これは何ぞわけがあるに違いないなあ。

　　　　二郎兵衛は、自分の知らないことが目の前で起こっているので苛立つ（いらだ）。が、きさの身に何が起こっているのかが心配で、川辺りにたくさんある材木の倉庫の一つの陰に身を隠してその場の様子を窺う。
　　　　風も凪ぎ倉庫の陰は蒸し暑い。

　　　　由兵衛が久三から提灯を受け取り船に吊る。

きさ　（船に走り寄り、その場に座って挨拶をしてから）今日は皆様お揃いで舟遊びをお楽しみなされたと、道々この久三から聞きました。なによりのことでございます。（せっぱ詰まった様子で）あの、病気がようなったわけではないんです……。お楽しみのところを私事で誠に申し訳ございません。お上様、お家様に是非お願いしたいことがございましてここにまいりました。（辛そうに）大変なことになりまして、風邪も余計に悪うなり、気分も一層すぐれぬ次第でございます。（ため息をつく。）

315

TEIHO [*taken aback by KISA's unusual behaviour and speaking gently*]: What is the matter with you? What do you want us to do for you? Tell us, Kisa. [*Sympathetically*] If we can do anything whatever to help you, we'll do it.

KISA: Old Mistress, thank you very much for your kind words. The thing is…last night suddenly my father from Sanda Village came to see me and said, "The mother of your fiancé from your childhood in Sanda is unwell, and they want to have their son's wedding as soon as possible. You must leave your service immediately and return to Sanda for it. I want to take you back with me." As you know, Old Mistress, I have been brought up in Osaka and haven't done any physical farm work all my life. Also I'm rather weak. How will I be able to manage the life of a farmer's wife at my age? I…I fabricated a story for the moment to get out of the difficult situation. I said to my father, "My old mistress cares a lot about me and has promised to find me a good husband among the Hishi-ya's employees. She even said to me, "You and your future husband will be independent of the shop and can start your own shop together. So you must never make any promise to marry someone else." I said, "I can't ignore the kind consideration of my old mistress. I can't go home with you, Father." Then my father said, "You must come with me. Otherwise I'll lose face!" He was so angry with me. We've been quarrelling since last night. I think that my father is coming after me. He will be here shortly. I know it's very selfish of me to say this but will you please, please tell him the same thing to corroborate my story and make him abandon my marriage in Sanda? Please, please help me out of this?

JIROBEI [*listening to KISA*]: I think that Kisa's come up with all this because she loves me. She thinks that I am more important than her parents whom she must love and care about more than anyone else. Oh, I am so happy! [*JIROBEI clings to the timber leaning against the wall of the warehouse beside him as if embracing KISA.*]

> *KISA's father, TARŌ SABURŌ of Sanda Village, comes, trudging, from the hanamichi Right.*
> *KISA quickly hides herself behind the tree nearby.*

TARŌ SABURŌ [*approaching the boat and bowing*]: Excuse me, please. I wonder if this is the boat carrying the people of the Hishi-ya. I'm Kisa's father, Tarō Saburō of Sanda Village. My daughter works for the Hishi-ya. [*He bows deeply.*]

TEIHŌ: Well, well, you're Kisa's father, Tarō Saburō-dono.[32] How do you do? It is a pleasure to meet you. I'm Hishi-ya Teihō, the old mistress of the Hishi-ya. Kisa is an excellent kimono seamstress. She has been wonderful in our shop. I would like to express our gratitude on behalf of my son, the master of the shop, Hishi-ya Shirōemon.

「今宮の心中」

貞法　（きさのただならぬ様子に驚き、優しく）どうしましたんや。願い事とは何かいな？話してみなさい。（慈悲深さの滲み出る物腰で）私どもで出来ることやったら力になりましょう。

きさ　お上様のいつもながらのお優しいお言葉、忝のうございます。あの…、昨夜、突然在所の三田村から父様が出てまいり、『幼い頃から在所で結婚の約束のしてあった男の母親が病気になり、先方が急にお前の嫁入りを急いできた。すぐに菱屋のお店からお暇をいただいてお前を三田に連れて帰り祝言させる。』と、申します。お上様もご承知の通り、私は幼い頃から大阪で育ち、力仕事はこれまでしたことがございません。それに、いたってひ弱な性質。なんで田舎の野良仕事など出来ましょう。それで、その場の言い逃れに、『菱屋のお上様がご親切に私のことを思ってくださって、長年店に奉公し功をなした者の中からお前の婿を選んで夫婦にし、独立させて店を持たせてやる。決して他に嫁に行く約束なんぞはせんようにと常々言われている。そのような有難いお心遣いを無駄にすることは出来ん。在所には帰れまへん』と、申しました。父親は『それでは親としての面目が立たん』と、えろう怒りまして、昨夜から親子の諍いです。じきに、私を追って、父様がここに参ります。勝手なお願いではございますが、どうか今私の申しましたことに口裏をお合わせ下さいまして、在所での嫁入りを諦めさせて下さい。どうか、お願い致します。

二郎兵衛　（聞いていて）きさは私のことを思うてあんなに言うてくれてるんや。何にも変えられん大事な親よりも私を大切と思うてくれている。ああ、嬉しい。（傍に立ててあった木材にきさの代わりに抱きつく。）

　　　　　　きさの父、三田村の太郎三郎が下手花道をとぼとぼと来る。
　　　　　　きさは慌てて近くの木の陰に身を隠す。

太郎三郎　（御座船のところまで来て会釈をして）お尋ねいたします。こちらは菱屋の皆様の乗っておられる船ではございませんか。私は御店でお世話になっておりますきさの親の三田村の太郎三郎でございます。（深く頭を下げる。）
貞法　まあまあ、きさの親父殿[32]か。初めてお目にかかります。菱屋の隠居の貞法です。きさは腕の立つ針子で菱屋の店でよう働いてくれております。誠に有難いことでございます。四郎右衛門に代わってお礼を申します。

SUKEGORŌ: How do you do? It is a pleasure to meet you. I am Hishi-ya Sukegorō, Hishi-ya's son. Please come on board and have a cup of sake with us.

SHIZUE: How do you do? How good to meet you. I'm Hishi-ya Shirōemon's wife. If you prefer tea to sake, we have tea as well. Please feel free to relax. Now, now, please come on board.

TARŌ SABURŌ: Thank you so much. But I've already had plenty of tea at Kisa's sister's house, so please do not worry about it. [*Kneeling formally on the ground and addressing everyone on the boat*] I think that my daughter has already told you this. Her fiancé in Sanda wants to marry her immediately. I know that she's your employee and if she leaves her job abruptly, it may cause you a problem. But marriage is the most important moment in one's life. So I've been trying to persuade her to speak to you and to arrange leave since last night. But Kisa insists on her own way and says that she won't go back to Sanda, she will marry someone in Osaka. I was much distressed to hear this and said to her, "Won't you listen to what your father says?" But she didn't listen and only talked back to me. She said, "I've already left the matter in my old mistress's hands. She will find me a suitable husband. If you force me to marry the man in Sanda, I'll kill myself. Will you be happy with that? Do you want to kill your daughter?" Then she cried loudly. [*Shedding tears*] Mistresses and the young master of the Hishi-ya, will you please speak to my daughter as a parent in place of me? Please do so, I beg you. Her fiancé's family in Sanda is wealthy. They live a comfortable life. I'm sure that she will be happy and content in her marriage. It may sound terrible, but the teachings of Buddha and prayers to Buddha are ultimately a way of helping us through life. Marriage is the same. How to feed ourselves, how to make one's living is the main thing. It appears that Kisa has got it all wrong and snapped up a man in Osaka instead of the one in Sanda. [*To KISA hiding behind the tree*] Hey, my stupid daughter hiding over there! Listen! An Osaka man and a Sanda man are both men and no different. [*Crying*] Why would I as a father want my beloved daughter to marry an unworthy man? Oh, it's awful! Children do not think of their parents as much as their parents think of them. [*He cries.*]

KISA breaks down crying; she is torn between her filial affection for TARŌ SABURŌ and her love for and promise to JIROBEI.

CHORUS 1: Kisa must be feeling awful making her own father cry.

CHORUS 2: But she's pledged her love to her darling Jirobei in this world and the next.

CHORUS 3: There's nothing left for her but to cling to the old mistress's sense of compassion.

「今宮の心中」

介五郎　初めてお目にかかります。菱屋の倅の介五郎です。親父殿、さあさあ、こちらへ。お酒でもお一つ。

静江　菱屋四郎右衛門の家内です。お茶のほうが良ろしかったら、お茶もございます。どうぞ、遠慮なさらずに。さあさあ、こちらへ。

太郎三郎　有難うございます。お茶はきさの姉の所で十分貰うております。どうぞ、ご心配なされませんように。（その場に座り船に向かって）既に娘のきさがお話したことと思います。在所三田のきさの許婚の方が急に嫁入りして欲しいと申してきました。奉公中ではございますが、一生の事でございますので事情をお話してお暇をいただくよう、昨夜から言い聞かせておるのでございますが、きさの奴が『在所には帰らん。所帯は大阪で持つ』と、わがまま言うて困っております。『親の言うこと聞かれんか』と、きつう叱っても聞き入れよりません。反対に『私の婿になるお人は御店のお上様にお任せしてある。親の威光で無理矢理に在所の男を婿に持てと言うのなら死んでみせる。それでもよいか。お前は娘を殺す気か』と、大声上げて泣きよります。（自分も泣いて）ご主人様方、お慈悲でございます。どうかこの親の代わりに娘に意見してやって下さい。在所の婿になる者の家は食べるに困らん身代のゆとりのある暮らし向き。娘が嫁ぎましたら身の果報となること間違いなしでございます。こう申すのも何でございますが、仏法も念仏もつまるところは生活の手段、方便。嫁入りも同じで、食べることが一番大事でございます。それを、きさの奴は食べる相手間違えて、大阪の男に食いつきよりましたようでございます。（木の陰に隠れているきさに向かって）やい、そこに隠れているアホ娘！在所の男も、大阪の男も男に変わりはない。（泣いて）親として大事の娘に何で味ない男食べさせよう。ああ、情けない。親が子を思うほど、子は親のことを思てはくれん。（泣く。）

きさは父親への気持ちと二郎兵衛との約束の板挟みで泣き崩れる。

コーラス１　きさも父親を泣かして辛いことやなあ。
コーラス２　けど、二郎兵衛との二世かけて誓った約束がある。
コーラス３　ここはもう、お上様のお情けに縋るしかない。

LOVERS' SUICIDES AT IMAMIYA

TEIHŌ [*weeping in sympathy*]: I think what you've just said is very true and stands to reason. However, your daughter is rather weak. I think if she is forced to do farm work or manual labour, she will be ill in a year's time. Meanwhile she has acquired the skills to earn a good deal of money. The Hishi-ya is a kimono maker who runs the shop in Honmachi, the centre of Osaka. You don't think that we would pay an ordinary girl as much as two hundred *monme*-silver[33] for her wages. There are many jobs that women can take in a large city like Osaka, but Kisa's job, seamstress, is one of those jobs that earns enough to support their husbands. If they wanted, with a needle in their hands, they could even keep more than a few men. When I think about it, I don't believe that it is a good idea to take her back to the mountain village. It'll only ruin her health. Tarō Saburō-dono, how about giving up the marriage in Sanda this time and leaving Kisa's future to me? We have many employees in the Hishi-ya. Some have been brought up like family members since they arrived as apprentices. There must be a suitable man for her among them. Please let us choose a good man for her. We will support the couple. Then, there will come a day when they will invite you to Osaka to stay with them.

YOSHIBEI [*smiling complacently and speaking in an aside*]: Wonderful! Teihō-sama is considering me for Kisa's husband. How good of her! My long held dream will at last come true. [*To TARŌ SABURŌ*] Listen, Kisa's father-dono. I think that it'll be wise to leave Kisa's marriage to the old mistress and to break off the engagement in your home country. My name is Yoshibei. I run a shop in Andōji-machi and employ one junior shop assistant. My business has been going very well; as a result, I can spend a couple of *ryō*-gold[34] to invite my master's family for a day out like this. It's all owing to the good reputation of my master. As a matter of fact, the reason I haven't got a wife yet is because I have left the matter to the old mistress, too. Depending on her choice, you and I may become father and son-in-law. [*To KISA*] Isn't that so, Kisa?

KISA [*her head on one side, looking doubtful*]: Well, I don't know. [*KISA looks down.*]

TARŌ SABURŌ [*nodding*]: I wasn't much convinced by what my daughter said to me. But, Old Mistress, after you told me your thoughts on Kisa's marriage, the doubts in my head have cleared. You are quite right. If the person you recommend has been brought up as a member of the Hishi-ya family, he is as close as our relations to us. We'll have no problem with him. So I would like to leave Kisa's marriage to you from this time on. Please find a good man for my daughter. Now, as the problem has been solved, I must leave. Please excuse me. [*TARŌ SABURŌ rises to his feet.*]

YOSHIBEI [*cutting into the conversation, wearing a serious expression*]: Teihō-sama, you've just taken on a very important role. As Kisa is still young, some unexpected thing may happen and trouble you in the future. I think that you had better ask Kisa and her father

「今宮の心中」

貞法　（貰い泣きして）親父殿の言われること、誠にごもっとも、理に適っております。けれど、このきさはどちらかというとひ弱な性質。在所での野良仕事、力仕事をさせたなら、一年とはもちますまい。それに、この子は充分にお金の稼げる技術を身に付けております。本町に店を構える新物の仕立屋の菱屋が二百目[33]近い給金をただの女子に出すとはお思いではございますまい。この広い大阪で男を養うことのできる商いとは針子という名のあれらが仕事のこと。男の三人や五人は針一本で養えるほどの手を持っております。それを、郷里の山里の家へわざわざ体を壊すために嫁がせるのはどうかと思われます。太郎三郎殿、この度の嫁入りは止めにして、きさのことはどうかこの貞法にお任せ下さらんか。菱屋にも幼い頃から家族同様にして養い育てた者、結婚させる者がようさんおります。良い婿を取らせて、ゆくゆくは親御達も大阪に呼べるようにしてしんぜましょうほどに。

由兵衛　（傍白、にんまりして）そうか、ご隠居はきさを私の嫁にと思うて下さっているのか。有難い。これで日ごろの念願が成就する。（太郎三郎に）これ、親父殿。きさのことはご隠居様にお任せして、在所での約束は破談にしたが良かろう。この由兵衛も菱屋のお陰で安堂寺町に一軒店を構えて手代も一人置くほどの商いさせてもろてます。今日のようなもてなしに二両、三両[34]のお金を使うことが出来るのも、みな親方の御威光あるがゆえ。私がまだ女房を持っていないのはお上様に仲人をお任せしてあるからです。お上様のお心次第でお前と私が婿、舅にならんとも限りません。（きさに）なあ、おきさ。そうではないか。

きさ　（困惑して首をかしげ）さあ、どうでしょうか。（と、下を向く。）
太郎三郎　（頷きながら）娘が言いますことには承知出来ませんでしたが、ただ今、お上様のお心を聞かせていただいて納得致しました。尤もな事でございます。親方様が取り持とうと思われるお相手で、しかも身内同様に躾けられた方なら親類も同じ。私どもには何の異論もございません。この先はきさの縁組はお上様にお任せいたします。どなたか良いお人をこれにお願い致します。さて、そうと決まりましたら、私はこれでお暇いたします。（立ち上がろうとする。）

由兵衛　（傍らから、尤もらしい顔で）貞法様、これは大事な引受け事でございます。おきさもまだ若い身。後日この件でごたごたがあっても面倒でございます。ちょっとこの場で、きさ親子に「きさの縁組は貞法様のお考え通りにする。他からの

to write out a sealed deed for you. The document should say "We Tarō Saburō of Sanda Village and his daughter Kisa will leave Kisa's marriage to Teihō-sama. Nothing can change this." How about that?

TEIHŌ [*nodding to herself*]: Yoshibei could be right. Then, would you mind writing a sealed deed, Tarō Saburō-dono?

KISA: But Old Mistress, my father is illiterate. I will draw up a deed and bring it to you tomorrow. Please leave things as they are today…

YOSHIBEI: Don't worry, it isn't a problem. Also if you haven't got your personal seal here with you, the end of the brush will do as a substitute. I don't mind writing it on behalf of you and your father. [*Quickly he takes out a sumi-stone case*[35] *and letter paper from the tobacco tray drawer and start writing a deed under the light of the lantern.*]

JIROBEI: Damn! This is terrible! Yoshibei is forcing Kisa and her father to put their promise in writing. Bastard! I'm sure he'll work hard to gain the old mistress's favour in order to get Kisa as his wife. If Kisa puts her seal to his deed, it will become irredeemable. How can I stop her? Oh, that's it! I'll throw a stone and put out the candle in the lantern!

JIROBEI looks for a stone nearby.
YOSHIBEI finishes the deed while JIROBEI is searching for a stone.

CHORUS 1, 2 & 3 [*chanting together in a low voice*]: Yoshibei the scoundrel! Yoshibei the beast! The scheming villain!

CHORUS 1, 2 & 3 [*together in a low voice anxiously*]: Quickly Jirobei! Haven't you found a stone yet? Hurry up!

YOSHIBEI [*showing the completed deed to TARŌ SABURŌ*]: Well, I've addressed it to Hishiya Shiroemon-sama and Teihō-sama from Kisa's Father Tarō Saburō of Sanda. Kisa's father-dono, would you put your seal here?

TARŌ SABURŌ: Oh, I am grateful! It's so reassuring! [*Taking a seal out of his purse and sealing the deed*] Now I'm relieved of my burden. Kisa, you must do the same.

KISA: No, father, I can't. I haven't got a seal.

TARŌ SABURŌ: Oh, I see. Then, your father will seal it for you using the reverse side of my seal.[36] [*Turning his seal upside down, sealing the deed in place of KISA and then holding it out to TEIHŌ*] Teihō-sama, here is the deed. Will you please keep it? Please look after my daughter well.

TEIHŌ [*receiving the deed*]: Thank you, Tarō Saburō-dono. Now I'll have to do my best. [*She puts the deed into her small bag of Buddhist prayer beads.*]

「今宮の心中」

邪魔は入れない」との証文を書かせて取っておくほうが良いのではございませんか？

貞法　（頷いて）確かに、由兵衛の言うとおりかもしれません。それでは証文を書いて貰っておきましょうか。
きさ　けど、お上様、父様は字が書けません。明日にでも、私がお上様に書いたものをお渡しいたします。今日のところはどうかこのままに……。
由兵衛　いやいや、字が書けんでもかまいません。判がなければ判の代わりに筆の軸を使うたらええ。証文は私が書いてあげましょう。（由兵衛はさっさと煙草盆の引き出しから硯箱[35]と紙を取り出して、提灯の灯りの下で証文を書き始める。）

二郎兵衛　あれっ！えらいことや。由兵衛の奴が皆に勧めて証文書かせとる。お上様に取り入ってきさを嫁に貰うつもりやな！きさがあの証文に判を押したら取り返しのつかんことになる。とないしょう。そや、石投げて提灯の灯い消したろ。

　　　　　二郎兵衛はあたりに石がないか探しまわる。
　　　　　その間に、由兵衛は証文を書き終える。

コーラス1、2、3　（小声ではやし立てて）由兵衛の悪党！犬畜生の鬼畜生！

コーラス1、2、3　（小声で心配そうに）二郎兵衛のぐず！石まだ見つかれへんのんか？早しいや！
由兵衛　（書き終えた証文を太郎三郎に見せて）えーっと、宛名は菱屋四郎右衛門様及び貞法様、差出人はきさ親三田村太郎三郎としておきました。さあ、親父殿、ここに印を押されんか。
太郎三郎　ああ、有難い。念の入ったことでございます。（巾着から印判を出して証文に押し）これで、肩の荷が下りました。さあ、おきさ、お前も判を押しなされ。
きさ　いえ、父様。私は判を持っておりません。
太郎三郎　それなら、父がこの判の裏判[36]を押してやろう。（自分の印判の反対の端に刻んだ判をしっかりと押してから、証文を貞法に差し出し）貞法様、この証文、どうぞお納めください。きさのこと、どうぞ宜しゅうお願い申します。

貞法　（証文を受け取りながら）確かに受け取りました。これで私も手落ちのあるようなことは出来まへんなあ。（証文を数珠袋に入れて懐にしまう。）

LOVERS' SUICIDES AT IMAMIYA

JIROBEI finally finds a stone in the ditch and throws it at YOSHIBEI. The stone hits the boat and plunges into the water with a splash, wetting YOSHIBEI.

YOSHIBEI [*wringing the water out of his kimono, standing up and looking around*]: Some roughneck has thrown a stone at me!

JIROBEI throws a few stones at YOSHIBEI. One of them hits YOSHIBEI's forehead.

YOSHIBEI [*covering his forehead*]: Oh, oh, Ouch! It's very dangerous here! Everyone, please hide yourselves under the roof of the boat. Kisa, you must get on the boat, too, and then close the door! [*He pushes KISA onto the boat.*] Father-dono, you'd better leave for Sanda now. You must be careful. Don't get hurt!

TARŌ SABURŌ [*talking to himself with joy*]: Oh, this is really good. When we were talking about Kisa's marriage, someone threw a stone at us. It's just like the tradition of "Stone Throwing,"[37] when friends and neighbours of newlyweds' throw stones at their house on their wedding night, wishing them a marriage as solid as a rock. Good luck is already with us. How joyous! It's wonderful! [*A stone hits his head.*] Ouch! Dear, dear! Namu-sanbō! Goodness! It is so auspicious that I see stars! [*He runs away from the hanamichi Right, covering his head.*]

JIROBEI keeps throwing stones at YOSHIBEI. YOSHIBEI is dismayed at this sudden disturbance. One of the stones hits the lantern on the boat and breaks it.

YOSHIBEI [*realising something*]: I've got it. This must be the work of the man who has taken a fancy to Kisa. [*Getting off the boat hurriedly*] Boatman, please row out! Kyūza, come with me. We'll catch the man who threw stones at us and stamp on him.
KYŪZA: Yes, sir! Why not?

YOSHIBEI and KYŪZA, crossing the bridge, run in the direction of the stone throwing.
JIROBEI runs away down a byway.
THE BOATMAN slowly rows the boat out.

Blackout.

「今宮の心中」

　　　　　二郎兵衛はやっと溝に落ちている石を見つけて由兵衛に投げつける。石は舟板に当たってザブンと大きな音を立てて川に落ち、跳ね返った水が由兵衛にかかる。

由兵衛　（水がかかって濡れた着物の水を絞りながら、立ち上がって見回し）どこぞの乱暴者が石投げてきよった。

　　　　　二郎兵衛は由兵衛めがけて幾つか石を投げる。石の一つが由兵衛の額(ひたい)に命中(めいちゅう)する。

由兵衛　（額を押さえて）あっ、痛っ！これは危ない！皆様、どうか屋形の中にお入り下さい。きさも早船に乗って、戸閉(は)めて！（無理矢(むりや)理(り)きさを船に乗せる。）親父殿も早う三田にお帰りなさい。怪我の無いよう気いつけなされや。

太郎三郎　（嬉しそうに独り言を言って）いや、これはめでたい。きさの嫁入りの話をしていたら石が投げられた。こりゃ、まるで婚礼の夜、祝いに近所の者が婚家へ小石を投げ込む「石打ちの石の祝い」[37]のようじゃ。縁起が良いわ。めでたい。めでたい。（頭に石があたる。）痛っ！南無三宝(なむさんぼう)。こりゃどうじゃ。めでた過ぎて目から火が出たわ！（頭を抱えて、下手花道から去る。）

　　　　　二郎兵衛は石を投げ続ける。由兵衛は突然のことでうろたえる。船の提灯に石が当たって破れる。

由兵衛　（気付いて）そうか。これは、きさに気いのある奴の仕業に違いない。（急いで船から降りて）船頭さん、どうぞ船出して下され。久三、一緒に来てくれ。石投げよった奴を捕まえて足で踏みつけたろ。
久三　　へえ。合点でおます。

　　　　　由兵衛と久三は橋を渡って石の飛んでくる方角に向かって走る。
　　　　　二郎兵衛は横道にそれて逃げ去る。
　　　　　船頭がゆっくりと櫓をこぎ出す。

　　　　　暗転

325

LOVERS' SUICIDES AT IMAMIYA

SCENE THREE
On the Kawara-machi Bridge

On the Kawara-machi Bridge. Dusk.
An old retired SAMURAI walks in from the hanamichi Right. His servant, the YAKKO, a moustached man, comes after the SAMURAI.
YOSHIBEI and KYŪZA are off-stage Left saying, "Where is he?" "Which way did he go?" After a moment KYŪZA comes running onto the Kawara-machi Bridge from Stage Left. He is wiping the sweat from himself.
The SAMURAI walks past KYŪZA on the bridge in a calm and leisurely manner. When KYŪZA and the YAKKO pass each other on the bridge, KYŪZA abruptly grabs the YAKKO from behind, throws him to the ground and kicks him in the head.

KYŪZA [*to the YAKKO*]: Here! Take this! I'll teach you!
SAMURAI [*astonished*]: You vulgar devil! What are you doing to my servant? [*The SAMURAI holds KYŪZA, hits him, and kicks him.*]

At this moment YOSHIBEI arrives at the bridge from Stage Left running. He is out of breath.

YOSHIBEI [*seeing the SAMURAI*]: Oh, here you are! How dare you throw stones at my boat? [*He is about to grab the SAMURAI from behind.*]
SAMURAI [*turning around and grasping YOSHIBEI by the hand*]: What did you say? I threw stones at your boat? What on earth are you talking about? You stupid insolent thing!
YOSHIBEI [*looking at the SAMURAI properly for the first time and astonished*]: Goodness! You're an o-samurai-sama. I'm so sorry! Please, please forgive me, sir. I mistook you for someone else. I…I was very careless! Please, please forgive me. Have, have mercy on me, sir. [*He cries and screams.*]
SAMURAI: What? Have mercy on you? How dare you? (*Twisting YOSHIBEI's arm, kicking his shin and knocking him to the ground*) Come, Yakko! Kick this crook till his bowels come out!
YAKKO: All right, master, leave it to me. [*Kicking YOSHIBEI hard*] You insolent devil! How dare you make your man hit me like that? I'll teach you a lesson now! [*He kicks YOSHIBEI's torso and buttocks repeatedly, good and hard.*]
YOSHIBEI [*screaming as if about to die*]: Owww! Owww!
SAMURAI: Enough! That's enough, Yakko. You mustn't kill him. Now we'd better go.

「今宮の心中」

第三場
瓦町橋の橋上

　　　瓦町橋の橋上。夕暮れ。
　　　年配の浪人侍、その後を浪人侍に奉公する髭奴が下手花道から来る。
　　　上手袖から「どっちや！」「どっちに逃げた！」と由兵衛と久三の声が聞こえる。すぐに、久三が上手から汗を拭きながら瓦町橋を走って来る。
　　　浪人侍は橋の上で久三の横を悠々と行過ぎる。次に髭奴が同じように行過ぎようとするところを、久三がすれ違いざまに、突然後ろから髭奴を掴んで横倒しにして額の真ん中を続けざまにぶん殴る。

久三　（髭奴に向かって）こいつ、思い知ったか！
浪人侍　（驚いてひき返して）こやつ、何をする！（久三を掴んで叩いてから、踏みつける。）

　　　久三から遅れた由兵衛が息を切らして上手から瓦町橋を走って来る。

由兵衛　（浪人侍を見つけて）ああ、ここにおりくさったか！ようも、わしの船に石ぶつけよったな！（近づいて後ろから浪人侍を掴もうとする。）
浪人侍　（振り返って由兵衛の手を逆に取り）何と！石をぶつけたとは何のことだ！無礼者めが！
由兵衛　（相手の顔を見て、侍であることに気付き、仰天して）あっ！これはお侍様！御免なされて下さいませ！人違いでございます。粗忽(そこつ)なことを致しました。どうか、お許し下さい！お慈悲でございます。（泣き喚く。）
浪人侍　何を！お慈悲だと！（由兵衛の手をねじ上げて向こう脛を蹴り、うつぶせに倒して）これ、奴(やっこ)、はらわたが出るほど、こやつを踏んでやれ！

髭奴　お任せ下され！（由兵衛を踏みつけながら）貴様、よくもこの身を打たせたな！思い知らせてやる！（由兵衛の胴や尻を力いっぱい幾度も踏みつける。）

由兵衛　（踏まれるたびに今にも死にそうに喚く。）ぎゃあーっ！ぎゃあーっ！
浪人侍　もうよい、もうよい。死なぬくらいにしておけ。行くぞ。

The SAMURAI and the YAKKO walk off Stage Left calmly.

YOSHIBEI [*rubbing his back and buttocks and managing to stand up*]: Ouch! Oh, it hurts! Kyūza, are you there? What a cold-hearted man you are! How could you keep quiet and do nothing when I was having such a hard time?

KYŪZA [*raising himself painfully*]: Ouuuch…it hurts. How dare you say such a thing to me? You told me to come with you, so I did. Then I was beaten up and kicked. I had free sake, took his side in return and had an awful experience. The free sake has gone and the aching buttocks are left. Dear me! Well, shall we go now? Let's go back to the boat. (*He gets up and goes off Upstage Right.*)

YOSHIBEI [*mumbling*]: At least you enjoyed free sake and free food. But I paid for it, entertained people, and then I was kicked and stamped on in return. I don't think I'll give anyone a treat in future. [*Murmuring to himself*] When I gave a treat to the people of the Hishi-ya, I got a stroke of bad luck. It's just like the saying, 'Pouring sake roaring with pain in return.'

YOSHIBEI follows KYŪZA.

Blackout.

「今宮の心中」

　　　　浪人侍と髭奴は来た時のように悠々と上手に去る。

由兵衛　（背中やお尻を摩りながら、ようよう起き上がり）痛い！ああ、痛い！久三、そこにおるのか？あんまりやないか。人がさんざんひどい目におうているのを黙って見ているということはあるまい。
久三　（痛そうに身を起こして）うう、おお痛た！どちらがあんまりですんや。あなたに来いと言われてついて来たばっかりに、殴られたり踏まれたりしましたんやで。ちょっと振舞うてもろたばっかりに、余計な人の味方して阿呆みた。振舞うてもろた酒が吹っ飛んで、蹴っ飛ばされた痛い尻だけが残ってしもた。さあ、ほな行きまひょか。船へ戻りまひょ。（久三、立ち上がり下手奥に去る。）
由兵衛　（ぶつぶつと）そっちはただ酒を飲んだり食べたりしたが、こっちは金出して振舞うた挙句に足で踏みつけられた。もう二度と人に振る舞いなんかはすまい。（独り言で）菱屋にご馳走したばっかりに災難受けた。「酒盛って尻踏まれ。」人に酒を振舞うたのがあだになる。とは、ほんまにこのことや。

　　　　由兵衛、久三の後を追う。

　　　　暗転。

ACT TWO

**At the Hishi-ya
On the 23rd of May**

Honmachi in Osaka, several days after the previous scene.
The main shop and residence of the Hishi-ya stands Centre Stage Right. Naniwa Bridge Street[1] which runs north and south of central Osaka goes from Upstage Left through the hanamichi Left. The shop front of the Hishi-ya faces this street. The branch shop of the Hishi-ya is located across Naniwa Bridge Street off-stage Left.
The shop consists of an earth-floor and a raised living area comprising a large tatami-matted room and a small anteroom.
A large noren,[2] on which the shop name 'Hishi-ya' is printed, hangs at the front of the shop. The entrance hall is a large earth-floor. There is a stepping platform[3] to the anteroom by the entrance on the right. The anteroom functions as the passageway to the large tatami-matted room and to the kitchen Off-upstage. The large room is the main part of the shop; there is a doorway to the interior of the house Upstage Centre the room. A long noren hangs over the doorway.
The earthed area stretches to Downstage Right from the entrance hall; it leads to the storeroom and the servants' quarters Off-stage Right.
A side street goes east and west Downstage; it crosses Naniwa Bridge Street Stage Left and joins the hanamichi Right.

SCENE ONE
Lovers' Quarrel

Afternoon.
The employees of the Hishi-ya are busy working in the shop.
Several people are sewing at the long narrow sewing table in the main room. Among them KISA is working on a padded kimono. JIROBEI sits next to KISA straightening a kamishimo ceremonial top[4] with a mallet. He looks sulky.
The senior shop assistant, CHŌBEI, is using an abacus at the book-keeping counting desk. GONBEI, another shop assistant, is counting the completed goods, checking the order sheet and packing, with the other junior shop assistants and apprentices.

中之巻

菱屋内の場
五月二十三日

　大阪の本町。前場から数日後。
　舞台中央から下手に向かって菱屋の店兼住まい。大阪の町を南北に通る難波橋筋[1]が上手奥から上手花道へと通っていて、菱屋の店はこの難波橋筋に面している。舞台上には見えないが、菱屋の出店がこの通りを挟んで向かい側にある。
　店の中は舞台前が広い三和土、奥側が畳敷きの大きな部屋と小さな中の間である。
　店の入り口には「菱屋」の屋号を染め抜いた暖簾[2]がかかっていて、中に入ると、先ず三和土の玄関があり、入ってすぐ右手に座敷への上がり框[3]がある。小さな中の間が座敷への通り道になっている。この座敷の中ほど、舞台奥に菱屋の主人方の住まいへの入り口があり、ここにも暖簾がかかっている。中の間は奥の台所への通り道でもある。
　三和土は下手の出入り口まで延びている。下手袖の方には使用人の部屋や倉庫がある模様。
　舞台手前を難波橋筋と交差するかたちで横道が走っていて、横道は下手花道にも繋がっている。

第一場
痴話喧嘩

　午後。
　菱屋の店内では使用人たちが忙しく仕事をしている。
　数人の手代と針子が座敷に置かれた細長い仕立て板の周りで縫物をしている。その中に綿入れの着物を縫っているきさの姿がある。きさの隣に二郎兵衛が座り、不機嫌な様子で乾いて反り返った修繕の裃[4]を仕立て用の打ち盤にかけて槌で打っている。
　帳場では重手代の長兵衛が算盤を手に帳面をつけている。別の手代の権兵衛は下手代や丁稚たちに手伝わせて、仕立て上がった商品の数を数えたり、出荷伝票と照らし合わせたり、荷造りをしたりしている。

LOVERS' SUICIDES AT IMAMIYA

CHORUS 1: Men and women are working together at the kimono-maker's Hishi-ya.

CHORUS 2: As the young men of the Hishi-ya mix with the seamstresses, you may think that they are rather womanly, but they are not at all so.

CHORUS 3: When a man and a woman are stitching together; accidentally they may develop a relationship, and then end up tying a fatal life-long knot…

CHORUS 1: However, when the thread is not properly knotted, their love is nothing like the blossoms blooming on the weeping cherry[5] in the spring.

CHORUS 2: It only comes apart and we don't know how to repair the ripped knots of lovers.

CHORUS 3: Jirobei pretends he has returned from his home and has been working harder than usual for these last couple of days. But he's been sarcastic to Kisa and getting on her nerves…

JIROBEI [*knocking the hakama[6] on the board in an angry mood*]: Dear, dear! How badly starched this hakama is! It's just like someone around here who turns in all directions… this direction…that direction…it's as changeable as the weather. Listen, O-Kisa-dono, when you marry the man in Andōji-machi through the good offices of the old mistress, you should dress your husband in this one. You should also hold him tight on your wedding night so that he isn't hit the side of his head by a stone. How about it, O-Kisa-dono? Well, O-Kisa-dono?

KISA: Oh, stop shouting! I'm not deaf! Look! Look at this padded cotton kimono I'm sewing now. I've been doing my best to sew straight, but the stitches keep going sideways. I think that this sort of impossible garment will suit you well. Wear this! Well! Won't you wear this, as I don't like it?

JIROBEI: Humph! If you don't like it, why don't you tear it up?

KISA: Are you sure that I should tear it up? Tell me how?

JIROBEI: Umm, let me think…all right, you can tear it up like this. [*Taking up the mallet once again, knocking the hakama on the board as if cutting seven spring herbs for a new year broth,[7] while humming a tune*] 'A certain someone and a woman thereabouts are ton, ton, ton… Before wading across the river ton, ton, ton… Let's tear it up ton, ton, ton…'

CHŌBEI [*from behind the counting desk, clearing the abacus, irritated*]: Hey, hey, you two! Stop messing about! The figures do not add up at all.

GONBEI: Look over there. Can't you see the master coming home?

> *All the seamstresses and shop assistants are suddenly quiet.*
> *HISHIYA SHIRŌEMON comes back from the branch shop across the road. He looks tired as he has been suffering from an eye problem.*
> *The employees say severally, "Welcome home, Master."*

「今宮の心中」

コーラス1　菱屋では手代と針子、男と女が混じって仕事をしている。
コーラス2　ここ本町の新物の仕立屋菱屋の若い衆は、女と一緒に針仕事はしていても女のようではない。
コーラス3　針仕事の間のふとした一針の交わりが、男と女のそれとなり、長い一生の縁の結び目となる……。
コーラス1　糸尻を結んでいない結び目は、糸桜[5]がほころんで春を呼ぶのとは違うよう。
コーラス2　二人の仲のほころびはどう繕(つくろ)うのやら、困ったもの。
コーラス3　二郎兵衛は在所から戻ったような顔をして、ここ二、三日、常より精を出しているものの何やらえらい拗ねて、わざときさの気に障るようなことばっかり言うては当てこすり……。
二郎兵衛　（反り返った袴[6]をトントンと打ち盤に木槌で打ちつけながら、腹立たしそうに）ああ、これは糊の付け加減の悪い袴や。そこらへんにいる者の心のように、あちらへぺったり、こちらへぺったり……移りやすいと根性。なあ、おきさ殿、お前がやがてお上様の肝いりで安堂寺町に嫁入りされる時にはこの袴を婿殿に着せたらええわ。それから、嫁入りの晩には石投げつけられて婿殿の小鬢先を割られんようにしっかりと抱きしめてやりなはれ！なあ、おきさ殿。おきさ殿。

きさ　ああ、喧しい！私はつんぼでありません！ほれほれ、私の仕立てるこの木綿の綿入れは誰やらの根性によう似て、なんぼ真っ直ぐに縫うても針目が横へ横へそれてしまう。こういう聞き分けの無い着物は二郎兵衛殿、お前によう似合う！お前がこれを着たらええ。ほれ、これ着なはれ。私の気には入りませんよってに。
二郎兵衛　気に入らんのやったら、破ってしまえばええやないか。
きさ　ほんまに破ってしもてもええのんですか？ほな、一体どうやって破るんです？
二郎兵衛　そやな、こんな風にして破ったらええわ。（再び木槌で打ち盤を打って、正月の七草粥(ななくさがゆ)の菜(な)を切る調子で、鼻歌交じりに）「どこやらの男とそこらの女が渡らんうちに、トントントン、トントントン……」

長兵衛　（イライラして算盤を御破算にして、帳場から）こらこら！二人とも、ほたえるの止めなはれ！一向に帳簿が合わへん！
権兵衛　ほれほれ、向かいの出店から旦那様がお帰りになるのが見えまへんのか！

　　　　針子や手代たちがいっせいに静かになる。
　　　　菱屋四郎右衛門が出店から戻ってくる。四郎右衛門は目を患っていて少し疲れた様子である。
　　　　奉公人たちが口々に「お帰りなさいませ、旦那様。」と言う。

SHIRŌEMON [*nodding to the employees, and then to GONBEI*]: Gonbei, have we completed the order from Sendai?
GONBEI: Yes, Master. [*Pointing at the finished goods stacked in the corner of the shop*] Here they are. All completed.
SHIRŌEMON [*examining the goods*]: Yes, yes, very good. These are very well done. I think they will be happy with them. [*To the people at the sewing table*] Thank you for your hard work. I'm grateful to you.
CHŌBEI: Master, we've also completed the order from Akita. We've already written out the slip for the goods and they are ready for shipment.
SHIRŌEMON: Oh, you have. Well done. Thank you so much all of you. One more thing, Chōbei, when they finish loading the goods to Akita, I want you to send someone to Imabashi to collect the payment for the other day.
CHŌBEI: Yes, Master. [*To GONBEI*] Gonbei, I'm sorry to ask you this, but do you mind going to Imabashi now?
GONBEI: Of course, not. I shall leave the rest of the loading to the others and go there now.
CHŌBEI: Oh, thank you. It's very good of you. [*Getting the invoice out*] Here is the invoice for the Iwata-ya in Imabashi.
SHIRŌEMON: Thank you, Gonbei. I'm sorry to put you to all of this trouble.
GONBEI: Not at all, Master. [*Receiving the invoice from CHŌBEI, GONBEI bows to SHIRŌEMON, and leaves the shop.*]

> *The employees go back to their work.*
> *SHIRŌEMON goes to the counting desk and starts looking through the book. But soon he stops as the state of his eyes is not good. An old shop assistant CHŌBEI looks at him anxiously.*

SHIRŌEMON [*to CHŌBEI*]: Has Doctor Bokuan come yet? My eyes aren't very good today. I want to have a moxa teratment[8] tonight. When the doctor comes, I'd like to ask him to mark the moxa points on my back with sumi ink. Hum, it works better when it's done by a woman. O-Kisa, I want you to do it. Get Jirobei to help you. You can stop sewing for the day as I want you to do it well. And the rest of you, you must also finish here and go to the branch shop to help them. It's been very busy over there today.
CHŌBEI [*to the employees*]: Now, everyone, you've heard the master. Please stop work here and go to the branch shop. Kisa and Jirobei, you two are preparing for the moxa here.

「今宮の心中」

四郎右衛門　（皆に会釈してから、権兵衛に）昨日言うてた仙台からの注文の品はもう出来ましたんか？
権兵衛　へえ、旦那様。（仕上がった商品を指して）この通り全部出来ております。

四郎右衛門　（商品を手で触って見ながら）ふんふん、きれいに仕上がってる。これでええわ。（針子らに）皆、おおきに。礼を言います。ご苦労さんでしたな。

長兵衛　それと、旦那様、秋田からの注文の品も出来ました。もう出品伝票とも合わせてありますし、出荷の用意もほぼ出来ております。
四郎右衛門　そうか、ご苦労さんでしたな。皆、おおきに。それからな、長兵衛、秋田への荷積みを終えたら、今日中に誰ぞに今橋へ行かせてこの間のお金いただいて来るようにしてくれるか。
長兵衛　分かりました。権兵衛、すまんけどなあ、お前ちょっと今から今橋へ行ってくれるか。
権兵衛　へえ、よろしおます。荷積みの方、後は他のもんに任せてすぐ行て参じます。
長兵衛　そうか。すまんけど頼みます。（請求書を取り出して）これが今橋の岩田屋さんへの請求書や。
四郎右衛門　すまんな、権兵衛。ご苦労さんやなあ。
権兵衛　とんでもないです、旦那様。（長兵衛から請求書を受け取り、四郎右衛門に挨拶をしてから出てゆく。）

　　　　　皆はそれぞれの仕事に戻る。
　　　　　四郎右衛門は帳場に行って帳面を見始める。が、目の調子が思わしくないので直ぐに止める。そんな主人の様子を年のいった手代の長兵衛が心配そうに見ている。

四郎右衛門　（長兵衛に）卜庵老先生はまだお見えにならんか？今日は目の調子がどうもあきません。先生がみえたら墨で灸点を書いてもろうて、今夜はお灸据える[8]ことにします。女子の手の方がよう効く。おきさ、お前に据えてもらおか。二郎兵衛にも手伝わしてな。手元が狂たらあかんよって、今日はもう針仕事は終わりにしなはれ。それから、他の皆もここはええから出店に行ってくれるか。今日は向こうがえらい忙しい。
長兵衛　（店の皆に）旦那様の言われるように、皆、もうこっちは終わりにして、出店の方を手伝うようにしなはれ。きさと二郎兵衛はお灸の用意をしてくれるか。

335

> *The employees stop their work, clear things away and leave for the branch shop. KISA and JIROBEI stay in the shop to prepare for the moxa treatment.*
>
> *At this point BOKUAN enters from the hanamichi Left. He arrives at the shop soon after the employees have gone.*

BOKUAN [*calling out*]: Hello, excuse me please. Doctor Shibukawa Bokuan here. [*Entering the shop and noticing SHIRŌEMON*] Oh, good afternoon, Shirōemon-dono, you are here.

SHIRŌEMON: Good afternoon, Doctor Bokuan. I've been waiting for you. Please come up.

> *BOKUAN takes off the setta,[9] the leather-soled sandals, on the stepping platform and goes to the tatami-matted room.*
> *JIROBEI places za-buton[10] floor cushions for SHIRŌEMON and BOKUAN and then goes to sit in the corner of the room.*
> *BOKUAN takes the seat of honour. SHIRŌEMON sits next to BOKUAN.*
> *KISA brings tea from the kitchen, serves it and then sits by JITROBEI.*

BOKUAN: Today is the twenty-third of May. It's the day of 'the long illness.'[11] Usually people dislike having moxa treatments and acupuncture on this day. But I know the Hishiya-san belongs to the Ikkō Sect,[12] the True Pure Land Sect[13] of Buddhism and the people of your sect are open-minded about old traditions because the Buddhist faith is of prime importance. I imagine you don't care too much about things like that either, so I want to give you a moxa treatment today. Tomorrow will be the start of the Hassen period before summer Doyō,[14] it is the day when a moxa treatment works particularly well. I hope that today's treatment will be more effective than usual for your eyes. Now let me examine your pulse. [*BOKUAN takes SHIRŌEMON's left hand and feels his pulse. Nodding, satisfied*] I see that you have been eating food nutritious for your eyes. Hem, hem, your pulse is much better. It is beating softly. You must've been eating eggs. I can tell. I've told you not to eat fish such as grey mullet as they tend to raise the body temperature. I believe that you wouldn't dare eat it. [*Taking the right hand this time*] Hem, hem, the right pulse starts strongly, then becomes weak. I wonder if you eat miso soup. You don't have a cold. Very good. [*Content*] Well, then I want to mark the moxa points on your back. Could I borrow sumi and an inkstone?

SHIRŌEMON: Doctor Bokuan, today I'd like you to treat me in the inner room. Please come this way. [*Standing up and leading BOKUAN to the inner part of the house*] Kisa and

「今宮の心中」

　　　　奉公人達は皆仕事の片づけをして出店に向かう。きさと二郎兵衛は店に
　　　残り、お灸の用意を始める。

　　　　このとき、渋川卜庵が上手花道から登場する。奉公人達が出店に行くの
　　　と入れ違いに卜庵が店先まで来る。

卜庵　（店の中に向かって）御免くだされ。お見舞い申します。渋川卜庵が参りました。
（店に入り、四郎右衛門に気付いて）おお、四郎右衛門殿、おいでになりましたか。

四郎右衛門　卜庵先生、お待ちしておりました。どうぞ、こちらへお上がり下さい。

　　　　卜庵は上がり框で雪駄[9]を脱いで座敷に上がる。
　　　　二郎兵衛は四郎右衛門と卜庵に座布団[10]を出した後、座敷の隅に行って
　　　座る。
　　　　卜庵が四郎右衛門の上座になり、二人が座る。
　　　　台所からお茶を持って出たきさもお茶を出した後、二郎兵衛の隣に座る。

卜庵　今日は「長病の日」[11]の二十三夜で、普通は灸や鍼は忌み嫌います。けど、菱屋さんは浄土真宗[13]の一向宗[12]ですので、ま、いっこうに構かまなしということで、お灸をすることにいたしましょう。明日からは夏の土用前の八専[14]です。この時期のお灸は特効があると言われております。ですので、お灸も一段と目にようございましょう。どれ、脈を拝見いたしましょう。（四郎右衛門の左手を取り、脈をはかり、頷いて）私の申しあげておいたように目に滋養のあるものを食されておられるようでございますな。ふんふん、脈も大変良うなっております。卵を食べられた印に左の脈が卵焼きのようにふわふわと軽やかに打っております。おや、魚は鰤などは体温を上げますのでお召し上がりになりませんようにと申し上げましたぞ。まさか、食されてはおられませんでしょうな。（今度は右手を取って）右の脈は初めが強く、後は弱い打ち方をしておる。味噌汁を飲まれるのかな？風邪はひいてはおられないようですな。結構です。（納得して）それでは、灸点を打つといたしましょう。墨と硯を下さらんか。

四郎右衛門　卜庵先生、今日は灸点は奥で打っていただきとうございます。どうぞ、奥の座敷においで下さい。（立ち上がり卜庵を奥座敷へ通し）きさに二郎兵衛、先ず

Jirobei, will you please light the oil lantern and start making a couple of hundred moxa balls?[15]

KISA: Yes, Master.

JIROBEI: Yes, Master.

> SHIRŌEMON *and* BOKUAN *go to the inner part of the house through the noren.*
>
> *JIROBEI lights the andon lamp stand.*[16] *Then he takes an unglazed pottery bowl and a wooden pestle, a large packet of moxa, a pair of moxa chopsticks,*[17] *and a few sticks of insence from a medicine box on the shop shelves. He warms up the bowl with the lamp, puts in some moxa to dry. Then he starts rubbing moxa with the pestle. While JIROBEI is doing this, KISA stares fixedly at him.*

KISA [*suddenly going to him and seizing him by the kimono collar*]: You've been so cruel! You are awful! How dare you! [*Sobbing*] The shop has been busy these few days, so I had no chance to speak my mind to you. And when I found a moment and came up to you to have a talk, you were sulky and nasty to me. On top of that you said, "When you marry Andōji-machi…" How, how dare you! Oh, even thinking about it disgusts me. Please, Jirobei-dono, I want you to listen to what I say. I know that boys of your age love sixteen or seventeen-year-old girls who are still wearing long-sleeved kimonos. But you chose me, a woman who is five years older than you. I was touched by your strong feelings for me and decided to live my life with you, deserting the love of my parents and brothers and sisters. Sanda Village is my home where I was born and, I think, there isn't a woman who doesn't want to marry a man who lives near her parents. Why on earth, do you think, I've chosen Osaka to live? It is only because I do not want to be separated from you that I acted against my father's will and lied to my old mistress. I've already given up living an upright moral life. But it seems that you don't appreciate my conduct at all. Instead it seems to me that you enjoyed tormenting me. Do you want me to kill myself? If you want me to, I'll be happy to die for you, Jirobei-dono! [KISA *clings to* JIROBEI *and sobs.*]

JIROBEI [*regretful*]: I'm sorry. Please, please forgive me, O-Kisa-dono. [*Caressing KISA's back and sobbing*] But tell me…what did Yoshibei write in the deed? It's been worrying me sick…

> *When KISA is about to speak, BOKUAN returns from the inner part of the house. KISA and JIROBEI jump apart.*

「今宮の心中」

油火を灯して艾[15]をよう揉んでから、二、三百ほど捻っておいてくれるか。

二郎兵衛　へえ、承知いたしました、旦那様。
きさ　はい、旦那様。かしこまりました。

　　　　四郎右衛門と卜庵は暖簾を分けて奥に入る。

　　　　二郎兵衛は行灯[16]の火を灯してから、店の棚に行き、素焼きの器やすりこ木、薬箱から艾の袋、灸箸[17]、線香などを取り出す。それから、行灯の火で器を温め、艾を入れて乾かして擦ったりし始める。
　　　　きさはそんな二郎兵衛をじっと見ている。

きさ　（つと二郎兵衛のところに行き、胸ぐらを掴んで）もう、お前は。あんまりではないか。酷い。酷い。（泣いて）先日からゆっくり話をする暇もなかったので、この胸の思いをお前に伝えることがなかなか出来ないでいた。お前と言う人は私がそばへ寄ったらつんつんとして思いっきり拗ねる。おまけに『安堂寺町へ嫁ぐ日には……』などと、よくもあんなことを。ああ、考えただけでも汚らわしい。なあ、二郎兵衛殿、私の言うことよう聞いて欲しい。誰しもお前の年頃では十六、七の振袖姿の若い女子を好き好む。それを四つも五つも年上のこの私に惚れて下さった。私はお前のその心が嬉しゅうて、親、きょうだいをも捨てる覚悟をしました。三田村は私の生まれ故郷。二親の住むすぐそばに嫁に行きとうないもんは誰もおらん。何の所縁で大阪という土地を選んだと思われるのか。ただ、お前という人と離れとうないばっかりに、親に背きご主人様に嘘ついて身持ちを狂わせている。そんな私の気持ちを可愛いとも言わずに、お前は面白そうに拗ねごとばかり。そんなに言うんなら死んでみせよか？お前のためなら死んでもええ。二郎兵衛殿。（二郎兵衛に抱きつき、声を殺して泣く。）

二郎兵衛　（しょんぼりとして）どうか、堪忍、堪忍して下さい、おきさ殿。（きさの背中を撫で自分も泣く。）そやけど、由兵衛はあの手形に何と書きよったんですか？わたしはそれが気になって……。

　　　　きさが話そうとした時、奥から卜庵が出てくる。二人は弾かれたように離れる。

339

JIROBEI [*instantly smiling at BOKUAN and speaking pleasantly*]: Doctor Bokuan. Are you leaving already?

BOKUAN: Well, I'm not sure...either going straight home or staying here a little longer and joining Shiroemon-dono for the moxa-treatment dish[18] such as cooked beans. Which one shall I choose? [*BOKUAN draws the tobacco tray near to himself and sits down.*]

KISA and JIROBEI start making moxa balls impatiently, as they want to talk about YOSHIBEI's deed. But BOKUAN shows no sign of leaving.

CHORUS 1: At last when Jirobei and Kisa were about to discuss Yoshibei's deed,
CHORUS 2: Once again they were interrupted.
CHORUS 3: Why doesn't Bokuan go home immediately?
CHORUS 1, 2 & 3 [*together in a low voice*]: Go home, Bokuan! Go home! Go home quickly!
BOKUAN [*no sign of leaving at all*]: Now, O-Kisa-san, have you heard what I'm eating tonight? Is it hiyamugi[19] noodles or sōmen[20] noodles? Well, if it is tea on boiled rice,[21] I'd rather go home and lie on the futon. Will you tell me in secret what the Hishi-ya-san is preparing for me tonight?

KISA [*pleased as things are looking up*]: Sir, as he must consider his health, my master hasn't had a night snack recently. And I'm sorry to say this, but as a matter of fact, the mistress has told me to serve you tea on boiled rice and freshly salted aubergine.[22] So sorry about tonight's dish, but you'd better go straight home and have a good rest.

BOKUAN [*pleased*]: Did you say 'freshly salted aubergine'? How wonderful! It'll be lovely to have it with good freshly brewed tea and rice. How marvellous! [*He seems to have decided to stay.*]

KISA [*making a face sour with disappointment*]: If you like it so much, why don't you stay overnight, doctor?

While KISA and BOKUAN are talking, JIROBEI has a bright idea. He goes to BOKUAN's setta sandals on the stepping platform, turns them over, places the lit moxa on them and fans them with his kimono sleeve until they begin to smoulder.

CHORUS 1: Jirobei is casting a spell on Bokuan's setta sandals. It's been said that burning moxa on someone's footwear makes the person want to leave. But I'm not sure whether or not it really works.

CHORUS 2: Reason cannot explain how a spell works.

「今宮の心中」

二郎兵衛　（とっさに卜庵に愛想をして）卜庵先生、もうお帰りでございますか。

卜庵　そうですな。このまま帰っても良ろしいが、もう少しここに居て灸饗[18]の煮豆のお相伴をさせてもろても良い。さて、どっちにしょうかいなあ。（言いながら店の煙草盆を引き寄せて座りこむ。）

　　　　きさと二郎兵衛は由兵衛の書いた証文の話が出来ないので、やきもきしながら艾をひねり続ける。卜庵はいっこうに帰る気配がない。

コーラス1　やっと証文の話が出来ると思ったら。
コーラス2　また邪魔が。
コーラス3　早よ帰ってくれたらええのに。
コーラス1、2、3　（小声で）早よ帰れ。帰れ！帰れ！
卜庵　（全く帰る様子もなく）これ、おきささん、灸饗を言いつけられておりませんか？冷麦[19]か素麺[20]か？もし、お茶漬け[21]くらいやったら家に帰って寝たほうがましやな。菱屋さんでは今夜は何を用意されているのか内緒で教えてくれんか。

きさ　（これ幸いと喜び、真しやかに）旦那様はただ今ご病気のための毒断ちをされておられるのでお夜食は上がられません。お家様からは卜庵先生には茄子の浅漬け[22]でお茶漬けをお出しするよう申し付かっております。今夜はお茶漬けですよって、早うお帰りになって家で休まれたほうがおよろしいのではございませんか。

卜庵　（嬉しそうに）なに、茄子の浅漬けとな。それは有難い。茄子の浅漬けに出花でお茶漬けか。それはよろしい。（腰を落ちつける。）

きさ　（期待が外れたので、仏頂面になり）いっそのこと、お泊まりになったらよろしゅうございます。

　　　　きさが卜庵と話している間に、二郎兵衛は思いついて、脱いであった卜庵の雪駄を裏向けにして艾に火をつけて置き、着物の袂で扇いで燻ぶらせる。

コーラス1　二郎兵衛が「履物の裏に灸を据えると長居の客が帰る」というお呪いをしている。あんなことして効くのんかいな。
コーラス2　お呪いたらいうもんは普通の道理では推しはかれまへん。

CHORUS 3: Let's wait and see.

CHORUS 1: How marvellous!

CHORUS 3: It appears that the spell has worked on Doctor Bokuan.

BOKUAN [*suddenly moves restlessly*]: Strange! I don't know why, but suddenly I feel that I want to go home. I'm leaving. I really want to go home, I don't know why but I just want to go.

KISA: What's the matter, Doctor Bokuan? Please stay a little longer.

BOKUAN: No, no, I have an urge to go home. Ah, my feet are itching. [*He moves towards the entrance way while rubbing his itchy feet on the tatami floor.*]

JIROBEI [*placing BOKUAN's setta sandals in front of BOKUAN with his face beaming with smiles*]: Doctor Bokuan, your moxa treatment always works excellently. I'm sure my master's eyes will get better soon.

BOKUAN [*unaware of JIROBEI's reference to the moxa on the setta*]: That's right, that's right. I'm a master-hand at moxa treatments. My patient sees the effects even after one treatment. [*Looking at his heels nervously and putting on the setta*] Now, excuse me.

> BOKUAN *shuffles off the hanamichi Right.*
> JIROBEI *sees off BOKUAN politely, putting on a serious look.*

JIROBEI [*hurriedly going back to KISA*]: I think the master will be here soon. Now, O-Kisa-dono, please tell me quickly what Yoshibei wrote in the deed before the master comes in.

KISA: I'm afraid but I, I can't tell…because Yoshibei-dono didn't read it out….We only know it was addressed to the master and the old mistress…and my father and I sealed it.

JIROBEI [*shocked*]: What? Goodness! You say that Yoshibei didn't read it out to the old mistress or you and your father! How treacherous! He may have written, 'I Tarō Saburō of Sanda Village want my daughter Kisa to marry Yoshibei.' A man like him would easily do such a thing. He has been making passes at you persistently. A man such as Yoshibei is likely to do things to his own advantage. Really, your father was very careless to seal a deed he didn't know the contents of. Later that deed may come between us. We must steal it at all costs and tear it up.

KISA [*taken aback by JIROBEI's fury*]: What are you saying? Do you truly want to steal something that belongs to our master? What a terrible thing to say!

JIROBEI [*in earnest*]: But the thing I want to steal does not relate to trade or to Hishi-ya's money. I'm not going to steal out of greed. It's the deed relating to the fight over you between Yoshibei and me. Our master won't suffer any loss. [*Looking around the shop*]

「今宮の心中」

コーラス3　ものは試しでおます。
コーラス1　あれまあ！
コーラス3　卜庵先生の気いに通じたんとちゃいまっか。
卜庵　（急にもぞもぞと動いて）不思議千万なこと。急に家に帰りとうなった。もう、帰ることにします。なんや知らんがむやみに帰りとなってきました。

きさ　どうかされましたか、卜庵先生。もちょっと、遊んでいってくださいな。
卜庵　いやいや、ものすごう帰りとうて、なんかこう足の裏がこそぼうなってきました。
（こそばゆい足を畳みに擦りつけながら店先の方に行く。）
二郎兵衛　（卜庵の雪駄を上がり框に揃えて出し、満面の笑みを浮かべて）卜庵先生、先生の灸がよう効きますので旦那様の目もじきに治ることでございましょう。

卜庵　（雪駄のお灸のことと気付かずに）はいはい。この卜庵は灸の名人。一回の灸で効果が表れます。（自分の足の踵を気味悪げに見てから雪駄を履き）では、ごめん。

卜庵は気味悪気に足を気にしながら摺り足で上手花道から去る。
二郎兵衛は真面目な顔を取り繕って丁重に卜庵を見送る。

二郎兵衛　（急いできさのところに戻り）すぐに奥から旦那様が出て来られる。さあ、おきさ殿、その前に早う由兵衛の証文に何と書いてあったか教えて下さい。
きさ　さあ、何が書いてあったのやら……。由兵衛殿は証文の文面を読んで聞かせても下さらんかった……。宛名は菱屋四郎右衛門様、貞法様とあり、それに三田村の父と私が印をつきました。
二郎兵衛　（ぎょっとして）ええっ！何やて！由兵衛の奴はお上様やあなたやあなたの親父殿に証文の文句を読んで聞かさんかったてか。油断ならん奴や！あいつのことや、「娘きさを由兵衛殿に嫁がせる」と書いたやもしれん。常日頃からあなたにしつこう言い寄ってる由兵衛のことや、どない転んでも、自分にええように書きよったに決まっている。あなたの三田村の親父さまという人も、証文の文面も見んと判を押すとは……。後々、あの証文が私らの仲を邪魔することになるやもしれん。何とかしてあれを盗んで破り捨てんとあかん。
きさ　（二郎兵衛の剣幕に驚いて）ええっ！仮にも旦那様の手にある物を盗むと言われるのか？そんな怖いことを……。
二郎兵衛　（本気で）商売の銭金の証文やない。欲や損得で盗むのではないのや。あれはわたしと由兵衛との間のあなたを巡る争いごとの証文。旦那様のご損にはならんもの。（店の中を見渡して）旦那様はいつも手形類を店の箪笥に入れておられる。

343

He usually keeps things like deeds in the cabinet. Have you seen the key to the cabinet somewhere around the shop?

KISA: Have you lost your mind? Why would our master leave the keys in the shop? They're so important that only the master, the mistress and the old mistress have them. Even Sukegorō-sama isn't allowed to keep them. I promise you. I will ask the old mistress to let me read Yoshibei's deed when the moment is right. I don't think that it'll be too late. I hope that you'll agree with me, Jirobei-dono?

SHIRŌEMON comes back to the shop from the inner part of the house.

SHIRŌEMON: Have you finished making moxa balls yet? If not, go over the road and ask the mistress to make them, too. I don't know why, but I feel impatient tonight. I don't want to be up all night.

KISA: Master, both the moxa balls and the fire are ready for you. Please tell us what to do. Where shall we treat you?

SHIRŌEMON: Oh, You've done it. How good of you. In that case here should be all right, I'll have it here this evening. (*Pointing*) Jirobei, will you bring a small futon from inside and spread it here? I'll sit down facing the inner part of the house. And don't forget to bring rice-crackers, roast-beans, and seaweed and pepper crackers[23] on the cake tray.

JIROBEI: Yes, sir. All will be ready in a moment. [*He leaves for the inner part of the house.*]

SCENE TWO
Moxa Treatment

JIROBEI carries in a small futon and spreads it on the spot indicated by SHIROEMON, and then goes off to the kitchen for the cake tray. SHIRŌEMON, turning his back, helped by KISA, puts on his kimono back to front in order to reveal his back and sits on the futon, facing the inner part of the house. KISA places moxa balls, a pair of moxa chop-sticks and a few sticks of incense for the treatment and sits behind SHRŌEMON. JIROBEI brings a tray from the kitchen and places it within SHIRŌEMON's reach. Then he sits by KISA and hands the tiny twisted moxa balls to her. KISA picks them up with the chopsticks and places them skilfully at the marked moxa points on SHIRŌEMON's back. JIROBEI lights the incense with the fire from the tobacco tray and hands it to KISA. KISA starts lighting the moxa balls on the back of SHIRŌEMON. The smoke of the moxa begins to rise. SHIRŌEMON sometimes

「今宮の心中」

箪笥の鍵、そこらへんにありませんか？

きさ　何をアホな事を。旦那様が大事な鍵をそのへんに置いておかれるはずがないではないか。旦那様、お上様、お家様のお三人の他は、介五郎様さえ店の鍵は持たされておいででない。また、いつかのついでにお上様にお願いして証文の文句を見せてもろたらええ。な、二郎兵衛殿、そのときでも遅うありませんやろ。

　　　　　四郎右衛門が奥から現れる。

四郎右衛門　何やまだ艾捻れまへんのか。まだやったら向かいの出店へ行って、あっちにいるお家様にも捻ってもろてきておくれ。なんや今夜は気いが急く。夜が更けんうちに灸を据えてしまいたい。
きさ　あ、いえ、旦那様、灸も火いもちゃんと用意できております。どうか、お好きなようにゆうて下さい。何処でお据えいたしまひょ？
四郎右衛門　そうか、用意出来てるんか。そんならここでええ、今夜はここで据えて貰うわ。二郎兵衛、（指し示して）ここへ奥から小蒲団持って来て敷いてくれるか。私は向こう向きに座りますよってにな。それから、菓子盆に霰と炒り豆と、昆布と山椒の茶菓子[23]のせて持って来てくれるか。
二郎兵衛　へえ、旦那様。すぐに用意いたします。（奥に去る。）

第二場
灸据え

　　二郎兵衛は奥から小蒲団を運び、四郎右衛門に言われたところに敷く。その後、菓子盆を取りに台所に引っ込む。四郎右衛門はきさに手伝わせて着物を後ろ前に背中を出して着て、奥を向いて蒲団に座る。きさは捻った艾、灸箸、線香などを順序良く並べて、四郎右衛門の後ろに座る。二郎兵衛が菓子盆を持って出て、四郎右衛門の手の届くところに置く。その後、きさのそばに座り、捻った小さな艾をきさに渡し始める。きさはそれを灸箸でつまんでは器用に四郎右衛門の背中の灸点に置いてゆく。二郎兵がたばこ盆の火で線香に火をつけてきさに渡す。きさはその線香で四郎右衛門の背中の灸に火をつけてゆく。灸のうす煙が立ち上り始める。四郎右衛門は時々頷き、菓子盆の菓子を食べては熱さに堪えている。灸がうまく効いているようである。

> *nods, and now and then stretches out for the tray for a bite in order to endure the pain of the treatment. It appears that the moxa treatment is working well.*
>
> *The ill feeling between the lovers for the last few days has been dispelled and they seem to think more tenderly of each other. Now KISA and JIROBEI hold each other's hands, kiss and caress each other as much as they want. For SHIRŌEMON does not know what is going on behind him as his back is turned to them, and there is no one else in the shop.*
>
> *The afternoon sun of May has set and dusk is falling.*
> *Someone in the neighbourhood is playing the samisen.*

CHORUS 1: One of the therapeutic points, 'meimon' the gate to life, just below the fourteenth vertebra, works for people who cannot sweat enough or has been low in energy....

CHORUS 2: When a woman in the prime of womanhood and a man still in early manhood fire moxa together, they sweat a great deal...it flows out and out and...[*looking at the couple*] really, there is no need to say any more...

CHORUS 3: Our first moxa treatment can give us small burns which cut through the skin...

CHORUS 1: These new burns could well be the start of their fatal love...

> *Gradually KISA places the moxa balls on the lower part of SHIRŌEMON's back. Unconsciously SHIRŌEMON loosens the obi*[24] *and then turns it round against the burning moxa to soothe the pain. His money pouch hanging at the front of the obi is pushed to the back. This accidentally loosens the drawstring of the pouch, which opens slightly and a bunch of keys half emerges from it.*
>
> *JIROBEI and KISA notice the keys. JIROBEI signals with his eyes to KISA and points to the shop cabinet. Then he presses his hands together momentarily as if praying to the heavens giving thanks for the 'divine present' and tries to steal the keys. KISA is astonished at the sight and motions to stop JIROBEI. But JIROBEI nods his head to reassure KISA. The lovers repeat these movements.*

CHORUS 1: The woman waves her hand to stop her man.
CHORUS 2: The man nods his head to reassure his woman.
CHORUS 3: The man holds out his hand.
CHORUS 1: The woman pulls back her hand.
CHORUS 2: They look like a cat playing with red-hot charcoal, trembling with fear and excitement.

「今宮の心中」

　　　二郎兵衛ときさは先日来の喧嘩の後なので余計に互いを愛おしく思う様子である。四郎右衛門が後ろ向きなのと店に誰もいないのを良いことに、二人は手を握りあったり、時折接吻したり、おもいっきり体を撫ぜあったりといちゃいちゃする。

　　　五月の午後の陽光が沈み、時が夕刻へと移って行く。
　　　どこかの家で弾く三味線の音が聞こえる。

コーラス1　「十四の灸に泉湧く。」背中の十四椎の下の灸のつぼ「命門」は汗の出ない病や精力減退によう効くとか……。
コーラス2　水の出盛りの若い女と盛りの若い男が二人して灸を据えると、汗も水も何もかも、沸き出でて、沸き出でて（二人を見て）……ほんまにもう……。
コーラス3　灸を初めて据えた時には肌を焼いて切ってしまうけれど、
コーラス1　これが因果の縁の事の初めか……。

　　　四郎右衛門の背中の灸の位置が徐々に下に下がる。四郎右衛門は灸の熱さをそらそうと、知らず知らずに帯を緩めて後ろに回す。この時、帯の前に提げてあった巾着が帯と一緒に後ろに回り、はずみで巾着の紐が緩んで巾着の中の鍵束が半分出る。
　　　きさと二郎兵衛は鍵束に気付く。二郎兵衛はきさに目配せし、箪笥を指差し、「天の恵み」と手を合わせてから鍵束を盗もうとする。驚いたきさはそれを止めさせようとして「駄目だ」と手を振る。二郎兵衛は「大事無い」と頭を振る。二人は互いにそれを繰り返す。

コーラス1　女が手を振る。
コーラス2　男は頭振る。
コーラス3　男が手を出す。
コーラス1　女は手を引っ込める。
コーラス2　まるで猫が赤ういこった炭火に触ろうとするような、

LOVERS' SUICIDES AT IMAMIYA

CHORUS 3: Ve-ry dan-ge-rous!

SHIRŌEMON touches his obi once again.

KISA [*concerned about SHIRŌEMON's condition*]: Master, if it is too hot, I'll press your back close to the moxa points to divert the heat. Shall I do that for you?

SHIRŌEMON: No, no, it's all right, I can bear the heat, but I feel rather exhausted. I think I want to finish the treatment for tonight.

JIROBEI [*stretching his hand to the bunch of the keys in SHIRŌEMON's money pouch*]: It'll be over in a moment. Please be patient for a little while...[*stealing the keys*] there, now it's over, very well done.

KISA is so astonished that JIROBEI has actually stolen the keys; she drops the lit moxa ball from the chopsticks onto SHIRŌEMON's back.

SHIRŌEMON [*shocked*]: Aaaah! Hot! It's hot!

KISA [*hurriedly brushing the lit moxa ball off SHIRŌEMN's back*]: Oh, what have I done! I'm so sorry, Master!

SHIRŌEMON: Oh, that was hot! I'll stop there tonight. I'll return to my room and go to bed. [*Re-arranging his kimono*] You've done enough today. I thank you for your work. When you finish clearing things away, you two should go to bed, too. Good night. [*SHIROEMON retreats to the inner part of the house.*]

KISA [*praying with her hands pressed together, thanking for SHIRŌEMON's kind words*]: I'm so sorry, Master. Thank you so much. Good night, Master.

JIROBEI [*also praying with his hands pressed together*]: Thank you so much. Good night, Master.

CHORUS 1: Unfortunately this time SHIRŌEMON's merciful mind let his employees slip from right to wrong.

CHORUS 2: Divine protection is blinded,

CHORUS 3: And now it's beyond reach.

KISA and JIROBEI spring up and clear away the items for the moxa treatment going in and out of the inner part of the house and the kitchen. When they finish clearing and return to the room, KISA and JIROBEI stare at each other and sink to the floor, shivering with fear at their crime.

「今宮の心中」

コーラス3　あ・や・う・さ。

　　　　四郎右衛門がまた帯にさわる。

きさ　（気遣って）旦那様、熱いようでしたら、少しお灸の横を押さえて熱いのをそらせてしんぜましょうか？
四郎右衛門　いや、いや、熱さは構わんのだが、ちょっと気力が失せてきました。今夜はこれくらいで止めにしたい。
二郎兵衛　（巾着の中の鍵束に手を伸ばしながら）もうちょっとでございます。それ、もうちょっとだけで……（鍵束を盗み取ってから）ああ、結構でございます。うまくいきました。

　　　　二郎兵衛が本当に鍵を盗んでしまったことに驚いて、きさは火のついた艾を四郎右衛門の背中に落としてしまう。

四郎右衛門　（びっくりして）熱っつ！熱い！
きさ　（あわてて火のついた艾を四郎右衛門の背中から払い落して）ああ、どうしよう。申し訳ございません、旦那様。
四郎右衛門　おお、熱。もう、今夜は……これでおしまいにしよう。私は奥に帰って休みます。（着物を着なおしながら）今日はよう働いてくれました。礼を言います。お前達も後片付けが済んだらもう休みなはれ。ほな、おやすみ。（奥へ退く。）

きさ　（四郎右衛門の心のこもった言葉に手を合わせ）ほんまに、申し訳ありませんでした、旦那様。有難うございます。お休みなさいませ、旦那様。
二郎兵衛　（同じく手を合わせ）有難うございます。お休みなさいませ、旦那様。

コーラス1　悪事と気付かぬ仏の心持つ主人の慈悲が仇。

コーラス2　目に見えぬ神仏の加護も、
コーラス3　今は尽きたり。

　　　　二人は弾かれたように店、奥座敷、台所を忙しく行き来して灸の後片づけをする。片付けを終え、二人は店の真ん中に立ってじっと見詰め合う。そして、あらためてやってしまったことの恐ろしさに身を震わせ腰が抜けたように座り込む。

JIROBEI [*looking at the bunch of keys, in a shaking voice*]: I've succeeded in stealing the shop keys from my master by deceiving him, yet I cannot stop trembling with fear at the seriousness of the crime I've committed.

KISA [*trembling with guilt, clinging to JIROBEI*]: Oh, I'm terrified. I'm so frightened.

JIROBEI [*holding KISA tightly for a second*]: No, no. We don't have time to be like this. Now, O-Kisa-dono, will you please keep a good lookout for anyone coming in?

KISA [*involuntarily*]: Yes, yes. [*KISA staggers up and watches in the directions of the doorways to the inner part of the house, the kitchen and the shop entrance.*]

> At this point YOSHIBEI *enters from the hanamichi Left. He sees the noren of the Hishi-ya still out at this time of the day. He thinks it is strange and looks into the shop through the noren. Then he quickly notices something unusual in the way KISA and JIROBEI are behaving, and decides to keep watching them from behind the noren.*
>
> JIROBEI *goes to the shop cupboard, inserts one of the keys into it and unlocks it easily. He opens the door and looks for the deed, but only finds items such as clothing, a Mihara dagger,*[25] *an antique medicine case and a box. He opens the box and finds a scroll, which says 'Namu Amidabutsu: Save us, merciful Buddha' written by the great monk Rennyo.*[26]

JIROBEI: It's strange. I don't think the master keeps the box of deeds in the storehouse. Oh, I know where. It might be in the shop cabinet. [*JIROBEI chooses another key and unlocks the cabinet without difficulty. He opens the cabinet door and finds the deed box. He opens the box and finds a headed deed.*] Thank Buddha! I've found it. Here it is! This, this is the thing that has driven me to behave like a mad man. [*JIROBEI holds the deed up momentarily so as to show his gratitude to Buddha. Then he tears it up and pushes the torn deed into the bosom of his kimono. He is about to lock the cabinet.*]

YOSHIBEI [*nodding his head to himself and suddenly speaking loudly*]: Who's done this? The shop entrance has been left open again. What a careless fellow!

> JIROBEI *hurriedly hides himself in the cabinet. But he drops the keys in front of it. KISA tries to pick them up quickly but YOSHIBEI comes in to the shop before she does it.*

KISA [*hastily standing in front of the cabinet with her back against it*]: Oh, why, it's Yoshibei-dono. Please come up. [*While speaking, she carefully shuts the cabinet door behind her.*]

YOSHIBEI [*standing on the earth floor, looking around the inside of the shop and then sniffing*]:

350

「今宮の心中」

二郎兵衛　（鍵束を見て、震える声で）主人の目を誤魔化して鍵を盗るには盗ったけど、罪の深さが恐ろしゅうて身が震える。

きさ　（犯した罪の恐ろしさに慄き、二郎兵衛にしがみ付き）ああ、怖い。怖い。
二郎兵衛　（きさを強く抱き締めてから）こうはしておれん。さあ、おきさ殿、誰も来えへんか、見張っていて下さい。
きさ　（無我夢中で）はい、はい。（よろよろと立ちあがり、奥座敷や台所、店の入り口に目を配り、我知らず見張り役をする。）

　　　　　ちょうどこの時、由兵衛が上手花道から登場する。由兵衛はこの時刻に菱屋の店がまだ開いているのを不審に思い、暖簾の隙間からこっそりと中を覗く。店内の二人の只ならぬ様子に気づき、素早く暖簾の陰に身を隠して中を窺い続ける。
　　　　　二郎兵衛は店の箪笥のところに行き、箪笥の錠前に鍵のひとつを差込む。錠前が簡単に外れる。扉を開けて箪笥の中を探すが、衣類、三原の匕首[25]、時代物の印籠などしか入っていない。箱があるので蓋を開けると、中には蓮如[26]の「南無阿弥陀仏」の掛け軸だけが入っている。

二郎兵衛　おかしいなあ。証文箱はいつもお蔵にはお入れにならんはず。そうか、戸棚の方かもしれん。（今度は戸棚に行き、見知った鍵を鍵束から選び、造作なく錠前をはずして扉を開け、証文箱を見つける。箱のふたを開けると中に一通の表書きのある証文が入っている。）あった！あった！ああ、有難い！これや、これや、これが欲しさの気違い沙汰。（有難そうに手形を一瞬押し戴いてから、二、三度破ってから懐にねじ込み、戸棚に鍵をかけようとする。）

由兵衛　（頷いて、急に大きな声で）誰や？また店の表を開けたままにしてるのんは。無用心な奴っちゃなあ。

　　　　　二郎兵衛は慌てて戸棚の中に隠れる。その時、戸棚の前に鍵束を落とす。きさが急いで鍵束を拾おうとする。しかし、そうする前に由兵衛が店に入って来る。

きさ　（急いで戸棚を背にして立ち）ああ、由兵衛殿か。まあ、お上がりになって下さい。（後ろ手でそっと戸棚の戸を閉める。）
由兵衛　（店の土間に立ち、じろりと店内を見渡して、鼻をひくひくさせ）今夜旦那様

LOVERS' SUICIDES AT IMAMIYA

It seems that our master had a moxa treatment this evening. [*Going up to the tatami-matted room through the anteroom and picking up the bunch of keys thrown on the floor*] Why? What's happened? Whoever left the precious shop keys here? [*Looking at the shop cupboard*] What? Why is the shop cupboard open? [*Going to the shop cupboard, locking it and turning to KISA*] O-Kisa, will you please move away from the cabinet? [*Going to the shop cabinet, pushing KISA away from it and seeing the cabinet unlocked*] You must know that the world isn't safe these days. Why, the cabinet door hasn't been locked, either? [*Pushing the string of the keys in between his kimono and obi*] Now, I'll keep the keys at my side safely like this...we must lock the cabinet firmly and properly, too. [*YOSHIBEI locks the cabinet carefully.*]

The metal jangling of keys echoes in the quiet shop.
KISA shudders with the noise and sinks to the floor, trembling all over. She is at a loss.

YOSHIBEI [*grasping KISA by the hand forcefully*]: Look, O-Kisa! [*Pointing at the scar on his forehead*] This scar on my forehead was made by someone the other day when he threw stones at my boat. The scar hasn't healed yet, but I've found out who did it. Perhaps it is the same person who's got into the shop cabinet tonight. My guess is that you desperately want to save the burglar. Shall I unlock the cabinet and let the burglar go while no one knows about it? Or shall I tell our master about it? Now what do you think? Whether to save or to kill him is completely up to you.

KISA [*clasping her hands in prayer and pleading*]: Look, I beg you and pray to you. Please, will you please help me, Yoshibei-dono? I think that you must have a grudge against me for the things that I've done to you in the past. Yet now you're kindly saying that you can bury the unhappy past. I won't forget it. I promise you, I'll return the favour whatever happens to me. [*Throwing herself on YOSHIBEI*] Please, Yoshibei-dono, will you please give me the key? Please let me open the cabinet.

YOSHIBEI [*pushing KISA off*]: Humph! Damn it! Stop the sweet words! I've heard enough. I was duped by your honeyed words and dreamed of the day we would be together so many times. I've fancied you since you worked for Doctor Tsuyama Genza. I know how to twist a cloth into your mouth and make love to you, if I just wanted to satisfy my desire, but then if I did it, it wouldn't be love. Now, if you want to open this cabinet, I will let you. But before that, you must let me sleep with you for a little while, just briefly. Just this once...say yes, O-Kisa, let me have you, O-Kisa....

は灸をされたようやなあ。(店に上がり、素早く落ちている鍵束を拾い)これは、どうしたことや！大事な鍵をこんなところに取り散らかして。(箪笥を見て)それに、箪笥の戸も開けっ放しや！(箪笥のところに行き戸を閉め施錠してから、きさの方に向いて)おきさ、そこ退いてみ。(今度は戸棚に行き、きさを押しのけ、鍵がかかっていないのを見て)この頃世の中が物騒やというのに、なんで戸棚の鍵閉めてへんのや？(鍵束を帯の間に挟みながら)大事な鍵束は私の腰にこうつけてと……戸棚の鍵もちゃんと下ろしとこか。ちゃんとな。(戸棚にしっかりと鍵をかける。)

　　　　　　鍵をおろす音が静かな店内に響く。
　　　　　　その音を聞き、きさはわなわなと震えその場に座り込む。きさはなす術がなく途方に暮れる。

由兵衛　(きさの手をぐっと掴み)おい、おきさ、(額の傷を指して)これはこないだ船に石投げられてこのでぼちんに当たった時にできた傷や。まだ治れへん。けど、犯人はもう分かってる。恐らく、今夜、旦那の戸棚に入った盗人と同じ奴や。察するに、定めてお前もその盗人を助けたかろう。このまま戸棚を開けて表沙汰にせんとこか、それとも旦那の耳に入れよか？どや、そいつを生かすも殺すもお前の気持ち一つや。どうするんや？

きさ　(手を合わせて)これ、この通り手を合わせて頼みます。どうか、助けて下さい。日ごろの恨みもあるはずなのに、それを堪えてのあなたの今のその言葉、未来永劫忘れません。一生のうちにこのご恩はどうしてなりともお返しします。(由兵衛に取り付いて)どうか、どうかその鍵、私に貸して！戸棚、開けさせてください。

由兵衛　(きさを押しのけて)ふん。うまいこと言わんといてくれ。いついつにはと、今まで何十回も甘い言葉で気を持たされてきた。以前お前が医者の津山玄三殿のところに奉公していた時からこの由兵衛はお前に惚れていたんや。ぜひともこの胸の想いを晴らそうと思うなら、お前の口に手ぬぐいねじ込んでお前と寝ることも知ってはいる。けど、それでは恋が実ったとは言えん。この、戸棚の戸が開けたかったらそのお返しにちょっとだけお前の肌、私に許してくれ。ちょっとだけや、なあ、ええやろ、ちょっとだけや、おきさ……。

LOVERS' SUICIDES AT IMAMIYA

YOSHIBEI chases KISA in the shop. KISA pushes YOSHIBEI back and flees from him. YOSHIBEI keeps chasing KISA and finally gets hold of her. But KISA uses all her strength to push YOSHIBEI away and breaks away from him.

KISA [*trembling all over with fear and anger*]: Go away! You filthy shameless beast! You drew up a deed without telling us what was in it and forced my good-hearted father and me to seal it! How dare you! You bastard! What! What did you say just now? You'll let me have the key if I let you have me? [*Deeply sarcastic*] Oh, how grateful I am! Don't you understand that I'm doing all this just to avoid it? If you want to tell our master, do so! Please yourself! I don't care! Jirobei-dono and I are in love. As you've guessed, the person in the cabinet is my Jirobei-dono. We opened our master's cabinet together, so I am also guilty and cannot escape the charge. Accuse me of stealing the master's keys out of spite for not loving you. You dirty beast! Loathsome brute! [*KISA dissolves into tears.*]

YOSHIBEI [*in a fit of anger and loudly*]: Hey, hello! Where're the young employees? Are they all in the branch shop? There's a thief in the main shop! Kyūza! O-Take! Where are you? It's still early in the evening?

CHŌBEI, GONBEI and other employees of the Hishi-ya come running barefoot from the branch shop. KYŪZA comes running from the servants' quarters and TAKE from the direction of the kitchen. TEIHŌ comes from the inner part of the house.

YOSHIBEI [*losing his temper*]: Please have a look at these, Old Mistress! [*Taking the keys out of his obi and carefully handing them to TEIHŌ*] I think that the keys are our master's which he always carries at his side. [*Pointing at KISA*] These people stole them and unlocked the shop cupboard and the cabinet with them. When I came in, the other thief jumped into the cabinet, so quickly I locked it up to keep him in there. The thief in the cabinet is Jirobei and Kisa was his lookout, and I'm a living witness to the scene. [*He is elated and rolls up his sleeves.*]

*KISA continues crying.
All the people of the Hishi-ya are shocked and look at one another.*

TEIHŌ [*attaching the keys which she received from YOSHIBEI to her side and calmly*]: Has Shirōemon gone to bed already? When he hears this, he will have his own thoughts.

YOSHIBEI [*getting agitated*]: As a first step we must send for a town official, and then go and

「今宮の心中」

  由兵衛はきさを自分のものにしようと店の中を追い回す。きさは由兵衛を幾度も突き離して逃げ回るが、思いを遂げようと執拗に追いかける由兵衛に捕まってしまう。乱暴しようとする由兵衛を、きさはもがき渾身の力を振り絞って突き倒して逃れる。

きさ　（恐怖と怒りに身を震わせて）ああ、汚らわしい！由兵衛の生き畜生！ようも、ようも文面も分からん証文を勝手に書いて私ら親子に判を押させよったな。何やと？今、お前と寝たら戸棚を開けてやると？（皮肉いっぱいで）何と有難いこと！お前とそうなるのが嫌さにこうして苦労しているのが分からんのか。旦那様に言いたかったら、言うたらええ！かめしまへん！二郎兵衛殿と私は深い仲。お前の思う通り、戸棚の中のお人は二郎兵衛殿。大切な旦那様の戸棚を開けたのは私も同罪。その咎は逃れられまへん。お前に靡かん仕返しに訴え出たらよろしい！この生き畜生の死に畜生！人でなし！（泣き崩れる。）

由兵衛　（腹立ちまぎれに、大声で）おーい、若い衆は皆出店か！店に盗人が入ったぞ！久三！お竹！まだ宵の口やというのに皆とこにおるんや？

  長兵衛、権兵衛ら奉公人達が出店から裸足で駆けつける。
  久三と下女の竹がそれぞれ裏や台所から走って出る。
  貞法が奥から出て来る。

由兵衛　（いきり立って）お上様、これをご覧下さい。（帯に挟んでいた鍵束を大事そうに貞法に渡して）旦那様方の腰から離されることのないお店の大事な鍵束です。（きさを指して）それをこれらが盗んでお店の箪笥や戸棚を開けとりました。私が入って来たので、盗人が慌てて戸棚の中に逃げ込みましたところを、私が、がちゃんと鍵をかけました。戸棚の中にいるのは二郎兵衛で手引きしたのはここにいるおきさ、この私が生き証人です。（得意顔で腕まくりする。）

  きさは泣き続ける。
  他の奉公人達は驚いて顔を見合わせる。

貞法　（由兵衛から受け取った鍵束を腰に付け、落ち着いて）四郎右衛門はもう寝ましたのか？旦那様にお知らせしたら何ぞお考えもあろう。
由兵衛　（いきり立って）とりあえず町役人を呼びにやり、町年寄殿にも知らせて

tell the town elders…

> *The employees become agitated and commenting variously, "We must tell the neighbours, too!" "Prepare the lantern!" "Bring the rope and a stick here!"*

SHIRŌEMON [*Off-stage, clasping his hands*]: Yoshibei! Yoshibei!
YOSHIBEI: Yes, sir. [*He goes to the inner part of the house through the noren.*]

> *SHIRŌEMON has emerged from the mosquito net in his room and beckons YOSHIBEI over. YOSHIBEI goes to SHIRŌEMON.*

SHIRŌEMON [*in a calm low voice*]: I've heard it all from here. Jirobei has been with us since he was a small boy, so I was off my guard. I'm very angry with him. How wrong of him to steal my keys when I was taking a moxa treatment! It is a terrible thing to do. However, if the others are told that I know about it, things will get complicated and serious. And we mustn't make a big noise about something like this late in the evening as we need to think of our reputation in the neighbourhood. I'll pretend not to know anything about this. If nothing has been stolen from the shop, there will be a way of burying the matter. Now it's getting late. Jirobei is a caged bird and won't be able to fly away. As for Kisa, we must take her to her guarantors', her sister and her sister's husband's, this evening without delay, and leave her in their charge. Haste makes waste. We must think carefully, before we act. I do not wish to frighten my wife and children. Will you tell them to sleep in the branch shop tonight? The employees should also go to sleep there. But ask my mother to stay. You'd better go home tonight and come back tomorrow morning. We must deal with things calmly…make everyone go to bed early tonight. Have you got it?
YOSHIBEI: Yes, I have, Master.

> *After finishing his speech, SHIRŌEMON retreats to his room. YOSHIBEI returns to the shop.*

YOSHIBEI [*pretending that SHIRŌEMON called him for something else*]: Master wanted to talk about the business. Well, we mustn't let our master know this and make his eyes worse. Why don't we deal with it tomorrow? Chōbei, I'm sorry to trouble you, but will you take Kisa to her sister and brother-in-law and put her in their charge. When you return, will you go to the branch shop and sleep there tonight? Gonbei, you tell our mis-

「今宮の心中」

　……。

　　　　　奉公人達は口々に「町内の人々にも知らせんと！」「提灯の用意や！」「縄と棒持って来い！」などと騒ぎ立てる。

四郎右衛門　（奥から手を叩いて）由兵衛！由兵衛！
由兵衛　へえ。（暖簾を分けて奥へ行く。）

　　　　　寝所の蚊帳から出て来た四郎右衛門が由兵衛を手招きする。
　　　　　由兵衛は四郎右衛門の傍に行く。

四郎右衛門　（落ちついて、静かに）ことの次第は奥で聞きました。小さい頃から家に居る奉公人と思うて気を許していました。憎い奴や。灸を据えている間に店の鍵を盗むとは恐ろしいことを。けれど、私の耳に入ったということにすると面倒になる。また、夜分に騒ぎ立てると町内への外聞も悪い。紛失したものさえなければ、私は何も知らんことにして、上手く済ませてしまうことも出来よう。夜も更けてきた。二郎兵衛の奴はどこにも逃げられん籠の鳥。そのまま戸棚の中に入れて置いたらよろしい。きさの方は今夜のうちに、間違いのう身元保証人の姉夫婦のところに預けに行きなはれ。何事も急いではことを仕損じる。じっくりと考えてから対処することにしよう。女房や子供らが怖がってはようない。今夜は出店のほうで泊まらせてくれるか。手代達も皆向かいへ行って寝るようにさせなはれ。母上だけはこちらでお休みになるようにとゆうておくれ。お前も今夜のところは一旦帰って、明日の朝またおいで。何事も穏便にすませるようにして、皆を宵のうちに寝させなはれ。よろしいな。

由兵衛　へえ、かしこまりました、旦那様。

　　　　　四郎右衛門はこれだけ言って、蚊帳に戻る。
　　　　　由兵衛は奥から店に戻ってくる。

由兵衛　（他の用事で呼ばれたかのように装って）商売の御用やった。こんなことを夜中にお耳に入れて、旦那様のお眼に障るようなことになるといかん。何事も明日にしたほうがよかろう。長兵衛、ご苦労やけど、お前、これからきさをこれの姉夫婦のところに預けに行ってくれるか。戻ったら今夜は出店で寝るようにしてくれ。権兵衛、お前はお家様方に今夜は出店でお休みになるよう申し上げてくれ。

tress and the others to sleep in the branch shop just for tonight. Old Mistress, would you mind staying here? Perhaps our master would like that. Everyone else, except Kyūza and Take, must go to the branch shop and have an early night. Now, Kisa, you must stand up! [*YOSHIBEI makes Kisa stand up and pushes her towards CHŌBEI.*]

KISA [*kneeling and sobbing*]: Old Mistress, please, please, hear me out. I'll go to my sister's. I don't mind whatever punishment you give me. I'll accept it, but Jirobei-dono is innocent. There is a reason for all this. Will you please intercede with the mistress for Jirobei-dono, too? Old Mistress, please, please help me. I can't bear to see Jirobei-dono treated like a thief… It's distressing… [*Sobbing bitterly.*]

> *CHŌBEI helps to stand KISA up and leads her off the hanamichi Right. An apprentice boy lights their way with a lantern. The three of them go off to the hanamichi Right.*
>
> *TEIHŌ stands still, seeing off KISA in a terrible state while thinking about JIROBEI in the cabinet.*

YOSHIBEI: Now now Teihō-sama, please go back to the inner part of the house and make an early night. For the time being I'll go home now, too and come back first thing tomorrow morning. Everyone, go over the road! Kyūza, you must lock up the front door and go to bed, but watch out for any noise at night. O-Take, you do the same. Is that all right?

KYUZA [*half yawning*]: Yeeees, sir.

TAKE: Yes, sir. I'll listen out for any noise while I sleep.

> *TEIHO retreats to the inner part of the house deep in thought.*
> *All the employees except KYŪZA and TAKE go off to the branch shop.*
> *KYŪZA locks the entrance of the shop firmly and returns to the servants' quarters Off-stage Right.*
> *TAKE brings out her futon and a mosquito net to the anteroom. She spreads out the futon and hangs the mosquito net, and then lights an oil burner.[27] She immediately falls asleep.*

CHORUS 1: It is about ten o'clock in the evening and people are still out on the streets in Osaka.

CHORUS 2: But everyone here has gone to sleep and the house of the Hishi-ya is very quiet.

「今宮の心中」

　　それから、お上様はこちらでお休みになって下さい。旦那様もそれをお望みになると思います。他の者も久三と女中の竹以外は皆出店に戻り、今夜はあっちで早う寝るように。さあ、きさ、立たんかい。（由兵衛はきさを立たせて長兵衛の方に押しやる。）

きさ　（その場に跪いて、泣きながら）どうか、お上様、お願いでございます。お聞きください。姉のところには参ります。私の身はどうなっても構いません。けど、二郎兵衛殿には何の罪もございません。これにはわけがございます。どうか、お家様にもおとりなしして下さい。お願い致します。お上様、どうか、お助け下さい。二郎兵衛殿が盗人扱いされるのが……それが悲しゅうございます。（泣きじゃくる。）

　　　　　長兵衛はきさを促して立たせ、下手花道に向かう。提灯を提げた丁稚が長兵衛ときさの足元を照らしながら二人について行く。三人、下手花道から去る。
　　　　　貞法はきさの哀れな姿と戸棚の中の二郎兵衛のことを思ってその場に立ち尽くす。

由兵衛　さあさあ、貞法様。どうかもう早う奥にお戻りになってお休みになって下さい。私も今夜はひとまず帰って、明朝早々まいります。皆も早う向かいへ行くように。久三は表をちゃんと閉めて、夜中の物音にはよう気いつけるようにして寝や。お竹も。分かりましたな。

久三　（半分欠伸で）あああ、へえ。
竹　へえ、よう気いつけて寝ます。

　　　　　貞法は何か思案しながら奥に退く。
　　　　　久三と竹を店に残して他の奉公人達は出店のある上手に去る。
　　　　　久三は皆が去った後、しっかりと戸締りをして使用人の寝所のある下手に去る。
　　　　　竹は座敷の中の間に蒲団を敷いて蚊帳を吊り紙燭[27]に灯を点して直ぐに寝入る。

コーラス1　人声もまだある夜十時の大阪の町。

コーラス2　菱屋の内はひっそりと寝静まる。

SCENE THREE
Lecture

The night advances. The town of Osaka is covered in darkness. No one is on the street. Now and then the howling of a dog is heard in the distance. TAKE is fast asleep in the anteroom in the Hishi-ya.

CHORUS 3: As the night advances, the narrow wick of the andon lamp tilts helplessly, as if reflecting the helpless mind of Jirobei.

TEIHŌ comes out from the inner part of the house and approaches the shop cabinet stealthily.

CHORUS 1: When one wishes to enter the Buddhist Paradise, one has a merciful mind.
CHORUS 2: Teihō has woken up in the middle of the night and comes back to the shop.
CHORUS 3: She approaches the cabinet stealthily and stands beside it.
TEIHŌ [*in a low voice*]: Oi, Jirobei! What a scoundrel you are! [*Knocking on the door of the cabinet*] Can you tell who's here? You, fool!
CHORUS 1: Jirobei feels as if he has met a Buddha in the pit of hell.
JIROBEI [*in the cabinet*]: Oh, that voice…it's my Old Mistress! Oh, how ashamed I am! Please get me a kitchen knife or a vegetable knife, or whatever…take the handle off… and slide it through the gap in the cabinet door. Please let me kill myself with it. Teihō-sama, you've been very kind to me all these years. Please show me one last mercy. I beg you! [*He sobs.*]
TEIHŌ: If you had had the guts to kill yourself, you wouldn't have done a shameful thing like this. [*Covering the cabinet door with her kimono sleeve in order to deaden the noise of unlocking and opening it*] Come out here! [*Deliberately in a vehement tone*] I'm just an old townswoman, but if you want me to help you to your death so badly, I don't mind chopping off your head with a vegetable knife or with anything.

JIROBEI crawls out of the cabinet, hanging his head in shame dejectedly. His summer kimono is soaked with sweat. He is worn-out in a short period of time.
TEIHŌ is moved to tears involuntarily when she sees the state of JIROBEI.

CHORUS 2: Jirobei is the boy whom Teihō has loved and cared for since he came to the

「今宮の心中」

第三場
説教

  夜が更けて大阪の町に闇が訪れる。
  人通りも絶え、時折、犬の遠吠えが聞こえる。
  菱屋の中の間では女中の竹が熟睡している。

コーラス3 二郎兵衛の心映すか行灯の灯火、灯心細く心細げに、静かに夜が更けてゆく。

  奥から貞法が出て来てそおっと戸棚の前に行く。

コーラス1 ものごとへの哀れみ深い心が極楽浄土を願う人の心。
コーラス2 夜中に目覚めた貞法が店に戻ってきた。
コーラス3 忍び足で戸棚に行きその前で立ち止まる。
貞法 （声を潜めて）こら、二郎兵衛。このど悪党！（戸棚をこつこつと叩いて）この声が誰か分かるか。阿呆めが！
コーラス1 二郎兵衛は地獄で仏に合う心地。
二郎兵衛 （戸棚の中で）ああ、そのお声はお上様！ああ、恥ずかしい！包丁なり、薄刃の菜切り包丁なり、なんなりと、どうぞ柄を抜いて戸の隙間からそおっと入れて下さい。どうか、死なせて下さい。常日頃からお心をかけて下さっているこの二郎兵衛への最後のご慈悲です。どうか、お願いでございます。（啜り泣く）

貞法 死ぬほどの根性があったら、こんな浅ましいことはせんはず。（音がしないように戸棚の錠前を袖で覆って鍵をはずして扉を開け）そこへ出なはれ。（わざと言葉を荒げて）町人の年寄りの婆ではあるけど、そんなに斬って欲しいのなら、菜切り包丁でなとお前の首を斬ってやる。

  二郎兵衛はしょんぼりとうなだれて戸棚から這い出て来る。単衣の着物は汗にまみれてぐっしゃりとしていて、少しの間に驚くほど憔悴している。
  貞法は哀れな二郎兵衛の姿に思わず泣く。

コーラス2 幼いときから養い育てた二郎兵衛の何とやつれた悲しい姿。

Hishi-ya as an apprentice. How haggard and pitiful Jirobei looks!

CHORUS 3: Teihō is too sad to say anything to Jirobei; tears flow down her cheeks.

JIROBEI [*looking up*]: Old Mistress, I'm so sorry. I am ashamed of myself. I betrayed my master and have been punished for it. [*He hangs his head low and sobs.*] As you know, I've not stolen even one *sen*-cupper[28] since I came to the Hishi-ya. I was proud of that. Then, you may ask why have I done this? No, I haven't lost my mind. Umm…I'm not sure whether or not I should tell you this. But…Kisa and I are in love. Yoshibei was jealous and bore a grudge against me. The other day when he invited you on the boat-trip, he schemed to take advantage of me and drew up a deed the contents of which no one knew. He addressed the deed to you and the master, made Kisa and her father seal it and hand it to you. I am embarrassed to say that this deed worried me very much… I was on tenterhooks…and finally my anxiety drove me to open the cabinet and to steal it. This evening in the cabinet I could hear people saying that our master does not know anything of this yet. Old Mistress, please don't tell him about this. I beg you. It would be worse than having my head chopped off if he knew and despised me as a thief. [*JIROBEI clings to TEIHŌ's knees, falling to the floor and bursts into tears.*]

TEIHŌ: I don't think what you've just said would persuade people and win their sympathy. Do you truly think that your story will be taken as a justification of what you've done in a work place? You stole your own master's shop keys from his pouch in order to steal the contract of your girlfriend's marriage. I thought that Yoshibei had drawn up something advantageous for him, too. But that day he was our host. So I received his composition without saying anything. I tried not to spoil the pleasure of the day. But I tore it up ages ago. Jirobei, I'd been thinking of marrying you and Kisa, and giving you independence to open your shop…I'd been working hard to achieve that. But now things have turned out like this, all my plans and efforts are in vain. I can't pretend something unreasonable is reasonable, even if I dearly wished to support you. If I did, Yoshibei would speak out. He would say that the master of the Hishi-ya was blind and couldn't see right from wrong. And if the other employees listened to him, the shop could lose control over them. If that happened, honestly it would become impossible for me to give you a helping hand. Jirobei, I think that in this situation the best you can do is to give up Kisa to Yoshibei. Then everyone will be happy; you'll be forgiven and keep your job. You'll have a chance to repay an obligation to your master. It's all up to you, Jirobei. There are a few good girls among my nieces in Ikeda who'll make you a good wife. What do you say? Will you give up Kisa to Yoshibei? Jirobei, what are you going to do? [*She bursts into tears while scolding JIROBEI.*]

CHORUS 1: Teihō scolds and persuades Jirobei in tears as if talking to her own child.

「今宮の心中」

コーラス3　あまりの哀れさに叱る心も忘れてしまった涙の貞法。

二郎兵衛　（顔を上げて）お上様、面目ございません。ご主人の罰が当たりました。（うな垂れて泣く。）ご承知のように、これまで一銭[28]のお金も誤魔化したことのない私でございます。気が違うたわけでもございません。お上様にこんなことを申し上げるのもなんですが、私ときさが好きおうているのを由兵衛の奴が根に持って、何が何でも自分に有利なことを作ろうと、先日、お上様方を舟遊びに招いた日に、文言の分からん証文を旦那様とお上様宛てに書き、きさ親子に判を押させ、それが旦那様のお手に入ってしまいました。お恥ずかしいことに、その証文のことが気がかりで気がかりで……もう、どうもこうも、居ても立ってもおられんようになり……その証文欲しさに戸棚を開けました。さいぜん、戸棚の中でかすかに聞いておりますには、今夜のことはまだ旦那様のお耳には入っていないとか。どうか、旦那様のお耳に入れずに済むようにしてください。お頼み申します。あの正直な旦那様から盗人と蔑みを受けるのは首を斬られるより辛うございます。（貞法の膝にすがり、畳に突っ伏して激しく泣く。）

貞法　そんなことで言い訳が立つと考えるのはお前だけ。今、お前の話したことが、主人の巾着から家の鍵を盗み取ってとんでもない事をしてのけた言い訳として公の場所で聞いてもらえるとでも思うたら大間違い。私も由兵衛が自分勝手なものを書いたとは思った。けれど、あの場は由兵衛がもてなす主人方。客の私が拒むのも座が白けると思うて黙って受け取っておいただけで、とうの昔にあの証文は破って捨てました。きさとお前を夫婦にして、やがては店を一軒構えて独立させてと、この年寄りもいろいろ苦心してきました。しかし、こうなってはこれまでの私の努力も水の泡。どれだけお前達二人に情けをかけてやりとうても、道理の通ったことを通ってないとは言えまへん。もしも由兵衛が「菱屋の主人の目は真実が見極められないほど悪うなっている、もう道理も見極めることの出来ない、分別もつけられないお人になられた。」と言い立てでもして、皆がそれに感化されでもしたら、その後は奉公人への睨みも効かんようになります。そうなったら、お前に情けもかけられんようになる。二郎兵衛、もうこうなったからにはどないもできん。思い切ってきさを由兵衛に譲りなはれ。そうすれば四方丸う収まり、お前もこれまで通りここで働くことが出来て主人への恩返しも出来るようになる。すべてはお前の心一つや。池田にいる姪たちの中にもお前の女房にしてもええような娘が幾人かいる。どうや？きさを由兵衛にやるか？二郎兵衛、お前はどうするのや？（叱りながら泣いてしまう。）

コーラス1　我が子に意見するように、泣きつ叱りつ、ことを分けて話す貞法。

LOVERS' SUICIDES AT IMAMIYA

CHORUS 2: Jirobei is so sad and mortified that he cries and writhes in agony.

JIROBEI [*after crying a while, resolved*]: What you've just said is truly reasonable. I know that I should listen to you otherwise I'd be worse than an animal. But I can't say yes to it and repay my master's kindness. [*Angrily*] Yoshibei kept bullying me even after I celebrated my coming of age. He looked down on me more than he did on the other apprentices and often beat me up over a petty matter. I endured the insults which even a worm would find hard to take. Because I thought if one day Kisa and I married with the help of the Hishi-ya and lived together, even if our marriage lasted only for a day, it would mean the same as putting him to shame. Keeping this in mind I worked as hard as I could. If I give up Kisa to Yoshibei now, shamelessly, I'll be a complete loser and Yoshibei will be a conceited arrogant winner. No, no, I can't have it…I would be humiliated…
[*JIROBEI sheds tears of frustration, bites his kimono sleeve and is convulsed in tears.*]

CHORUS 1: JIROBEI is wracked in tears.

CHORUS 2: It's natural. I am sorry for him! He must've been given a hard time.

CHORUS 3: Cry as much as you want, and wash away the anger in tears!

JIROBEI [*pulling himself together*]: I'm sorry. The more I say, the more I offend you and my master. I'll go back to the cabinet. Please lock it up in the same way as Yoshibei did. [*Looking straight at TEIHŌ*] Old Mistress, if I am sent to prison straightway after I'm arrested… this will be my last moment with you in this life. Please forgive your Jirobei for being unable to repay you for your kindness. [*He crawls into the cabinet, crying.*]

TEIHŌ [*pulling out JIROBEI from the cabinet*]: What an ungrateful man you are! You stubborn wretch! [*With anger and tears of sorrow*] Have you forgotten the time when you were called Jiroshichi?[29] When you came to the Hishi-ya as an apprentice, you were twelve years old and we named you Jiroshichi. You were ill every couple of days, and so everyone said, "This boy should be taken back to his parents' because he can't possibly serve out his time here." Stubbornly, I alone was against it and said, "If we send back a boy who is as feeble as this, he won't survive. It will be more merciful if we bring him up here." As a result you were kept and raised here. When you were ill, I got you medicine and often asked a shaman to recite an incantation to cure you. And it went on until you arrived at manhood. Have you forgotten those days? I looked after you more than I did my sons and grandchildren. Shirōemon had to spend extra money because of you. I brought you up and made a man of you. I took good care of you and even made the other employees envious [*crying*]… If you are sent to prison, people will say, "That old woman of the Hishi-ya did her best with their apprentice and brought him up to be a thief." I'm sure that they'll speak ill of Shirōemon, too. They'll say, "Well, it seems that the blind master of the shop couldn't see his fortune being stolen!" And yet, do you still

「今宮の心中」

コーラス2　悲しさ、口惜しさに、身もだえして泣く二郎兵衛。
二郎兵衛　（しばらく泣いて、ようやく口を開き）一つ一つごもっともなお言葉。それを聞き入れん二郎兵衛が畜生にも劣るのはよう分かっております。けど、どうしても「はい、分かりました。」と承諾して親方様のご恩に報いることは出来まへんのです。（怒って）由兵衛は元服も済ませた私を丁稚よりもまだ下に見下して、些細なことを口実に踏みつけんばかりに打ち叩きました。そんな虫でも我慢でけへんほどのくやしさに耐えてきましたのも、いつか菱屋のおかげできさと所帯を持たせてもらい、一日でも二人一緒に暮らすことが出来たら由兵衛を見返したのと同じになると思うたからです。それを思うて、これまで精一杯、まめにお勤めに励んでまいりました。それを、おめおめと由兵衛めにきさを渡し、あいつにそれ見たことかという顔をされるのは嫌です。それだけは口惜しゅうて我慢できまへん。（悔しさに涙を流し、袖を食いしばり、身を震わせて泣く。）
コーラス1　悔しさに身い震わせ身悶えして二郎兵衛が泣く。
コーラス2　泣くのも道理や。可哀そうに、さぞ辛かったんやろ。
コーラス3　思いっきり泣きなはれ。泣いて悔しさ流しなはれ。
二郎兵衛　（気を取り直し）どうか、堪忍して下さい。言えば言うほど、お上様とご主人への無礼になります。とにかく私は戸棚に戻ります。どうぞ、あの由兵衛がしたように錠を下ろして下さい。（貞法の顔を見て）お上様、捕まってすぐに牢屋に入れられることになったら、これが今生のお別れです。ご恩返しもできない二郎兵衛をどうぞお許し下さい。（泣きながら這って戸棚に入る。）
貞法　（二郎兵衛を戸棚から引っ張り出して）この恩知らず！わからずや！（腹立ちと悲しみの涙を堪えて）十二の歳から養い育ててもろうた、あの丁稚の二郎七[29]の頃のこと忘れたか！三日にあげず患うので、誰もが『この子はとてもここでは勤めおおせまい。早よう親元に住なせた方が良かろう』と言うのを、この婆独りが強情を張って『こんな弱い子を在所の親元に住なせたら死んでしまう。誠の慈悲の心とはここで育てること。』と言い、お前が十八の春を迎えるまで呪いをしてもろたり薬を飲ませたりと、子や孫にもせんほどの世話をしてきた。四郎右衛門にも余分なお金を使わせて、そうやって、ようようお前を一人前に育てました。他の奉公人が妬むほど可愛がってきたのに（泣く）……。もしもお前が牢屋に入るようなことになったら、「あの菱屋の婆が愚行の限りを尽くして盗人を養い育てた！」「お店の主が眼病を患っていて、店の身代盗まれているのも見えなんだ！」と四郎右衛門まで悪しざまに言われることになる。それでもお前は自分の面目を立てたいのか。朝早うから下女や丁稚を起こして、あれらに苦労かけては極楽往生を願うことも叶わんと思い、お御堂への朝事参り[30]にもお前を連れてお参りしてきた。けど、明日からはそれも出来んようになる。この年寄りが仏様に極楽浄

want to save your honour? It has been my wish to enter the Buddhist Paradise in the next world and I chose you to accompany me on a visit to the morning service[30] at the Midō Temple. For, I thought that my wish wouldn't be heard if I woke up our maids and young apprentices and gave them an early start. If you go, I won't be able to make a visit from tomorrow. Have you become a man who doesn't care whether or not an old woman like me will have to give up her wish? I'm a woman who hates to see anyone or anything, even a dog or a cat, treated badly, once they've belonged to the Hishi-ya. I care about you. That's why I'm telling you these things. But if you are determined to have your own way and want to die, please yourself. Get into the cabinet! [*She scolds while crying.*]

CHORUS 1: By crying and threatening in any number of ways,

CHORUS 2: By concealing her tender heart behind harsh words, Teihō tries to reason with Jirobei.

CHORUS 3: She is truly merciful as one in the Buddhist Paradise.

JIROBEI [*listening to TEIHŌ intently*]: I, I think…you're right. I've understood. I'll give up Kisa. Yoshibei can take her.

TEIHŌ: If you mean it, you should make a vow.[31]

JIROBEI: It'll be the seventh anniversary of my mother's death[32] next month. I've already held her memorial service early. I wanted my mother's spirit to rest in peace in Buddhist paradise, but I will even send it to hell if I ever break my oath to you.

CHORUS 1: If you break an oath, you'll be punished for it, yet Jirobei is saying he'll send his mother to hell…

CHORUS 2: He is promising it without considering the consequences at all.

CHORUS 3: He should be punished for saying such a thing!

TEIHŌ [*relieved*]: Well done, Jirobei. Well said. Yoshibei has been with us for a long time. He used to be a senior shop assistant of the Hishi-ya and is still an important figure. Even if you won Kisa from Yoshibei this time, you've as bad as lost. It'd only put you in a more difficult situation. Leave it to me. I'll settle the matter once and for all. No need to worry. Now, you must go upstairs and sleep. (*Locking up the cabinet firmly*) You are a fool. Kisa isn't the only woman you can fall in love with. She has already seen much of life. I'll find you a good girl who is a virgin and suitable for you. Namu Amidabutsu. Save us, merciful Buddha! [*She retreats to the inner part of the house.*]

CHORUS 1: Namu Amidabutsu. Save us, merciful Buddha!

CHORUS 2: Namu Amidabutsu. Save us, merciful Buddha!

CHORUS 3: Even his true parents wouldn't care about him as much as she does.

JIROBEI is absent-minded for a while.

「今宮の心中」

土を願うことも叶わんようにする、そんな情けない気持ちがお前に付き始めたのか。私はこの家に来たものは、犬や猫でも酷い目に合わされるのは見とうない性分。お前が可愛いと思うからこそこんなふうに話している。それでもどうでも我を押し通して死ぬというんやったら、勝手に戸棚に入りなはれ！（泣きながら、叱る。）

コーラス1　泣きつ、脅しつ、いろいろに
コーラス2　死ぬこと、止めたく、意見する

コーラス3　老女の心、既に後世安楽のもの。
二郎兵衛　（じっと聞き入って）お上様の言われることごもっともでございます。合点いたしました。思い切ります。きさを由兵衛にやります。
貞法　そしたら、それがほんまやったら、その証に誓文[31]たてなはれ。
二郎兵衛　来月は母の七年忌[32]です。先頃年忌の法事は早めに済ませました。けど、もしも、この誓いを破ったら、この年忌の済んだ母を地獄に落とすことにいたします。

コーラス1　誓文とは背けば自らが罰を受けると誓うもの。「母を地獄に落とす」などと……。
コーラス2　前後の見境すらない誓いの言葉。
コーラス3　このこと一つですでに二郎兵衛の罰当たり！
貞法　（ほっとして）そうか。よう言いました。由兵衛は店の古参の重手代。その由兵衛ときさを張り合うて勝っても負けたと同じこと。かえってお前の立場が悪うなるだけ。この度のことはすべてこの貞法が綺麗さっぱりとかたをつけてやる。もうお前は二階へ上がってお休み。（戸棚の錠前をしっかりとかけて）阿呆めが。おきさばかりが女じゃない。あんな世慣れた者よりも、純真無垢の穢れのないお前に似合うた生娘を探してやる。南無阿弥陀仏。南無阿弥陀仏。（奥へ去る。）

コーラス1　南無阿弥陀仏。
コーラス2　南無阿弥陀仏。
コーラス3　親にも勝る深い情けの貞法の言葉。

　　　　　二郎兵衛は暫く放心状態になる。

JIROBEI [*suddenly coming to himself*]: Old mistress has just said that she tore up Yoshibei's deed ages ago. Then, what on earth did I tear up just then? [*Taking the torn deed out of the bosom of his kimono in haste, putting the pieces together and reading it*] Goodness! What shall I do? This is the deed for the mortgage on the house in Uehonmachi, the amount of money is seven *kan* and five hundred *me*-silver. It says both the principal and interest should be paid back at the end of this month. It's a business deed. Err…err… err… [*Open-mouthed, he collapses to the floor.*]

CHORUS 1: He's committed an irredeemable crime.

CHORUS 2: One misfortune brings another; they seldom come alone.

CHORUS 3: It's like the sky being filled with dark thunderous clouds. I'm afraid!

JIROBEI [*staggering to his feet and looking at the torn deed once more*]: Oh, no, I've torn the seal. [*Carefully putting the pieces of the deed together with trembling hands*] No, I can't…I can't put them together. They won't be restored to their original state. I've torn an important business document. I've committed a serious crime. Hell! There is no doubt that I'll be caught and sent to prison for this. This, this one can't be paid for even with my life. [*JIROBEI tries to put the pieces of the deed together one last time but fails. Having lost the last vestige of hope, he cries in despair, trembling with fear. Making up his mind*] whatever I do, I don't think that things will get better from now on. Since things have turned out like this…either I stay alive or die, whatever fortune or misfortune comes upon me…I, won't be separated from Kisa. I won't leave her! First I must run away from this place…

JIROBEI staggers to his feet and steps forward stealthily. He opens the fusuma[33] *sliding door of the anteroom quietly and looks into the room. TAKE is sleeping on her futon, half-naked, in the mosquito net. The oil burner is burning brightly beside her.*

JIROBEI: Oh, no, O-Take-don[34] is sleeping. What a nuisance! When I go through the room, she'll wake up and make a racket. What shall I do? [*Having an idea*] Oh, yes, let's do it.

JIROBEI goes to the shop shelves and takes out a fan. He fans the oil burner with it and extinguishes the light. The anteroom becomes dark.

TAKE [*waking up with a start, looking around restlessly and noticing the light is out*]: Oh, how annoying! The wind has blown out the oil burner. Fleas and mosquitoes are going to bite me tonight. They'll be on my soft fair skin. Oh, what a waste! Oh, I wish Kyūza would come to me. Oh, I envy Jirobei and O-Kisa-dono so much. When I go back home for

「今宮の心中」

二郎兵衛　（ふと我に返り）お上様はあの証文はとうに破って捨てたと言われた。そしたら、さっき破ったのは一体何やったんやろ？（急いで懐から破った証文を取り出し、突き合わせて見る）ああっ！どないしょう！これは上本町の家を抵当に七貫五百目貸し付けたという商いの証文。今月末に元金と利子残らず返済してもらうと書いてある。ああ、ああ、ああ……。（口を開いて座り込む。）

コーラス1　手形破りの大罪犯した身の咎。
コーラス2　災いは一つ起これば、二つ続く。悪いことは重なるもの。
コーラス3　雨雲の暗い空のようでほんに空恐ろしい。
二郎兵衛　（ふらふらと立ち上がり、もう一度、証文をよく見て）ああ、印判のとこを破ってる。（手を震わせながら、注意深く破れ目をいろいろと突き合わせてみて）あかん、これは継ぎ合わしようない。元通りにはなれへん。大事な商売の証文を破ってしもた！手形破りの大罪犯してしもた！どないしょう。間違いのう後ろに手えが回る。こ、これは、命にかかわる難儀や。（二郎兵衛はもう一度破れた証文を継ぎ合わせてみようとする。が、やはり継ぎ合わせられない。一縷の望みも絶たれ、絶望して、ただただ罪の大きさに震え慄いて泣く。心を決めて）もう、この先、生きていてどうなるものでもない。こうなったからには、死んでも生きてもどうなろうとも、きさとは別れん離れへん。先ずこの家から抜け出して……。

　　　　　二郎兵衛は気が動転してヒョロつく足を踏みしめながら、店の中の間のところまで行き襖[33]をそっと開ける。中の間では蚊よけの紙燭を赤々と灯し、竹が蚊帳の中で半裸で寝ている。

二郎兵衛　ああ、邪魔やなあ。お竹どん[34]が寝てる。ここ通ったらお竹どんが起きて騒ぐやろなあ。どないしょう。（思いついて）そや。

　　　　　二郎兵衛は店の棚にあった扇子を持ち出して扇いで紙燭の灯を消す。中の間が真っ暗になる。

竹　　　（はっと目を覚まし、紙燭の消えていることに気付いて）ああ、憎い！風が吹いて虫よけの紙燭の火を消してしもた。今夜は蚤と蚊に肌を捧げることになる。せっかくのこの柔肌を、ああ、もったいない。久三でも来ればいいのに。あの二郎兵衛とおきさ殿の仲を見ていると羨ましゅうてたまらん。わしも今年の盆の藪入り[35]

the servants' holiday[35] in the midsummer Bon Festival this year, I'll sleep with the men of my country in the millet field. [*TAKE lies down on the futon and starts snoring.*]

JIROBEI passes by TAKE stealthily, descends to the earth floor past the stepping platform and puts his setta in the bosom of his kimono. He tries to unbolt the wicket door of the front door, but the bolt has been locked. Not knowing what to do JIROBEI pauses.

KISA comes running from the hanamichi Right with a bundle of furoshiki cloth[36] in her arm, trying to avoid being seen.

CHORUS 1: Carrying a bundle of furoshiki cloth with a decorated with the chrysanthemum of partings pattern,[37] she is coming back to the Hishi-ya.
CHORUS 2: She knows well that her sister will be in trouble if she leaves the house.
CHORUS 2: She also knows very well that she must forget Jirobei. But she can't. She can't be separated from him. She can't leave him.

KISA comes to the Hishi-ya and peeps through the key hole of the wicket door. The inside of the shop is just quiet.

CHORUS 1: Kisa looks through the keyhole, but only hears the buzzing of mosquitoes.

KISA sobs convulsively with helplessness and misery.
JIROBEI catches the sound of KISA's sobbing, goes to the keyhole and puts his face to it.

JIROBEI [*startled*]: That's the smell of plum-flower hair oil…[38] Is that you, O-Kisa, standing outside?
KISA: That voice! It's Jiro-sama! Yes, it's me. Oh, Jiro-sama, I've so much to tell you. Oh, I've run away from my sister's…
JIROBEI: Oh, O-Kisa, I've so much to tell you, too. I, I've done a terrible thing! But, oh, I can't open this, this door…

JIROBEI and KISA try to open the wicket from both sides, but it does not open. They use all their strength and collapse in tears.
There is a dog howling in the distance. This wakes up a dog, sleeping on the street

「今宮の心中」

には田舎に帰って粟畑で男といっぱい寝たろ。（再びコロリと横になって、すぐに鼾(いびき)をかき出す。）

　　　　二郎兵衛はそおーっと竹のそばを通って、上がり框から三和土(たたき)に降りて自分の雪駄(せった)を懐に入れる。そして店の入り口の潜り戸を開けようとする。が、門の鍵(かんぬき)が下りていて開かない。二郎兵衛はどうしてよいかわからず立ち尽くす。

　　　　この時、風呂敷包み(ふろしきづつ)み[36]を一つ抱えたきさが、人目を避けるように下手花道から小走りに来る。

コーラス１　別れ割り菊、菊の紋[37]の風呂敷包み手に抱え、きさが菱屋に戻ってくる。
コーラス２　預かりの身が外に出たら姉の迷惑になることは分かっている。
コーラス３　分かっていても、別れさせられても、愛しい二郎兵衛のことは思いきられへん。別れられへん。

　　　　きさは菱屋の門口まで来て店の潜り戸(くぐりど)の枢(くるる)の穴から中を覗(のぞ)く。
　　　　店の中は静かで物音ひとつ聞こえない。

コーラス１　目を凝らし耳を澄まして探れとも、聞こえるものは蚊の声ばかり。

　　　　きさは心細さと情けなさでしゃくり上げる。
　　　　二郎兵衛がその声を聞きつけて、店の中から枢(くるる)の穴に顔を付ける。

二郎兵衛　（はっとして）梅花油(ばいかあぶら)[38]の鬢付(びんつ)けの匂い……そこにいるのはおきさか？

きさ　その声は恋しい二郎様。ああ、二郎様、言いたいことがいっぱいあって、姉の家を抜けてきました……。
二郎兵衛　おきさ、私も言いたいことがある。大変なことをしてしもたんや。しかし、ああ、この、この戸がどうにも開けられへん。

　　　　二郎兵衛ときさは潜り戸の内と外で何とか戸を開けようとするが開かない。二人は力尽きて泣き崩れる。
　　　　遠くで「ウォーン」と犬の遠吠えが聞こえる。その声で辻に寝ていた犬

near the Hishi-ya. The dog notices KISA and starts barking at her. This wakes up several more dogs. All the dogs come to KISA, barking and frightening her. KISA trembles with fear and stands still.

JIROBEI stands still at the entrance, not knowing what to do.

TAKE wakes up.

TAKE [*addressing KYŪZA in the servants' quarter at the back of the shop*]: Kyūza! Dogs are barking outside the shop. Will you please get up and have a look? [*After speaking, she falls back to sleep immediately.*]

KYŪZA [*Off-stage Right, half-sleeping*]: A-lr-ight!

KISA: Oh, no! Kyūza's coming! [*She hides herself in the direction of Sakai Avenue Off-stage Left.*]

JIROBEI: Goodness! I must hide myself.

JIROBEI quickly hides himself in a dark corner of the shop.

KYŪZA, in underwear, enters with a long stick and a key in his hand. He unlocks the latch of the wicket door and goes outside.

KYŪZA [*looking around the streets puzzled*]: How strange! No one's here! I wonder if a beggar has passed by. [*Seeing a dog and beckoning it*] Hoi, dog! Come! Come here!

The dog comes to KYŪZA.

[*Petting the dog*] It's sultry inside the house, but outside you've got westerly winds, and it's nice and cool here. Isn't it good? It's like paradise here. [*Enjoying the cool air and petting the dog*] Don't you think so? Oh, you do. I see, I see, you feel cool, too. What a clever dog!

There are bolts of white silk cloth for dying piled up in the shop. JIROBEI picks up one of them, wraps it around himself from head to toe and goes out of the shop abruptly.

KYŪZA [*extremely frightened at the sight of JIROBEI*]: Aaaah! I'm afraid! It's a ghost! There's a ghost here! I'm afraid! [*He rushes into the shop and shuts up the wicket.*]

JIROBEI removes the cloth covering his face and looks around for KISA.

「今宮の心中」

　　が一匹目を覚まし「ワン、ウーウゥン、ワン！」と、きさに吠えかかる。声につられて方々から七、八匹が「ウー、ワン、ワンワン。ウーウゥン、ワン！」と、きさを脅して吠えかかる。きさは恐ろしさに震えて門口に立ち尽くす。
　　　二郎兵衛もなすすべなく潜り戸の内に立ち尽くす。
　　　竹が目を覚ます。

竹　（久三の寝ている裏の方に向かって）久三！表でえらい犬が鳴く。何もないか起きて見て来てくれんか！（言い終わると、またすぐ寝入る。）

久三の声　（下手袖から、半分寝た声で）おう。
きさ　あれ、久三が来る！（上手袖、堺筋の方に逃げる。）

二郎兵衛　えらいこっちゃ！隠れんとあかん。

　　　二郎兵衛はとっさに店の物陰に身を隠す。
　　襦袢姿の久三が眠そうな様子で寄り棒を引っさげて下手から出て来る。手に持った鍵で門の錠前をはずして潜り戸を開けて表に出る。

久三　（辻辻を見て、不思議そうに）あれっ、誰もおらん。乞食でも通ったんかいな。（一匹の犬を見つけて手招きして）ほれ、来い、来い！

　　　犬が尾を振って久三のところに来る。

　　（犬を撫でてやりながら）家の中は蒸し暑いが外に出ると西風が吹いて涼しいのお。有難い。極楽じゃ。（涼んで、尚も犬を撫で）なあ、そやなあ。おうおう、そうかそうか。お前も涼しいか。賢いのお。

　　　二郎兵衛は店の中に積み重ねてあった染め用の白絹を一反取って解き、くるくると頭から体まで巻きつけて、潜り戸からぬっと出る。

久三　（二郎兵衛の姿に驚き）ああーっ！怖い！幽霊じゃ！幽霊じゃ！怖い！怖い！（急いで店の中に逃げ込んで、潜り戸をぴしゃっと閉める。）

　　　二郎兵衛は白布の間から顔を出してきょろきょろときさを探す。

373

KISA [*beckoning JIROBEI from Downstage left*]: Jiro-sama! Here! I'm here!

JIROBEI [*running to KISA*]: O-Kisa, There's a problem. I've done a terrible thing! The deed which I tore up earlier wasn't Yoshibei's. It was the deed of the mortgage, an important business deed of the Hishi-ya.

KISA [*astonished*]: What! You tore up of the mortgage deed? Goodness! Tearing a deed is a serious crime... You'll be arrested for that...

JIROBEI: I'm sorry, O-Kisa. Forgive me. We must leave here immediately. I have nowhere to go, but let's go south. Oh, if someone sees me, they'll think this is very odd. [*He unties the cloth and folds it up.*]

JIROBEI and KISA run off through the hanamichi Left.

Blackout.

「今宮の心中」

きさ　（上手袖近くから呼んで）二郎様！こっち、こっち。
二郎兵衛　（駆け寄り）おきさ、大変や！えらいことしてしもた！さっき破った証文は由兵衛の書いたもんやない。あれは菱屋の大切な商いの家質の手形！

きさ　（びっくりして）ええっ！破ったのは家質の手形！手、手形破りは大罪……。お、お咎めを受けるのは必定……。
二郎兵衛　堪忍してくれ、おきさ。早うここから逃げんとあかん。行く宛てはないけど、南に向かおう。あ、人が見たらけったいに思うなあ。（二郎兵衛は巻つけた白絹をくるくると解いてたたむ。）

　　　　　二人は手に手を取って上手花道から去る。

　　　　　暗転。

LOVERS' SUICIDES AT IMAMIYA

ACT THREE

On the 24th of May

SCENE ONE
The lovers' journey

The streets of Osaka in the small hours.
JIROBEI and KISA enter from the hanamichi Right, walking south.

CHORUS: One, one stream of a waterfall[1]
    Made of lovers' tears rolling down their cheeks.
    Two, two lovers make a journey along the stream of tears to the River Styx.[2]
    Three, let the lovers' three wishes come true before they leave for the next world.
    They wish to have a writing brush and ink.
    For they want to write a last letter to their parents.
    They wish to dream a last dream.
    For they want to see their fathers' faces and to hear their mothers' voices left behind in their home countries.
    They wish to return to this world and live together when they wake up from the dream.
    For they want to visit their parents as a married couple on servants' holidays on At New Year and the Midsummer Bon Festival.
    They've looked forward to it ever since they met.
    But their wishes won't be heard on their journey over the mountain of death.[3]
    Now it's most unlikely.
    What'll await them then?
    The lid of the iron pot in hell[4] will be opened!
    Lovers' hearts are filled with regret and resentment.
KISA: My love.
JIROBEI: My sweetheart.
KISA: I'll be with you forever.
JIROBEI: I'll never leave you.
CHORUS: The lovers cling to each other and cry in each other's arms.

「今宮の心中」

下之巻

五月二十四日

第一場
道行

　　　真夜中の大阪の町。
　　　南に向かう二郎兵衛ときさが下手花道から来る。

コーラス　一つとや[1]　一つ涙の滝の糸
　　ひとつ思いであふれる涙　滝と流して三途の川[2]へ
　　二つとや　筆があるならこの心　書いて残して　去りゆくものを
　　三つとや　見たい　聞きたい　せめては夢で
　　在所に残した　父様の顔　母様の声
　　それは叶わぬ　夢も叶わぬ　きびしい責めの　死出の山[3]
　　願い叶い　その夢見られても　夢覚めた時は　この世に戻れぬ二人連れ
　　藪入りに　夫婦連れでと約束し
　　盆、正月の十六日　心待ちした幸せも
　　今は悲し　地獄の釜[4]の蓋　開くのを　待つ身なり
　　後悔の心　無念の涙

きさ　愛しいひと。
二郎兵衛　恋しいあなた。
きさ　離れない。
二郎兵衛　離さない。
コーラス　すがり　抱き寄せ　溢れる涙

LOVERS' SUICIDES AT IMAMIYA

The street dogs are barking.

CHORUS: The street dogs condemn the lovers, and bark at them mercilessly.
The lovers are chased off to hell to see the abyss in this world.
KISA: This is the punishment for lying to my parents.
JIROBEI: My punishment is for my master and my old mistress. I've repaid their kindness with ingratitude. The old mistress prayed to Buddha for a charitable deed in the evening and chanted a prayer to Buddha at night for everyone. I've squandered her generosity.
KISA: Oh, the eastern sky is turning light in the ray of the white midnight moon.
JIROBEI: Led by the moonlight, we've come to the Higashi Yokobori Canal. I can't bear to see the reflection of my tarnished self in its clear water. I'm so ashamed.
CHORUS: No need to feel ashamed of being in love.
It is the way people think in this life.
Let us be model lovers.
We've come to the street of Honmachi,[5] the central area of Osaka.
We walk through Kome-ya-machi, Rice Shop Street.
How to weigh the rice? Five shō, seven shō[6]...
We'll be saved in our future lives in paradise, in our seven lives through eternity.[7]
My husband is a good man rarely found in Japan, nor on the street of Karamono-machi, the Chinese Goods Quarter.
My wife is a sweet but hard-working young woman.
We'll have a boy as beautiful as a cherry blossom.
We've come to Kyūtarō-machi.
Oh, let us name our boy Kyūtarō.
Soon our Kyūtarō starts his elementary temple school near the Kyūhō-ji Temple in Kyūhō-ji-machi.
We often talked of moments like these, dreaming of our future and listening to the temple bell.
Now everything is just like a passing dream.
We've come to Bakuro-machi, the Town of Horse Dealers.
Baku, a tapir, has devoured our dream![8]
We're in the Junkei-machi, whose name suggests happiness.
But how can we use this name when children die first and elderly parents are left alone.
Our parents remain alive while all around life withers away.
We're walking in Andōji-machi, the Town of Relief!
Children should relieve their parents' anxiety;

「今宮の心中」

　　　　二人を吠え立てる野良犬の声。

コーラス　奈落に旅立つ恋人を　咎めて吠える　犬の責め
　　この世で地獄を見るような
きさ　思えば、これも親の罰。恩ある親に嘘ついた。
二郎兵衛　私は親より旦那様とお上様の報い。慈しみ育ててもろうた情けに水かけた。
　　お上様は宵には仏の功徳、夜中には念仏を唱えておられた。私はその情けあるお
　　心を無駄にした。
きさ　ああ、東の空が真夜中の月の光で白み始めた。
二郎兵衛　月の光に助けられ、東横堀まで来たけれど、澄んだ川面に映される濁った
　　我が身が恥ずかしい。
コーラス　恋する身を恥と思うはこの世のこと。
　　恋する者の手本となりましょ。
　　ここは手本の手・本町[5]
　　二人の心を一つ思いに込める　米屋町
　　五升七升[6]と思いを量り　後生七生[7]　永久の来世で救われましょう
　　私の殿御は　日本はおろか　唐物町の　唐の国にも稀なるお方
　　嫁御は　ちょきりこっきり　小さくかわいい若女房
　　二人の間に　花のような男の子もうけて　久太郎と呼びましょ　久太郎町
　　その子が　やがて寺子屋入りする　久宝寺町
　　寺の鐘の音聞きながら　かねて話したことも　今は独り寝のあだ夢
　　獏[8]に夢を食われてしもうた　博労町
　　親よりも子が先に逝く　老人の残る逆の世を　順慶町とは呼び難い
　　私もあなたも　後には親が枯れ残る
　　安堵させたい　安堂寺町も
　　かえって　子ゆえの闇に迷わす　親不孝

LOVERS' SUICIDES AT IMAMIYA

Instead we are leaving them with remorse and grief.

KISA: I lied to my parents, and now am departing to the next world leaving them behind… I won't escape the punishment. Oh, how despicable! [*Crying*]

JIROBEI holds KISA gently. The lovers embrace each other closely and cry together.

CHORUS: The tide is in Shioya-machi, the Salt Merchant Town.
  Bitter salty tears flow down cheeks.
  The Nagahori is a long canal flowing through Osaka, while we passers-by only live short lives.
  We change pleasure into trouble on the Kunosuke-bashi, the Bridge of Agony.
  Now we've come to the Kawara-ya-bashi, the Bridge of Roof Tile.
  We hear the sound of oil being extracted[9] in the oil shop in the north corner of the bridge.
  It is a reminder of the suicide pact of the lovers O-Some and Hisamatsu, an only daughter of the oil shop and their junior shop assistant.
  Like a drop of late autumn drizzle falling on green leaves, drenched in the colour of love, the young lovers lost their lives.
  The story is still sung in utasaimon, 'Lovers' Suicides of O-Some and Hisamatsu.'[10]
  It's no longer someone else's story. When the dawn comes, it will be our own.
  We pray in tears for the lovers of the oil shop.
  We burn the votive light at the altar with oil from the oil shop.

  The Two-Wells stand side by side at the end of the Dōton Canal.
  It's sad enough to lose one life.
  Tonight two lives are to be lost.
  We'll die falling together, tied tightly to each other.
  We've just crossed Yamato-bashi, the Bridge of the Mount of Sins.[11]
  There's smoke from Sennichi-dera, the Temple of a Thousand Days.[12]
  The smoke of cremated criminals, the smoke of mortality.
  Before the May rain of a merciless cloud, we must travel to our place of death.
  As we hasten, we are drenched to the skin with night dew.
  A kimono with hazy flowers on the shoulders and the hem,
  A boat sailing for the Buddhist paradise[13] on the waist,
  And pine woods by the seacoast on the lower hem,
  We'll put it on when we finally reach Kyō-bashi, the Kyō Bridge.

「今宮の心中」

きさ　親に嘘ついて先立つ親不孝(おやふこう)の罪……。ああ、浅ましい。（泣く。）

　　　　　二郎兵衛が優しくきさを抱き寄せる。二人、ひしと抱き合い泣く。

コーラス　潮のよう　寄せる涙の　塩屋町(しおやまち)
　　長くない　現世(げんせ)の時を　なんで長堀(ながほり)
　　楽しいこの世を　苦(く)に変えて　九之介橋(くのすけばし)
　　ああ、ここは瓦屋橋(かわらやばし)
　　橋の北の角(かど)の油屋(あぶらや)の　油搾(しぼ)る木[9]の音(おと)は
　　三味(しゃみ)の音(ね)に　流れて悲しい　娘お染(そめ)の恋物語
　　時雨(しぐれ)の一雫(ひとしずく)が　木(き)の葉(は)あに　沁(し)み入るように
　　洗(あろ)ても　落(お)ちへん　恋の心に染められた
　　お染久松恋衣(ひさまつこいごろも)　歌祭文(うたざいもん)の　心中話(しんじゅうばなし)[10]
　　その歌祭文の一節(ひとふし)も　もう他人事(ひとごと)でなくなった
　　明日(あす)は　我が身　我らのこと
　　灯明(とうみょう)の油に縁(えん)ある油屋に　回向(えこう)するも　悲しい縁(えにし)

　　道頓堀(どうとんぼり)の堀詰(ほりづめ)に　二つ並んだ　二つ井戸(いど)
　　命(いのち)　一つ落とすさえ　惜(お)しいものを
　　二つの命を　落とす今日(きょう)
　　そんなら　落ちて行きましょ　深い縁のまま
　　往生(おうじょう)させてくれない　罪障(ざいしょう)の山[11]の大和橋(やまとばし)
　　千日寺[12]から立つ煙(けむり)　火葬(かそう)の煙(けむり)　無常(むじょう)の煙(けむり)
　　無情の雲の五月雨(さつきあめ)　降らん先に死に場所へ
　　急げば　夜露(よつゆ)にびっしょりぬれた
　　帷子(かたびら)の肩と裾(すそ)におぼろ花
　　腰に弘誓(ぐぜい)[13]の帆掛(ほか)け舟(ぶね)
　　褄(つま)に磯馴(そなれ)の松原映(まつばらうつ)す
　　この帷子(かたびら)を最後に着よう
　　ここは京橋(きょうばし)

In the west we see the masts at the mouth of the Aji River.
This is the field of the pine forest of Ebisu.
Is that the shadow of the forest or a rain cloud?
We must hurry to avoid the rain.
Travellers are making their way!
Has the dawn already come?

    (*In tune of utanenbutsu*[14])
    Some people have decided to commit suicide.
    (Interlude) Yoooh!
    Others don't notice these things and engage in idle talk.
    (Interlude) Yoooh!
    Others don't notice these things and chant a prayer to Amida.
    (Interlude) Yoooh!

Please chant a prayer to Amida for us.
The moon is sinking in the west and guiding us to the Pure Land in the west.[15]
We hear the sea roaring in the far distance.
It may be the sound of the waves on Naruo Beach?
No, no, it's thundering somewhere else.

    There is the sound of a thunderbolt.

KISA: Ah, it's thunder. [*Covering JIROBEI's ears with her kimono sleeves*] If lightning must strike, please spare my Jiro-sama.
JIROBEI: Why do you say such a thing? I'm a man. I want you to be spared. [*He covers KISA in his kimono sleeves.*]

    A streak of blue lightening splits the sky. The sound of thunder.
    JIROBEI and KISA are frightened by it. They start walking toward the south once again. They go off the hanamichi Left.

    Blackout.

「今宮の心中」

　　西に　安治川(あじがわ)の川の口　船の帆柱(ほばしら)
　　ここは戎(えびす)の松の原
　　松の黒みか　雨雲(あまぐも)か
　　雨を避けましょ　道急ぎましょ
　　もう　夜明けか　旅人が行く

　　　（歌念仏[14]の節で）
　　　死にに　行く者
　　　（囃詞(はやしことば)）よおーっ！
　　　知れへん　世間の人々の　無駄口(むだぐち)
　　　（囃詞(はやしことば)）よおーっ！
　　　知れへん　世間の人々の　歌念仏(うたねんぶつ)
　　　（囃詞(はやしことば)）よおーっ！

　　浮世念仏(うきよねんぶつ)　お頼みします
　　傾く月が　西方浄土(さいほうじょうど)[15]の　道しるべ
　　空を拝(おが)めば　どろどろどろと　遠く鳴る
　　「遠く鳴尾(なるお)」の海の音か
　　いやいや　あれは他所(よそ)で轟(とどろ)く雷(かみなり)の音

　　　　雷の音。

きさ　ああ、雷！（着物の袖で二郎兵衛を覆って）落ちるのなら、どうぞ、二郎兵衛殿は避けて。
二郎兵衛　何を言う。私は男。お前こそ。（着物の袖できさを覆う。）

　　　青く稲妻(いなずま)が走る。落雷(らくらい)の音。
　　　二人は怯え、再び南に向かって足を速める。上手花道から退場する。

　　　暗転。

LOVERS' SUICIDES AT IMAMIYA

SCENE TWO
In the forest of the Imamiya Ebisu

Dawn. In the precincts of the Imamiya Ebisu Shrine[16] where a large pine tree stands.

CHORUS: Lightning is fearful to see in life even for the ones about to die.
  The glow of a firefly by the waterside,
  We must not mistake it for the votive light of the Imamiya Ebisu, the shrine of the god of wealth.
  It's been said that the infant Ebisu[17] toddled much, and now that is how we are walking.
  We have walked and walked, and cannot walk any more.
  But we are here now!
  We've arrived at the place of our death.
  It's the forest of the Imamiya Ebisu Shrine.

JIROBEI and KISA enter from the hanamichi Right. When they arrive at the shrine, they collapse beneath the pine tree, looking at each other. Both are exhausted and miserable and helpless. They cry in each other's arms for a while.

JIROBEI [*stoping crying and in the manner of a typical young fainthearted man*]: Oh, what have I done! I should have killed myself with a vegetable knife from the kitchen in the Hishi-ya… I've made you the companion of my journey into death… I'm bringing shame on the shop, and trouble to your family. I'm going to embarrass my master. People will stare at my death mask and think of me a shameless man. All my hard work as a good and honest man will have been in vain. They'll also laugh at you as a woman who fell for a pathetic man like me. Please forgive me, O-Kisa. [*He bursts into tears with remorse.*]

KISA: You worry about me on the verge of your own death. Thank you. I'm, I'm very happy.

The lovers throw themselves to the ground and cry.

KISA: [*stoping crying*] But why Jiro-sama, there's no point in lamenting what we've done. It's idle remorse. Although you're tall and sturdily built, it is not long since you became a man. People will say that Kisa has done a terrible thing to young Jirobei and that he had to kill himself because of her; she is old enough to be his eldest sister… I don't mind

「今宮の心中」

第二場
今宮の戎の森

　　　夜明け。今宮戎神社[16]の境内。大きな松の木が一本。

コーラス　死に行く者でも　生きる身の
　　目に恐ろしい　稲妻の閃光
　　水辺を飛ぶ　蛍の光を
　　今宮戎神社の　灯明の明かりと　違えまいよ
　　稚児の戎のよろよろ歩き[17]
　　もう、足も立たへんほど　歩きに歩いた
　　さあ、つきました
　　ここが死に場所
　　今宮の戎の森

　　　　　二郎兵衛ときさが下手花道から登場する。二人は今宮戎神社の境内まで来て松の木の下にへたれ込むように座る。疲れきった二人は情けなさと心細さで暫く泣く。

二郎兵衛　（泣き止んで、いかにも気の弱い若者らしく）ああ、えらいことしてしもた。店にいるとき、流しの前の菜切り包丁でなりと死んだら良かった……。死ぬのにわざわざ道連れを拵えてしもて……旦那様には不自由な思いをさせる、お店の名は出す、女房の親や兄には難儀かける、ずうずうしい奴と、死に顔を見つめられ、日頃立てた正直もみんな無駄になる。そんなしょうもない奴と契りを交わしたと、あなたまでもが世間に取り沙汰される。おきさ、どうか許して。（後悔の心から、前後不覚に泣き崩れる。）
きさ　あなたは死ぬ間際まで私のこと思うてくれる。嬉しい。嬉しゅうございます。有難いこと。

　　　　　二人は地面に伏して泣く。

きさ（泣き止んで）二郎様、それは言うてもせんないこと。体格こそ大柄なあなただけれど、前髪を落として間もない若い者を、姉と言うてもおかしくない年かさのきさの奴がむごたらしいことした、二郎兵衛を殺しよったと、世間に憎しまれるのは私の方。私一人が非難されるのはちょっともかまいません。ただ……私は、晴れ

being criticised. My regret is only...oh, how I wanted to marry you and to have a small house to ourselves! Then I wanted to work as hard as I could and to sew for as long as I had these two hands... People may laugh at me and said, "A young man like Jirobei has got an old woman like Kisa for his wife." But after we had endured those jibes and continued what we believed in for fifteen years, you would be thirty-six and I forty-one. Then I would want to hear, "Well! What an achievement! The husband could buy a house like that because he's got a wife who's much older than him." I wanted to make all of them envious. I wanted to help you gain prestige as a merchant... But everything has turned out so differently... Life in this world is filled with many unexpected things. In the next world it is harder to foresee what will await us. They say that after death we'll journey in limbo for seven weeks[18] before we are reborn. Even if we lose each other in the thick clouds or the deep fog on our journey, you will never think that your death was in vain, will you? We'll meet again at the Crossroads of the Six Paths which branches into the six worlds: Hell, the Inferno of Starvation, the Realm of the Beasts, Pandenomium, Earth and Heaven,[19] Jiro-sama.

JIROBEI: Of course we will. Even if we fall into the Realm of the Beast and reborn as worms, let's be reborn as the same worm... [*Pause*] Umm, are you ready, O-Kisa?

KISA: Yes, I am. I'm ready.

JIROBEI: But, whatever we've said, we don't know what we will be when we are reborn and return to this world. Please let me have a good look at you once more. This is the last time we'll see each other as a man and a woman here on Earth.

KISA: I want to see your face, too.

The lovers cling together and gaze at each other fixedly.

JIROBEI: You're going to die because of me?
KISA: No. You're going to kill yourself because of your wife?
JIROBEI: Oh, how dearly I love you! O-Kisa!
KISA: How dearly I love you, too! Jiro-sama!

They embrace passionately, and then cry aloud.

CHORUS: Many things they regret!
Their lament too great and sorrow too deep.
The lovers fall to the summer grass.
Confused and distraught, they do nothing but cry.

「今宮の心中」

てあなたと夫婦になって小さな家を持ち、「若い者が年いった女房を結婚相手に持った」と人が笑おうが謗ろうが、この両手のある限り、命の続く限り働いて稼いで、もう十五年も辛抱したら、あなたは三十六で私はちょうど四十一。そのとき、「たいしたもんや。年いった女房を持ったおかげで男は家を買うことが出来た。」と、謗った人らを羨ましがらせ、自分の夫に箔をつけようと思うていました……。けど、なにもかもがこんなに違うてしまいました。現世でさえこんなやから、来世のことはなおさら分かりません。死後は四十九日の中有の旅[18]に出るといわれている。旅の途中で雲や霧で互いにはぐれるようなことになっても、決して無駄死だと思うて下さいますな。そして、地獄、餓鬼、畜生、修羅、人間界、天上界の六つの世界の分かれ道の六道の辻[19]で必ずまた巡り合いましょう。ねえ、二郎様。

二郎兵衛　もちろん、言うまでもないこと。たとえ畜生界に落ち、虫けらになって生まれ変わっても、同じ虫に生まれましょう。（短い間）おきさ、覚悟はええか。
きさ　はい、もうとうに覚悟は出来ています。
二郎兵衛　けど、そうは言うても、次にこの世に生まれてきたときには、何に生まれ変わるのか分かりません。人の姿で生きるこの世の見納めに、もう一度、あなたの顔をよう見たい。
きさ　私もあなたの顔がとくと見たい。

　　　　　　二人、互いを引き寄せあって、じっと顔を見合う。

二郎兵衛　私ゆえにあなたを殺すことになるのか。
きさ　女房ゆえに死になさるか。
二郎兵衛　おきさ、ああ、好きや。
きさ　二郎様、あなたが好き。

　　　　　　二人は激しく求め抱き合う。やがて声を出して泣く。

コーラス　悔めども　嘆き尽きず　思い乾かず
　　　思い乱れて　夏草の上　二人　しおれ伏し　泣くばかり

KISA [*noticing*]: Oh, over there, those travellers are making an early start. Dawn is just breaking. Now, Jiro-sama, I have heard that lovers committing suicide do this…Let's tie our obis together. [*She is about to untie her obi.*]

JIROBEI [*stopping KISA*]: No, no, we won't look respectable if we wear no obi. We'll use this silk cloth from the Hishi-ya. I didn't mean to steal it, but I have as I took it without our master's permission. When we tie the cloth to the pine tree and hang ourselves with it, it'll be as if we are being punished by our master. And we will also be freed of the guilt of stealing kimono fabric from the shop.

> *The lovers hold each end of the cloth firmly and start climbing the pine tree. As it is raining and very dark under the branches, and the trunk of the tree is crooked, they slip and have difficulty climbing.*
> *Finally KISA succeeds in ascending first.*
> *JIROBEI tries to climb up many times, but he keeps failing.*

CHORUS: The narrow trunk of the pine tree in the darkness!
    The man tries to climb it, but misses his footing.
    Is the trunk the bridge of confusion?
    Does his guilt make him falter?

KISA [*reaching her hand out to JIROBEI, worried*]: What happened? Are you all right? I've managed to climb up, a weak woman.

JIROBEI [*tears trickling from his eyes*]: Oh, it's terrible! I've been punished by my master. One of the tabi socks[20] I'm wearing has been passed on from my master. In normal circumstances it would be fine, but on an occasion like this, my master's tabi should be held above my head, [*sobbing*] I shouldn't have climbed in it. My feet slipped and couldn't climb up the tree. Master, please forgive me! [*He takes off the tabi, holds it above his head momentarily and puts it on the ground. Then he climbs the pine tree successfully.*]

> *There is a flash of lightning through the branches of the pine tree.*

JIROBEI: The lightning's flashed. In a moment we'll hear the roll of thunder. O-Kisa, please don't fall from the tree with fright.

> *The thunder roars loudly. It rains like an evening shower. It is pitch dark under the pine tree.*

「今宮の心中」

きさ　（気付いて）あれ、もうちらほらと人が通ります。夜明けが近うなってきた。さあ、二郎様、心中者はこうするものと聞いている……二人の帯を結び継ぎましょう。（帯を解こうとする。）

二郎兵衛　（止めて）いやいや、帯を解いて死んだら見苦しい格好になる。この白絹（しろぎぬ）は店の商（あきな）いもん。盗むつもりはなかったけれど、親方に断って持って出たわけやないから盗んだも同じこと。これをこの松に結わえつけて、この絹で首をくくれば、旦那のお手にかかったも同然。それで、お店の反物（たんもの）を盗んだという罪からは逃れられる。

　　　　二人は白絹の反物の端と端をそれぞれの手にしっかりと掴み、松の木に登り始める。しかし、雨が降って暗いのと松の木の幹が曲がりくねっているのとで滑ってなかなかうまく登ることができない。
　　　　きさが先に登り始める。
　　　　二郎兵衛は足を踏みしめて幾度も試みるがどうしても登ることが出来ない。

コーラス　迷いの橋か
　　　闇の中の松の幹
　　　登ろうとすれど
　　　心の罪に踏み滑る

きさ　（手を差し伸べて、心配そうに）女の身でも登れるのに、どうしました。

二郎兵衛　（はらはらと涙を流して）ああ、恐ろしい。主の罰が当たりました。私が今履（は）いている足袋[20]の片方は旦那様のお古（ふる）。常はどうであれ、こんなときは頭の上にいただくべきもの。（泣いて）それを土足にかけたその咎（とが）で足が滑って登られへんのです。旦那様、どうか堪忍してください。（足袋を脱ぎ、一瞬頭上に押し戴いてから置く。松の幹に登るが、今度は滑らない。）

　　　　松の枝越しに稲妻が走る。

二郎兵衛　それ、稲妻が走った。すぐに雷が鳴る。おきさ、びっくりして落ちんようにしいや。

　　　　雷が激しく轟く。雨が夕立のように降りしきる。松の木の下は真っ暗になる。

KISA: I can't see a thing as it is so dark here. I know this may be asking too much, but Jiro-sama, will you please move your face closer to me? I want to see your face in the lightning flash.
JIROBEI: I want you to look at me as much as you can.

> *The lightning flashes.*
> *The lovers move closer and look at each other. They burst into tears, overcoming with a sense of sorrow. The sounds of thunder and the lovers' cries echo sorrowfully in the darkness. Then they wind the silk cloth around one of the branches of the tree and firmly tie each end of the cloth around their necks.*

CHORUS: Thunder cannot separate lovers in love.
  Rain and tears fall onto the pine tree shrine.
  The silk is wound around the branch twice or more.
  Two ends of the cloth hang down quietly.
JIROBEI: We've tied our bodies together. We'll be born on the same lotus leaf in the Pure Land of Amida Buddha and live our whole life together.
KISA: Now shall we go? There isn't much time left before sunrise.
JIROBEI: Have you tied the cloth tightly, O-Kisa?
KISA: Yes, I have, Jiro-sama. I've tied it very tight never to be separated from you.
JIROBEI: This'll be our last moment. After this we won't be able to speak.
KISA: Jiro-sama, have you said everything you have to say?
JIROBEI: My sweetheart, how about you, O-Kisa?
KISA: I, I have only one thing…it's about my mother and father…I miss them so much.
JIROBEI: In my case…I'm thinking of my master and my old mistress…but, I can never say enough. I think the only thing left for us to say is a prayer to Buddha.
KISA: I think so too. Let's pray Namu Amidabutsu, Save us, merciful Buddha together.

> *The lovers look at each other, nod approvingly and say a prayer together.*

JIROBEI: Namu Amidabutsu, Save us, merciful Buddha.
KISA: Namu Amidabutsu, Save us, merciful Buddha.

> *After saying a prayer together, they take their feet off the branch. For a while they hold each other's sleeves, cling to each other and writhe in pain. They swing towards and away from each other. Soon they kick their legs or stretch their arms in mid-air in agony.*

「今宮の心中」

きさ　暗うて何も見えません。欲深いこととは分かっているけれど、二郎様、私のほうへ顔を寄せて。稲光の光でなりとあなたの顔が見たい。

二郎兵衛　お前に私の顔、見て欲しい。

　　　　　稲妻がピカッと光る。
　　　　　その光の中、二人は顔を近づけ、見つめ合う。そして、悲しさに号泣する。闇に雷と二人の泣き声が悲しく響く。二人は互いに助け合いながら、反物を松の枝に巻きつけ、その端をそれぞれの首に括る。

コーラス　思いあう二人の仲は　雷さえも裂けられん
　　降る雨と　涙の雨の　松の枝
　　絹の反物　二重三重　締め付け締めて
　　そっと　二筋　垂れ下がる
二郎兵衛　これで二人は一蓮托生。極楽浄土できっと添い遂げよう。

きさ　死にましょう。夜明けまでもう一刻の猶予もなくなってきました。
二郎兵衛　おきさ、首の結び目はほどけんよう堅結びになっているか。
きさ　はい、二郎様。あなたと離れることのないようにきつう結んである。
二郎兵衛　これが最後。もう、この後は、物言うことも出来んようになる。
きさ　二郎様、何か言い残したことはないか。
二郎兵衛　あなたこそ。何か言い残したことはないか、おきさ。
きさ　私は父様、母様が懐かしい……の、そればかり。
二郎兵衛　私はお上様、旦那様のこと……。いくら言うても尽きることはない。今はもう南無阿弥陀仏を唱えるだけ。
きさ　二人一緒に南無阿弥陀仏を唱えましょう。

　　　　　二人は見詰め合い、覚悟の時と頷き、同時に南無阿弥陀仏を唱える。

二郎兵衛　南無阿弥陀仏。
きさ　南無阿弥陀仏。

　　　　　二人は南無阿弥陀仏を同時に唱えて、足を松の枝から踏み外す。暫くの間、互いの袂を引き寄せ、抱きつき、もがき苦しむ。二人は寄ったり離れたりを繰り返す。やがて、苦しさに足を縮めたり、手を伸ばして虚空を掴

LOVERS' SUICIDES AT IMAMIYA

As they cannot speak, they stare at each other; they weaken little by little.

CHORUS: Like two branches of wisteria hanging under the pine tree in a storm,
    The lovers swing towards and away from each other, writhing in discomfort,
    See the other weakening little by little,
    They can't talk any more, only stare at each other.
    Their eyes meet, the knotted cords of love.

The night is shifting to the grey of morning.
Their last Namu Amidabutsu echoes in the divine forest.
The two breathe their last and close their eyes.
The lovers' love burns out and the lovers' lives die away.

A shop assistant and a seamstress died honourably.
They looked beautiful in their well-fitting kimonos.
A sword has become old-fashioned for suicide.
Kimono cloth is the appropriate choice for their leaving.
People praised the uniqueness of their method and prayed for the dead.

    Blackout.

END

「今宮の心中」

んだりする。口のきけない二人は徐々に弱って行く互いの姿を見つめ合う。

コーラス　松の枝　嵐に抗う下がり藤二つ
　　　　もがき苦しみ　寄っては離れ　離れては寄る
　　　　互いの弱り死に行く姿
　　　　口きけず　見つめ合う
　　　　目と目だけが今は絆

　　　　闇の向こうに　朝の気配
　　　　これが最期の南無阿弥陀仏
　　　　二人一度に　息絶え目閉じる
　　　　愛燃えて　命燃えつく

　　　　綺麗に逝った　新物屋の手代とお針子
　　　　死に姿　二人揃うて乱れなし
　　　　刃物で死ぬは古手なり
　　　　反物使った新手の心中
　　　　これこそ心中の新物と　聞く人回向したという

　　　　暗転。

　　　　　　　　　　　　　　　　（幕）

Lovers' Suicides at Imamiya
Notes

CHARACTERS
1. Hishi-*ya* is a ready-made kimono-maker.
2. '-*ya*' of Hishi-*ya* is a suffix, meaning a shop. Kanji (Chinese characters) of Hishi-*ya* is 菱屋.
3. Hon-*machi* is in Chūō ward of Osaka City, which is a prefectural capital of Osaka in the present-day Kinki Region. In the Edo period the Tokugawa shogunate had the direct control over Osaka. As a result many *kurayashiki*, a warehouse and a sales office for rice and other local products of a daimio, were built and the city became a centre for commercial transactions called '*Tenka no Daidokoro,* the Public Kitchen.' The city had many rivers and canals, and bridges, and the products were carried by a waterway.
4. *shimo-tedai* in Japanese: one of the posts of a shop in pre-war time Osaka. The top rank is *danna*: a master and the owner of the shop, followed by *bantō*: a head shop assistant, then *tedai*: a shop assistant and *decchi*: an apprentice. An apprentice is engaged in manual labour, while a shop assistant serves customers and takes part in business, and is paid wages. *Shimo-tedai* is placed lower than *omo-tedai*.
5. It is a common name for a seasonal worker.
6. It is in the south-east part of Hyōgo prefecture of the Kinki Region.
7. Many *yakko* had a moustache. Some had a false moustache or a painted one.

ACT ONE
SCENE ONE
1. The tenth bridge spans the West Yokobori Canal
2. The Yokobori Canals ran north-south, from the Tosabori Canal to the Dōtonbori Canal, in present-day Chūō ward of Osaka city; they were the West Yokobori Canal and the East Yokobori Canal. Only the East Yokobori remains.
3. (See Notes No. 5 of ACT ONE, **Woman-Killer in Oil Hell**)
4. The Tenma River was the old Yodo River and is also called the Ō River. It diverges from the Yodo River at the Kema Floodgate in North ward, runs through the central area of Osaka and flows into Osaka Bay.
5. It stood on the east side of the north corner of the Tenma Bridge.
6. A small boat works for a large cargo-vessel in the rivers and bays of Edo and of

「今宮の心中」
（註）

登場人物
1 新品の既製の着物の仕立屋。
2 「－屋」は商店・商人を指す。

3 大阪は近畿地方中部の大阪府中部に位置する都市。江戸時代は大坂（おおさか・おおざか）と称し、幕府の直轄地として諸大名の蔵屋敷が集中、諸国の米や特産物の取引の中心地となり「天下の台所」と言われた。河川や運河に囲まれた地形で橋が多数あり、水路が発達していた。本町は現在の大阪市中央区にある。

4 船場商家の役職。旦那・番頭・手代・丁稚の順で位が低くなる。現代の会社組織でいうと係長や主任に相当する。丁稚が力仕事や雑用が主な仕事であるのに対し、手代は接客など、直接商いに関わる仕事に携わる。手代になると給与が支払われるのが一般的。手代の中では重手代のほうが下手代より高い位置にある。
5 季節奉公人の通称。
6 近畿地方の兵庫県の南東部。
7 江戸時代に武士に仕えて雑務に従った。髭奴（ひげやっこ）はほおひげのある武家奴。作りひげや描きひげの者もいた。

上之巻
第一場
1 西横堀川十筋目に架かる橋。
2 大阪市中央区を南北に土佐堀川から道頓堀川まで通じる運河で西横堀川と東横堀川があった。現在は東横堀川だけ残っている。

3 川遊び用の屋形船。（「**女殺油地獄**」上之巻（註）5 参照）
4 旧淀川のことで大川とも呼ばれる。大阪市北区にある毛馬水門で淀川から分かれて大阪の中心部を通って大阪湾に注ぐ淀川水系のひとつ。天満橋の下流。

5 天満橋の北詰の東側にあった。
6 近世、江戸大阪などの河川や港で大型回船の貨物の運搬用に用いた小舟。お

LOVERS' SUICIDES AT IMAMIYA

Osaka in early-modern times. As the boat sold tea, it was called a tea boat.

7   *Sake* produced in Itami area, the south-east part of Hyogo Prefecture, was regarded one of the best *sake* in the Edo period.

8   *hamanaya* in Japanese

9   *moshiho-gusa* is seaweed for gathering up salt. The magazine gathers up the stories about the most popular kabuki actors.

10 It is a bridge built between Enoko Island and Ebisu Island in Osaka Bay in the Edo period.

11 It was a wholesale district for dried fish and salted food in present-day Nish ward of Osaka city. Salt, *shio* in Japanese, has a connotation of charm or attractiveness.

12 A bridge spans the Nishi-Nagahori Canal.

13 It was the bridge spanning the Shijimi (Corbicula) River. The river flowed between Sonezaki and Dōjima and joined the Dōjima River. (See Notes No. 3 of CHARACTERS, **Woman-Killer in Oil Hell**)

14&15 Located in Nishi ward of present-day Osaka city

16 Nanba-*midō* of the Higashi Hongan-ji Temple in present-day Chūō ward of Osaka city.

17 It is a homonym of 'to wash', '*arau*' in Japanese, and the '*Araya*' Bridge, which is the fifteenth bridge from the north spanning the Nishi Yokobori Canal.

18 It is a homonym of 'a kettle', '*chabin*' in Japanese, and '*Bingo-bashi*.' The Bingo Bridge is the eleventh bridge spanning the Nishi Yokobori Canal.

SCENE TWO

19 '-*san*' is a suffix to put after people's names or an official title; it is an honorary term of address. (See Notes No. 9 of ACT ONE, **Woman-Killer in Oil Hell**)

20 '-*sama*' is a suffix to put after a person's name or names of gods, goddesses and Buddha or things personified; it is an honorary term of address. '-*sama*' has a politer implication than '-*san*.' (See Notes No. 9 of ACT ONE, **Woman-Killer in Oil Hell**)

21 A female blind musician who plays the samisen and sings a folk song or a ballad, going from house to house for money. In the play a *goze* goes from a boat to boat.

22 The area where the Hōryū-ji Temple is located. (See Notes No. 7 of ACT ONE, **Woman-Killer in Oil Hell**)

23 It is a type of dramatic recitation, in a traditional style of narrative, accompanied by samisen, which is associated with *Bunraku*, the Japanese Puppet Theatre.

24 '*O-*' of O-Kisa is a prefix that expresses politeness. (See Notes No. 12 of ACT

「今宮の心中」

茶などを売ったのでこの名が付いた。
7　兵庫県南東部伊丹地方で産する酒。江戸時代から最高酒とされた。

8　川岸の物置小屋。
9　藻塩草は塩を取るための海草。塩を「掻き集める」のと「書き集める」をかけている。ここでは評判記のこと。
10　江戸時代の大阪湾岸にあった江の子島と戎島との間に架かる橋。

11　現在の大阪市西区にあたり魚類の干物・塩物を売る問屋町であった。「塩」には愛嬌の意味がある。
12　西長堀川に架かる橋。
13　蜆川（しじみかわ）に架かる橋。蜆川は大阪市北区の曽根崎新地と堂島新地との間を流れて堂島川に合流していた川。（「**女殺油地獄**」登場人物・註3参照。）

14&15　現在の大阪市西区にある。
16　今の大阪市中央区の東本願寺難波御堂のこと。

17　「洗や」と「荒屋」をかける。西横堀筋十五筋目の橋。

18　「茶瓶」と「備後橋」をかける。備後橋は西横堀筋十一筋目の橋。

第二場

19　（「**女殺油地獄**」上之巻・註9参照。）

20　（「**女殺油地獄**」上之巻・註9参照。）

21　盲御前（めくらごぜん）の略。鼓を打ったり三味線を弾いたりして、歌をうたい、門付（かどづ）けをする盲目の女芸人。民謡・俗謡のほか説教系の語り物を弾き語りする。
22　（「**女殺油地獄**」の上之巻・註7参照。）

23　三味線に合わせてかたる語り物の総称。特に義太夫節（ぎだゆうぶし）。

24　「お（御）－」接頭語。体言・用言の前について尊敬・丁寧・親しみなどを表

ONE, *Woman-Killer in Oil Hell*)

25 'U*ta*' is a song and '*s(z)aimon*' is a written paean to the gods and goddesses. It is a ballad originated from *saimon*: a miraculous virtue of Buddha, the gods and goddesses chanted by a mountain priest. In the Edo period it became a public entertainment, chanting about a recent incident accompanied by samisen.

26 *nenki* in Japanese: it is the anniversary of someone's death or an annual memorial service for the dead in Buddhism.

27 It is in Kawara-machi, Chūō ward of present-day Osaka city.

28 *ri* is about 3.927km. (See No. 5 (1) of **Measuring System in the Edo Period**)

29 The translation of the phrase is 'I believe in the three Treasures of Buddha, laws and priests.' The phrase is used as an interjection to express surprise or a mistake. (See Notes No. 7 of ACT THREE, *Drumbeats Over the Horikawa*)

30 *chō* is about 109 meters. (See No. 5 (1) of **Measuring System in the Edo Period**)

31 *nankin-wata* in Japanese: the remanufactured cotton wool was called under this name in Kyoto and Osaka, while it was called '*uchinaoshi*' fluffed-up, in Edo (Present-day Tokyo).

32 '-*dono*' is a suffix put after a person's name or an official title. (See Notes No. 9 of ACT ONE, *Woman-Killer in Oil Hell*)

33&34 Money of the Edo period. (See No. 4 of **Measuring System in the Edo Period**)

35 *Suzuri-bako* in Japanese. It is a writing case in which *sumi*: a black ink stick, *suzuri*: a *sumi*-stone, *fude*: a writing brush and a small pitcher for water are kept. A stick of *sumi* is rubbed down in the *sumi*-stone with little water to make black ink.

36 The other end of someone's registered seal

37 There was a custom that the neighbours and friends of the newly-wedded couple threw stones into their house on the night of the marriage ceremony.

ACT TWO
SCENE ONE

1 A street going north-south through the town of Osaka; the street name comes that it runs through Naniwa Bridge.

2 *noren*, a shop curtain (See Notes No. 2 of ACT TWO, *Woman-Killer in Oil Hell*)

3 *agari kamachi* in Japanese: it is the timber step entering the living area of the house.

25 神仏の霊験を語った山伏の祭文に始まる江戸時代の俗謡の一つ。三味線の伴奏で市井の事件などをいち早く読み込み、その伝播の役も果たした。芸能化した祭文で浪花節の源流。

26 仏教で人の死後毎年めぐってくる命日。また、その日に行う法要。

27 今の大阪市中央区瓦町二丁目あたり。
28 「里」は尺貫法の距離の単位。(**江戸時代のものの数えかた　5（1）参照。**)
29 仏・法・僧の三宝に帰依する意。三宝に呼びかけて、仏の助けを求める語。驚いた時、失敗したときなどに発する語。しまった。なむさん。ここでは後者の意。(「**堀川波鼓**」下之巻・註7参照。)
30 「町」は約109メートル。(**江戸時代のものの数えかた　5（1）参照。**)
31 古綿を再製したものを京都・大阪ではこう呼んだ。江戸では「打ち直し」と言った。
32 「－殿」は接尾語。人名・役職名などに付けて敬意を添える。(「**女殺油地獄**」上之巻・註9参照。)
33 「－目」は尺貫法の重さの単位の「－匁・文目」のこと。一匁は約3.75グラム。(**江戸時代のものの数えかた　4参照。**)
34 「－両」江戸時代の通貨単位。金一両は慶長小判1枚（4.74匁、役17.8グラム）(**江戸時代のものの数えかた　4参照。**)
35 硯や筆や墨などを入れておく箱。

36 実印の他方の端に刻んだ印判をいう。
37 婚礼の夜に「石打ち」といって、近所の者などが婚家に石を投げうつ習慣があった。石の祝い。

中之巻
第一場
1 淀大川に架かる難波橋のある南北に通る道。

2 (「**女殺油地獄**」中之巻・註2参照。)
3 玄関などの上り口に取り付けた横木あるいは板。

4   *Kamishimo* in Japanese: the formal attire of samurai. (See Notes No. 17 of ACT ONE, ***Woman-Killer in Oil Hell***)

5   *Ito zakura* or *shidare zakura* in Japanese. *Ito* means thread.

6   *hakama* is a pair of loose-legged pleated trousers for formal wear. (See Notes No. 4 of this ACT.)

7   It is rice porridge/broth with seven spring herbs such as a dropwort, a shepherd's purse, a cudweed, chickweed, a henbit, a turnip and a garden radish traditionally eaten on the seventh of January to be in good health for the New Year.

8   One of oriental medicine: it is to burn moxa on the moxibustion points of the skin to stimulate the body. It is thought that this increases the healing power of the body.

9   A pair of bamboo *zōri* with leather sole and some metal fittings at the heel. (See Notes No. 16 of ACT ONE, ***Woman-Killer in Oil Hell***, for *zōri*.)

10   *za-buton* is a small square futon to sit on.

11   The 23rd of May is 'the day of lengthy illness' which was thought unlucky to start taking new medicine or to have a moxa treatment or acupuncture.

12   *Ikkō-shū* was originally started by Ikkō Shunshō (1239?-1287?), one of the priests of *Jōdo-shū*. But by the time of the play it was meant the True Pure Land Sect of Buddhism.

13   The True Pure Land Sect, *Jōdo-shin-shū* in Japanese. (See Notes No. 11 of CHARACTERS, ***Woman-Killer in Oil Hell***)

14   *doyō* is the periods of eighteen days before *risshun*: the first day of spring, *rikka*: the first day of summer, *risshū*: the first day of autumn, and *rittō*: the first day of winter. It was regarded that moxa treatment on the summer *doyō* especially works well. *Hassen* is a special eight days before the summer *doyō* period.

15   Moxa is made of a Japanese mugwort (a hedgerow plant). First people dry a mugwort, grind it with a hand mill and make mugwort wool called moxa. The damped moxa is dried by passing over a flame before use.

16   A paper-covered lamp stand, *andon* in Japanese (See Notes No. 11 of ACT ONE, ***Drumbeats over the Horikawa***)

17   They are made of peach twigs or bamboo.

18   *yaito-gyō* in Japanese: it is a dish when they had a moxa treatment. It was said that bleeding was stopped by biting something hard when they bled.

19   Dried thin white Jananese noodles made of wheat. Normally boiled and served in a large bowl of ice cold water, then dipped in sauce and eaten in summer.

20   Dried thin white Jananese noodles made of flour, thinner than hiyamugi. Mostly

4	江戸時代の主に武士の礼服。同色の肩衣と袴からなる。(「**女殺油地獄**」上之巻・註17)
5	シダレザクラの異名。
6	着物の上に穿いて下半身を被うひだのあるゆるい衣。(同巻・註4参照。)
7	正月七日に春の七草(セリ、ナズナ、ゴギョウ、ハコベラ、ホトケノザ、スズナ、スズシロ)を入れて炊く粥。新年の健康を祈って食べる。
8	漢方医術の一つ。艾をつぼにあたる皮膚の特定の位置に据え、線香で火をつけて燃やし、その熱の刺激で病気に対する治癒力を促進する療法。やいと。
9	竹の皮の草履の裏に牛革を張り、かかとの方に金物を打った履物。(「**女殺油地獄**」上之巻・註16参照。)
10	座るときにしく布団。
11	二十三日は「長病日」に当たり灸や鍼、初めての薬を飲むのを良くないとする。
12	もとは浄土宗の僧侶一向俊聖(1239?-1287?)の起こした宗派であったが、この作品の時代には浄土真宗のことを指す。
13	浄土宗から分かれた宗派。親鸞(1173～1262)によって創められた。(「**女殺油地獄**」登場人物・註11参照。)
14	土用は立春・立夏・立秋・立冬の前の各十八日間を言う。夏の土用の灸は特効があるといわれる。八専は陰陽道で壬子の日から癸亥の日までの十二日のうち丑・辰・午・戌の日を除いた八日。
15	ヨモギの葉を干して臼でついて作る綿状のもの。灸に使う。湿気を含んだ艾はあぶって乾かして使う。
16	英語版では an *andon* lamp stand とする。(「**堀川波鼓**」上之巻・註11参照。)
17	桃の枝、竹などで作られた。
18	灸を据えた時に食べるもの。血が出た時などに噛んでいれば血が止まるといわれている。
19	細打ちしたうどんを水や氷で冷やし、汁をつけて食べるもの。
20	塩水で捏ねた小麦粉に植物油を塗り細く引き伸ばして日干しした麺。茹でて

eaten in the same way as hiyamugi are. The dough of sōmen is stretched with the help of vegetable oil to make thin noodles, and then air dried.

21 A bowl of rice with hot green tea.
22 *nasu no asa-zuke* in Japanese: *nasu* means aubergine. *Asa-zuke* is a vegetable pickled for a short time with salt or in salted rice-bran paste.
23 At the time when the play was written, there was confectionery called *mizukara*, which are made of dried cooked kombu kelp and a Japanese pepper.

SCENE TWO

24 *obi* in Japanese : man's *obi* is narrow. (See Notes No. 8 of ACT ONE, **Woman-Killer in Oil Hell**)
25 It is a dagger without a sword guard made by a sword smith in Mihara in Bingo country, present-day Hiroshima prefecture.
26 Rennyo (1415-1499) was a priest, a restorer of the True Pure Land Sect of Buddhism.
27 *shisoku* in Japanese: it is a light made by burning oil with a twisted paper string as a wick. Here it is used as an insect repellent.

SCENE THREE

28 Money of the Edo period (See No.4 of **Measuring System in the Edo Period**)
29 Jiroshichi was Jirobei's name when he was an apprentice. An apprentice and a junior shop assistant were named often by adding '- matsu' '-kichi' '-shichi' to their own name in a shop.
30 *asaji mairi* in Japanese: a believer of the True Pure Land Sect of Buddhism goes to the temple for the morning religious service.
31 *seimon* in Japanese.
32 The day a person died is counted as the first anniversary. The seventh anniversary is the sixth year after the person's death.
33 *fusuma* in Japanese (See Notes No. 4 of ACT TWO, **Woman-Killer in Oil Hell**)
34 '-*don*' is a suffix, used for servants and apprentices.

35 *yabuiri* in Japanese: employees of a shop and servants were given a day off and go home or go to their guarantor's place on the sixteenth day of the months of January and August. It is the day even the Ogre in Hell stops his job of tormenting sinners.
36 *furoshiki* in Japanese: it is a piece of square cloth for wrapping things.

「今宮の心中」

21 飯に熱い茶をかけたもの。
22 大根や瓜、その他のものを、すぐ食べられるようにぬか漬けや塩漬けにしたもの。
23 当時、昆布を結び山椒を入れた「みずから」という茶菓子があった。

第二場

24 英語版でも *obi* とする。男帯は女帯よりも細い。(「**女殺油地獄**」上之巻・註8参照。)
25 備後国(現在の広島県)三原の刀匠正家が作った鍔のない短刀。
26 蓮如(1415-1499)は室町中期の僧。浄土真宗中興の祖。宗旨を平易な文で説く「御文」を送って布教し、門徒派の組織化に尽力した。(浄土真宗はこの項の註12参照。)
27 油を浸したこよりで火をともすためのもの。ここでは蚊よけに用いられている。

第三場

28 (**江戸時代のものの数えかた** 4 江戸時代の貨幣 参照。)
29 二郎七は二郎兵衛の丁稚の時の名前。名前の後に「-松」、「-吉」、「-七」などを付けて丁稚や下手代の名前にした。
30 浄土真宗で信徒が朝早く御堂で行われる勤行に参ること。
31 神仏にかけて行う誓いの言葉。
32 七年忌または七回忌は死後六年。死んだ日から数えて七回目の回忌。
33 英語版では *fusuma* sliding door にしている。(「**女殺油地獄**」中之巻・註4参照。)
34 「-どん」接尾語。下男、下女や丁稚など目下の者を呼ぶときに名の下につける語。
35 正月と盆の16日に奉公人が親元、または請人の家に帰ること。この日は「地獄の釜の蓋もあく」、地獄の鬼でさえも罪人を責めるのをやめて休息するそうだから、この世でも仕事をやめて休むことになっていた。(「地獄の釜」は同作品の下之巻・註4参照。)
36 「風呂敷」は英語版では *furoshiki* cloth にしている。

37 It is a name of family crests: there are different names by way of dividing a chrysanthemum.

38 The plum oil (See Notes No. 4 of ACT THREE, ***Woman-Killer in Oil Hell***)

ACT THREE
SCENE ONE

1   A counting song, which often includes rhyme.

2   A Buddhist term. It is the river in Hades where the dead cross on the seventh day of their death. There are three different ways of crossing points; good people walk on the bridge, whilst light sinners ford shallows and heavy sinners cross at the rapid depths.

3   A Buddhist term. It is a mountain of severe torment to climb over after death.

4   It is a pot in Hell that a sinner is put in.

5   Tehon-*machi* and Hon-*machi* are in rhyme. The following names mentioned are the towns through which the lovers are walking as they travel south.

6   *shō* (See No. 5 (3) of **Measuring System in the Edo Period**)

7   It is thought that people are reborn for seven times after death. While being reborn in this world for seven times, if the dead person achieves spiritual enlightenment, he or she is able to go and live in Buddhist paradise.

8   Baku is an imaginary Chinese animal that eats up people's dreams. It has a body of a bear, the eyes of a rhino, a nose of an elephant, the legs of a tiger, a tail of a cow.

9   There is an apparatus made of timber for extracting oil from fruit and seeds

10 There was an oil shop in the northeast corner of the Roof Tile Bridge in Osaka. In 1708 there was an incident which the daughter of the oil shop O-Some and its junior shop assistant Hisamatsu, committed lovers' suicide pact owing to a difference in social standing. The *utasaimon* was written based on that. (See Notes No. 25 of ACT ONE of this play for *utasaimon*)

11 It is an idea of Buddhism; when a person commits one sin after another in this world, he or she comes across the Mount of Sins after death, which is hard to cross over and an obstacle to go into the paradise.

12 (See Notes No. 7 of SCENE TWO, ACT THREE, ***Woman-Killer in Oil Hell***)

13 It is an allegorical picture that a bodhisattva saves people and take them to nirvana.

14 A ballad in the Edo period: it was sung to the tune of a Buddhist invocation. It took the song lyrics from *sekkyo-bushi* preaching songs, and was sung accompanied

「今宮の心中」

37　家家で定めている紋章、紋所の名前。菊の花の割り方で二つ割菊、三つ割菊などがある。
38　(「**女殺油地獄**」下之巻・註4参照。)

下之巻
第一場
1　数え歌形式。「一つとや（一つとせ）…二つとや（二つとせ）…」などと順に数えてうたう歌。多く頭韻を踏む。
2　仏語。死後七日目に渡るという冥途にある川。三つ瀬があり生前の業によって善人は橋を、軽い罪人は浅瀬を、重い罪人は流れの速い深みを渡るという。
3　死後に越えるという厳しい責めのある山。
4　地獄で罪人を煮るという釜。
5　手本町は「手本」と「本町」で、「本」と韻をふんでいる。以下、本町から南に向かって町の名を言い掛ける。
6　「升」は尺貫法の体積の単位。(**江戸時代のものの数えかた　5 (3) 参照。**)
7　この世に七度生まれかわること。永遠。仏教で悟りの初段階である「預流果」を得たものは人間世界に七度生まれ変わる間に必ず涅槃に入るといわれている。
8　「獏」は中国の想像上の動物。形はクマに、目はサイに、鼻は象に、脚はトラに尾はウシに似て、人の夢を食うといわれている。
9　油搾木。原料から油を搾り取る器械。
10　「油屋お染久松心中」。1708年、大阪の東横堀川に架かる瓦屋橋の北東の角にあった油屋の一人娘お染と丁稚の久松とが身分違いの恋から心中に至ったという、実際の事件をモデルにしている。(歌祭文は同作品の上之巻・註25参照。)
11　「罪障の山」。仏教で往生の妨げとなる罪業が大きいことのたとえ。
12　(「**女殺油地獄**」下之巻その二・註7参照。)
13　「弘誓の帆かけ船」。菩薩が人々を苦から救って彼岸に送るのを、船が人を渡すのにたとえた。
14　江戸時代の俗曲。念仏の節をつけて歌ったもので説教節などの文句を取り、鉦に合わせて歌う門付け芸となった。元禄年間（1688－1704）に流行した。

by a hand bell. It became a strolling entertainment and was prevailed in the Genroku time (1688-1704).

15   A Buddhist term: it is the place hundred thousand of hundred million in the west from this world where Amida lives, the Pure Land of Amida Buddha.

SCENE TWO

16   The Imamiya Ebisu Shrine is located in Ebisu-chō, Naniwa ward of present-day Osaka city. Enshrined deities are the Sun goddess, Ebisu the god of Shipping, Fishing and Commerce and some others. The Ebisu Festival on the tenth of January is well-known.

17   Ebisu is one of Seven Deities of Good Fortune, usually depicted carrying fishing pole and sea bream, and is famous for the power of answering prayers for good business. It was said that Ebisu toddled until he became three years old.

18   In Buddhism people's life has four stages. The first stage is the moment of the birth. The second is from the birth to the death. The third is the moment of the death. The fourth is the time from the death to the rebirth, which is seven weeks.

19   In Buddhism people are sent to six different places according to their deed in lifetime after their death. The six places are Hell, the Inferno of Starvation, the Realm of the Beast, Pandemonium, Earth and Heaven. The Six Paths lead to these destinations.

20   *tabi* in Japanese: it is a thick-soled Japanese ankle sock with a separate section for the big toe.

15　仏教でこの世の西方、十万億土の仏土をへだてたところ存在する阿弥陀仏の浄土。極楽浄土。

第二場

16　大阪市浪速区恵美須町にある神社。祭神は天照大神、事代主命（えびす）らで、商売繁盛の神として信仰される。一月の十日戎は有名。

17　えびすは古くは豊漁の神。後に七福神の一人として生業を守り福をもたらす神と崇められる。三歳まで足が立たなかったといわれている。

18　仏教では人が生まれて死に、さらに生まれるまでを四つに分けて四有、即ち生有、本有、死有、中有とする。中有は人が死んでから次の生を受けるまでの期間。七日間を一期とし、第七期の四十九日までとする。

19　死後に人間が生前の行いに応じてゆくという地獄、餓鬼、畜生、修羅、人間、天上の六つの世界への分岐点。

20　「足袋」は英語版では *tabi* socks にしている。

BIBLIOGRAPHY (Books in English)

Malm, William O. (1959) *Japanese Music and Musical Instruments*. Rutland, Vermont, Tokyo: Charles E. Tuttle Company.

Brandon, Malm and Shively. (1978) *Studies in Kabuki*. Honolulu: University Press of Hawai'i.

Adachi, Barbara C. (1985) *Backstage at Bunraku*. New York & Tokyo: Weatherhill.

Gunji, Masakatsu. (1985) *Kabuki*. Tokyo: Kodansha International.

Gerstle, Andrew C. (1986) *Circle of Fantasy: Convention in the Plays of CHIKAMATSU*. Cambridge, Mass and London: Harvard University Press.

Nakamura, Matazô (1988) *Kabuki Backstage, Onstage*. Trans. by Oshima, Mark. Tokyo: Kodansha International.

Banham, Martin. (1988) Ed. *Cambridge Guide to Theatre*. Cambridge University Press.

Ortolani, Benito. (1990) *The Japanese Theatre*. Princeton: Princeton University Press.

Kawatake, Toshio (1990) *Japan on Stage*. Trans. by O'Neill, P. G. Tokyo: 3A Corporation.

Cavaya, Ronald. (1993) *Kabuki a Pocket Guide*. Vermont, Tokyo: Charles E. Tuttle Company.

Shively, Donald H. (1953) Trans. *The Love Suicide at Amijima – A study of a JapaneseDomestic Tragedy by Chikamatsu Monzaemon*. Cambridge, Mass.: Harvard University Press.

Keene, Donald. (1961) Trans. *Major Plays of Chikamatsu*. New York, Oxford: Columbia University Press.

_____. (1970) Ed. *20 Plays of the Nō Theatre*. New York: Columbia University Press.

_____. (1971) Trans. *Chūshingura – The Treasury of Loyal Retainers*. New York: Columbia University Press.

_____. (1990) *Nō and Bunrakau*. New York, Oxford: Columbia University Press.

Motofuji, Frank T. (1966) Trans. *The Love of Izayoi Seishin*. Rutland, Vermont, Tokyo: Charles E. Tuttle Company.

Jones, Stanleigh H. Jr. (1985) Ed. &Trans. *Sugawara and the Secrets of Calligraphy*. New York: Columbia University Press.

_____. (1993) Ed. &Trans. *Yoshitsune and the thousand Cherry Trees: a master piece of the eighteenth-century Japanese puppet theatre*. New York: Columbia University Press.

Brandon, James R. (1992) Trans. *Kabuki Five Classic Plays*. Honolulu: University of Hawai'i Press.

_____. (1993) *Cambridge Guide to Asian Theatre*. Cambridge University Press.

_____ & Leiter, Samuel L. (2002) Eds. *Kabuki Plays on Stage Volume 1, Brilliance and Bravado, 1697-1766*. Honolulu: University of Hawai'i Press.

_____. (2002) Eds. *Kabuki Plays on Stage Volume 2, Villainy and Vengeance, 1773-1799*. Honolulu: University of Hawai'i Press.

_____. (2002) Eds. *Kabuki Plays on Stage Volume 3, Darkness and Desire, 1804-1864*. Honolulu: University of Hawai'i Press.

参考文献（和書）

新編日本古典文学全集74『近松門左衛門集①』　小学館　1997.03
新編日本古典文学全集75『近松門左衛門集②』　小学館　1998.05
新編日本古典文学全集76『近松門左衛門集③』　小学館　2000.10
名作歌舞伎全集第一巻『近松門左衛門集一』　東京創元社　1969.10
名作歌舞伎全集第二十一巻『近松門左衛門集二』　東京創元社　1973.02
岩波セミナーブックス31『近松への招待』　岩波書店　1989.11
岩波講座　歌舞伎・文楽　第一巻　『歌舞伎と文楽の本質』　岩波書店　1997.09
岩波講座　歌舞伎・文楽　第八巻　『近松の時代』　岩波書店　1998.05
日本文学研究叢書『近松』有精堂出版　1976.03
上方文庫7『上方の文化　近松門左衛門をめぐって』　和泉書院　1988.06
上方文化講座『曽根崎心中』　和泉書院　2006.08
浦山政雄・他　『日本演劇史』　桜楓社　1978.02
広末保　『近松序説　近世悲劇の研究』　未来社　1957.04
井口洋　『近松世話浄瑠璃論』　和泉書院　1986.03
鳥越文蔵　『虚実の慰み　近松門左衛門』　新典社　1989.03
松平進　『曽根崎心中』　和泉書院　1998.04
松平進　『近松に親しむ　その時代と人』　和泉書院　2001.12
渡辺保　『近松物語』　新潮社　2004.11
石川了「紀海音『今宮心中丸腰連理松』臆説」『芸能文化史』第五号　芸能文化史研究会　1982.12
諏訪春雄　『愛と死の伝承』　角川書店　1968.12
諏訪春雄　『心中ーその詩と真実』　毎日新聞社　1977.03
田中澄江　『近松という人』　日本放送出版協会　1984.10
田中澄江　現代語訳日本の古典17『女殺油地獄』　学研　1980.01
富岡多恵子　『近松浄瑠璃私考』　筑摩書院　1979.01
水上勉　『近松物語の女たち』　中央公論社　1977.05
戸板康二　『女形』　駸々堂　1975.10
髙田衛・阪口弘之・山根為雄　日本の古典を読む⑲『雨月物語・冥途の飛脚・心中天の網島』　小学館　2008.07
『摂津名所図會』全二巻　古典籍刊行会　1975.04
渡邊忠司　『大阪町奉行所異聞』　東方出版　2006.05
野田宇太郎　『関西文学散歩　大阪・堺・淀川両岸編』　人物往来社　1967.09
林豊　『大阪を歩く』　東方出版　2007.06
歴史の旅7『大阪　＝天下の台所＝』　小学館　1974.06
町人文化百科論集4『浪花のにぎわい』　柏書房　1981.07
町人文化百科論集5『浪花のにぎわい』　柏書房　1981.07

BIBLIOGRAPHY (Books in English)

_____. (2003) Eds. *Kabuki Plays on Stage Volume 4, Restoration and Reform, 1872-1905*. Honolulu: University of Hawai'i Press.

Waley, Arthur. (1921) Trans. *The Nō Plays of Japan*. London: George Allen and Unwin Ltd.

Komparu, Kunio (1983) *The Noh Theatre: Principles and Perspectives*. Trans. by Corddry, Jane & Comee, Stephen. New York: Weatherhill & Tokyo: Tankosha.

Rimer, Thomas J. & Yamazaki, Masakazu. (1984) Trans. *On the Art of the Nô Drama - The Major Treatises of Zeami*. Princeton: Princeton University Press.

Sekine, Masaru. (1985) *Ze-ami and Theories of Noh Drama*. Gerrards Cross: Colin Smythe.

Tyler, Royall. Ed & trans. (1992) *Japanese Nō Dramas*. London: Penguin Books.

参考文献（和書）

児玉幸多　『日本の歴史16「元禄時代」』　中央公論社　1966.05
奈良本辰也　『日本の歴史17「町人の実力」』　中央公論社　1966.06
石川英輔　『ニッポンのサイズ』　淡交社　2003.08
吉原健一郎　『江戸の銭と庶民の暮らし』　同成社　2003.07
中村元・紀野一義訳註　『般若心経　金剛般若経』　岩波書店　1960.07
九鬼周造　『「いき」の構造　他二篇』　岩波書店　1979.09
釘町久磨次　『歌舞伎大道具師』　青土社　1991.09
和角仁・樋口和博　『歌舞伎入門辞典』　雄山閣　1994.04
渡辺保　『カブキ　ハンドブック』　新書館　1993.05
「歌舞伎図鑑」『別冊太陽』No.76 WINTER 1991　平凡社　1992.01
「文楽」『別冊太陽』No.80 WINTER 1992　平凡社　1993.01
「丸本歌舞伎」『演劇界』増刊第53巻第2号　演劇出版社　1995.01
「特集・近松の大阪」『大阪人』第58巻5月号　大阪都市協会　2004.05
「歌舞伎入門シリーズ—④　道具・衣装百科」『演劇界』第六十二巻第八号　演劇出版社　2004.04
『能・狂言事典』　平凡社　1978.06
『日本大事典』第一巻　平凡社　1992.11
『日本の子守唄100選』　日本子守唄協会　2006.08
『大辞林』第三版　三省堂　2006.10
岩田アキラ（写真）『扇雀　上方芸と近松』　京都書院　1989.04
青木信二（写真）『吉田蓑助写真集』　淡交社　2001.05

POSTFACE

I owe many people a great deal of gratitude in making this book.

I have revised both Japanese and English texts for the book. Rachel Christophides, Terry Ram and Richard Tall proofread the texts and the other writing for the book. They also gave me precious comments and advice. They did this from the time I started writing the stage scripts. Hiroko Okuma proofread all the Japanese play texts and writing for the book. All have answered my detailed questions and helped me to move towards the right answers. There is no word to express my gratitude to them.

Others also contributed their knowledge to the stage scripts. Emeritus Professor Bunzō Torigoe kindly read the Japanese adaptations for the staging texts. I am thankful to all the support from the Workshop Theatre at Leeds and the School of Drama, Music and Screen at Hull. Comments by their members of the staff and the student-actors were extremely valuable and essential.

The picture of the back book jacket is drawn by my sister Ikuko who is an oil painter. When I started the adaptation of **Woman-Killer in Oil Hell**, my sister and I visited Imai-chō in Nara. It is a place where the townscape of the Edo period has been conserved. I wanted to experience what a shop of the Edo period was like. My sister gained an inspiration from the visit and painted this picture, which, I think, also depicts my feelings at that time well. I am grateful that she kindly contributed the picture to the book.

I am much indebted to Professor Yoshie Inoue of Toho Gakuen College of Drama and Music in innumerable ways. She introduced me to my publisher, Mr Kenji Matsuda of Shakai Hyōron-sha. When my work for the book was making little progress, she urged me on and advised me to complete the manuscript soon. She saw performances in both England and Japan, and collected her theatre review of the project in her own book. If there had not been her vigorous encouragement, the timing of publication must have been further delayed or my plan of publishing a Chikamatsu book would have come to nothing. I am truly grateful for all that she has done for me and the project. Mr Matsuda always listened to me and made the book. I am very grateful to that.

Finally I must mention that the project owes its existence to the encouragement of two women, my dearest friends Kitty Burrows and Joan Hall.

MY

おわりに

　本書の出版では多くの人々のお世話になった。

　出版に際し公演に用いた英語版テキストと日本語版を見直した。英語版のプルーフリードは、公演テキストの時からレイチェル・クロストフィデス、テリー・ラム、リチャード・トールに労をかけた。貴重なコメントやアドヴァイスも貰った。出版のための日本語版は奥間博子さんに目を通していただいた。皆、忙しい中、時間を割いて幾度も原稿に向かって下さった。細かな疑問点をそのつど一緒に考えて解決の糸口を見つけてくれたプルーフリーダー達にはただただ感謝の言葉しかない。

　この外にも公演テキストには多くの人々の知識が込められた。鳥越文蔵先生は「堀川」と「今宮」の上演台本の日本語版を読んで下さった。リーズ大学英文学部ワークショップ・シアター及びハル大学演劇・音楽・映画学部の先生方や出演してくれた学生たちのコメントは非常に有意義でなくてはならないものであった。彼らのプロジェクトに対するすべての支援にとても感謝している。

　裏ブックカバーの挿画は油絵画家である姉郁子の作品である。「女殺油地獄」の翻案を始めた時、私は姉と一緒に江戸時代の家並みの保存地区である奈良の今井町を訪ねた。江戸時代の商家がどんなものかを肌で感じたかったのである。絵はその時に姉が構想を得たもので、今井町の情景だけでなくプロジェクトを始めたころの自分が見えるようである。この絵を提供してくれた姉に感謝している。

　私の親しい友人の桐朋学園芸術短期大学の井上理恵さんは出版社を紹介して下さっただけでなく、仕事の捗らない私を叱咤激励して下さった。理恵さんはイギリス公演も日本公演も観に来られて、ご自分の著書にもプロジェクトの劇評を載せて下さっている。彼女に背中を押して貰っていなかったら、出版はまだまだ遅れていただろうし、そのうちに立ち消えになってしまっていたかもしれない。すべてに心から感謝している。そして、私の要望に黙って耳を傾けて下さった社会評論社の松田健二さんにもとても感謝している。

　最後になるが、二人の女性、キティー・ボロワとジョーン・ホールのいつもの励ましがなかったら、近松プロジェクトは始まってさえいなかったことを付け加えて感謝の言葉としたい。

湯浅雅子

Yuasa, Masako

Masako was born in Osaka. She lives in Sakai city in Osaka and Leeds in th UK. She is a member of the Japanese Society for Theatre Research. She received her master's degree in Theatre Studies at the University of Leeds, UK in 1986 and also received her doctorate in Theatre Studies at Leeds in 1990. The title of her master's dissertation was *Kunio Shimizu and his work*, and that of her doctorate theses *The Plays by Minoru Betsuyaku*. Masako taught Japanese theatre and Japanese at Leeds from 1990 to 2000. She taught story-telling at the Osaka Kyoiku University from 2002 to 2011. She is an honorary research fellow in drama translation at the University of Hull, UK.

She has translated and staged several contemporary Japanese plays at the Workshop Theatre at Leeds, including **He Died at His Peak** *(Hana no Sakari ni Shinda ano Hito)* by Kunio Shimizu, **The Kangaroo** *(Kangarū)*, **I am the Father of the Genius Idiot Bakabon** *(Tensai Bakabon no Papa nanoda)*, **A Corpse With Feet** *(Ashi no Aru Shitai)* and **The Story of the Two Knights Travelling around the Country** *(Shokoku o Henrekisuru Futari no Kishi no Monogatari)* by Minoru Betsuyaku, **Futon and Daruma** *(Futon to Daruma)* and **The Man Next Door** *(Tonari no Otoko)* by Ryō Iwamatsu, **Paper Balloon** *(Kami Fūsen)*, **New Cherry Leaves** *(Ha-Zakura)* and **Love Phobia** *(Renai Kyōfu-byō)* by Kunio Kishida. **A Corpse with feet** was broadcast on BBC Radio 3 in October, 1991.

Translated works with annotations: *The Story of the Two Knights Travelling around the Country, Futon and Daruma, Kunio Kishida - three plays* by Alumnus. "A Corpse with Feet by Betsuyaku Minoru and the Snail Theatre Company," *Asian Theatre Journal* by University of Hawai'i.

Joint works: *20 Seiki no Gikyoku I and III (The Criticisms on Japanese Playwrights' Works in the 20th Century Vol. 1 and 3)* by Shakai Hyōronsha, *Half a Century of Japanese Theatre: 1990 Part 1 and Part 2* by Kinokuniya Company Ltd, *Kishida Kunio no Sekai (The World of Kishida Kunio)* by Kanrinshobō and *Toshi no Fikushon (Fiction of a City)* by Seibun-do.

Contributions to *The Cambridge Guide to Theatre* by Cambridge University Press; *Who is Who in Contemporary World Theatre* by Routledge.

Articles: "*Gendai Nihon-Engeki ni okeru Junsui-Engeki kara Fujōri-Engeki eno Nagare no Kōsatsu* (Aspects of Contemporary Japanese theatre from the Pure Theatre to the Theatre of the Absurd)," *The Journal of the Japanese Society for Theatre Research*, No. 34 (an English full version, *Leeds East Asian Paper* No. 53).

湯浅雅子（ゆあさ　まさこ）

　大阪生まれ。堺市と英国リーズ市に住む。演劇学専攻。日本演劇学会会員。英国リーズ大学大学院修士・博士修了。修士論文　KUNIO SHIMIZU AND HIS WORK（1986）、博士論文　THE PLAYS BY MINORU BETSUYAKU（1990）。1990～2000年英国リーズ大学レクチャラー。2002～2011年大阪教育大学非常勤講師。現在、英国ハル大学名誉研究員。

　これまでにリーズ大学ワークショップ・シアターで英訳・演出上演した作品：He Died at His Peak（「花の盛りに死んだあの人」作・清水邦夫）、The Kangaroo, I am the Father of the Genius Idiot Bakabon, A Corpse With Feet, The Story of the Two Knights Travelling around the Country（「カンガルー」「天才バカボンのパパなのだ」「足のある死体」「諸国を遍歴する二人の騎士の物語」作・別役実）、Futon and Daruma, The Man Next Door（「蒲団と達磨」「隣の男」作・岩松了）、Paper Balloon, New Cherry Leaves, Love Phobia（「紙風船」「葉桜」「恋愛恐怖病」作・岸田國士）。英訳 A Corpse With Feet は1991年にBBC Radio 3から放送される。

　翻訳と解説：*The Story of the Two Knights Travelling around the Country*（Alumnus 出版）, *Futon and Daruma*（Alumnus 出版）, *Kunio Kishida-three plays*（Alumnus 出版）。"A Corpse with Feet by Betsuyaku Minoru and the Snail Theatre Company," *Asian Theatre Journal* No. 2, Vol. 14.（「英訳「足のある死体」作・別役実とかたつむりの会の仕事」『アジア演劇』ハワイ大学出版）。

　共著：『20世紀の戯曲』1巻と3巻（社会評論社）、*Half a Century of Japanese Theatre 1990s Part 1 & Part 2*（紀伊国屋書店）、『岸田國士の世界』（翰林書房）、『都市のフィクション』（清文社）。

　寄稿：*The Cambridge Guide to Theatre*（Cambridge University Press）、*Who's Who in Contemporary World Theatre*（Routledge）。

　論文：「現代日本演劇における純粋演劇から不条理演劇への流れの考察」『日本演劇学会紀要』34（同論文の英語版 *Leeds East Asian Paper* No. 53）。

A Bilingual Edition of
Three Sewa-mono Plays by Chikamatsu Monzaemon

First Published in Japan in 2014
By Shakaihyoronsha Co., Ltd. 2-3-10, Hongō, Bunkyō-ku, Tokyo 113-0033, Japan

Copyright© 2014 Masako Yuasa
Masako Yuasa has asserted her moral right to be identified as the author of this work

Book designed by Taeko Nakano
Typeset by Jungetsusha, 3-28-9, Hongō, Bunkyō-ku, Tokyo 113-0033, Japan
Printed and bounded by Kurashiki Insatsu, 14-16-17, Kinshi, Sumidaku, Tokyo 130-0013 Japan

ISBN978-4-7845-1131-0

対訳　湯浅版近松世話物戯曲集

2014年6月10日　初版第1刷発行

著　　者────湯浅雅子
発 行 人────松田健二
発 行 所────株式会社 社会評論社
　　　　　　　東京都文京区本郷 2 - 3 - 10
　　　　　　　☎ 03（3814）3861　FAX 03（3818）2808
　　　　　　　http://www.shahyo.com

製　　版────閏月社
印刷・製本────倉敷印刷
装　　幀────中野多恵子

printed in Japan